For

Laurie and Scott
on their wedding day

from
Uncle Stoyan and Aunt Margaret

June 22, 1984

THE EAGLE

AND

THE STORK

Harper's
MAGAZINE PRESS

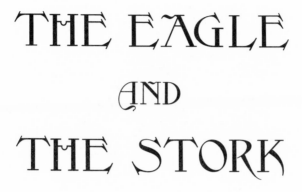

THE EAGLE
AND
THE STORK

Stoyan Christowe

Harper's Magazine Press
Published in Association with Harper & Row
New York

FOR MARGARET

THE EAGLE AND THE STORK. Copyright © 1976 by Stoyan and Margaret Christowe. All rights reserved. Printed in the United States of America. No part of this book may be used or reproduced in any manner whatsoever without written permission except in the case of brief quotations embodied in critical articles and reviews. For information address Harper & Row, Publishers, Inc., 10 East 53rd Street, New York, N.Y. 10022. Published simultaneously in Canada by Fitzhenry & Whiteside Limited, Toronto.

FIRST EDITION

Designed by Janice Willcocks Stern

Library of Congress Cataloging in Publication Data

Christowe, Stoyan, 1898–
   The eagle and the stork.
   1. Christowe, Stoyan, 1898– —Biography.
I. Title.
PS3505.H93Z47   813'.5'2   75-9359
ISBN 0-06-121545-7

76 77 78 79 10 9 8 7 6 5 4 3 2 1

PART
ONE

The land was ours before

We were the land's.

—ROBERT FROST

1

America was not discovered by my native village in Macedonia until the first years of this century. Our Columbus was a man named Michael Gurkin. I was a child when Gurkin left the village and I had no memory of him, but I shall never forget the first letter he sent from America or, later, his return to the village an *Amerikanetz*. No one in the village had known about Gurkin's great adventure until that first letter, written in America, had found its way to the village. There being no local post office, the letter was addressed in care of a merchant in the market town of Lerin (Florina). Mrs. Gurkin, a fine, stately woman in her prime, illiterate like all women in the village but shrewd in the way of peasant women, got word from the merchant to appear in person in order to be handed the letter. The villager who delivered the message, instead of saying "letter," used the word for "paper," and Mrs. Gurkin's mind was filled with forebodings concerning her husband. At the next market day she went to the merchant to pick up the "paper." The man dipped a pen into a small brass inkwell and handed it to her to make a cross on a piece of paper on which he had written her name. Then the envelope, ornamented with various seals and colorful stamps and secured in the back with red sealing wax, was handed to Mrs. Gurkin.

Despite urgings from fellow villagers with whom she had gone to market, Mrs. Gurkin did not open the envelope until she got home. She carried it in her bodice, postponing knowledge of the bad news she feared the "paper" carried. The opening of the letter was an event and a revelation. People gathered about Mrs. Gurkin, wagged heads and clicked tongues in wonderment at the appearance of the letter, at where it must have come from, and at what it must contain. Mrs. Gurkin, never before having opened an en-

3

velope or even seen one, carefully cut the edge at one end with a pair of scissors and pulled out the contents. I say contents because there was more than a letter in the envelope.

Those able to read took turns reading the letter to Mrs. Gurkin and to those who could not read, which included all the womenfolk and all the older folk. One by one, like stitches in a piece of embroidery, the readers unraveled the individual letters to make out the words. Each word, as it was deciphered by the reader, was uttered separately as though it carried an independent thought.

The letter was not written by Gurkin, who was himself innocent of the mystery of reading and writing, but by some literate Macedonian from the city who had preceded Gurkin to the New World. Gurkin must have dictated the letter, but the scribe used some learned words like *mashineria* or *industria,* the meaning of which neither the readers nor the listeners comprehended.

Though the several readings varied somewhat, depending on the reader's ability to discern the letters and knit them into words and then, in spite of pauses, to link them into a sentence, the readings matched, so one had to believe the unbelievable wonders the letter recounted. What was hardest to believe were the instructions Gurkin had given his wife about a blue slip of paper he had enclosed in the envelope. The slip of paper was in itself a beautiful thing, bright blue, with ornamental scrawls and intricate patterns along the edges that the womenfolk admired and regarded as difficult to reproduce in their embroideries. The letter instructed Mrs. Gurkin to take the slip of paper to the *sarafs* (money changers) in the city and to exchange it for ten *napoleons,* not a *para* less. Now that was more money than Mrs. Gurkin could dream of, let alone calculate in *piasters.* Only the Jewish merchants and the Turkish beys in the market towns could deal in such sums. Though not entirely convinced of what her husband had written, Mrs. Gurkin nevertheless held the slip of paper tenderly, reluctant to let too many hands touch it, for—who knows—if it should be true what Michael had written, every touch might tarnish the gold or cause some of it to melt away. Those privileged to touch the paper did so with trepidation, as though it were a magical thing that might either disintegrate into air at the touch or tinkle out into ten glittering gold coins. But the paper did neither. How could it? Didn't such things happen only in the folk tales?

The following market day Mrs. Gurkin again drove her donkey across the hills and descended into the city of Lerin, which straddled a sluggish river at the southern end of the Pelagonian plain. With some skeptical but curious villagers at her side, who afterward related the occasion in detail, Mrs. Gurkin approached a stall where sat a Jewish *saraf* with rows of gold and silver coins of different sizes and values neatly arranged before him like cartridges. Mrs. Gurkin hesitated but, urged on by her entourage, produced the slip of paper and, blushing, handed it to the *saraf.* The man studied the paper carefully, stroked his luxuriant beard, and asked to see the envelope. Reading thereon the name of the local merchant in whose care the registered letter had come, he offered to buy the paper for nine napoleons.

"Don't take it, Mrs. Gurkin," the erstwhile doubting Thomases now counseled. "If it's worth nine, it's worth the ten Michael says it's worth."

After some haggling the *saraf* made a final offer of nine and one half napoleons, and Mrs. Gurkin agreed.

Everyone was then convinced that Michael Gurkin had really gone to this mythical world called 'Merika and that all he wrote about it must be true, including the boastful statement that he was earning there more in one day than he could earn in a week at home. And it was that slip of paper, so magically converted into gold pieces, that caused, more than the wonders the letter recounted, the Americamania that changed the life of the village. People mortgaged fields and vineyards and meadows to the merchants in the towns for enough money for passage to this new world discovered by the unassuming Michael Gurkin.

As more people went to America, more letters came. Every letter told of the marvels there, and every letter, in one way or another, contradicted the others, though they all purported to tell the same story. In their zeal to give some notion of the New World the emigrants confounded their descriptions—if descriptions they were —so that there were as many different conceptions about America as there were people in the village. Some of the letters were not written by the senders themselves, who could not write, but by others only slightly more literate than themselves, who colored the texts with their own impressions. The contents of the letters, exaggerated and distorted in the writing (and in the understanding or misunderstanding of those who heard them read), were passed from mouth to ear until all manner of queer and fantastic beliefs and opinions about America came into being. Everybody had formed his or her own idea of what America was like. Although the letters did not say so, some people insisted that Americans had only one eye, a large one in the center of the forehead. One of the emigrants had sent a picture card showing an American drinking beer from a keg balanced on his huge stomach. This gave rise to the belief that Americans were orbicular as well as Cyclopean.

5

Even though many went to America and many letters arrived with those varicolored slips of paper that the *sarafs* converted into gold, no one had yet returned from there to prove that, while it was possible to go there, it was also possible to return from there. Some people had the notion that America might be like "the world beyond," to which one could go but whence one could not return. Besides, there was something worrisome about this America because of the word *merak,* which meant "anxiety." Most people elided the "A" and called the new country 'Merika, land of worry.

It was most fitting and proper, then, that none other than Michael Gurkin should be the first to return and dispel the doubts about the non-returnability from the New World. Gurkin had been a sawyer, one of those itinerant up-and-down sawyers of those days. When he had left the village to seek work after the suppression by the Turks of the Macedonian uprising in 1903 he had not the remotest notion that he was setting out on a journey of discovery. From job to job, moving northward across Macedonia, he wandered into the principality of Bulgaria, where he felt at home because of the language. There he joined a band of sawyers and with them crossed the broad Danube into Rumania, to lose himself somewhere in the deep forests of Transylvania. It was here that agents recruiting laborers for American industries persuaded him and some others to cross the Atlantic. As a result, the simple sawyer changed not only his own life but also the life of his village and of other villages in his native mountains. In all the centuries before, nothing had happened that had such a profound effect on the lives of the people.

And so it was that one day the news spread through the village that Michael Gurkin, himself and no other, had returned from America. It was true! It was Michael Gurkin who *had* returned, and it *was* from America. For if anyone had the slightest doubt that it was from America Gurkin had returned one had only to look at him. As I have said, when Gurkin left the village I was too little to have had any recollection of him, but by the time he returned I had heard so much about him—as who hadn't—that I felt I knew him. When he had emigrated he certainly must have worn the traditional village garb of rough homespun dyed in walnut hulls or alder bark. Around his waist he must have worn the broad dark woolen girdle, on his head the red fez that all Christians in the Ottoman Empire were forced to wear; and his feet must have been encased in raw-hide sandals.

People crowded into Gurkin's house to view him, to hear his voice, to touch him. They saw a new, different, transformed Gurkin. A splendor radiated from the once shy, withdrawn sawyer; he was now a man set apart from his fellow men, a man with a star

6

shining on his head. Never before had a man been seen in a costume such as Gurkin wore. People recalled a *Franga* (Frenchman) who, before I was born, had come to explore our hills for mineral deposits. He spoke some Bulgarian, and he had said that he was an *engineer,* whatever that meant. The Franga wore queer clothes, but that was to be expected. After all he was a Franga. For Michael Gurkin to rig himself out in the kind of costume he now wore was something else. Yet nobody questioned his right to do so. One did not have to ask oneself who gave Michael Gurkin the right to sport such attire. Of course it was America. That must be one of the wonders of this new land, that it could change people, make them over; that it could take a simple Macedonian up-and-down sawyer and make him over into a new kind of human being. That was one wonder none of the letters had mentioned—the wonder that was happening to the human being who emigrated to America. The emigrants, dazzled by America, told of what they saw, of the money they earned, the work they were doing, but not of what was happening to themselves.

There were skeptics, not to say cynics, and my father was the foremost of them. He quoted the well-worn saying that clothes do not make the man. He questioned Gurkin's right to come home and pose as an *Amerikanetz.* A wolf can change his clothes but not his habits was one of my father's favorite sayings. There *was* change in Gurkin, but to my father it was only an outward change. What counted was the inner man. Anybody could array himself in Gurkin's American fineries and still within be the same simple villager, the plowman, the sheepherder, the grist miller.

Now Gurkin did not boast, did not say that he was an *Amerikanetz,* did not condescend or patronize. He did not have to. Everything about him bespoke the new man. And it wasn't only the clothes. There emanated from him, in spite of his unpretentiousness and humility, an air of superiority or a broadening and enlargement of the man. Regardless of what he said or did not say, the *new man,* the embryo Amerikanetz, showed himself in many ways—in gestures, in mannerisms, in body language, and in oral language. He would say *yea, yea* instead of *da, da; no, no* instead of *né, né.* And he would wag his head sidewise to indicate dissent and nod his head up and down to indicate assent, which confused the people. It was the external Gurkin—the clothes, the gestures, the shaven mustaches, the gold teeth—that irritated my father, however much they might have fascinated the others. Now, who ever saw a man with gold teeth! Must a man put gold in his mouth to show how rich he was? Gurkin's four upper front teeth glittered like napoleons he brought from America.

7

I was eight years old and too young to be thinking of migrating to that magnetic land, but my father must have read in my eyes the enchantment and fascination with Gurkin. "Bah," he said, "you can caparison a donkey in silver and gold, but that doesn't make him a stallion."

On the first Sunday after his historic return Gurkin attended church, setting a pattern for all future returnees. His attendance at church caused more excitement than the visit of the bishop who, two years before, had come to the village to dedicate the new church. Nobody paid much attention to the liturgy, or to do the reading of the psalter, which I was now doing myself. Instead of worshiping, people gaped at the new transfigured Gurkin. Many had not gone to his house to view him, and he had not shown himself around the village until after he had "churched" himself, as if his new-manness, his Americanness, needed some kind of confirmation before it could be paraded around the village. There were no pews in the church, but on either side of the nave there were stalls in which worshiped the more prominent men of the village. Gurkin now occupied the one nearest to the altar. He stood there conscious that all eyes were upon him, the resplendent returnee from a new planet that might be closer to heaven than our poor earth.

His gift to the church—a brilliant, scintillant chandelier that would have done credit to a cathedral—was temporarily suspended by ropes from a beam above the nave. No village church was ever before enriched by such a treasure. Its shimmering crystals tinkled like tiny bells, irradiating the hues and sound of heaven, a fitting symbol of the opulence of the world whence Gurkin had returned. After church I described the chandelier to my blind grandfather, but never having seen anything like it in the days of his sight, he could not visualize it. I had guided my grandfather about and had described for him many remarkable scenes, including the visit of the bishop and a natural phenomenon involving a fierce, bitter and bloody war between storks and eagles, but one of the hardest tasks I faced was to make him see the new Gurkin.

Gurkin did not go home directly after church but lingered on the green to give the people a chance to view him and answer their questions about America. And the people listened spellbound to him tell of things they never dreamed existed. Many crossed themselves at the wonder of it all. Though the weather was fair and warm and the usually muddy byways of the village were dry, Gurkin had come to church wearing two pairs of shoes, one over the other, and carried a new kind of cane that opened into a small tent to protect him from the rain. This thing, which he called an "oumbrella," so

8

intrigued the people that repeatedly he had to open it and close it to satisfy the general curiosity. I tried as best I could to describe to Grandfather the ingenious mechanism which when pushed up caused the tent to open and when pulled down made the silky black tent wrap itself around the stick. What really astonished Grandfather was when I told him that Gurkin was wearing two pairs of shoes. I explained that the outer pair were made of some new kind of shiny leather that Gurkin called "goumma." Because most people in the village couldn't afford a pair of shoes and went barefoot or wore home-made *opinitsi* of raw pigskin or oxhide, Grandfather was offended by Gurkin's ostentation. To wear two pairs of shoes at the same time when people didn't have a single pair to call their own!

Gurkin wore a double-breasted jacket with heavy gray stripes and matching trousers that he called *pantaloni* and which were cuffed at the bottom and sharply creased in front and back. Most men in the village wore woolen frocks. Among the young, breeches began to appear, but they were of the knee-length type with a band that buttoned just below the knee. All this I described to Grandfather as best I could, and he shook his white head and made clucking sounds with his tongue.

Those who had dear ones in America whom they had doubted of ever seeing again were much heartened now that Gurkin had returned. Simple souls, they probably thought that America was no larger than a dozen villages and everybody there knew one another, and they asked Gurkin about their own. It was news to Gurkin that so many had followed in his footsteps, but he was most discreet and careful not to cause anxieties, made reassuring answers, giving the impression that he had seen everyone inquired about on the very day he had left America.

We the youngsters were especially enchanted by Gurkin, and we clustered about him wide-eyed with admiration. To make a contemporary comparison, our attitude toward him was somewhat like that of American youngsters toward space men. I myself, like most of my agemates, had dreams of becoming a *komitadji,* perhaps even chief of a band, like legendary Delchev, who had organized the armed *chetas* to fight Turkish oppression and free Macedonia from the age-old Ottoman yoke. But this new Turkless, pashaless, beyless country that could work miracles in simple villagers like Michael Gurkin and that could be reached by traversing boundless lands and a vast, limitless ocean, which Gurkin called *okean,* already from afar began to invade my young mind and my being. Listening to Gurkin narrate the marvels of America, I saw myself returning from America twice as glorious as he and bringing as a gift for the church

9

not a chandelier or a candelabrum but a new bell to replace the cracked one whose voice sounded like the voice of a person long ridden with an incurable sickness.

As Gurkin answered questions and told of wondrous things that one never heard of even in the folk tales, with the ferule of his "oumbrella" he punched little holes in the earth, making a kind of pattern, which the people stared at lest it should reveal something that language itself was incapable of conveying. Now in retrospect, as I write this after more than half a century of American life and a lifelong preoccupation with the meaning of Americanness, it seems to me that if it had been some wiser man describing what Gurkin attempted he would first have made some remark about the inadequacy of human speech to give even a vague notion of what Gurkin called *Amerikanska tsivilizatsia*. But Gurkin saw no need of any prefatory, apologetic remarks. Straightway he plunged into a narrative that entangled his listeners into a skein of verbal confusions. His language was interlarded with expressions that amazed and confounded his audience, words never before heard by man, such words as *aiskrim, sodapap, krakerjak, biliardo*. The once shy and shallow Michael Gurkin had become too learned and too skilled in the wizardries of *Amerikanska tsivilizatzia*. All stared at him. Even my grandfather with sightless eyes gaped and shook his head at Gurkin's giddy tales of buildings so high their roofs were in the clouds.

"Don't people get tired of climbing all those stairs?"

"There are no stairs," declared Gurkin pontifically and punched another hole in the ground with the umbrella by way of emphasis.

"No stairs! Is that what you said—no stairs?"

"No stairs," repeated Gurkin.

"Then how do people walk up?"

"They don't walk. They stand. The room goes up and down."

"What's he saying?" Grandfather pulled at my arm. "Is he saying the buildings have no stairs and the rooms go up and down?"

"Yes, Grandfather, that's what he said."

Was Gurkin telling folk tales or was he telling of wonders that really existed? One couldn't tell, because Gurkin himself was a folk tale, an unbelievable one. No one had the courage to question him or contradict him. No one, that is, except my father. He looked contemptuously at this nobody of a Michael Gurkin whom, by some quirk of destiny, the wind had blown to this new world. Patiently my father listened to Gurkin's outlandish words, studied his fineries, sumptuous and unbefitting to a peasant, and then he spoke to him, sarcastically and enigmatically. "But, Michael Gurkin, you have returned with the same clothes you wore when you left the village." Some people blinked at my father's words, puzzled. Gurkin himself stared at his creased pantaloons, looked at his shiny rubbers and the ankle-high brown shoes that buttoned on the sides, pulled at the stiff white band around his neck, touched the wide ribbon that was fastened to it, and then turned his nonplussed eyes on my father.

"Now be yourself, Michael Gurkin," my father persisted. "Remember, you were cradled and nourished by these same hills as the rest of us. Now you come here and tell us tall tales of tall buildings, of rooms that go up and down in the buildings in which they are supposed to be rooms."

These challenging words went deep and touched the old pre-American Gurkin. And the peasant in him re-emerged from under the American accouterments. The simple man crossed himself and summoned God to be his judge if he told a single untruth. " 'Tis the truth I tell. May lightning strike me and may the gold I brought from America turn to dust!"

The folk watched Gurkin go through the ritual of crossing himself and they believed him, for he was again one of them and had come home and was talking their own language.

"Go ahead, Michael, we believe you. Tell us more. Are there storks in America?"

"I can't say. I never saw any. But I don't think there are any. It's too far, much too far. The *okean* is too big for them to fly over."

Another man wanted to know if there were donkeys in America. This occasioned some laughter and Gurkin himself grinned, that being his way of indicating that he considered the question rather foolish.

"Don't be a hollowhead," my father put in. "Wherever there are human beings there are donkeys."

"Don't ask foolish questions," a man said. "Just let Michael tell us things. Go ahead, Michael, tell us more about 'Merika." Then Gurkin told in all seriousness that people in America talked to one another at great distances—distances of many days' journey. He explained that the talking and listening was done through horns connected by metal strings hung on poles. For some reason this did not seem so remarkable, but when he told how by the mere touch of a button a whole house was lighted—and not, mind you, by kerosene lamps or wax candles or pine splinters—there was much head-shaking and not a few *huhs* and *hmmms*.

"Then how is it lighted?"

"By *elektrichestvo.*"

"By what?"

"*Elektrichestvo.*"

"And what may that be, Michael Tomev Gurkin?"

Gurkin thought a moment, then he said confidently, *"Elektri-chestvo* is something you cannot see but gives light. It burns but it is not a flame. It is all light and there is no smoke. You press a button and it comes on. And you can't blow it out no matter how hard you blow."

"Then how do you blow it out when you want to blow it out?"

"You press the same button that brought it on, and that makes it go out."

And Gurkin told many more American wonders. Some sounded more incredible than others, but what's the use; you just have to stand there and listen to the man whether you believe or not.

2

Grandfather's gnarled hand held onto mine as I guided him up the winding path toward the treeless hillock on which stood the little chapel of St. Haralam. I didn't know how old Grandfather was, but to me he was as old as God, and he was dressed the way I believed God dressed. I could not imagine God wearing knee-length breeches like my father. In my childish mind the image of God was mixed up with my grandfather's appearance, except that God could fly across the heavens like an eagle and that everything about Him was larger, His face, His beard, His eyes.

Summer and winter Grandfather wore the same clothes, a *gi-urdia,* or frock, of bleached undyed wool, knee-length white socks in which were tucked the bottoms of white linen drawers. He was girded by a broad woolen sash, woven on the loom by my mother. It was wound around his waist several times to provide enough folds for his tobacco pouch, pipe, flint and tinder, some lumps of sugar to give a child. Looped on the girdle was a leather strap to which was fastened a crescent-shaped, horn-handled jackknife kept in the pocket of the frock.

Slowly we trudged up the winding path. The little shrine stood on a shelf near a solitary majestic oak in whose spreading branches roosted many birds. The chapel was built of bricks, mossy and discolored now, and was six-sided. The pantiles on the roof had turned green with age, and the roof itself conformed with the hexagonal shape of the building. At the apex of the roof, where the six riblike ridges converged, stood a wooden cross, tilted chidingly toward the village. I had often wondered why someone hadn't climbed up there to right the little cross. It had been like that for as long as I could remember, and no wind seemed to have had the force to dislodge it from its lopsided position. It seemed that it was held there in that precarious stance by some power other than the power of gravity.

Inside the chapel it was damp and cool and redolent with the odor of beeswax and olive oil. There was only one icon, that of the saint for whom the shrine had been built, nobody knew when or how long ago. The icon itself was old, its silver frame tarnished. An image lamp suspended from the ceiling hung before the icon. In a small, cylindrical, rusty tin there were matches. But they were damp, and I had to strike several against the bottom of the little box to light the taper Grandfather held. Then I guided his hand to the candelabrum where he stuck the taper, and I watched him cross himself three times, very devoutly, bowing low and describing wide arcs with the bunched thumb and two first fingers of his right hand. He leaned over and kissed the faded old icon.

Afterward we sat in front of the chapel, on the brow of the hill, warming ourselves in the sunlight. Down below in the hollow the village basked in shimmering heat. Our own house loomed above the others. Its two chimneys rose like sentinels at either end of the roof, and between them, on the roof ridge, reposed the huge stork nest, like a tree house.

To the left of us, as we sat there on the brow of the mound, stretched our beautiful mountain valley, with the peaks of distant Grammos, the boundary of our world to the west, veiled in purple mist. Beyond that were the lands of Greeks and Albanians. The latter we called *Arnauti,* proud descendants of men of the eagle, of noble Skanderbeg, but now reduced to the state of *gavaazi* (body-guards) of feudal Turkish lords. The native valley was flanked by oblong mountains, their beech- and oak-clad sides fringed by vine-yards and cornfields and bordered along the river by ribbons of bright-green meadows. Through the bottom of the valley coiled the limpid Bistra, watering fields and meadows, driving millstones, washing the sweat of villages on its serpentine course to the un-known sea. Nothing had changed here from the days when Grand-father could see, and he looked at the village with his blind eyes, knowing in his memory every house and who lived in it, every rise and dip on the mountainside, every turn and bend of the beautiful river. He leaned on his staff, his unseeing eyes fastened on the familiar scene.

His dream at my birth that I would be the medium through which he would view the living world was not without truth, for I had become, in a way, his recovered vision. The old man cherished me as one cherishes one's eyes. With his cane he could find his way alone within the house and on the grounds, and he could venture by himself through some parts of the village, but I was ever by his side. Even during harvest and haying, when children as little as six or seven helped with the work, I was allowed to stay with Grandfather, to guide him about, to help him with his carving, which he now did by touch and feel. From early youth he had shown an inordinate gift and zeal for carving. At first he had built carts, vats, wine casks, yokes, cupboards, cradles, and chests graven with leaves and flowers and other motifs from nature. People prized these artifacts, and well they might, for Grandfather would no more stoop to handcrafting such mundane objects. Since his pilgrimage to the chaste forests of Mount Athos, where he visited the renowned orthodox monasteries and served apprenticeship under the tutelage of the famous Debar carvers, he had forsworn the building of another cartwheel or vat or similar worldly objects and vowed to consecrate the rest of his life to the sculpting in wood of the benign images of saints and the re-creation in wood tracery of entire episodes of the New Testament.

The villagers paid for vats and casks and wheels and looms and barrows but not for the images of saints, and so Grandfather gave up his carving long enough to build a grist mill. While it chattered and ground grain into flour, he sat in front in the yard and carved rosettes and birds and strange animals and coiling serpents on walnut panels, which he would later assemble into an iconostasis for some church in a village nestling in the bosom of the mountain.

The grist mill was not like any other seen or heard of. It was like a toy, and it sang like a lark and its rattles made a sound like a woodpecker. Instead of damming the waters of the Bistra, as other millwrights had done, and conducting it down a millrace to the grist mill, he dammed the current of a little stream that purled between two slopes and conducted the water along the side of one of the slopes and into a long funicular tube girdled at intervals with dogwood hoops. No wider than a stove pipe at the bottom where the nozzle was, as it went up the slope the tube broadened until at the upper end where it received the millstream it was as wide around as a hogshead. The entire vessel was like a giant telescope peering into the earth. The nozzle was about the size of a saucer, and the mill wheel, the blades, the spindle that held the stone were all so magically constructed that one could put the waterwheel in motion by merely blowing at it. The water issued from the nozzle compressed like steel, struck slantingly at several blades simultaneously, and put the mill wheel into furious gyrations, causing a foamy whirlpool.

On the floor above, at the upper end of the spindle, the millstone whirred. From a wooden box shaped like an inverted pyramid the grain trickled into the hole at the center of the millstone. At an

15

opening in front, the lips of the stone sifted out the flour like foam from the mouth of a dragon.

Other millers had harnessed the waters of the Bistra to propel their millstones. Grandfather had dammed a mountain brook to power a mill that became the wonder of the village and the joy of the children. For it was like an organ, humming and droning at the foot of a hill near a walnut tree.

The mill had made it possible for Grandfather to do what he wanted, for while it chattered and droned he sat in the yard in the shade of the walnut tree to carve the famous iconostasis for the new church. He had started working on the panels even before ground had been broken for the church. When finally assembled, the immense wood tracery stretched from wall to wall and halfway up to the roof, thus separating the altar from the nave proper. Many times, while the priest went through the various steps of the liturgy amidst rows of fluttering tapers, I would stand there with my eyes glued to the fantastic world carved in wood by my grandfather. Had anyone seen such foliage, such fruits and flowers, such birds and animals? I was proud that it all had been done by Grandfather. Then he lost his sight but continued, stone-blind, to carve things by touch and feel. He did not confine himself only to reproducing objects from memory but instead created new things, some of them so fantastic they could only have come from his imagination.

I myself was ever aware of my special obligation to make Grandfather "see," to help him in his work. But my mother said that Grandfather was helping me more than I was helping him, for at a time when my agemates were hardly articulate, I had, thanks to helping Grandfather see, acquired a vocabulary and fluency of speech beyond my age. The old man had begun to teach me the art of expression as soon as I was able to talk.

"Ah, my child," he would say when I had described something to him. "I see twice. I see as an old man and I see with the eyes of a child." He would press my hand and stroke my hair. His hands were gnarly and knuckly from a lifetime of wielding chisels and mallets.

I was too young to realize it then, but for a long time I have known that my grandfather had a profound influence on my development as a child and as a man. Gurkin was to plant the seed of Americanness in me while he himself was barely touched by it. My grandfather Bogomir, as he handcrafted chunks of wood into recognizable creatures of nature or into the images of saints, was in a real sense molding my own character. He was a balladist, a blind bard who intoned no ballads but built them out of wood. Since I had to guide him to church, to funerals, festivals, saints' feasts,

16

processions, I came to participate with him in all these observances, and the "seeing" I did for him enlarged my own world.

Outside of his undying urge to work wonders with wood there were two powerful forces working within the blind man's being: to see the bishop, who had promised to come to dedicate the new church, and to see Macedonia freed from the Ottoman yoke.

"Ah, the bishop, child. When will he come to put his blessings on our church? He promised to come a long time ago."

I asked him if he had seen a bishop during his stay at the monasteries at Mount Athos.

"No," he sighed. "I've never seen a bishop. I saw two archimandrites, but a bishop! Bishops are rare. There's only one bishop to a thousand priests. They carry silver-capped staffs and wear vestments of gold and on their heads miters studded with precious stones. Bishops are so rare and so pious, wherever they set foot the ground is hallowed."

"Are they big, Grandfather? The bishops?"

"You never heard of a small bishop."

"Are they like human beings? Are they like us?"

"They are born of mothers just like us. But there's something of heaven in them. They are touched by God."

Grandfather believed in signs and omens and looked in nature for some portent that would foretell the end of the half a millennium of Turkish dominion over our country. Time and again he said to me, "Ours is the only Christian land in Europe still under the crescent, and yet it was here on our own Macedonian soil that St. Paul planted the cross." He prayed for delivery from the Turks. In school we were reading the poems of Khristo Botyov, the famous Bulgarian revolutionary poet, and I told Grandfather that in one of his poems Botyov said that freedom needs the rebel, not prayer.

"If freedom needs the rebel, then the rebel needs prayer," he said.

As we sat there on the hillock under the clear blue sky and warm sun, nothing was further from our minds than that we should presently be witnessing a unique natural phenomenon in which Grandfather would try to read meanings that might betoken the dawn of freedom for us. In the distance between the two oblong mountains that flanked the valley there appeared two clouds, one black and the other white. There was something strange about those clouds appearing so suddenly out of nowhere against a cloudless sky. There was no wind, yet the clouds were moving up the valley quite perceptibly. As I peered at them I became aware that there was something too precise about their formation. Though distinctly

17

separated, they floated on evenly, uniformly. And as they moved closer I began to discern that they were made up of perhaps hundreds of separate bodies quivering in the air. And soon those bodies began to grow larger and to take on the shapes of birds with outstretched wings. Presently I was able to make out that the white birds were storks and the dark ones eagles. Perfectly parallel, like two aerial phalanxes sailing uniformly, the two flocks continued on until they reached the meadows below the village. Here they cut their flight as to a command and in beautiful, sweeping waves, with the sun rays playing on their plumage, began to descend to the meadows on either side of the river.

I grasped Grandfather's arm. "Look, Grandfather, look! Eagles and storks, hundreds of them."

The old man passed his hand across his opaque, sightless eyes and stared ahead, bewildered. "What eagles and what storks, child? What are you saying?"

"They just alighted. They came up from the lower end of the valley and are now in the meadows not far from the village. The eagles are on one side of the river, the storks on the other."

The old man's eyes peered down on the meadows where the birds had settled. "There'll be war," he said, his voice quavering. "They'll fight. This is an omen."

"Whom will they fight, Grandfather?"

"They'll fight each other. It will be a battle between the cross and the crescent. You must help me see everything, child."

I knew as did everybody else that the storks were favored by the Moslems. I did not know the reason for it. In Kostur (Kastoria), which was as far as I had ever been, I had seen stork nests on the roofs of mosques or on the balconies of minarets, and I had also watched storks pace undisturbed like gendarmes about the market place and snatch fish from the stalls. The vendors didn't harm them for fear of inviting the wrath of some Turk. Storks built nests on house roofs in the village and returned to them year after year to raise their young. People thought it good luck for a stork couple to settle on their roofs, and to entice them to do so they placed old cartwheels to serve as foundations for their huge nests. We children always looked with excitement to the coming of the storks in spring, and we welcomed them with joy. We had names for them—the Frogger, the Fisher, the Snaker, the Abbot. We also believed that the storks were real people who became storks in order to fly to our land from their winter homes across the seas. To turn into storks, the legend said, they had to immerse themselves in the waters of a spring. Upon their return there in the fall they turned human again by immersing themselves in the same spring.

18

As for the eagles, I was yet to learn that they were the symbol of royal and military power, that the eagle was carried on standards by the armies of Rome and of Napoleon. What I knew was that the eagle was a bird beloved of Balkan rebels who had fought the Turks. In school we recited Botyov's famous ballad about the wounded rebel on the mountain. It was an eagle, heroic bird, that cared for him, fanned him, and shaded him from the scorching sun.

A sudden deafening, earsplitting scream chilled my spine. It came from two eagles that had detached themselves from the ranks and wheeled loftily above the meadows.

"It's the war cry," said Grandfather animatedly. "The eagles have given their signal."

In response to the eagles' shriek two storks soared above the meadows, their broad, black-tipped wings slowly cleaving the air, their long pink legs extended. When they attained the height of the eagles, they wheeled majestically and then answered the eagles' screams with a furious clattering of their mandibles.

And then the plumaged meadows on each side of the river stirred. Hundreds of wings flapped, and the two hostile flocks began to rise for battle. Fierce, blood-chilling eagle screams were answered by an artillery of clattering storks' beaks.

The flocks rose halfway up between the bottom of the valley and the spines of the mountains. Here they formed fronts and the battle began. It seemed as if the two mountains, which had faced each other in tranquillity for millenniums, were suddenly roused to fury and discharged living bullets from their great sides. The space between them became a sea of savage, screaming, tumultuous waves. Sharp, hooked eagles' claws dug into white storks' crops and dragged great birds earthward to rip and disembowel with their powerful beaks. Bright-red stork beaks stabbed and slashed, impaling frenzied eagles as though they were frogs in the marshes.

It didn't seem real. So strange, so improbable it all was—the grappling, the tearing, the rending of flesh by the eagles; the bayoneting and harpooning by the storks; the hellish screaming of the eagles and the artillerylike rattle of the storks' beaks.

Grandfather was trying to say something, but his words were drowned by the uproar. He shook my arm. "Are the eagles winning?"

"It's hard to tell, Grandfather. They're all mixed up. It's too terrible. You never saw such a sight."

A phalanx of storks zoomed above the plane of battle into the serene air above and then swooped down on a contingent of eagles, using their beaks like cutlasses to hack at their enemies. To avenge their bleeding comrades, squadrons of rageful eagles rent the air with trumpetlike cries and clutched and grappled, only to be over-powered by the bulk and mass of their foes, by the deadlier thrust of their bayonetlike beaks.

Grandfather kept staring into the holocaust. His eyes had lost their blankness and a strange light as of restored vision had come into them. I knew those eyes were unseeing, but I knew also that he was seeing with his whole being, with the cells of his body and the pores of his skin, with his heart and his soul. Without a word to me he stood up and faced the tilted little cross on the roof of the shrine. Amidst the hellish noise of the battle I caught snatches of his prayer, his expressions of gratitude to the saint for his guardian-ship of the village, his supplications that he not forsake his wards at this fateful moment.

He tugged at me. "The eagles must win. They must. Are they favored?"

"It's not clear, Grandfather. It's hard to say." I wished with all my heart for the eagles to win. But my heart ached as I watched one raging white wave after another fall on a dark one like an avalanche and beat it down to the earth. The eagles fought bravely, fero-ciously, and it appeared they outnumbered the storks, but the latter overwhelmed them by their greater size and the deadlier hacking of their spearlike beaks. Dozens of storks, white plumage blood-spattered, wings no longer able to hold them in the air, wavered and floundered as they were relentlessly clawed and mangled by platoons of infuriated eagles, but far many more mutilated eagle carcasses darkened the meadows.

"Tell me, child, are the eagles gaining?"

I didn't have the heart to tell Grandfather that it looked hopeless for the eagles. Battered, decimated, still flurries of them uttered clarion calls and rose high in the air to catapult themselves in suicidal rage on their enemies.

The battle did not last long. It ended abruptly. The surviving exhausted eagles suddenly withdrew from the scene as though blown away by a gale. Some bellicose diehards, in pairs or in threes, still pursued some stray enemy, only to be beaten to the ground by a detachment of storks that rushed to the aid of their imperiled comrades.

Soon what was left of the eagles fled the scene, and a deathly silence fell upon the valley, over which wheeled serenely trium-phant storks. Voiceless, they made no drumming sounds with their mandibles, nor did they show any other sign of jubilation. In their silence they were all the more majestic. Some of them swooped down on the meadows perhaps in search of a wounded mate. And then, leaving the scene of their triumph, they floated silently over the village. A wearied one, injured perhaps and unable to support the pain, fell upon a rooftop. Having passed the village, the storks formed echelons and headed north for the mountain pass on the other side of which lay the broad Pelagonian plain.

Again the sun shone on the wounded bosom of the earth; again the valley began to breathe. Some frightened animals, which had fled in terror to the woods, drifted back, eying the fallen birds suspiciously and snorting at the blood-smirched grass.

From the strange silence that enveloped us on the little mound where we sat and whence we had "witnessed" the savage battle between the two bird tribes, Grandfather knew that the battle had ended. His lusterless eyes still gazed unblinkingly at the meadows, as if they were trying to see what had actually happened.

"It's all over, Grandfather," I said.

"I know that, child."

It was the first time I had ever lied to him, and I did not do it consciously, deliberately. I just heard a voice say, "The eagles won, Grandfather."

He said nothing.

I helped him up and guided him on the winding path down the hillside. At the foot of the hill I stopped and faced him.

"Grandfather," I said.

"Yes, child."

"Will you forgive me? The eagles did not win."

He put his hand on my head. "I know. Cross yourself, child."

3

Of all the seeing I did for Grandfather the visit of the bishop was the most difficult. For weeks before the expected arrival of that dignitary the old man talked of nothing else. "Ah, child, it will be a glorious sight when the bishop comes."

The church had been built years ago but had not yet been consecrated. For generations the village had worshipped in a mud-brick, whitewashed low building with a stone cross on the pantiled roof but no bell or cupola. It had been built back in the days when Turks forbade cupolas or belfries and permitted only such Christian houses of worship as hugged the ground. The voice of the muezzin was heard from the minarets in the cities, and no bell was allowed to interfere with that voice.

All that had changed, but the village continued to worship in the squatty old chapel until the *Amerikantzi,* while transforming the face of the village, had the moldy old chapel torn down and replaced by a granite-walled "edifice" with tall arching windows, French tiles on the roof, and a graceful cupola topped by a gilded cross. For some years then the village had worshipped in this handsome but unconsecrated church built with money earned in carshops, roundhouses, mines, and foundries in America. The church had not been consecrated because it had no bell with which to welcome the bishop. And then, again largely due to the discovery of the New World by Michael Gurkin, the fanatic zeal of Simeon the beadle, plus sacrifices of the worshippers themselves, the village had acquired, for the first time, a real, large, and wondrous bell.

Like Grandfather, Simeon the beadle was a man of profound piety. He too had three overpowering ambitions: to see a new church in place of the dingy, unbelfried old chapel; to see a real bell take the place of the pine plank by which he summoned the village to worship; and to become a priest. To thank God for the new church and for the discovery of America (for all was God's gift) Simeon made a pilgrimage to Jerusalem, thereby gaining the title of *hadjia,* or pilgrim, a religious honorific that did little to assuage his thirst for the priesthood. On his return from the holy city Simeon told many stories, stories of hermitages and ennobling piety and self-abnegation. He also brought back icons and little painted wooden crosses in which one could see, through a tiny lens in the center, magnified episodes of the Old and New Testaments in brilliant colors. He would have preferred to come back an ordained priest but had to console himself with the title of *hadjia.* Like the good beadle that he was, he once again took up the duty of calling the village to worship by clapping the old plank whose clear, sharp sound carried for a mile or so down the valley. On a calm, weather-breeding day it could be heard farther. Simeon regarded this seasoned sounding board with due reverence for the service it had rendered the village, but since his return from Jerusalem he began crusading for a metal bell as ardently as he had crusaded for the new church. In Jerusalem he had thrilled and marveled at the voices and the sizes of the church bells. From the monks and priests there he heard of bells of immense sizes, like the Great Bell of Moscow, as well as of churches that had not one, not two but a whole set of bells that chimed simultaneously like a chorus of angels.

We knew that bells were part of the ritual and symbolism of our faith. Moslems in the cities were summoned to worship by the human voice—the call of the muezzin. For years after the conquest the Turks had forbidden the use of bells, and when they did permit them they levied taxes on them to discourage their use. As a symbol of Christian worship the bell was distasteful to the Turks, perhaps because its voice, chiming above the voice of the muezzin, gave intimation of an authority higher than the conqueror. And this power sometimes showed its censure of Ottoman oppression by causing church bells miraculously to swing by themselves and ring out without anyone's striking them.

Another thing about bells that moved our hearts was their association with freedom. The *Amerikantzi* had not said anything yet about the most famous bell in history in this connection, but the Ilenden Insurrection in 1903, when I was five years old, was proclaimed by the ringing of bells throughout Macedonia. In speaking about the bells of Jerusalem Simeon had told of how in other lands bells had been rung to proclaim the triumph of Christian arms.

"We do more than merely pray for the day of our deliverance," said Simeon, alluding to the liberation movement. "When that blessed day comes, will it be by striking a piece of wood that we shall welcome it?"

The beadle also kept reminding the villagers that the church

23

remained unhallowed, like a grown-up child unbaptized, because there was no bell. To welcome a bishop with a wooden plank was a sacrilege, and to continue to worship year after year in a house ornamented with icons and chandeliers and scented with incense and olive oil but still unconsecrated was a sin before God.

And so the villagers, emulating the *Amerikantzi* who donated napoleons, opened their hearts to the appeal for contributions. Women took off from their waistbands silver clasps the size of saucers and from their thick braids coins worn smooth by the centuries. Rings and necklaces and bracelets and brooches and earrings and other prized adornments they threw in the common "bell pile." Men parted with cherished objects—silver and brass inkhorns, embossed buckles, silver powder horns, snuffboxes and tinderboxes. Grandfather brought out his *kiostek,* an ornament that men of his day wore in a loop across the breast. It was made of many silver strands threaded into a ribbonlike band more than an inch wide.

All these treasures were taken to some distant place to be melted and cast into a bell, and I had thought that in a week or two we would have our bell; but it was months before the bell arrived in Florina. To haul it to the village three teams of oxen were needed and a specially built cart with oversize wheels and stout axles. Scores of us children went a good distance to meet the bell. With horns curving like lyres above their heads, the oxen tugged at the precious load.

For the raising of the bell to its place in the cupola it seemed half the men of the village lent a hand. By the ingenious manipulation of thick hempen ropes, fulcrums and levers and other primitive craning devices, plus the judicious application of human power, the great bell was hung upon the strong oaken beam in the cupola with the shining cross above it.

The whole village gathered on the plaza for the "sounding," or the testing of the bell. A new bell may turn out to have a full, resonant, beautiful tone or a dull, raspy, metallic one. From one of the arches of the cupola Simeon looked down on the people who waited to hear the voice of their bell. For this was no ordinary bell. Into it had gone precious objects, cherished heirlooms kept in chests and bequeathed from generation to generation. Sentiments were attached to those objects, vows made by sons to fathers, by daughters to mothers, pledges given when youths had offered them to their loved ones. All that was now in the bell. And the sweat of roundhouses in America.

There was something profoundly spiritual in the pallid, bearded face framed in the arch of the cupola. In a quavering voice Simeon spoke to the people. "Brothers, listen now to your bell. I shall ring it." A pall of silence fell upon us. Not a child cried, not a babe whimpered in its mother's arms. The whole of nature hushed in expectation; the birds in the trees seemed to understand the import of Simeon's words and interrupted their songs. The fruit trees, the slender tall poplars, the spreading old grandmother willows, all seemed eager to hear the first sound of this first church bell.

Simeon crossed himself three times, and the sign was repeated by many people down below. Grandfather didn't have to be told. In the silence he sensed that others were crossing themselves, and he released my arm and crossed himself the way he always did, touching his forehead with the thumb and first two fingers bunched and then describing wide arcs in three directions. To me his outreaching, embracing crosses were expressive of his profound piety and goodness.

Through the arches of the cupola we now watched Simeon seize the piece of rope that hung from the clapper. He held the rope firmly for an instant, then pulled it a little to one side and gave the bell a gentle, measured stroke. A mellifluous sound wave, full and resonant, beautiful and sustained, floated over our heads like an immense silvery bubble, like a benediction from above. Before striking again Simeon allowed this first peal to die out completely, and it died out slowly, sustainedly—a prolonged moan, a prolonged hum, and then a barely perceptible sigh. Then Simeon pulled the clapper farther to one side and swung it with greater force against the brim on the opposite side of the bell. The new sound wave, fuller, deeper-toned, more resonant, more timbrous, floated out from the cupola and engulfed the people, the plaza, and the whole village. No sound like that had ever been heard in the village. Other villages had bells but none like this, none with such a voice. This was not the voice of mere fused metals; this was the music of heaven caught in the burden of a bell, the voice of angels blended into heavenly harmony. I could feel Grandfather quiver as he held my hand.

Again Simeon swung the ringer and again the bell responded, sending forth succeeding sound waves before the preceding ones had died out. It was heaven's response and reward to the people for their sacrifices.

As I looked at the entranced, transported faces, with tears in many eyes, I imagined that to them the bell sounds appeared in the forms of the objects they had donated, every donor seeing his or her own silvery gift or gold napoleon glinting in the sunlight and emitting its own enchanting melody; every coin ringing with the accent of its own century; every medallion echoing the vow and

25

love voice of the maiden whose bosom it had once adorned; every heirloom echoing the good will of its generation.

I was not "seeing" for Grandfather now. There was no need for it. He heard the bell and saw with his inner being. He always imputed meanings and divinations to things that it was hard for me to understand. He invariably addressed me as "child" or "boy" but treated me as a grownup and attributed to me an adult's capacity of comprehension. On our way home he talked to me about the bell as a symbol of man's innate goodness. He said the bell was proof that God was present in every being. The treasured pieces amalgamated into the huge, cuplike shape had brought the village closer together, had fused its hopes and desires into a single aspiration. He saw hope for freedom in the village's realization of its dream for a bell. Now that we had a bell with which to welcome it, freedom would not be long in coming.

With time the bell's voice expanded; it grew more sonorous, more heavenly. There was no bottom to its depth, to those mysterious caverns whence issued the mellow tonality that inundated the valley with its sustained, prolonged hum. Not alone did its voice grow more timbrous and melodious, but the bell itself became more sensitive. And Simeon loved the bell, loved its responsiveness. He made friends with it and translated its silvery tones into meaningful phrases that the villagers understood as jungle people read the meaning of distant drums. Simeon could evoke from the bell moods of pathos or of joy, of despair or jubilation, of submission or defiance. For the bell was rung not only to summon the village to worship but to give warnings of fires, break the spell of hailstorms, prevent lightning from striking people and animals. It called the villagers to meetings, announced the commencement of harvests, the gathering of the grapes, the arrival of notables. It tolled a dirge when someone died. For every purpose the ringing was different.

Though soon after the bell was hung the bishop was informed, for a long time he did not come. Bishops cannot be ordered about. They come when they come. And the longer they delay their coming the more solemn it becomes. Their coming is a blessing that can only be beseeched, supplicated, and people said prayers for the coming of the bishop.

In the meantime the old priest died. In expectation of being ordained a priest, Simeon let his hair grow long so that it might be plaited and the braid tucked under the black priestly hat. And he had visions, as village priest, of being the first to welcome the bishop when he would come for the consecration, the first to kiss his saintly hand and march beside him in the great welcoming

26

processional. He would be the one to assist him in the solemnizing rites.

But fate decreed otherwise. To be ordained priest, the village chose a younger man. Simeon humbly accepted the verdict as the will of God but kept his hair long. He appeared to find solace in a more devoted attachment to his duties as beadle and to such other humbler ecclesiastical duties as reading the psalter, lighting and snuffing the tapers, and refilling the image lamps before the icons.

Thus it was with Simeon, with the bell, and with the village, when finally tidings came that to dedicate the church the bishop had chosen a Sunday in the middle of June. For this long-awaited memorable event many things were done, many preparations made. Dooryards were swept clean, the churchyard and the whole plaza between the church and the schoolhouse were raked of sticks and stones, house walls were whitewashed, windows cleaned, roofs mended, fallen fences or lopsided gates propped up. Things that people had neglected for months or years they now attended to as though they feared the bishop would chide them for their shiftlessness. The whole village brightened and adorned itself like a bride, to be blessed by the bishop.

Though the great day was to be the day of the dedication, the one preceding, on which the bishop arrived, was the fateful one. On that day the thousand-odd inhabitants of the village, together with hundreds of pilgrims who had come from other villages, marched up the valley to the foot of the mountain to welcome the prelate. But Simeon the beadle had to stay behind, perched like a stork in the cupola whence he commanded a view of the road up the valley that the bishop would travel. At sight of the bishop's approach he was to commence ringing the bell and continue ringing it until the princely visitor had reached the churchyard.

One other person besides Simeon did not march in the welcoming procession. It was Grandfather. He insisted that I go alone and that he would wait for me on the balcony of the schoolhouse, which faced the church and overlooked the plaza. I had helped him up the steps to the open balcony and was to rejoin him there as soon as the bishop appeared so that I might help him "see" him. Like everybody else, Grandfather was dressed in what he called his Easter costume, which he also wore on Christmas, on All Souls' Day, and other major holidays. Everything about him was white, except his shoes. His frock was made of the choicest wool, which had been bleached in the sun by the river and carded so thoroughly by my mother that it had become light and soft like silk before it was spun into yarn and woven on the hand loom into the velvet-textured cloth. This rich white garment, embroidered in black braid all along the edges and around the pockets, was sleeveless, so that the sleeves of Grandfather's white linen shirt flapped about him like the wings of a giant bird. As I regarded him there on the balcony he looked sublime and apostolic, a living saint, his snow-white hair a veritable halo around his forehead.

In all the "seeing" I had done for Grandfather I had lied to him that one time about the eagles and the storks and in confessing I had vowed never to deceive him again no matter what. And yet I broke my vow when the bishop came. The bishop was a wizened little man with a weary, hollow face and a frizzy beard like shriveled corn silk. There was nothing princely or rotund or resplendent or bishoplike about him. He wore no miter studded with rubies and emeralds but a flat-topped stiff black hat covered with a black cloth that hung on either side of his face like blinders. We had come to welcome him at the northern end of the valley, an hour's walk from the village. He had come by train from Bitola, the seat of the episcopate, to Florina and thence on horseback over the mountain and down into the valley escorted by an Albanian *gavaz.* The bishop dismounted here and allowed his hand to be kissed by the priest and a dozen village elders. Then the procession started. The bishop refused to ride his horse and insisted on marching on foot together with the people who had come to welcome him. And he did so march, at the head of the procession, disdainful of the mud. If these simple folk could draggle through the mud for the sake of God, then why could not God do the same for them? In keeping with the occasion, the day was a blessed one. The two preceding days it had rained, but at dawn on this historic day the sky had cleared and the sun had come out, itself eager to welcome the prelate, though the road was muddy.

With his feet on the ground the bishop looked even less impressive than when mounted. His black cassock reached to his ankles, but you could see his shoes; they too were black, the kind with elastics on the sides at the ankles. I never thought of shoes in connection with the bishop, the kind of shoes they would be, or how they would look, any more than I would have thought of angels wearing shoes.

The bishop's horse and the stately Albanian bodyguard made up in part for the bishop's unbishoplike appearance. The horse was sleek and ebony black and had beaded fringes across the forehead and red, green, and yellow tassels on the halter. It was the kind of steed one imagined the sultan and his viziers might ride. The guard was a Christian Albanian, of the Tosk tribe, and wore the Epirotic pleated white skirt, gold-braided jacket, and the gondola-shaped footwear with the multicolored pompoms at the upturned toes.

A silver cross dangled at the bishop's chest, but instead of a silver-capped crozier he carried in his left hand a commonplace wooden staff, while with the right hand, or rather with the first two fingers of it, he kept blessing the people. He draggled along, making holes in the miry earth with the ferule of his staff, his shoes sucking the mud as he lifted one foot and then the other. The hem of his dark robe drabbled behind, and behind that plodded the procession, flanked on one side by wheatfields and on the other by cornfields. Despite the bishop's unprepossessing appearance it seemed to me that the wheat stalks inclined their ears toward him, like some flowers that always turn to the sun. And the endless rows of luxuriant cornstalks, freshened by the two-day rain, seemed legions of devout communicants bowing their cruciform tassels toward the bishop as though they were church insignia.

The warm sun fell down on everything like a special benediction, and the earth heaved its panting bosom to it. I looked at the faces of the people and saw no disappointment there, only an ecstatic glow, an answer to a prayer, a blessing. Hundreds of feet trudged through the mud—men, women, children, privileged to march through nature with a bishop. Many of them had prayed for this moment, to see a bishop, to be walking in his foot tracks, to be with him in this serene procession which trod the soil, marched through the heart of nature, where the birds singing in the trees, the fluttering butterflies, the lowly grasshoppers could rejoice.

Young as I was, just entering my teens, after the initial disappointment over the appearance of the bishop I began to feel in some part of my being that there was about this bishop something of the original, rough-garbed, bread-and-water disciples we studied about in the *Evangelium*. I began to see the bishop as a humble apostle come to our mountain valley to flounder through the mud in order to refill the image lamps in the hearts and souls of the people, as well as to bolster our national spirit; for, because we lacked self-government, the church was the only prop to our nationality. And this little man with his scraggly beard and thin, pallid face and sunken eyes was not only the representative of God, the embodiment of our faith, but also the symbol of our identity as a nation. We were not a state, only a subject province of a dying empire, which still stretched over three continents. We had no governor, king or president; our church held us together as a separate and distinct people, provided us with free schools and kindled in us the hope of freedom and the pride of nationhood while we were a subject people without any rights, civic or political.

From his perch in the bell tower, as soon as Simeon had sighted the procession, he started to ring the bell. Under his controlled, well-measured, well-timed strokes, the bell sent forth its glorious voice to welcome the prelate. Wakened by Simeon to its innermost being, the bell filled the valley with the burden of its sweet voice. A flock of singing angels issued from the arches of the cupola and winged jubilantly through the valley. And listening to this angelic choir, the villagers waded through the mud as though it were a sacred stream—the Jordan River. And why should it not be? Wasn't the bishop in the fore? Did he not hallow everything he touched? This was not the consecration of the church alone; this was the baptism of the village, the confirmation of ourselves as a people apart from the Turks, who governed us.

As the procession approached the village I ran ahead so as to be with Grandfather on the school balcony when the bishop would enter the plaza. The old man grasped my hand. "At last, child, at last! You will help me to see him. I mustn't miss anything. All my life I've waited for this, to see a bishop of our own who prays in our tongue. Ah, child, how fortunate we are. God has not forsaken us."

Then the bell drowned his voice, and I saw that the bishop had made the corner by the bridge. With the young priest by his side he slowly paced toward the common. The bell, which had been ringing continuously, now paused, and Simeon gazed down on the people milling about the bishop like a swarm of bees around its queen.

"Is he here, child? Can I see him now?"

"Yes, Grandfather. He has just crossed the bridge and is now walking toward the church."

"Well, then, why am I not seeing him?" The old man's hungry eyes stared toward the little bridge over which the procession still flowed in a stream toward the church grounds. He could tell that from the tramping of feet on the planks. Speechless, I stood there on the balcony, myself gazing at the bishop, at his weary face and frizzy beard, his mud-splotched robe. When some minutes passed and I had not spoken, Grandfather became restless. "Why are you silent? Why am I not seeing the bishop? Is anything wrong, child? Is this not a bishop? Have they sent an abbot instead?"

"No, Grandfather, no. It's the bishop. He came himself."

"Then why are you not telling me? Are the people kissing the hem of his golden robe, are they worshipping the ground hallowed by his foot track?"

"Yes, Grandfather, the people bow and cross themselves."

The old man's thirst for a graphic description of the prelate was not quenched by these few words. "How does he look? How big is he? What does he wear? I've waited for this all my life and thank

30

the Lord I can see if only you'd help me. Don't be selfish, child. Don't see only for yourself.''

Again as at the time of the battle between the storks and the eagles something stirred in me and a voice other than my own began to speak within me. "He's tall and stout, Grandfather, the bishop is. He towers above the others like the belfry above the rooftops. His face is full and round and his cheeks are like ripe apples. His beard is thick and black. A huge silver cross sways on his breast. The cross is large, larger than the one our priest makes us kiss when he smacks us on the forehead with the hyssop drenched in the holy water."

The old man trembled. Tears ran down his cheeks, wetting his white beard. The procession kept moving into the plaza, the bishop still at the head. His mud-spattered shoes shuffled on nimbly. The hems of his black cossack flapped at his ankles.

"Again you are silent. Does he wear a jeweled crown? Is he robed in gold? Tell me.''

"Yes, Grandfather. He's clothed in gold and silver. His hair is plaited and the braids are tucked under his miter, which is big and round and is set with many jewels."

"And his staff, and the way he walks?''

"His staff is bigger than your cane, its handle not crooked but round, shaped like a pear, and of silver. He walks very slowly, Grandfather, the bishop does, and very gravely. When one foot is set on the ground it is stayed there until the other is lifted. You never saw anyone walk like that."

"Is he saying anything?''

"No. He keeps blessing the people. He does this like the priest does, by lifting the first two fingers of his right hand and making signs in the air and then slanting his fingers toward the people. The people bow in waves, like the wheat before the wind, so that the blessing may fall on their heads."

Thus I continued "seeing" the bishop through Grandfather's eyes, telling him what he wanted to hear, to sustain his image of the bishop. Tears trickled down his old cheeks. He embraced me and kissed me. "Cross yourself, child, cross yourself, and thank the Lord that we have seen a bishop."

I felt wretched for deceiving him. Why did I not describe the bishop as he really was, thin and pale and worn, with his wispy beard, his black bonnet, his faded black cassock? For a moment I was comforted by the thought that I was not lying to Grandfather, that I was seeing the bishop with *his* eyes, not mine, and that that was not sinful.

For some reason the bell started to ring again. At the first blow

31

it flooded the plaza and the whole valley with the swell of its burden. Then followed a pause during which the bell kept filling the atmosphere with its sustained, slow-dying hum. Then a mightier blow brought forth from the depth of the bell's being the full splendor and resonance of its celestial voice. Then somewhat alarmingly stroke followed stroke in rapid succession, giving the bell no pause or respite between the strokes, and the bell responded with all its depth and breadth.

Grandfather grasped my hand. I felt the quivering of his body as I detected something unnatural in the submissive bell, as though its soul were troubled. Before I even had become aware of this, Grandfather, more acutely attuned to sounds because of his blindness, had perceived that something was wrong and said so. In the bell's wonderfully responsive voice he perceived overtones of protest, even of anger, as though it were driven beyond its endurance. Now the ringing became erratic. From jubilation it passed to sudden alarm as of fire or tumult, then abruptly it reverted to exultant tolling and again to a succession of sharp, dinning claps as for a hailstorm.

Something tragic, dreadful, was happening up there in the belfry, in the soul of the beadle; the bell communicated this to the people and to the bishop, who raised his right hand and pointed it toward the cupola. There was hierarchical power in that uplifted hand, but it did not silence the tempest of sounds. For Simeon continued to belabor the bell with what now seemed ruthless, fiendish zeal, and the bell kept responding with all the burden of its voluminous voice. Yet under the ceaseless, cruel blows the bell moaned and whined.

Simeon kept striking with greater and greater force and celerity. Before the peal of one merciless blow had hardly issued from the belfry, another pursued it, and another, until the whole atmosphere became a universe of clashing, agonized sounds. And then in an instant it seemed that the baser alloys had separated themselves from the nobler metals and jangled their brassy whimpers through the silver-toned crescendos. It was then that the bell's voice broke. In that final blow all the precious relics that had blended their individual voices into the angelic chorus tumbled on the heads of the people like a heap of ironmongery.

And then the atmosphere became calm. Nature, which had been stifled by the tempest, resumed its respiration. And the people were stunned, unbelieving in the finality of the calamity, some hoping that the bishop might yet have the divine power to repair the damage. The bishop himself stood transfixed. His hand, which had failed to stay Simeon's blows, now clasped the cross at his breast.

When Simeon, having descended from the cupola, set foot on the ground, he swayed drunkenly and then staggered toward the bishop. His long black hair, cultivated for the priesthood, was tangled as though hedgehogs had prowled through it; his deep-set eyes glowed with a strange light. With a great sob he fell to the ground before the bishop, seized the mud-spattered hem of his robe with trembling hands and kissed it frantically. For a while the bishop stood straight and immobile, his eyes peering ahead as though they were seeing visions, and then he raised his somber face and lifted the first two blessing fingers toward heaven. Having beckoned or invoked something from up there, he transferred the two fingers to Simeon's disheveled head as if to anoint it with that which he had drawn from the sky. And then the bishop helped the broken, sobbing man to his feet. The red mud on the hem of the bishop's robe into which Simeon had sobbed had mixed with his tears, but some of the people didn't realize this at once, and seeing the red streaks on the sallow cheeks, they believed Simeon had wept tears of blood. And as they watched the bishop wipe Simeon's tears with his sleeve, from that episcopal act a feeling of humility mingled with pity communicated itself to the people.

Soon after this Simeon left the village, and it was learned later that he had gone to Mount Athos, there to live on bread and water in a hermit's cell. The cracked bell, despite the flaw in it, still could be heard all over the village and far beyond it, but it had to be struck gently, since hard blows evoked from it a medley of discordant sounds that brought memories of the day Simeon had cracked it. And it was never again rung to give warnings of fires, to break the spell of hailstorms, to prevent lightning from striking people or animals, nor for any other purpose save to call the villagers to church on Sundays and holidays and to toll the quiet dirge when one of them was being buried.

4

Grandfather lay on a sedge mat inside the garden apiary on the sunny, southern side of our house. Near him was his time-worn dogwood cane, with the dragon handle that he had himself carved. From the dragon jaws stuck out a tongue, still bearing traces of the red paint Grandfather had put on it. It was pleasant in the garden, but Grandfather and I were not here for the enjoyment of it. We were playing midwife to the apiary. The swarming season had already begun, and one swarm had escaped into the forest because we were not on hand to prevent its flight.

Ours was one of the few families in the village that kept bees. Our neighbor, an aunt whose husband (my mother's brother) had been killed by the Turks in the 1903 insurrection, also kept bees, and she was an expert at it. My father had no interest in the bees; he was busy with his varied tradings and village affairs. Grandfather and my mother were both bee enthusiasts. And it was with them, and from them, that I learned a great deal of bee lore. Years later, in America, I read a good deal about bee culture, including Maeterlinck's fascinating *Life of the Bee,* and I was astonished how much of what the famous author of *The Blue Bird* and *Pelléas and Mélisande* had written scientifically about these complex, remarkable creatures Grandfather and my mother, both of them illiterate, had known.

The teeming, ceaseless life, the drama that went on through spring, summer and fall in that garden-orchard-apiary behind our house is as fresh in my memory as though it all happened the day before yesterday.

The bees swarmed at that interval when spring slides into summer, when it is neither spring nor summer and when nature is at its best. The cherry trees in the orchard part of the fenced-in garden had long since shed their pink blossoms, and their boughs were now fringed with reddening beadlike fruit. Jade-green embryo clusters hung from the arbor that twined about the wattled fence on the courtyard side. The hedge of bushes shielded the garden on the brookside, bemantled with flowers that looked like garlands suspended from the necks of the dwarf willows. The bees whizzed and swirled continuously, alighted on the flowers and returned to the hives with wings yellowed and bags stuffed with precious pollen.

From their nests under the eaves of the house swallows dived down and filled the air with cheering notes. On the leafless branches of a dying walnut tree a pair of crows perched occasionally to utter their ill-boding screeches, mindless of the curses I addressed to them. And from the tangled growth of the brookside a weasel would sometimes dart out to flash before my eyes like a streak of lightning. And often in the serene quietude of a perfect day, when the sun's warmth would reach into damp and mouldering recesses of the earth, an old lizard would wobble out from the mysterious hedge and drag its cream-colored belly through the garden. The lizard was bright green on top. On the sides the greenness turned to tarnished gold and toward the flanks to orange and then to cream. And, chameleonlike, it seemed to change hues without any atmospheric influence. The quaint reptile would crawl close to me and leer at me with its bulging, lidless eyes, which glistened like gems. Then the creature would lie in the sun. Nothing disturbed its lordly composure, neither the droning bees nor the spinning, playful swallows, nor the multitude of other birds that kept up a perpetual chatter in the trees. Did the bees know that Grandfather had warned me not to annoy the lizard or the weasel, not to harm them in any way, that they were the spiritual hosts, or guardians, of the household, had supernatural powers to protect the family against misfortune? Since it seldom showed itself, the weasel had no need of any such veneration, but the old lizard availed itself of Grandfather's attributions and sunned itself in the garden undisturbed, not stirring even when we stirred. And no bee ever stung it. Did those sensitive creatures also believe what Grandfather believed?

Grandfather was not absolutely certain which of the two animals was the incarnate symbol of the "genius" of our household, but since the bees, wiser and instinctively more knowing, never stung the lizard even when slumbering directly in front of the hives—invariably they attacked any slug or strange creature coming near their homes—Grandfather inclined to the belief that the lizard represented the beneficent spirit. There was also an old toad that did not live in the garden but somewhere about the stone foundations of the house. This was no ordinary toad, not the kind garden snakes swallowed for breakfast. It was enormous, with the patina of the ages on its crinkled skin. You might come upon it sitting on its haunches in some damp and cool spot, its gemlike eyes fixed on you, its broad, field-marshal breast puffing like a bellows. It did not have the lizard's coloring, was in fact almost colorless, its warty skin being a dull brown. A gray stripe ran lengthwise along its back.

In those, my pre-American, days my world was limited by the mountains that enclosed our valley. Of the varied worlds that existed beyond the rim of those mountains I knew only what little was taught us at the village school. The lizard with its iridescent body gave me an intimation of a wider world and, as in a dream, fed my imagination with visions of tropics and jungles inhabited by fantastically shaped and colored creatures.

As for the lizard's protective powers, I was yet to learn how out of bronze and gold and silver man from primitive times had fashioned the likenesses of scarabs, beetles, salamanders and other creatures to wear at his throat or wrist as phylacteries of his health and well-being. I was yet to see in unsuperstitious America men wear as watch fobs the teeth, claws or paws of animals that were supposed to possess protective or luck-bringing powers.

The mystery the big toad exuded was geologic rather than physiographic. He made me think of the deep, dark bowels of the earth rather than of its surface. You had the feeling that the toad was not born of a toad, or hatched of an egg, but that it had been fragmented of the earth itself. You had the feeling that it was ageless, that it lived without food or water or air, that it contained within itself all the solid and atmospheric elements necessary for its viability, for its millennial existence. And you suspected that in its skull, like a pearl in an oyster, was a stone of talismanic powers.

As between the lizard and the toad, I myself inclined to the belief that the toad was the living reincarnation of the guardian host of the family, and I tried to visualize it as having derived from the blood of the ram my great-grandfather had slain in the foundations of our house a century before. Depending on the size of the building or the economic condition of the family, in the building of a new house a calf, a sheep or at least a rooster was sacrificed in the foundations. Of the flesh a feast was prepared for the builders, and of the blood in the foundations there would come into being the *talasum,* the beneficent ghost that sometimes manifested itself in the form of an animal, such as a huge harmless snake, a lizard, a frog, or a weasel, to abide within the immediate environs of the building.

For all his artistic nature, Grandfather was a realist, a practical person who in his blindness could see more clearly through things than most people with good eyes. But he did believe in natural phenomena, in signs and portents, in the existence of a world of the spirit, and in the magic of creating a ghost through the slaughtering of an animal or causing the death of a human being through magic. He believed the old legends about the sacrifice of human beings in the foundations of bridges to create ghosts to keep the bridges from being washed away during floods.

Our apiary consisted of a score of hives terraced in two rows one above the other against the back wall of the house. The architecture of the hives was primitive. The younger ones were housed in rectangular wooden boxes that had come to the village with kerosene cans—two large five-gallon cans in each box, with the word *Batum* stamped on the cans. These cans, when empty, were cut and flattened and the tin used by the villagers for roofing. The older hives, established before the availability of the boxes, were housed in conical hampers of osier plastered on the outside with cow dung and thatched with straw bonnets to keep the rain from washing away the plaster. The hampers reminded me of the African hut villages in my geography book.

One hive was lodged in a truncated log, shaped like the bushel measures we made out of hollow tree trunks. Its interior had been the hatchery of generations of bee tribes. My great-grandfather had found the hive in the hollow of an oak tree. He had carefully sawed off the section in which the bees had settled and brought home the hive at night while the bees slept. It was the only way to found an apiary, for nobody would sell or barter a hive or make a gift of it. To do so would be to lose one's luck with the bees. Bees resented being sold, bartered, or made a gift of.

As if conscious of its age, and proud of being the progenitor of countless colonies of bees, the log reposed in patriarchal dignity amidst its brood of boxes and hampers. The bark had long since peeled off, and the sun had baked and bleached the bare wood to the hardness and color of bone. Some knots on the wood suggested the knuckles of a prehistoric animal, and on one of them Grandfather had hung a calf's skull, which blended with the bone-bleached surface of the stump. The skull was put there to break the spell of the "evil eye." Skulls of sheep, oxen or other animals people stuck on poles or fences of their gardens or vineyards to keep them from being "bewitched" by envious, spellbinding eyes.

To the exterior of the log-hive, as well as to the outsides of other hives, now adhered clusters of bees, swarms in their prenatal stirrings, harbingers who had come out in advance of those propitious and historic moments when their queens would lead them to new

37

homes. The sun, the blossoming flowers, the warm day itself had also stirred the other bees—those that would remain in the parent homes—into feverish activity. They slipped through the wax-trellised entrances of their toylike homes, hummed and twanged in the sunlit air, spun about and dashed off into the fields to forage. Others would be returning from foraging, their honey sacks gorged with nectar. They dropped like bullets on the threshold of the hives and then scurried into the cavernous interiors to unburden themselves of their treasure. Thus bees streamed in an endless procession, hurrying out to gather pollen and hurrying back to stow away the precious stuff to be processed into honey.

Many bees warped close about us, their tiny bodies glinting, their strumming orchestrating itself with the trilling of the birds. I could see how the claws and antennae of some were yellowed by the pollen they had been gathering. A bee would alight on Grandfather's neck or on his face as he lay drowsing. The flesh would twitch where the bee crawled, but he never disturbed the creatures. It seemed to me that a bee would no more think of stinging him than it would of stinging the bark on a tree. I had seen him hive swarms by shoving bare hands into a boiling live mass of bees and scooping them into a box like so many handfuls of berries. And I felt certain that the bees in their omniscience knew that he was blind. From childhood, like myself now, he had cared for the bees, stood watch over them during swarming, and studied their habits. He attributed to them superhuman intelligence, and the bees, in their behavior toward him, seemed to confirm it. He was so familiar with their ways from the days when he could observe them that now when he lived in a world of sounds he could detect not only the temper and mood of a swarm but of a single bee, and from its hum he could tell whether the bee was a worker or a drone. Sometimes a bee would rush by with a hiss as though it brandished a sword, and sometimes it would glide by with a sweet hum like the soft thrum of a guitar. Oftentimes the jamlike masses that clung to the fronts of the hives, or depended from the edges of the platforms like clusters of berries, had a wildness in their throb and hover and agitation in the rustling of their wings. Grandfather would listen awhile, and if the agitation did not subside he would ask me to go fetch the priest to sprinkle the hives with holy water and calm them with Biblical incantations. He once asked me to call the priest when I myself had perceived no sword-rattling or spear-shaking in the shiver and rustle in the huge blister seething on the outside of a hive. But the old man had sensed the bellicose mood of the hive.

While Grandfather dozed two bees kept looping in front of me, causing a tense, angry buzz. Observing them closely, I discerned that one of them was trying to dodge the other in an effort to escape. But the assailant pursued skillfully, imitating its every maneuver as if it were fastened to it by an invisible cord. I noticed further that the pursued bee's wings and horns were tinted yellow while the aggressor's weren't. From this I deduced that the chased bee must have been foraging and was returning to the hive to deposit its load of nectar. Could it be that the other was a transgressor from our neighbor's apiary and was attempting to rob ours of its harvest?

The two bees collided in the air and, grappling, dropped to the ground like a single heavy drop of rain. With claws clasped about each other's cuirasses, they groveled in the dirt before me. Firmly interlocked, they bounced up and then dropped again to roll in the dust like a single pellet. I could not now tell one bee from the other, because the yellow on the horns and legs of the assaulted bee was covered with dust. I picked up a twig and tried to disengage them, but the instant they found themselves unclenched they flew at each other with redoubled zeal. They rolled in the dust, their narrow waists twisting, their little bodies quivering wrathfully. And all the time the sun shone warmly and brightly, and the whole garden brimmed with life. If there were such a day as could be called a bee-day, this was it. The duel continued even when the enfeebled bodies sagged, when legs and horns and fins strained. There didn't seem to be much life left in those tiny bodies but anger and vengeance, and it was these that still kept them writhing in the dust.

Then one of the bees ceased to move, or rather it ceased to struggle, for it still twitched. Again I could not tell which bee it was; coated as they were with dust, they looked alike. And then with one final straining, incredible effort, the other bee sank its claws into the bowels of its victim and ended its spasms. Then its own legs shuddered a few times; its body went through a single convulsive movement and became as still as the other.

I viewed the dead bees with equanimity. Two bees! Two dead bees! The sun shone so gently and caressingly, suffusing the atmosphere with gold. The garden, the orchard, the apiary, the whole surrounding world swelled and pulsated with the renewal of life. How often had Grandfather said that bees were wiser and more knowing than human beings! He had told me so much, so many things about the bees that I had affection and admiration for the creatures, so orderly in their communal life, so ready to sting at the cost of immediate death and yet so trusting that one could scoop them with bare hands like so much grain. Well, here were two bees who had lived in darkness and numbness through the winter. A minute or two ago they were buzzing around in the sun-drenched air, leaping from flower to flower and gorging themselves on nectar. And here they were now lying in the dirt like two crushed berries.

"Grandfather! Are you asleep?"

"No, child," the old man responded without stirring.

"I just watched two bees kill each other, Grandfather." I said this in a way to make him aware that I was alluding to his belief in the superior wisdom of bees.

Rising a little and moving forward, he coughed a few times to clear his throat. "You have, eh? Maybe one of them was a wasp."

"No. They were both honey bees."

"Well, there's good and bad among bees, too, boy. A nasty one may have molested a peaceable one who had to defend itself."

Presently, as we were talking, another bee buzzed and spiraled in front of us and then alighted on the fatal scene. It circled the bodies twice, poking and nosing as it did so. When it was satisfied that the bees were dead, it darted toward the hives and almost immediately a half dozen other bees arrived to inspect the scene like a guard from the sanitation or police department. I turned to Grandfather to tell him of this by way of confirming his belief that bees had a language of their own when I noticed that the old man's eyes were fixed on the rows of hives as if he were "seeing" something there. I could tell that he perceived no note of agitation. The sounds of those bees that warped about the trees, buzzed over the flowers and vegetable plants, and about ourselves, carried in them the sweetness and melody of peacefulness and neighborliness. They hummed and murmured as if they were ever so lightly touching cobwebby strings of some delicate instruments. And as they glided by, their tiny bodies glinted in the sunlit air like specks of gold, emitting faint sounds as though their wings were muted cymbals.

"There'll be a swarming," Grandfather said. "It is the log-hive."

I noticed the uncommon activity of the bee clump dribbling at the platform of the ancient hive. The bees there stirred like grain sifting in a sieve. The glimmering of thousands of silky wings with their emitting murmur was a sign that the bee pile was in its preswarming stirrings. Many bees detached themselves from the pendant cluster and maneuvered in front, spinning in the air.

Grandfather listened carefully, and I told him of the unusually large congestion of bees and described their movements. He said that their queen must have left the hive but that she was still attached to the outside of it and that I must watch closely because at any moment she might set forth to seek a new home for her brood. I had never seen a queen bee, that strange mysterious creature that could give life in a single season to a brood of one hundred thousand and then lead it on an exodus to a new settlement. In his lifetime of hiving swarms Grandfather had seen several queen bees. He said they were larger than any worker bee, larger than any drone. He also said that the queen had no sting. I wish I had known then what I learned later from books. How interested he would have been to know that a queen bee does have a sting but that she uses it only to sting a rival queen; that her sting is smooth and can be withdrawn, whereas the worker bee's lancet is barbed and cannot be retracted without tearing its own body and causing it to die. Likewise he would have been pleased to learn about the queen's mating—of how the virgin queen on her nuptial flight is pursued by drones, or male bees, high up into the atmosphere and how the male that pursues her to the greatest height and she chooses for her consort is destined to die after his single embrace up in the air, leaving the widowed queen fecund for life to lay millions of fertile eggs.

The shimmering thousands of silky wings with their murmur on the log-hive told me what Grandfather knew without seeing. The live mass, clinging to the hive, was visibly swelling without detaching itself from the log. The bees there shivered and rustled and sputtered like popcorn roasting in a pan. Some detached themselves from the pendant mass and scouted around, swerving in the air and then bouncing back to the fomenting pile as though they were attached to it by invisible strings. An ever-increasing number of bees kept bouncing back and forth, and the bee-ball kept distending into a huge brown blister that threatened to burst at any moment.

We kept watching, each in our own way, both certain that the tribe of a hundred thousand bees, led by their queen, the mother of them all, would take off to seek a new home. The swarm would follow its queen, its matriarch, going where she went, settling where she settled.

Suddenly the swelling blister burst at one point as though it were lanced by an unseen hand, and there spurted out a stream of dancing berries. The gushing stream thickened, the expulsive force at the font forcing the animated berries higher into the air and over the treetops. A low and sustained sound, like the bass drone of a bagpipe, filled the garden with its din. Thousands of bees were now leaving the mother hive never to return to it.

With increasing force the spout kept effusing bees, blowing them in flurries over the sunlit air, over the treetops. And the blister kept shrinking, distilling itself into the myriad of dancing drops. The gushing spout thickened, the explosive force at the font spinning off a continuous stream of bees, propelling them higher and wafting them above the garden. It was a prodigious swarm. The sunlit air shimmered with bees like a heat mirage. The birds in the trees, with alarmed chirrupings, fluttered away to safer places. And the old log-hive stood there relieved of its geniture, lonely and weathered but with an air of pride for being the progenitor of yet another offspring. It was a sight that put you in mind of things you never saw but heard of, about armies readying to set off on an expedition, of tribes or nations on the eve of transmigration.

Grandfather listened to the swarm's deep hum. "It's a good song it makes," he said, "a good, wise queen! We should keep this swarm for a mother."

Indeed there was no harshness in the swarm's din, no angry buzz or impatience. You could tell a swarm's mood from the bees' nervous movements, from their jerking, restless gyrations. Sometimes a swarm twisted like a whirlwind, uncertain of its aim, of its queen's aim, with bees prone to sting without provocation.

Under the dark cloud of bees we stood in the middle of the garden. I handed Grandfather two stones and he began to knock them against each other and to chant in a beguiling voice. Bees love music, and it was through the rhythmic clacking of the stones and the mesmerizing effect of the monotonous chanting, addressing the queen now as Mary, now as Mother, now as Darling, that Grandfather tried to coax the swarm to settle on one of the nearby trees or bushes.

"Come, Mary; settle, Darling; alight, Sweet One!" He twanged out the words with honeyed sweetness to the accompaniment of the stones. At times the rustling drapes swirled about a tree, as if to fringe its boughs, but instantly they unfurled, scintillating in the sunlight. Somewhere within this throbbing mass was the queen.

"Perch, Darling; alight, Sweet One." Though not settling, the swarm, beguiled by Grandfather's cantillations, kept wheeling above the garden. While Grandfather, with all his beekeeper's cunning, kept importuning the queen to alight, I myself made a posy of daisies and placed it on top of a bush in hopes that the queen might be drawn by the flowers. Bees are partial to daisies. But presently Grandfather called my attention to some commotion on the courtyard side, on the other side of the wattled fence. And looking over, I saw with consternation that a swarm had also issued from our neighbor's apiary. Its murmur, like the muffled drone of a bagpipe, began to blend with the deep hum of our own swarm. Like a conoidal, baseless tower, it was reeling in the direction of our swarm.

"Pick up stones, child, and hurry. Try to keep it from coming this way." He knew of the other swarm without my telling him. I rushed out and, as best I could, endeavored to entice the other swarm away from ours. It remained suspended above me for a few moments, but then, as if displeased by my blandishments and lured by Grandfather's, it began to veer slowly toward our garden.

Roused by these happenings, my aunt came out, wiping dough from her hands on her woolen apron. She too commenced the bewitching chant to the accompaniment of clacking stones. "Come, Queenie; this way, Mother; this way, Darling." She was an experienced bee breeder and with great skill she tried to charm her swarm away, but the dark teeming cloud revolved slowly toward ours.

We knew that if the swarms should commingle it would mean war and the end of both swarms. No holy water or priest's incantations could prevent it. Bees have many virtues but not the virtue of peaceable coexistence. Their highly developed social structure and communal life is entirely within the tribe, within the colony. Hives stand in rows side by side, but every one of the millions of bees in the apiary knows its own hive and at the tiny entrances of these homes stand guards ready to intercept intruders. How does a bee standing guard at the entrance of its own hive pick out of the millions of other bees one that doesn't belong to its own colony?

Neither Grandfather's nor my aunt's efforts to woo the swarms away from each other seemed to have any effect. Like two dark clouds destined to collide, the swarms gyrated toward each other. Neighbors came out to see what was happening but kept at a distance for safety and for fear their "eyes" might be blamed should the swarms intermingle and start a war. Children came running from their play, but they, too, knew enough to keep their distance, knew that the atmosphere bristled with a million stings. When a swarm of bees takes possession of an air space the space around it for some distance is a zone of fire into which no other creature dares to venture. Bees brook no interference from man or other creature.

The swarms came so close that at one point the fringes brushed and remained in that position for a few seconds like two animals sniffing at each other. The next instant the touching edges parted, shrinking away, leaving a narrow neutral zone, only to be filled in the next moment. But now there was no parting, and there began a gradual fusion and presently the two swarms dissolved into each other to form a single swarm.

Nothing like this had ever been seen or heard of—for swarms from different apiaries, or the same, to coalesce. I watched Grandfather's face and could tell that his ears were tuned to the sound the bees made. The din was deep and sustained, like a bass drum gently rolled. But the huge swarm was somewhat high, and we knew that when a swarm rose high more often than not it made for the hills.

Once a swarm started on such a flight it moved fast like a ghost, and no power on earth could check its flight. The instinct to return to the wild whence the bees were domesticated millennia ago was still in them.

I plucked handfuls of daisies and swayed them above my head while the two bee charmers caroled, their voices each with its own lulling sweetness never ceasing to intone affectionate names to the queens. In dulcet lullabies they implored the queens to alight.

The twin-sized swarm wavered, hovered over an apple tree, draped its boughs for a brief moment, and unfurled. Somewhere within this simmering mass were the two queens themselves, who must have reached an understanding, for there was no war. But would they both choose to alight together or would each queen choose a separate perch to gather its own family?

For a few minutes the giant swarm remained poised above the trees like a prismatic chandelier suspended from the heavens. And then, at last, yielding to the magic of the clacking stones and the suppliant voices, it began slowly, almost imperceptibly, to sag in the direction of the lilac bush on which I had stuck the posy of daisies. As it drifted nearer to the bush, the swarm began to assume the shape of an inverted pyramid, the apex of which began to twirl over the bush like a gimlet. There was no doubt now that the two queens had settled there, but lest the charm should be broken the canting and stone-clacking continued.

Now that the queens had perched, the cloud of bees began to precipitate itself on the lilac bush. Thousands of bees fell like hail on the congealing nucleus. In their mad rush they bounced against one another and tumbled in little cataracts. It was as if the atmosphere itself were filtering the inflated swarm through an unseen funnel. In ten minutes the huge swarm congealed on the bush into a viscous mass, looking like some oversized tropical fruit that would drop off unless immediately gathered.

"Bless them! Bless the little mothers," said Grandfather as he and my aunt proceeded to hive the bees in a box brought over by my aunt. She had scoured the box to get the kerosene smell out of it and had anointed it with honey to attract the bees. She officiated at the hiving like a priestess or midwife. She was flushed with excitement as her eyes peered at the boiling mass. Perhaps because their dimensional regularity made it easier to construct their combs, the bees preferred these rectangular boxes to the conical dung-plastered osier hampers. The hiving was done by holding the box over the clump of bees and smoking them into it with dry cow dung, which burns without flame. The smoke caused the bees to spume up the sides of the box, shedding away from the cluster in a continuous ferment without actually detaching themselves from one another. I peered at the mass, oblivious of any danger of stings. For an instant I thought I saw one of the queens, but it was only a drone, distinguishable from the worker bees by its larger body, the thicker plumage at the neck and saddle, the greater spread of wings and longer reach of horns.

In this way the two swarms were hived as a single family in a single home, and the box was set down on a plank near the bush, where it remained for the rest of the day, for many bees continued to spin about and did not enter the new home until twilight. Besides, one didn't move a hive in daylight. At nightfall my aunt came over and without saying a word lifted the box.

"Wasn't it fortunate that the *two* swarms didn't fight?" said Grandfather, putting emphasis on the word *two* so as to impress on the woman the fact that the hive was jointly owned. Our neighbor made no reply and, holding the box in her arms, started for her own apiary, which was separated by a picket fence from our own courtyard. We followed along in her footsteps. "It's all the same where our hive sets," said Grandfather good-naturedly. "Your garden or ours, it's all the same. It's got to set somewhere till fall. Then we'll spoil it and divide the honey." The old man was not angry or upset. He kept murmuring gently, as if talking to himself, or thinking aloud. "Too bad they had to go and get all mixed up like that. But praise God they didn't cut each other up." Grandfather's voice trailed after the woman, but she made no reply nor paid any attention to us. She pushed the wicket with her hip and entered her apiary. Gently, not to disturb the bees, she set the hive down on an empty platform in the front row. We leaned over the picket fence and watched her movements. When she was finished she padded along on her bare feet, closed the turnstile, and disappeared into her house.

"No harm done, child. The hive's hers as much as it is ours, and it's got to set somewhere. She's a good beekeeper, and the hive's as safe with her as in our own apiary." The words were calm and reassuring, but I could sense concern in the voice. The manner in which the woman had taken the hive, not saying a word to us, suggested to me that she might not be sharing our own view about the joint ownership of the hive.

"Mark the hive well, child. Remember where it is so there'll be no mistake which hive it is." By saying that Grandfather revealed his own suspicions in spite of his reassuring words.

Fall came. Reaping, thrashing, husking and corn-cribbing were all behind. Nature was divested of its fruits. The grapes had been mashed and their juice fermented in the big vats in the cellars. The sky, gray, bleak, hung low over the village. The fruit trees in the garden apiary stood sad and leafless, their twigs quivering in the breeze. The hedge of brambles and other prickly growth on the brookside was likewise denuded of its foliage. There were not even any late-ripening fruits or vegetables to be gathered except the frost-free cabbages and leeks to which the frost imparted a sweetness they did not have before. The bees had fallen for their sustenance on the honey they had stored for the winter.

Like the bees we, too, had labored hard in field, meadow and vineyard, and our house was brimful with the fruit of our labor. Plaits of unshelled yellow corn hung from the rafters in our large kitchen, forming a ceiling of grain; festoons of dried peppers, garlands of onions, bouquets of dry parsley and mint and basil and other aromatic herbs hung from pegs on the walls. On the tops of grain chests, on shelves, on the beams above the loom lay piled varicolored pumpkins and winter squashes, some gourd-shaped, some oblong, some broad-bellied like Ali Baba's jars and some looking human, squatting there like listless contented grandmothers. Down in the cellar were vats filled with pickled peppers and pickled green tomatoes. And in a row of bins—lentils, dry beans, walnuts, potatoes. Yet all of it could be destroyed or carried away by order of an army captain. If regular soldiers were billeted in a peasant's house he had to feed them. But at least nowadays he did not have to pay them *dish-taxasi,* or tooth tax, which the janissaries demanded from their hosts for using their teeth to eat their food.

It was worse with us and the bees. We not only robbed them of their winter provender but had to kill them first. We knew of no other way to take their honey. To me the spectacle of killing millions of little creatures to take their food seemed cruel. All through spring, summer and early fall the bees had made countless journeys to field and garden to stuff their honey bags with nectar, which they regurgitated into the waxen cells, so ingeniously and so precisely constructed. But what use their industry when we could kill them at will to take the fruit of their labor.

And now in the fall when there was nothing left in nature for them to feed on, and before they had made an inroad into their stores, we killed them to harvest their honey crop. But we never used the word *kill.* It was always the word *spoil.* Deep in our hearts we must have felt a sense of guilt, or remorse, else we would not have used this euphemism for the slaughter of the little creatures. Killing the bees was not the same as killing a pig or a calf or even a lamb. We pastured and fed and cared for the animals for the food their flesh would provide. They were the crop, like the corn and the wheat. But the bees themselves were not the crop. We did not

46

eat the bees; we ate their food. There was joy and satisfaction in haying and reaping and thrashing and the gathering of the grapes, but in the harvesting of the honey crop, the way it was done by us, there was always a sense of remorse.

The "spoiling" was done at night, when the bees, numbed by the cold, were helpless like chickens in a pitch-dark coop. This particular fall we "spoiled" all but eleven of our hives, which we retained for "mothers." The following summer every "mother" would swarm at least once and some more than once. Sometimes an early, healthy swarm would itself produce a swarm before the end of summer. Thus starting with a dozen hives in the spring, we would end up with more than twice that many by the time of the next honey harvest.

And now in late fall, with everything else harvested, all that remained was the honey crop. In the middle of the day when the sun would shine weakly bees, singly or in pairs, would slip out of the wax-trellised entrances and after a few loops in the air would drop to the platforms and crawl back into their quarters. Some braver one would venture farther, to alight on some withered autumn flower or troop even as far as the vineyards in hope of finding hidden grapes frost-shriveled but sticky and sirupy.

As we culled our hives Grandfather kept thinking of the common hive in our neighbor's garden. Every day he would ask if the hive were still in its place, and I would reassure him that it had not been "spoiled," that it was there in its place in my aunt's apiary.

One day Grandfather tapped his dogwood cane across the court-yard and knocked on our neighbor's door. I didn't go along and I didn't hear what was said, but I had never seen the old man so upset. He bristled with anger. "Come," he said to me, "we are going to the *Kommittet*," the *Kommittet* being the local cell of IMRO —Internal Macedonian Revolutionary Organization. Like its parent, the village committee was illegal and secret, but everybody knew that Trayko Gatso was its president and, as such, IRMO's factotum in the village. Starting out as an underground liberation movement, founded by schoolteachers and other intellectuals, it soon turned into a mass movement with *komitadji* bands (guerrillas) engaging Turkish troops in open battle. The bands also avenged atrocities committed by willful beys and other local tyrants. Primarily a conspirant society using terror as one of its weapons, IMRO also assumed the functions of a government—stern and paternalistic. Without losing sight of its primary aim, it concerned itself with practically every aspect of the people it hoped to liberate. Like a jealous parent it kept close vigil over our health, our well-being, our morals. It fought superstitions and instituted many re-

47

forms, some of them motivated by the need of money to buy arms from Bulgaria or Greece or sometimes even from Turks. Often the reforms accomplished a dual purpose—economy and hygiene, as in the case of the skullcaps that the women wore under their babushkas and the unhealthy foot-wide woolen girdles they wound around their waists until in some cases they weighed as much as twenty pounds. Skullcaps and girdles were banned as unhealthy and wasteful. On their long braids of hair at their backs women wore clusters of silver coins, at their waists silver clasps as large as saucers and at their throats and wrists silver necklaces and bracelets. All these IMRO banned. It also frowned on the use of makeup, such as rouge and "Spanish white," and it agitated against excessive dowries, against cash payments by the groom to the parents of the bride. It issued a decree reducing wedding festivities to a single day instead of the usual three or four. IMRO punished adultery, drunkenness, idleness, discouraged ostentation and prodigality or extravagance of any sort. All resources, human and economic, were needed for the revolution, for the achievement of statehood and nationhood. Under penalty of the rod it forbade people to take their disputes to the corrupt Turkish courts, where cases dragged on for months and years at the expense of plaintiff and defendant alike. IMRO justice was refreshingly prompt and bribeless. Minor cases, such as ours with the bees, were reviewed by the local civilian committees; more involved ones by the district committees, which could also impose death sentences subject to approval by the all-powerful central committee. IMRO had no jails, and jail sentences were never imposed. It reprimanded, flogged, fined the well-to-do, and sentenced to death. Loose women who trafficked with Turks were invariably executed as a safeguard against treason as well as for their immorality. IMRO was a government within a government, with its own constitution, postal service, its armed bands, and agents in foreign capitals.

And now as I guided Grandfather to IMRO to seek justice I gleaned what our neighbor had said to him. Imitating her voice and manner, he kept repeating, "Hollowheaded old fool! *Our* hive! It was *my* swarm and it is *my* hive. And it is in *my* apiary."

Gatso's old mother was in her courtyard winding warp onto a beam with the help of another woman. A notable village character, fearless and outspoken, the old woman had known the sting of the Turkish whip for her brashness. She had clawed at gendarmes for arresting villagers and reviled the sultan and his grand-viziers, calling them filthy swine, the worst possible insult to non-pork-eating Turks.

"What will you be when you grow up?" She would ask me the same question every time she saw me. And I always gave her the same answer: *"Komita."* And always she reached in the folds of her woolen girdle (which she wore in spite of the prohibition) and handed me a lump of sugar. The word *Komita* derived from *Kommittet* but was corrupted by the Turks into *komitadji* and as such found its way into dictionaries and encyclopedias of many languages.

Gatso was an austere man. Half my grandfather's age, he belonged in age and worldly-mindedness to a different generation. Instead of woolen frock and white linen drawers he wore knee-length breeches and a double-breasted vest and jacket of cloth woven by his mother on the handloom. He had suffered for a year as a political prisoner in the Fortress at Diar Bekir in Anatolia, and his language was more like that of a schoolteacher. He was stacking wood in a shed in back of the house when we got to him, and he continued doing so while Grandfather told him the story about the mingling of the two swarms and the common hive.

"I have heard about that phenomenon," said Gatso.

The word *phenomenon* was strange to us, but we both deduced its meaning, and Grandfather put in, "Yes, it is a wonder, but it happened and the woman now refuses to have the hive spoiled and share the honey with us."

I watched Gatso's face for signs of how he was reacting, but the lean, taut face was impassive as a mask.

"Is the hive in her possession?"

"Yes, we set it down in her garden. It's all the same where it is; it belongs to both of us. The swarms were hived in *our* garden."

Gatso stopped lining wood and stroked his chestnut-colored beard. It was a well-trimmed, slightly pointed beard such as schoolteachers cultivated in those days. I was thinking Gatso would make a good priest if he let his beard grow long. I had an urge to describe his appearance to Grandfather, but I knew it would be inappropriate to do so in his presence, and, besides, I didn't know how long Grandfather had been blind and he might have remembered Gatso from his days of light.

"Couldn't you go there and call your bees?"

Grandfather was stunned. He "stared" at me and I felt for an instant as if he could see. "What is the man saying?"

"He says to call our bees to us."

"Call our bees! May God forgive! Bees are not sheep to be called."

I couldn't tell whether Grandfather's face showed disgust or pity for the man. As for me, my boy mind was unable to divine whether the man was being sarcastic or just ignorant of the ways of bees.

After a brief silence, as if realizing he had gone too far, Gatso said, "What do you want me to do about it?"

"For the woman to agree to spoil the hive and divide the honey with us."

"Why does she refuse to do this?"

"I think she wants to keep the hive for a mother because it is two swarms in one, with two queens, and it is bound to swarm two and maybe three times next summer."

"Suppose I order her to give you the honey of another hive, one she would be willing to have spoiled. This way you would be likely to get more honey than the half of the other hive."

"That will not do. She will be keeping our bees."

"I don't understand. What do you want, the honey or the bees?"

"Both."

"How can you have both if you must drown the bees?"

"There is no other way I can have them back."

"But you can't kill just yours; hers have to be killed too. And she doesn't want hers killed. Is it right for you to demand that she kill her own bees?"

Grandfather never used the word *kill* with reference to the bees. And he said, "She spoils other hives. What right does she have to insist on keeping for a mother the one hive in which our queen and our bees are mixed up with her queen and her bees?"

The committeeman rubbed his forehead, pondering over what Grandfather had said. For the first time his firm, graven face showed signs of mobility. I felt for Grandfather that he was limited to the man's voice and words and could not follow the "language" of his face.

"I beg the *Kommittet*," urged Grandfather, "to consider that the matter is *bees* more than *honey* and especially the queens."

"But you can't have your bees, and your queen, by *killing* them."

I was glad that Grandfather could detect a note of mellowness in the voice.

"She will not have them either."

"Then what you want is for both queens and all the bees, yours and hers, to be killed."

"Spoiled," corrected Grandfather. "There is no way you can separate them. They are all mixed up, and they cannot be called. Mr. Kommittet, you may not know it—you are of the new generation and you are not a bee man—but bees must not be traded for honey; they must not be sold, bartered, or given away. They are not animals; they are *bees*. They are like us, like humans, except that unlike us they are free and have better instincts. We can learn much from the bees."

"But how would your bees know they haven't been bartered away if you kill them and they are dead?"

"The live ones in our apiary would know."

"How would they know?"

"That I can't say. They just know."

There was a pause. I could see the committeeman meditating, his jaws still set hard, but there was a different look in his eyes, a kind of faraway, dreamy, sad kind of look. I wondered if Grandfather's saying the bees were free had some effect on him.

"All right," said the committeeman, "I will talk to the woman."

A few days later we "spoiled" the common hive. It was a dark, cool, starless night. I carried a lantern to light the way to our neighbor's apiary. By my side my father carried a kettle of water to drown the bees. My mother, who always attended to these chores, would not come because my aunt was the widow of a brother. Grandfather needed no light and followed behind, tapping with his cane. Our neighbor must have heard us or seen the light moving across her courtyard, and I was just turning the wicket when we heard the squeak of her door and heard her crowlike scream. "Robbers, spoilers, get off my grounds!"

Father and I kept silent. Grandfather answered her. "Shush, woman. We aim to spoil nothing but the hive, which is half ours."

"There's no bees of yours here, you old scarecrow."

"Hold your tongue, woman. You have your orders."

"Orders! What orders? From those bandits. I'll go to the court."

"You do that and you know what's going to happen to you."

A volley of stinging imprecations, like angry bees, assailed us but otherwise she did not interfere with us, held in check by the invisible hand of the *Kommittet.*

I put the lantern down to take hold of one end of the case to help my father turn the hive over and set it down open side up. Then I held up the lantern so that the arc of light fell over the exposed hive. The disturbed bees rustled in the interstices of the combs. Some crawled sluggishly over the edges of the combs at the top. Benumbed by the chill air and dazed by the sudden light, they quivered as if to fight off impending disaster. Quickly my father emptied the kettle of water over the combs. To the bees it must have been a deluge. The water descended on them in cataracts and swirled them down the narrow corridors amidst the system of combs.

My aunt stood by like a fate, not interfering but continuing her curses, invoking the wrath of heaven on our evil heads and inviting the devil's own cunning on our own apiary. "May the evil eye cast its spell upon your hives; may all your queen bees be sterile as mules; may your honey be poison to you."

We paid no heed to her maledictions and proceeded with the task

51

of spoiling the hive. With a whisk broom my father began to sweep aside the layer of dead and twitching half-drowned bees and asked me to raise the light so he could see better. He kept staring at the combs and then took the lantern from me to angle the light to suit him.

"You see that!" he exclaimed.

I leaned over and what I saw made me hold my breath. I had assisted in the spoiling of dozens of hives, but I had never before seen an arrangement of the combs such as I now beheld. It took my young mind a few seconds to comprehend the significance of what I saw. And then I turned to Grandfather and said, "The two swarms never mingled, Grandfather."

"What are you saying, child?" The old man "stared" at me.

"There are two hives in the box, not one."

My aunt, overhearing, came close to peer at the combs. She spoke not a word, struck dumb by the phenomenon. I described to Grandfather as best I could that instead of constructing the combs widthwise, and strictly parallel, as was always the case with these rectangular boxes, the bees had in this case divided the interior into two equal square compartments, partitioned off by a thin but solid wax wall. The combs on one side of the partition ran parallel to it, those on the other side at right angles to the partition. And there was the same number of combs on either side.

Grandfather crossed himself three times and then leaned over the box to trace with trembling fingertips the pattern of the combs. Always looking for portents and revelations in nature, especially in the behavior of animals, he urged, "Cross yourself, child. It is God speaking to us. There may yet be peace in our land. Our poor Macedonia is homeland of different peoples, but peace will come and freedom, and we shall live in friendship and not kill each other."

My aunt was ashamed, and so were we. More than that, we were humbled by the example of the bees. It was clear that the two bee tribes had separated immediately after they were hived. What was puzzling was why they had chosen to commingle in the first place, when they had ventured forth from their homes for lack of space.

There was no need for us to weigh the honey or draw lots as to who took which half because the interior had been divided with mathematical precision, and, owing to the limited space, all the combs were stuffed with the purest golden honey. There wasn't a dark spot or a dry cell in those combs.

5

Grandfather could make anything, at least so I believed. I had been pestering him to make me a rifle, not a toy rifle but a real one that could shoot bullets. I never knew that a rifle had to be calibrated and that you had to have cartridges of different sizes for different rifles.

"What do you need a rifle for, child?"

"To kill Turks."

"You mustn't think of killing."

"But I'll kill Turks only."

"They are God's creatures, even if they are Turks."

"But they kill us, Grandfather."

"God knows it. Leave retribution to Him."

To take my mind off the rifle the old man made me a pinwheel. I watched him make it. When it was finished it was a toy such as a child never had. It was so skillfully, so magically constructed that even when there was not the slightest breeze if I held it in front of me and ran its wings whirred and hummed like a huge devil's needle. It had four wings turning on a wooden pin at the end of a stick about three feet long. I never tried this, but I was certain that if I ran fast and then let go of the thing it would have flown on by itself like a swallow. But all that was in the future, and now as I watched the old man carve each wing and wedge it like a spoke into the tiny hub a sudden chorus of dogs barking portended something unusual, and I left Grandfather to run down to the road to see what caused the commotion.

"It's Ivan the bear," some youngsters shouted.

Soon the barking stopped and the dogs, tails between their legs, slunk behind stables and woodsheds and Ivan the big bear took possession of the village.

Most performing bears in the Balkans came from the Carpathians, caught there as cubs and trained to dance and wrestle, but of Ivan it was said that he was born in the Ural Mountains. Now nobody in the village knew where the Ural Mountains were, but the name Uralski Planini had something awesome about it, suggesting mammoth and behemoth. And a mammoth of a bear was Ivan. His body, standing up, looked like the charred trunk of an oak with two spurs at the top. It was a wonder, the bigness of Ivan the bear, and a bigger wonder it was that the huge beast was led about by a puny, swarthy man with a jack-o'-lantern face. His name was Marin. Straight black hair came down low over his forehead and long black mustaches divided his face into half-moons. He looked like a gipsy and he didn't. Other bear-masters who brought their bears to the village were usually tall, strong-armed, long-legged men, and it seemed incongruous that spindly-legged little Marin with his mean-looking face and little beady eyes, like the bear's, should be leading around by the nose the biggest bear ever seen.

The diminutive bear-master made up in trappings what he lacked in stature. He was formidably girded by a broad mailed leather belt from which dangled two clanging chains, heavy like the ones loggers use. The end of one of these chains was hooked to the iron ring that hung to Ivan's nose like a padlock to a door; the end of the other chain was clasped to the leather halter that encompassed Ivan's stumpy head and muzzled his snout. Thus the big bear was doubly bound to his dwarfy but tough little master. Moreover, Marin held, scepterlike, a dogwood staff thick as his wrist and twice his height.

Followed by the entourage of us youngsters, Marin leads the bear from house to house. Slowly and heavily shuttle the big paws, the broad mane trembles, the whole gigantic mass lumbers behind the little master like a bumblebee behind an ant. Before every house Marin strikes the tambourine and his deep baritone, surprisingly full and resonant for the man's size, resounds through the village. His repertoire of ballads and ditties is limitless. He now intones the one about the dead warrior who, in his grave, yearns for battle:

> The earth I conquered while alive;
> In death to combat yet I strive.
> Here lies my body seamed with scars;
> My spirit thirsts for future wars.

The bear's woolly bulk, balanced on the powerful haunches, rocks and shakes like a tree in the wind. At the conclusion of the song and the dance Marin hands the bear the dogwood staff. "A

54

shepherd be thou, Ivan," says Marin, "three hundred sheep herd thou in Babuna Planina." Staff on the shoulder in the manner of a shepherd's crook, the great bear wags his stumplike head and sways his trunk, suggesting, no doubt, that holding the staff is much more to his liking than dancing to his master's bidding. Then giving back the staff, Ivan takes from his master the tambourine to hand to the housewife in whose dooryard he has just performed. In a moment the housewife returns with the tambourine half filled with flour, which Ivan receives with a bow and hands it to his master to empty into one of the sacks tied to the mare's pack saddle.

This done, Marin turns to the lemon-pale child who is clinging to his mother's skirt and Marin says, "Bless him, the little one. He looks sickly. Is he prone to the evil eye and to ailments of diverse kinds?"

The mother's rough hand presses the child's head to her. "He whimpers and moans in his sleep, and he's a ready victim for any pair of evil eyes."

"Mashala!" heartens Marin. "Have no fear, big Ivan will banish the evil things." Then he reaches out and takes the shy child in his arms, petting him and otherwise reassuring him, but as he tries to set him on the bear's back, the child screams and tries to squirm out of his arms. But Marin knows how to lull a child's fear with a ditty, which he sings in a gentle, beguiling voice:

> Have no fear, my little one,
> Something will I give to thee;
> Yes, a gift I'd make to thee;
> Ohrid fair and Bitolia,
> Istanbul with its jewels,
> Salonika with its vessels.

As he sings, Marin, ever so gently, places the child on the bear's back and leads the bear about the courtyard, giving the little one the bear-ride cure. Meantime Ivan, who knows his part, growls and grumbles to scare away the evil things that bother the little one in his sleep.

"This will outfear the fear in his heart," says Marin the bear-master. "He'll no more scream in the night, and a strong and fearless man he'll grow up to be."

The child's pale face blinks into a smile, which reflects itself on the mother's careworn face. The little one has ridden a bear and that bear Ivan.

But one thing more: a tuft of Ivan's hair for the sickly one to wear at his throat. Big Ivan's hulking haunches are bare as a monkey's.

55

The hair there has been clipped tuft by tuft for young and old to wear in lockets in their bosoms. If the spell of evil eyes can be broken and ailments of diverse and mysterious origins can be charmed away by amulets of hair from ordinary bears, as anyone will tell you, then how surely by that of Ivan, the biggest and scariest of bears. The grateful mother trustingly clutches the tuft of hair, holding in her very fist the health and growth of her young one. Carefully she will tuck it into a square of linen cloth dipped in beeswax, fold the cloth into a triangle, stitch it neatly, and attach it to a loop of string for the child to wear at his neck. But now she must hurry and from her scant supply of flour put a few more handfuls in the good man's tambourine.

We can never see enough of Ivan and, fascinated, watch him do the same dances, the same tricks over and over again, watch him bow like a bride, treat the sick, kiss the hands of men who hand him coins as to a bride, which he passes on to his master. And we can never listen enough to the jingling of Marin's tambourine and to his repertoire of ballads. We know the bear is well secured by the nose and muzzle and we know Marin holds the staff, big as a pole; still, we keep at a respectful distance, such a frightful-looking thing is Ivan. What we do not know is what the bear-master knows so well —that the mammoth bear is held to his tameness and to his fate not so much by the staff and the chains as by his own ignorance, by his not knowing that only an inch of gristle at his nose stands between bondage and freedom. Or perhaps the bear doesn't know what freedom is, having been a captive since cubhood.

At the end of every dance Marin hands over to the bear the dogwood staff—perhaps in commendation, perhaps as a token that the power the staff symbolizes is his, Ivan's, and he, Marin the master, holds it by virtue of his skill and superior knowledge and for Ivan's own good.

At the next stop, after the bear dances (always to the voice of Marin's ballads and the beat of the tambourine), when the housewife hands Marin the tambourine half filled with flour, she mentions what the whole village knows. With sadness in her eyes and hope in her voice, she tells the bear-man how her husband has been ill these many months, how Grandma Shimba had tried her sorceries and herb potions on him; the grains of salt that she tossed into the fire sizzled and sputtered and she yawned languidly and then sneezed violently, all very good omens; and the priest too had come twice and had read from his sacred books and had smacked the sick man on the forehead with the hyssop soaked in holy water and then had walked about the house chanting divine words and dipping the hyssop in the kettle of holy water and sprinkling walls and furniture and shaking puffs of incense smoke from the jingling censer and everything thereafter had smelled chastened and exorcised but still the poor man was unable to rise and yoke his oxen to plow his neglected fields.

"Your man's a victim of magics and witcheries," says Marin the bear-master. "He needs the bear's paws more than the priest's prattle. Come, Ivan, let's deliver the poor man from these evil spells."

With a frightening groan, which delights us youngsters, the big bear heaves across the threshold into the humble dwelling. Once inside, he shambles about, sniffs in this corner and blows in that, grunts here and grumbles there, mops the floor with his furry paws and shakes his woolly trunk like a mummer on New Year's Eve and comes to the corner where the sick man lies on the floor covered with a coarse hempen blanket. The bear now whiffs and scents the covered form and his nostrils blow breath like a bellows and then from his mouth issues a low, sustained, warning roar. Then he lifts one moplike forepaw and sets it on the prostrate form, then another, and thus cumbrously, hulkingly but cautiously, as though danger lurks beneath, he treads and scuffles. It is fortunate that all four paws are not pressing down simultaneously, that the bear knows better than to let his entire weight bear down on the sick, moaning man. On the back of the patient, on the shoulder blades, on the spread-out arms and stretched-out legs, the bear rubs and kneads while muffled groans issue from under the blanket.

If the evil things have not escaped through the chimney and the man doesn't rise to yoke his oxen, it is none of Ivan's fault.

After making the rounds in the upper quarter, bear and master, ever escorted by the retinue of fascinated youngsters, tramp over the plank bridge to the lower quarter of the village. Just beyond the bridge spreads the well-trod, grassless plaza flanked on one side by the church and the schoolhouse and on the other by the riverbank with its rows of slender poplars and gnarled, droopy old willows. On the benches in the shade of the willows are seated several village loafers who suddenly bestir themselves at sight of the bear lumbering over the bridge like an overloaded haycart. At the same time, as fate would have it, from the far end of the plaza a lone figure approaches. It is Boyko, Boyko the shepherd and none other. At sight of him we youngsters raise a cry. Crook in hand and skinbag over the shoulder, Boyko strides down like the man of the mountain that he is. The mountain has been Boyko's home and abode since he was a boy. A giant of a man, fearsome as any bear, Boyko summers his sheep and goats high up in the mountain and winters them in the Shkya, the lowlands along the Aegean. Bears and wolves and other wild creatures of the forest are no strangers to him, and he is the greatest wrestler since Koka the Albanian. Wrapped always, regardless of season, in his sheepskin coat, with the wool on the outside, and a *kalpak* of the same material on his massive head, Boyko looks like a man-bear and twice the size of Marin the bear-man. (In his youth he had been a *haiduk,* one of those defiant spirits who made of the forest a cradle of freedom long before there was a national revolutionary organization. He and his ilk, combining brigandage with protection of the defenseless peasantry, often swooped down from their mountain lairs to deliver some unfortunate village from the greed and lust of a local hireling of the Sultan. They were the precursors of the *komitadjis,* rough, uncouth half bandits, half apostles of freedom. Every Balkan nation had a galaxy of these semi-heroes who challenged the Sultan's authority and later formed the backbone of the national insurrections.)

At sight and scent of Boyko the bear paces nervously, his four paws treading a clumsy pattern, his enormous body swaying and his stumpy head jingling the chains. But there is no meanness and hostility in the small bear eyes as the chained nostrils sniff the freedom of the mountain that exudes from the shepherd.

"Wrestle him, Boyko," two or three voices urge at once. Boyko, leaning on his crook, looks at the beast with eyes full of warmth and compassion. From his *haiduk* days he has hated bondage in any form, be it of man or beast. Who knows, in the chains of the muzzled beast he might be seeing the iron fetters of hundreds of Macedonian "politicals" driven to exile in distant Anatolian fortresses.

A match between Ivan and Boyko is the last thing Marin wants, and to appease Boyko and divert attention from the urgings, Marin strikes the tambourine and sings out the famous ballad about the rebel-hero who lies on the mountain with a deep wound in his breast.

"Wrestle the bear, Boyko," more people prod when the song is concluded, but Marin is quick to strike the tambourine again and intone another *haiduk* ballad. He knows that one thing the *haiduks* feared most was to be caught alive and, to avoid it, always saved the last bullet for themselves, their favorite greeting being, "Good bullet to you, my comrade." The body of one caught alive and tortured to death they called a "carcass," but of one who died fighting or, wounded, was dispatched by his comrades they called a "victim." And of such a rebel Marin sings again.

> And cut my head from off my shoulders
> That the Turks may have it not;

58

For they'd carry it to the pasha,
On the palace fix it high;
My foes would rejoice to look at it,
My friends behold and sigh;
And my mother, too, would see it,
And would for sorrow die.

"Wrestle the bear, Boyko. Wrestle him."

"No, I'll not wrestle the bear. But I'd wrestle the fox that holds the chains."

Derisive laughter bursts on all sides. By now more people crowd around, bringing with them traces of the work they have left behind —the men with chaff in their ears and straw in their hair, the women with flour on their handkerchiefs and dough on their hands. They have hurried down to the plaza in response to some children who ran about shouting, "Come quick. Boyko the shepherd's here. He'll wrestle Ivan the bear."

The big bear puffs and pants but doesn't groan or growl. He paces nervously, his huge paws slapping the earth, his broad back swaying and shivering, causing the hair to bristle and stand on edge like the quills of a hedgehog poked by a stick. His small, shifty eyes, like two knots in a brown stump, slant inquisitively toward the mountain man whose own gray eyes regard the chained beast with friendliness and compassion. Then for a moment the bear stands still; not a muscle twitches in his body, his gimlet eyes riveted on the shepherd's, noting the warmth and pity in them.

"No, Boyko, the bear you must wrestle."

"The bear, Boyko, the bear. There's no strength in the man. You can crush him with one hand."

The shepherd's eyes turn from the big chained animal to the smaller one who has chained him. The eyes have momentarily lost their meekness and compassion and narrowed in hatred and contempt as they regard the bear-master.

"I'd like to wrestle the coward that holds the chains. He sings of freedom but has freedom chained by the nose and makes it dance and bow like a *kokona.*"

"I wrestle no man, nor beast," says Marin, accenting his words by tapping the earth with the bottom of his staff. "My bear Ivan will wrestle any man, or any beast, for a stake."

"For any stake?" several voices ask simultaneously.

"For any stake."

"Good enough!" says Boyko. "Let the bear be the stake. If I down him I get the bear. If not, I'll give the man a sheep and he can keep the bear."

No one takes exception to the oddness of the stake.

59

Boyko now puts aside his crook, removes his furry kalpak, un-slings the skinbag from his shoulder, sheds the sheepskin coat, and stands naked to the waist, revealing hairy chest and arms. Then he steps forth, facing the bear, his powerful arms spread out, his deep chest heaved out. The big bear shies away, paces to and fro as in a cage, his body trolling, his huge paws boxing the earth; the gleaming knotlike eyes in the brown stump keep shifting, now fixing on the half-man, half-animal shape, now glancing at the little master, who gently clinks the chain without tugging at it.

"A wrestler be thou, Ivan. With Boyko of the mountain match thou thy strength." And now he tugs lightly at the chain. But the shuttling paws keep sweeping the earth, and the whole shaggy mass sways like a bush in the wind.

With legs apart and arms spread Boyko waits for the bear's mighty trunk to rear up. But the trunk keeps wobbling, stomping and trembling, the huge paws shuffling.

"Stand up, Ivan. Thou art a wrestler now, not a dancer." And this time Marin gives the chain a measured pull, causing the nose ring to dig into the cartilage and the trunk to lift, forepaws hanging limply, chain dangling at the chin, hind paws tamping to steady the towering mass.

Nobody stirs. We all hold our breath. For an instant the hush is broken by the distant, solitary bark of a dog. Then all is silence again. In this pregnant silence Boyko's widespread feet grind the dirt, sidling toward the bear.

And then he charges, his powerful hairy arms clutching at the furry trunk, too large for the arms to encompass. The bear reels and staggers but quickly steadies himself; he rocks again and steadies himself again. Like one possessed, Boyko heaves at the unwieldy mass; he breasts and shoulders and lunges, summons strength from his every bone and muscle to down the great beast in one superhuman effort.

But the bear, all he does is keep from falling. He draggles, his hind paws scuff the earth, his hind legs tremble, his bushel-size head wags from side to side. Is the bear dancing, a slow, earth-thudding, ponderous, clumsy dance?

Silently, inwardly, we all pull for Boyko, for it looks as if the man is trying to uproot an enormous deep-rooted tree by sheer human tug and push. The man has mountain strength, primeval strength, and he repeatedly gathers concentrations of this strength and heaves them at the bear; but the bear is planted deep in his own Ural strength, and though he staggers a little and rocks a little, he keeps his stance, his furry surface wrapped about the struggling man, his arms dangling over his shoulders in a loose embrace, as though he were a dancing partner.

60

Now everybody knows Ivan is a trained wrestler, as he is a trained dancer, and Marin knows it better than anyone else, for it is he who has done the training. And he knows better yet how to conduct a wrestling match between his bear and a man, any man. And the people know, as does Marin, that they must be given due entertainment for the coins they are to drop in the tambourine that Ivan will pass around at the conclusion of the match. So Marin hops about on his short legs, accommodating the chain to the bear until the time comes for him to tell the bear to stop fooling.

Sweat trickles down Boyko's back as he digs his heels into the ground and again and again lunges at the bear bulk with all his might. Above him the bear rocks his head from side to side, his feet pedal the earth to keep the body upright, and there's a gleam of humor, of amusement, in the small black eyes, as if Ivan were merely hugging another bear whom he doesn't wish to hurt.

Marin now begins to jig and prance nervously as though he himself were chained, like a monkey, and the bear held the chains. He must think the moment has come, for he flicks the chain and taps the earth three times with his staff, the signal for Ivan's huge arms to clamp without strangling, his heavy bulk to bear down without crushing, that deftly and painlessly Boyko may be leaned over, hugged down, pinned to the earth with limbs extended, shoulders touching ground all along.

But there's no response from Ivan, no sign that he is taking the hint. He still dances rather than wrestles. His eyes have a roguish glint in them, and there is a bemused smirk on his face. And Marin frolics about like a jester before a monarch, and he gives the bear plenty of slack on the chain. Again he jingles the chain and again he sounds the earth with the bottom of his staff; still, the bear holds back, his arms hanging limply over the struggling man's back.

If there's one thing Marin cannot stand it is disobedience and rebelliousness in his bear. Anger flames up in his eyes like a fire-brand, and in a sudden fury he gives the chain an unmeasured pull and the iron ring digs into the cartilage at the nose. The bear gives out a protesting growl that enrages Marin the more, and before he realizes what he is doing he rams the pole at the bear's back.

From the depths of the animal the wakened wildness comes in a thunderlike roar, in a savage blazing of the eyes and a stiffening of joints and muscles. All at once the giant tree that Boyko has been trying to push down begins to fall on him with all its crushing weight. And it is now Boyko's painful moans that bring Marin back to his senses. He realizes now what he has done. Tugging hard at the nose and ramming the staff into Ivan's back has roused the slumbering wildness in the tameness of the beast. Quickly, in a flash, like the experienced bear-master that he is, Marin unhooks

61

the tambourine from his belt and, striking it with the flat of his hand, sings out the ballad about the hanging of *haiduk* Strahil. And just as suddenly as the bear has taken flight into the wild because of the tear in his nose and the blow in his back, he is returned to his tameness by the song of his master. The stiffness drops from his muscles, the arms relax their iron grip, the burst of savage fury ebbs away, and the troll-like bulk lifts away before it has broken a bone or bruised a muscle.

In his wisdom Marin announces that the match is over and that it is a draw. Nobody questions Marin's decision, not even Boyko, who is shaken but unhurt. And so the match *was* over between Ivan and Boyko but not between Marin and Boyko. For that night the village was wakened by a series of angry roarings of the bear. People whose windows overlooked the threshing lot where Marin camped observed the strange drama that took place there and told about it. Because the moon was blanketed at first by sailing clouds the threshing lot was shrouded in darkness and they could not see what was causing the terrible cries. But presently when the clouds passed and the moon shed its light on the campsite they saw the huge bear standing on its haunches, waving his arms and letting out wild roars that sent tremors through the village. Within striking distance of the pole but beyond reach of the chain to which Ivan was secured stood Marin's sinister little figure holding aloft the pole, both man and pole casting a grotesque silhouette on the moonlit lot. His short legs spread out, his feet hard on the ground and the pole held firmly in both hands to prevent its being seized, Marin swung with all his strength and brought the pole down on Ivan's shoulder. A deafening, terrifying bellow issued from the beast and rumbled through the village and the hillsides.

With one powerful jerk of the chain the bear could have yanked out the threshing post, but the chain was hooked onto the iron ring that hung from his nose. And that inch of gristle between the nostrils held the mighty beast to the post and to his fate. All Ivan did was beat the air with his arms and roll out thunders against his mean little master who would not be stayed and who, again and again, raised the pole and struck Ivan with all the strength of his agile body.

And then something happened that was wondered at and talked about for a long time and that had cheered the hearts of those who witnessed it. The pole lifted to strike again, but it struck no more, for another shadow, twice the size of Marin's, moved on the lot. A mighty arm of this shadow reached out, grasped the uplifted pole, wrenched it from the bear-master's grip, and sent it hurtling over the lot. But just then a bank of black clouds blotted out the bright lunar face and cast a pall of darkness over the bizarre scene.

What then took place in that murk and silence was not seen and was not revealed until morning, when the village was astounded to see chained to the stout threshing post not Ivan the bear but Marin the bear-master and no bear in sight.

6

To be doing the "seeing" for Grandfather I felt it a duty as well as a privilege. The old man was a living saint, and he looked like one, with his white hair and beard, his white homespun woolen frock, the knee-length stockings, the white linen drawers tucked in them. He never wore a fez or cap; his frock was girded by a broad woolen sash, wound at the waist several times. He wore rawhide moccasin-type sandals. We children thought of God as an ageless, eternal old man, with white hair and beard, flying through the heavens to oversee mankind, the human race that He had created. If, as the priest said in church, God had made man in His image, then Grandfather looked more like God than any other human being I had ever seen. I did not know how old he was, and neither did he. In the time of his birth no records of births and deaths were kept. Nobody ever saw a calendar, and people kept track of time by wars, plagues, floods, famines, uprisings, massacres, and other natural and man-made disasters.

Grandfather was all goodness, kindness, gentleness, forgiveness. I wondered why God had taken away his vision. We children knew, or believed, that God punished people for their sins. Had God punished Grandfather or, in His infinite goodness, made him blind for some special purpose? I also wondered whether it was his blindness that made him so saintlike or whether he was like that when he could see. He did not look on his blindness as an affliction, nor as a blessing, but as a condition the reasons for which were in God's keeping. It is embarrassing for me to put this in words, but he believed, even though he did not say it in so many words, that it was God's intent that I be his eyes. Except for this and for his dream at my birth, he never spoke of his blindness, never alluded to it, and neither did I. I never asked him, or my parents, how he lost his sight or how long he had been blind. And I was glad and eager to do the "seeing" for him. Yet in "seeing" for him I saw more for myself, saw things and through things that I might not have seen had I been looking for myself alone. And the old man, for all his gentleness, was exacting in his demands on me, especially when viewing new things, which, what with Gurkin's discovery of the New World, were fast finding their way into our own world. And I couldn't help suspecting that his eagerness for me to see for him was as much for my sake as for his own.

There was one chore I performed for Grandfather reluctantly, although it wasn't "seeing" so much as it was merely standing by or holding his hand as I guided him along. This was attendance at funerals. He believed he had a God-given as well as human obligation to attend the funeral of whoever died in the village, be it babe or centenarian. It was God's wish that the living should escort the dead to their final resting place. Whatever he might be doing, the moment the bell sounded the familiar dirge announcing death's visitation, he would stop, cross himself three times and say *"Bôg da prosti"* (God have mercy). Because the funeral rites were exactly as he remembered them from his days of light, I didn't have to do any "seeing" for him, but I had to guide him to the home of the dead, thence to church for the service there, then to the cemetery for the burial, and then back to the home of the bereaved to partake of food and drink, for it was a sin to bury a person and not afterward offer food and libation for his soul.

There was one other man in the village besides Grandfather who never missed a funeral. The decades have thrown a veil of mist over many childhood memories; the new and varied life in America has superimposed its own rich store of memories, overlaying the pre-American life with its own vast panorama. Yet it is a quirk of the memory to assign niches in its hallway to simple souls like "Setchko," who, like Grandfather, considered it a sin not to attend a funeral, no matter whose. This good man, whose baptismal name was Yovan, had been nicknamed Setchko (an unflattering epithet) and was so called by everybody except Grandfather. Setchko was nicknamed after the month of February. Only those with some pretense to schooling—and they were mostly young—called the second month of the year *Fevruary;* the others knew it only by the folk name Setchko, which meant a "cutter" or "chopper." And that the month deserved to be called. It was the worst month of the year. It brought cutting winds and squalls and sleets and drifts of snow that quelled the life of the village and made people surly and abrasive, forcing them to stay indoors to feed the fires. The flocks of sheep and goats bleated in their enclosures, munching dehy-

65

drated oak leaves and leafless, fresh-cut willow twigs. No weddings were planned for this month. Who would want to get married in Setchko? In it mothers feared to bear children lest they turn out bleak and sullen like the month itself. Worse yet, they might be nicknamed Setchko.

And yet it is not to be wondered at that I should remember this man through more than half a century of a crowded, variegated American life. I particularly recall his death and funeral and a hoax that was played on him by fellow villagers. He died at a most inconvenient time so far as his funeral was concerned. It was on a golden July day when everyone was promoting life, storing away nature's bounty for the winter. From every part of the village, from the flats down by the river, from the upper quarters where the threshing lots were terraced against the hillsides, were heard the voices of people, the squeaks and clatter of oxcarts hauling sheaves, the strident neighings and whinnyings of mules and horses threshing grain. This was no time for dying, let alone for funerals. Man and beast were engaged in the elemental labor of separating the grain from the straw. Whips came whistling down on the rumps of horses and mules, which galloped around the threshing posts, winding and unwinding the ropes looped about their necks and tied to the posts. The pounding iron-shod hoofs cut the straw, and the grain shot from the studded ears. Even the dogs helped, chasing chickens that snatched at the grain at the edges of the lots.

It had been a hot summer, and the wheat had ripened before its time so that the grain shed at the slightest breeze. People were reaping, binding, carting, and threshing all at the same time. In some fields sheaves lay scattered like beehives; in others they were piled in shocks, little temples to nature's generosity. Even donkeys and teams of oxen did the threshing, but mostly it was done by mules and horses, their hoofs drubbing the grain as in the time when Christ walked the earth. Every now and then the panting animals, their sweaty backs and rumps striped with welts from the whiplashes, would be led to the shade of a fruit tree and given oats, while the family, with pitchforks shaped out of tree branches, turned the straw to bring to the top the unthreshed underpart. When the threshing was done and the straw forked into the barns for winter fodder, the grain with the chaff was raked into a pile for the winnowing, which was done by the women. With long-handled, flat wooden spades, they tossed scoopings into the air like snow flurries, and the breeze wafted the chaff to one side while the grain dribbled into a pile at their feet. This was a time when strangers came to claim their share of nature's bounty—gypsies to barter their eternal loom reeds, spindles, shuttles, heddles, baskets, sieves; beggars astride shambling beasts swinging long staffs against the dogs while intoning endless ballads in droning, whining voices, invoking heaven's favor on people and animals for a bowl of wheat; monks came, too, in rough gray cassocks with crosses dangling at their breasts, their staffs surmounted with crucifixes. They canted benedictions in return for donations to their monasteries. But one never could be certain that a monk was a monk. He might be a courier or agent of the revolutionary organization or, with a prize on his head, an apostle preaching the gospel of freedom, or even the great Delchev himself, who traveled the length and breadth of Macedonia in different disguises.

It was in the midst of this all-embracing activity that the bell announced death had come to the village. *Danngg . . . danngg* moaned the bell, causing people to stop and say, *"Bôg da prosti."*

Anachronism! Were there not enough empty, fruitless, gloomy days in which death could do its work? Must he come now, when everyone was promoting life, storing for winter? Or could the tolling mean something else? No, the dirge was unmistakable— slow, prolonged, mournful peals, with measured pauses. *Dannngg . . . danggg!*

Who would die at a time like this? And who had time to go to his funeral? People called across threshing lots to ask whom God had taken to His bosom. In some voices there was irritation that at a time like this God should send down one of His angels to take a soul.

"Setchko died! Setchko's dead!"

"Setchko! Of all people! Who'd go to his funeral? He never missed one. God have mercy!"

Indeed Setchko should have died when everybody could go to his funeral. But death comes when it comes, when expected and when least expected. It is all God's work and *will.*

Setchko lived alone at the edge of the village in a low mud-brick house hugging the hillside. Facing the house and about fifty feet from it was a small barn also of sun-baked brick. The shelf of ground between the house and barn was yard and threshing lot. His wife, a goodhearted childless woman, used to give us children walnuts and Easter eggs not to call her husband Setchko. She had adopted a boy, an orphan, and raised him and loved him as though he were her own, but at age eighteen he too caught the virus of Gurkin's Americamania and joined the migration to America. (Years later I saw this foster son in Great Falls, Montana. He was a bartender at the Park Hotel, facing the Great Northern railway station hard by the bank of the Missouri River.)

Unlike his unwelcome namesake, Setchko was not squally and blustery, but he *was* shut in, wintry, overcast—a tall, lean man, meek but stern of appearance, with brows jutting like eaves. He rarely spoke and then in monosyllables. Except as he went to, or returned from, field, meadow, or vineyard, he was seen only at church on Sundays and holidays and at all funerals and weddings. And he never missed memorial services for departed souls, at which food was handed out. He loved the soil; it seemed that in the soil, in the land, in its responsiveness, he found what he failed to find in his fellow beings, save when they died. The dead he honored and with them he seemed to have some kind of communion that was lacking while they were alive. He usually worked on the land till dusk, but if there was to be a funeral or a commemorative service, even though the earth cried out to be plowed, he unyoked his hybrid team of a tawny ox and a mouse-colored donkey, planted the goad in the earth near the wooden plow, and started on the road to the village.

People never take things for what they are but always seek for a handle to the egg or a calf under the ox, as Grandfather sometimes put it. The villagers believed that Setchko attended funerals not so much for spiritual reasons as for the feasting that always took place immediately after the burial. Setchko also never missed weddings and the plenty to eat and drink that was a part of them.

But why was the man always silent, never saying anything? He would walk along the road slightly stooped, his head trembling, his lips moving soundlessly as in prayer, his eyes half hidden under his grizzly brows. When we children saw him returning from the mountain, nudging his donkey packed with firewood, or from the meadow with a clamped scythe balanced like a rifle on his shoulder, we would run after him as after a tame bear and shout, "Setchko . . . Setchko . . ." The man would glance at us sideways, the way people do at vicious dogs who bite without barking, and keep on walking. His lips moved, but as no sound came from his mouth, no one knew what he was saying. Only once, unable to contain his anger, he growled at us and muttered curses against our mothers for having brought us into the world. But this only served to spur our unwitting childish cruelty, and we closed in on him like a pack of dogs.

We never knew who gave Setchko that dark epithet. Was it because of what he was or had the nickname itself made him that? His silence and that single eruption of anger did not reveal Yovan to us or to the grownups. The soil he tilled, the ox that helped him till it, and the donkey, that constant companion with the large, compassionate eyes and ears flopped down like palm leaves, must have known him better. At the funerals I attended with Grandfather I sometimes would catch him open wide his grayish eyes and look about him as if searching for someone or something and then quickly retreat within himself to resume his customary silence and humility. Even the *Bôg da prosti* he said every time he crossed himself was a mere whisper.

One day of the long laborious village year was of greater import to Setchko than Christmas or Easter. This was *Zadushenitsa* (All Souls' Day), which came in the first week in November. It was the annual feast day of the dead, but it was the living who did the feasting. On this day no soul was forgotten, even those had to be remembered whose bones had been dug from their graves, washed clean at the river, and dumped onto the bone pile behind the apse. I recall vividly the observances of All Souls' Day, a sort of Memorial Day, because for Grandfather, too, this was a memorable day. On this day the women of the village vied in their skills for cooking and baking. For days before All Souls' Day the chimneys belched fleeces of smoke—a sure sign of extensive culinary endeavors. Then on the day itself, soon after sunup, the bell would spill holiday benediction over the low, pantiled house roofs. In response to it men, women, and children, singly and in groups, would stream by the many paths leading down to the white church on the village green. But long before the bell's summons, Setchko, silent as a sphinx, would be there waiting on the bench just outside the church door to watch the women carry into the church the broad rattan baskets packed with delicacies neatly separated within freshly laundered white napkins. There would be certain standard items— boiled wheat mixed with sugar and crushed walnuts, round wheat-flour buns. For the rest it all depended on the resources and resourcefulness of the basket carrier. There would be smelts fried in olive oil, shortbreads, biscuits, custards. Inside the church the women would set the baskets on the stone floor and with fingers dovetailed, or hands crossed like daggers into the folds of their woolen belts, would stand by motionless like costume models in an ethnographic museum, each with her eyes on her own basket, observing the arrangement there of the eatables and comparing them with those in other baskets and thinking of the dead for whom they were intended, thinking not of the dead collectively but individually, connecting each dead in the family with a portion of the food to be given, thinking of dead specifically when giving the portion, as she had done when preparing it, so that thus, through concentration, the food would reach the dead, reach his soul. And all the time the priest, in gold and silver vestments, would be mumbling benedictions and swinging the censer over the baskets.

While thus jingling and canting the priest every now and then would dip the basil in the copper vessel of holy water carried by an altar boy and shake it over the baskets.

Meantime on the benches outside the church and within the open arched gallery men and old women and children would be waiting with cloths spread in their laps. But the place next to the door, the most strategic of all, which no woman could overlook, would be occupied by Setchko, coming early in order to secure it. And so now on this particular All Souls' Day Setchko, as always, sat there patiently, the capacious cloth expectantly spread out before him. One never knew what would be deposited there; it could be the prosaic spoonful of wheat pudding, or a boiled egg, or a wedge of cheese, or one of those baked rarities made of rolled dough sheets stuffed with honey and crushed walnuts. Not unlikely, waiting would be rewarded with a generous square of that celestial concoction—a custard made of eggs and cream held together by flakes of home-made noodles. When a woman stopped before Setchko and her hand began to prowl over the arrangements in the basket, the man's eyes would brighten behind the bushy brows. Benign, invoking, ingratiating expressions would flit across his face from which a fortnight's growth of stubble had just been mowed for the occasion. Setchko knew every woman and the dead in the family for years back. When a woman who had buried a brother, cousin or other close relative of Setchko's own age stopped before him, Setchko would look up with a simple but concentrated expression as if he were envisioning the dear departed for whose sake the offering would be made.

Setchko knew that some baskets would pass him with only a tidbit offering, but there would be ample reward when a generous hand would dip into the basket and produce a wheaten bun, round and swollen like a bride's breast. One such would be sufficient for a meal; a dozen would provide bread rations for a week. But no matter what the bestowal, Setchko was genuinely grateful and never failed to say *Bôg da prosti.*

And now at that critical moment when the row of baskets began to file out of the church door, some youngsters ran pell-mell down to the church grounds screaming that Setchko's barn was on fire. And smoke in the vicinity of Setchko's barn did rise to support the alarm. There was instant commotion. A few men left their places and started toward the scene of fire. Others by word and gesture urged Setchko to hurry and save his barn. Setchko did not stir. Calm, imperturbable, his bushy brows drooping over his untroubled eyes, he sat there not budging or uttering a word, determined not to give up his place though his barn burned to the ground. Soon

70

the smoke subsided and drifted away in pale wisps. From the children's sheepish behavior it became evident that the whole thing was a hoax, and so it turned out to be. Some village pranksters, in order to defraud Setchko of his strategic place, had bribed several youngsters with a few coins to light a pile of straw on Setchko's threshing floor and to spread the alarm just as the women began to file out of the church with their loaded baskets. The ruse not only failed but boomeranged, for, the women's sympathy having been roused, they loaded Setchko with choicest delicacies. He went home with enough bakings and fryings and curdlings to last him a month.

The bell kept reminding the village, plunged in the feverish seasonal activity, that Setchko was dead and was not yet buried. The following morning, as soon as it recommenced its dirge, Grandfather and I started to build a coffin out of rough poplar boards. My mother took time from the threshing to dress me appropriately for the funeral and to lay out Grandfather's frock, linen shirt, and stockings. The funeral procession was pitifully small. Besides ourselves and the priest, there was Uncle Petko the *protoger;* the storekeeper Kuzman, who had lost a forearm in a West Virginia lumber mill; a vacationing schoolmaster; and a few old grandmothers dressed in black like crows. The field warden, the schoolteacher, and the two gravediggers were pallbearers. We trod slowly along the narrow road leading out of the village, clumped over the plank bridge of a tributary to the Bistra, and then turned into a lane of Lombardy poplars that led directly into the cemetery. The one-armed storekeeper had brought along a leaden flask of brandy, and one of the grandmothers had carried under a napkin a bowlful of boiled wheat to give for Setchko's soul.

When Setchko finally lay under a mound of dirt we all said *"Bôg da prosti"* and all but myself "tswirked" brandy and dipped into the bowl of wheat and once again invoked God's mercy. From the cupola came the three final strokes in rapid succession, without any pauses, announcing to the village that Setchko had been returned to the bosom of Mother Earth.

On the following Sunday, at the end of the liturgy, the priest announced that Setchko had left his two fields, his meadow, the two vineyards, his house and barn, the ox and the donkey and all his other worldly goods to the glebe, asking in return that at the end of forty days after his death, and at the end of one year, services be held in his memory and that the deacons arrange that at every All Souls' Day there be a woman with a basket "to give for his soul."

Setchko's was the last funeral Grandfather and I attended. I was no longer a child to guide him and see for him but a youngster of thirteen with visions of my own and dreams of that far new world discovered by Gurkin. And, too, Grandfather needed me no more as his "seeing eye," for he never ventured farther than the garden apiary, where through spring, summer, and fall he baked himself in the sun like the old lizard and listened to the somnolent thrumming and humming of the bees. His lips would move, but he wasn't saying anything; it was as if he were praying. A lethargy had come over him, and more and more he lived in a world to look at or see he needed no eyes, his or mine. Even though he needed me no more to see for him, he clung to me not as a link with life but as a link with the past. I tried to be with him as often as I could. I would sit with him in the garden, and he would feel my face with his bony hand. He had moments of perfect clarity, as if he were seeing things with his soul, as when he urged my father to let me go to "this new world they have found." Both his hair and his beard had thinned out, detracting from his old patriarchal appearance. His body also had shrunk, and there was not about him that evangelical appearance that, in my earliest childhood, made me think of God. He was not ill, only old, too old, and he knew he would soon die. He had never seen my face, and I had a feeling that in tracing my features with his bony but sensitive fingers he wanted to imprint on his mind, to carry with him to wherever one went when one died, a memory of the way I looked. For ten years, since I was three years old, his life had been bound up with mine. We shared the same world. When he would die, it would be like a man dying but leaving himself behind. "I would go, child," he once said to me, "to the everlasting world, and you, you go to this new living world they have found." Unlike most old men who remember minor incidents of their childhood but cannot recall something that happened a month ago, his most vivid remembrances were of his blind days, or scenes and episodes he had seen through me, through my own eyes. He thanked God for me and for having lived long enough to see a bishop of our own set foot on our soil and pray in native Slav words and grieved that he must die without seeing Macedonia freed of the Turkish yoke. He was too feeble to attend funerals, but his hearing was still good and he listened to the cracked bell toll the funeral dirge and he prayed for the repose of the soul of whoever it was Mother Earth had taken back to her bosom. He never used the word *die* when he spoke of death, only "when I will go." *Koga ke si oda.*

And he went from the garden apiary. One sunny day I found him there with one hand clenched on the old cane with the carved handle. A dozen or more bees were hovering over him and humming a chant but not alighting. Not a bee was on his face or hands. At his funeral my mother carried a basket with boiled wheat mixed with sugar and walnut kernels to give for his soul. I took a second pinch of it in remembrance of Setchko and for his soul.

7

As I write these lines in a Vermont farmhouse it is more than half a century since I landed at Ellis Island. All these years I have been preoccupied with the theme of America and the meaning and essence of Americanness. I have written in books and magazines and lectured on the processes and adventures of Americanization, a word tired and fatigued, no longer popular among the sociologists who have developed a new lexicon for the anatomy of the American nationality. The *crucible* is in disrepute; the melting pot has been melted down. Now it is *pluralism, acculturation, acculturation without assimilation, cultural integration, behavioral assimilation,* anything but Americanization.

I belong spiritually as well as chronologically to the generations of immigrants who had to Americanize as well as acculturate, integrate, assimilate, coalesce, all at the same time. With me the process had begun even before I had set foot on American soil. Robert Frost expressed it when he said at John F. Kennedy's inauguration that "We were the land's before the land was ours."

The moon rocks the astronauts brought back to earth had to be analyzed for strange germs or viruses that might infect our planet. The *Amerikantzi* of my boyhood days brought back to my native soil a powerful virus, an infectious Americamania that affected the young and middle-aged so that they were no longer content to till the thin mountain soil or dream of becoming *komitadjis* to fight the Turks.

But not for my father. He was the original anti-American. Still he did not resent America so much as he did the *Amerikantzi*—Gurkin and those who followed in his footsteps. After two or three years in roundhouses and foundries and coal mines in West Virginia, they returned to the village scrubbed clean and with gold not

74

only in their pockets but in their mouths as well. Gurkin, the trail blazer, had set the pattern for all returnees. They were all copies of him, the first Americanaut. These were new men, in striped double-breasted jackets, cuffed pantaloons, silk shirts and flowery neckties, leather gloves, spats over shoes that buttoned on the side with a little metal hook. They used strange words, words never before heard in the village. To pronounce these words the mouths twisted like flutes, the sounds guttered out as the lips and the tongue articulated the difficult Anglo-Saxon syllables.

In these early migration days no women went to America and no old folk. America needed muscles for her railroads, mines, heavy industries. Somewhere on the far confines of the planet this new land reached across water and land spaces and changed the life of the village as if by some powerful magic. And the magic was gold. Not America's civilization, not her idealism of those days, not her basic freedoms, her democracy, her Constitution, her Bill of Rights. It was none of these things. It was her gold, earned in driblets by sweat and grime but sizable in terms of the village economy, where a man laid bricks for ten hours for the equivalent of twenty cents. There was freedom in America, but it wasn't that freedom that gave the *Amerikantzi* the ability to tear down the old mud-brick, mud-plastered houses and rear new ones of stone or fired brick with large windows and spacious rooms and iron-grilled balconies.

There was no denying that the journey across continents and oceans and the two or three years in America cloaked the *Amerikantzi* with luster and glamour. But their beings were not inoculated with the leaven of America that worked so powerfully with earlier immigrants from other lands. They were familiar with the heat of steel mills and iron foundries and roundhouses but never came in contact with the heat of the melting pot. America had not put her finger on their minds or hearts as it had done to millions before them and as it would to their children and grandchildren. They were not pilgrims or transplants. Still, America had put her stamp on them. They *had* undergone a change, externally, and they *were* new men. *Amerikantzi!* The aura of America was upon them. Even at this distance of time, those *Amerikantzi* stand out in my memory as distinctly as if it all happened yesterday. Their show-offness, their putting on the dog—for that's what it was to him— my father resented. For years on end he had been mayor and factotum in the village, and although now his authority, and especially his magisterial functions, had been curtailed by the *Kommittet,* he still held court in the shade of the plane tree in the village green. He liked this spot for its shade but also because at the nearby riverbank the women, bare-legged and with skirts tucked up, did their wash. My father was a trader, kept a small general store, journeyed to Prilep and Bitola to buy livestock, which he sold in the villages in our valley. Wearing his long cloak lined with sheepskin, he received the Turkish civil and military officials who visited the village. They addressed him as *Chorbagi,* an honorific derived from the Turkish word *chorba* (stew) and literally meaning "steward" but connotatively "squire." The mess sergeants of the janissaries were also called *Chorbagi.*

Had my father been born in the New World he might have been a politician or a Yankee trader. As it was he passed for a local sage, and people from other villages came to consult him. He paid small heed to such scattered farming as our household did, hired people to plow and sow and do the haying and harvesting, except for the vineyards, to which he was devoted, cultivating them and pruning the vines with expert care. He wasted nothing of the fruit of the vine. When the vats in the cellar were drained out of the fermented juices, he raked out the residual mash and, sprinkling it with caraway seeds, boiled it in the still to produce the strong and aromatic distillate called *rakia.*

In the days before the *Kommittet* forbade the people to take their cases to the official courts, my father, as mayor, also performed certain minor judicial functions. I remember a man he disliked very much came to him with a complaint against another man whose dog had bitten him. My father was quite sober at the moment, and without any outward sign of sarcasm he fined the complainant ten *piasters* and turned the money over to the owner of the dog with instructions that he buy fresh liver for the discriminating animal. My father was also a veterinary of sorts. At any time of day or night he might be called to minister to some sick animal. He answered these calls with such zeal that I was much intrigued, because whenever one of our own animals had distemper he did nothing about it. So one day I went along with him to see how he treated sick animals. The moment we reached the ailing creature, an ox, he turned to the owner and in a voice full of foreboding said, "Quick, the brandy." The poor man rushed to the house and hurried back with a small bottle of brandy. My father took a long draught, put the bottle in his pocket, and proceeded to stuff some dry herbs into the animal's nostrils.

My father's anti-Americanism intensified when I, barely in my teens, became one of the worst, or best, victims of the American epidemic. He tried hard to break the spell. "An ox is an ox even if you put golden horns on him," he said contemptuously of the *Amerikantzi.* And with a diabolic pleasure he observed how, as time passed, those who did not make a second or third trip to America

76

wore out their fineries and reverted to the traditional village garb. Yes, and they went back to poking oxen and riding donkeys. He laughed derisively at all that was connected with America.

"You've let these American jackasses with their pantaloons and trinkets turn your mind."

"America has given them things they never had before," I would say.

"What things? Gold teeth and a pair of overshoes. They strut here like peacocks, but what do you think they do in America? They are *hamals* [porters], that's what they are. They carry iron on their backs. You get this America out of your mind. America is right here for you. We have fields, meadows, vineyards, trading to do, a store to tend."

My father's admonitions and his denigrations of America and of the *Amerikantzi* had no effect on me. The unseen, the as yet unclaimed and untouched America, had indeed extended her long arm across the vast spaces and put her hand on my shoulder and beckoned to me. I went about moping, irritable, constantly dreaming of the New World and the new life there. I was not to be a mere migrant, like the others, but an emigrant.

To break the spell my father began to take me on his journeys to the cities, where I met the merchants and began to learn the rudiments of bargaining. He also left the store pretty much to me and finally began to send me alone to Kastoria to do the purchasing. It was all calculated to divert my mind from America and involve me in activities at home. It was on the first of these solo journeys as an embryo merchant that I became the victim of a superstition. How I came to believe in this thing I do not know. Grandfather had never mentioned it to me, and I had never heard my mother or my father speak of it, but we youngsters believed in it, the way we believed in fairies, vampires, succubi that sucked the blood of people while asleep. I did not know then how widespread this belief was. We children had probably absorbed it from the grownups even though they did not speak of it openly.

On this maiden mercantile journey I started out in high spirits, having made a list of the items to be purchased. I wore at my neck a little silver medallion of St. Christopher, the patron saint of travelers, that Grandfather had given me. No bigger than one of the gold coins I carried, the saint's image was fastened to a thin-spun silver chain, which I passed over my head and tucked the medallion in my bosom next to the money pouch.

The mule had inherited equal parts of his lowly sire's characteristics and of the dam that foaled him. In his moments of "donkeyness" he could be balky and stubborn and you could break a cudgel over his rump without his budging. He could also be stoical as a philosopher and meek as a nun, regarding you with wide, friendly, and compassionate eyes. He threw you only when the "donkeyness" had the uppermost of his hybrid ancestry, and you fell so hard your bones ached for days. There were times, however, when he let you fall lightly like a feather, and at such times I always thought that the "horseness" had intervened just in time. It was on mounting that you had to be most careful, for sometimes just as you flung yourself onto the saddle he would lower his muzzle to the ground, and, using that as one point of a compass and his rump as the other, he would describe a quick circle before bucking. In this way he aimed to make you dizzy so as to effect your fall with greater ease. As I mounted the mule now he went through that maneuver, but I was prepared, for at the moment I flung myself onto the saddle I gripped the pommel with both hands, pressed my knees against the beast's flanks, and kept my eyes shut. When the revolution was completed the mule bucked violently, and then when he didn't see me on the ground he turned up his head and regarded me with a puzzled and disappointed eye. Then it was my turn. I dug the rowels into his flanks and swung the crop over his rump. With a final malicious kick he leaped ahead and shimmied out of the courtyard. Once he got going it was a pleasure to ride that mule. He did not wobble or flounder; he was all horse then, and his was a dense, rhythmic tread, neither a trot nor a canter but an interweaving of both.

As soon as I was out of the village and on the high road a feeling of bigness, or grownupness, welled up in me. The mule pattered on with his characteristic side movement, as if he were going off the road, and I could feel myself bobbing in the saddle, my arms flapping like wings. I did not think of myself as a boy but as a merchant carrying gold in my bosom. My father had given me the needed sum for the purchases in napoleons, those gold coins with the roosters on them which the *Amerikantzi* exchanged for the dollars they earned in America. I carried the money in my bosom in a little pouch of canvas dipped in beeswax. It felt good to have the gold warming my bosom; it gave me a sense of power and reminded me of a folk tale Grandfather had told me about a man who could, on a wager, jump across a wide stream. He did this on every wager until a wise old man noticed a string around the man's neck. The old man figured that there was a talisman or some kind of charm attached to the string that gave the man the strength to jump the stream, and he doubled the wager, provided the man, before jumping, took off the string and whatever was attached to it. This time the man landed in midstream. Attached to the loop of string was no talisman but a moneybag.

I crossed and recrossed the unbridged Bistra as I rode down the valley. In the fields by the roadside men—grown men—plodded after ox teams, kicking clumps of earth with their heels, while I, a mere boy, was a merchant with gold in my bosom riding to the city.

Maybe my father was right. Maybe America was right here for me. Sensing my mood of elation, the mare in the mule danced like a *kokona,* the beads and tassels on the halter shimmering in the sunlight. The valley narrowed at a point where a small tributary joined the Bistra, but soon the enlarged Bistra and the road to Kastoria parted. The mule scrambled up some gutted and gravelly hillocks, crossing and recrossing dry gullies until, leaving all this behind, the road zigzagged down naked hillsides for a thousand feet or more to descend to a semi-tropical basin in which the city lay on a promontory in the lake connected to the mainland by a narrow neck of land. From the water's edge to the top of the promontory the blue and white buildings, their red pantiled roofs gleaming in the sunlight, climbed in serried terraces to give the city the aspect of a single enormous structure rising above the waters like a bishop's miter.

By the time I was on the narrow isthmus leading to the town the sun was sinking behind the hills I had just traversed. The road here ran along the edge of the lake, and I recalled the first time I had passed here with my father. I had never until then seen a body of water larger than a mill pond or any kind of boat, and I marveled at the fishermen's *kayiks* floating on the water. I was familiar only with water running in one direction, but the water here ran in waves toward the shore, and then just when you feared it would flood the road it turned back and ran into the lake.

I entered the town through the ancient stone gate of the ruined fortress, or *Kastron,* which gave the town its name. The mule, from habit, hurried toward the inn where my father always stopped. Though twilight was now falling some shops were still open, the kerosene lamps inside throwing weak yellow light on the narrow cobbled street.

Through an archway I rode into the inn's court, really a small caravanserai, a flagstoned compound with mangers under the veranda, or gallery, that gave access to the sleeping quarters. I handed the halter cord to the stable boy. "Remove the saddle and rub the sweat off him. Fill his nosebag with oats but give him no water till he's rested." I was a merchant now and, instinctively, acted like one. But the groom, an Albanian youth wearing the white skullcap of his tribe, smiled wryly.

This not being a market day, there were only a few guests at the inn, which catered to villagers coming to market. The innkeeper, a Vlach friend of my father's, raised his brows when I told him I had come alone to buy goods for the store. I didn't order any *rakia,* which my father would have done, but with my dinner took a hundred-dram tankard of wine. The innkeeper not being busy did me the honor of sitting at my table while I dined. He was a dark little man with a humorous twinkle in his eye and a smirk on his mouth. I was self-conscious of my embryo merchanthood and felt some resentment against the innkeeper, but soon the sly grin faded and he fell to telling me anecdotes about people who stayed at his inn. I have forgotten them all except the one about the peasant who went across the street to the bakery and bought himself a small round loaf of fresh city bread. Peasants brought their own bread from home, dark, coarse bread of corn and rye. So it was a treat to buy a small loaf of white city bread. The peasant returned to the inn and walked over to the counter where a stewpot was simmering and held chunks of bread over the steaming stew. When the bread would be well impregnated with the steam and aroma of the stew he would swallow it and then do the same with another chunk until he finished the loaf. He then started to leave, but the innkeeper tapped him on the shoulder and demanded that he pay for the stew. "What stew? I never ate any stew," rejoined the peasant. But as the innkeeper would not let go of him until he paid for his lunch, the peasant took out a *medjidie* (a large silver coin), banged it on the counter, and put it back in his pocket. "There," he said. "You've heard the sound and you've been paid."

The next morning after a breakfast of hot milk and cheese-and-egg turnovers at a dairy stand I began my calls on the merchants. I first took care of the smaller orders, saving for the last the big order at Miralai's, the fabrics merchant. The merchants, who remembered me from visits with my father and seeing me alone, made discreet inquiries about my father. When I reassured them of his good health they did not offer me Turkish delights as previously but sent to the nearest coffeehouse for *finjans* of Turkish coffee, thus according me the status of a merchant in my own right.

By the time I got to Miralai's it was mid-afternoon. And here again coffee was ordered, but by now I merely took one or two sips for politeness' sake. Miralai, too, was duly impressed by my new status but swayed his head chidingly when told that I had spent the night at the inn.

"You are coming home with me this evening," he said flatly.

"But I have my mule at the inn."

"No excuses now. The groom looks after the beasts. As if you didn't know that."

He pulled out an ornate gold watch from the breast pocket of his caftan and clicked it open. "We have time before dark to take care of your purchases. I want you to see the stuff in daylight, not under lamplight. I have some new fabrics from Belgium."

There was something aristocratic about Miralai's appearance and bearing. Tall, gaunt, graceful of movement, fair of complexion for a Levantine Jew, with a reddish tapering beard and mustache trimmed Turkish-fashion, he could have been the scion of a distinguished banking family fallen on hard times. He did not regard as beneath his dignity his being a fabrics merchant in a small provincial Macedonian town far removed from mercantile centers like Salonika and Skopje. He took pride in his store, the finest in the city, and stocked fabrics imported from British, Italian, and Belgian mills. The first time I met him he had reminded me of a high priest. Despite his height and angularity he was not awkward and looked elegant in his dark-green caftan girded with a broad purple sash. I liked Miralai's habit of speaking in epigrams, which my father quoted in our village without identifying their source. "Wisdom is all Miralai is generous with," he would say. "He charges and overcharges for everything else."

I consulted my list of the goods I had to buy, but Miralai knew pretty much what was needed by a small village general store— mostly calicos, muslins, velvets, and such. He turned to the shelves and began to slide out rolls of textiles with his accustomed dexterity, causing the least disarrangement in the neatly lined shelves. He slung bolts onto the counter lightly and stroked them as though they were sleek living creatures of distinguished pedigree. He would unroll an *arshin* of some extra-fine material, twist it into a rope, and then, releasing it, watch it unfurl without a whorl or wrinkle on its smooth sheen.

By the time we got down to the ribbons, braids, laces, bandanas, threads, Miralai had to light the kerosene lamps. For each item there was a separate bargaining ritual, for to give the asking price was fatuous, yet to haggle beyond a reasonable point was as unmerchantlike as not to bargain at all. One had to feel instinctively when the bargaining threshold was reached. During bargaining you could simulate hurt feelings, even pretend that your intelligence was insulted, and yet there was no ill-feeling in it; it was like a play, like something staged.

Miralai totaled up the sum, and I counted out the right number of napoleons. His long fingers deftly picked up the gold coins one by one and placed each on a little brass balance. As the coin tipped the scale in proof of its worth and tinkled on the counter Miralai picked it up and put it in a pouch. Many thousands of such coins had passed through his hands, and the ones I handed him seemed to cling to his fingers like some flat gold bugs with glittering shells.

When we were finished Miralai let down the iron shutters and locked the store with a huge padlock. A phaeton with the top down was waiting in front, and we climbed in. The *phaetondji*—a Turk wearing a braided waistcoat and an unblocked fez—cracked the whip and the carriage clattered on the cobbles. Bunches of sparks played about their fetlocks as the horses struck the stones with their iron-shod hoofs. The street was zones of darkness checked by shafts of lamplight from the doors and windows of coffeehouses and shops still open.

The *phaetondji* was careful not to disturb the dogs lying in the street. Sometimes he had to stop the horses and shout to the dogs to move.

"Do you know why Turks are so kind to dogs?" asked Miralai.

"Are they kinder to them than we are?"

"Oh yes. No Moslem would dream of annoying a dog, let alone hurt one. That's why there are so many of them in the cities. They are a nuisance and a menace to health. In Stambul [Istanbul] there are more dogs than people in the streets."

"Have you been to Stambul?"

"Yes, twice. I have a brother there. He is a banker."

"You were going to tell me why Turks are so kind to dogs."

"A dog saved Mohammed from being robbed and murdered by bandits. The prophet was asleep in the desert when some bandits were about to pounce on him. Just at that moment he happened to be dreaming, and in his dream a dog bit him. This made him wake in time to save himself from certain death at the hands of the marauders."

We left the bazaar quarter behind and started climbing up into the residential parts of the city. There were no street lamps, and such light as there was in the street came filtering through latticed windows like splotches of moonlight through foliage. I had never been in this part of the city, but I knew we were passing through the Turkish quarter, for I saw veiled women dart across the street and disappear within walled courtyards. The carriage bumped along on the cobbles. We came into a completely dark street, and here I realized that there were lanterns attached to the front of the carriage.

By my side now Miralai was strangely silent, his hands crossed in his lap. His silence became disquieting to me, for it wasn't like him not to be saying something or telling some story or anecdote. I thought he must be tired.

Presently the carriage turned into a street so narrow that the overhanging balconies formed a kind of arcade. Occasional fragments of light trickling through grilled windows made weird, shivering patterns on the backs of the horses. Miralai kept up his un-wonted silence until the coachman stopped at the entrance to an alley too narrow to admit the carriage. Here we climbed down, and Miralai reached deep into his caftan and handed some coins to the coachman, who drove ahead because he couldn't make a turn here.

The alley we now entered was flanked by two- and three-story stone houses with low doorways and small, barred square windows. The sky could not be seen, but the moon must have swum out from under some clouds, and its phosphorescent light found this narrow corridor. My host's tall figure, in the ankle-length caftan and blocked cylindrical fez, appeared taller and ghostlike in the moon-light. As I trailed the merchant's elongated shadow, an eerie feeling came over me, and an uncanny, premonitory fear began to pervade my being. The silent houses silhouetted against the moonlit alley gave the scene a sepulchral, mortuary aspect, and with each step I took the fear grew in me and I felt as if I were descending into some labyrinthine mausoleum whence I would never come out.

My host stopped before an arched doorway cut into a stone wall. With a key that he fished out from the folds of his girdle he un-locked the door and, putting his hand on my shoulder, gently propelled me across the threshold. At that instant the vague fear dropped into my heart like a stone. And as a stone dropped into a pool causes ever-widening concentric rings on the water, so the fear undulated through my entire being. We had entered a walled, flagged courtyard at the far end of which was a house seeming to crouch there like an animal in the dark waiting for its prey. The door was opened to us by a stoutish middle-aged woman in a black velvet dress and yellow scarf. She was holding a small kerosene lamp.

"I brought a guest, Mama," said Miralai. "A young merchant friend of mine from upcountry."

"I am glad you came, son." The woman took my hand but did not shake it, just held it in hers and led me, with my host following, into a large living room the like of which I had never before seen. My hosts told me to make myself at home and left the room. No village house that I had ever been in had such a room. In village houses we used no chairs. We sat on rugs or blankets spread on the floor and ate our meals sitting cross-legged at low round tables. Here for the first time I saw divans and ottomans upholstered in damasks and somber velvets; carved oblong tables on which were silver and copper trays with curious devices engraved on them; on the walls pieces of tapestries, mosaiclike miniature rugs, lengths of black silks with strange scrolls in gold on them, framed pictures of bearded men in skullcaps, a print of an old worn stone wall against

83

which people leaned their foreheads. The floor was covered with a thick, soft rug of many colors woven in an intricate pattern of flowers and birds and strange animals. My eyes searched for some object, such as the photograph of a child, that might give me some reassurance, help quiet the fear that gnawed at my heart. But everything tended to augment rather than diminish my fear, especially the ponderous silver candelabrum on the mantel shelf ensconced by two silver chalices that I thought must be used in the sacrificial rites.

Presently Miralai returned, having replaced his red fez with a dark-red skullcap, which was scant comfort to me. His wife brought in a tray with a brandy bottle, two glasses of water, a little silver dish of preserves, and two small silver spoons. "You will like this," said Mrs. Miralai to me. "It is made of four different fruits—quince, apricot, plum, and cherry."

Miralai did not offer me brandy, and after he swallowed a couple of glasses a warm glow came into his broody eyes and a flush on his pale cheeks. "Do you like my house?" he asked. "I don't suppose you've been in a Jewish house before." He reached into his caftan and pulled out a string of amber beads. The beads were the size of grapes, and he read them with his thumb and forefinger, feeling them as if they were gold coins.

Mrs. Miralai came in to say dinner was ready. She had changed her dark velvet dress and had put on a light green one with braiding at the bodice and embroidery on the hem and on the loose sleeves. As I looked at her now she did not appear as old as at first she seemed, and since I was eager to seize on any sign or detail that might allay my forebodings, I connected the woman's look of premature age with the possible loss of a child. On this I pinned a slender hope, which was strengthened when the woman came over to me and placed her hand on my shoulder. "So a merchant you are now," she said affectionately. "And to the city all by yourself you have come. But such a shy merchant you seem to be."

"Shy! You should see him bargain. He can outbargain two Jews, a Greek, and an Armenian put together."

"It is nice to start early and learn how to trade," said Mrs. Miralai.

A new fright, like an icy wave, crept through me when I saw the food on the table. They are already putting me on the fattening diet, I thought. It was supposed to last six weeks, according to the belief, and then they put you in a vat set out horizontally, with sharp pointed nails on the inside. They rolled the vat, and the points of the nails pierced your flesh and your rich blood spurted out and was drawn out and drunk at the mysteries. But if I refused to eat, my blood would become weak as whey and unfit for the *kurban*. I could begin now. I didn't have any appetite anyway.

84

Mrs. Miralai, with maternal concern, noticed that I merely nibbled at the baked lake trout, chewed a lot but swallowed little. "Our young guest has no appetite. Our kind of cooking maybe he doesn't like."

"I am not hungry. I ate a big lunch at the inn."

Miralai ate with gusto. After the fish course he put choice pieces of roast lamb on my plate, but I barely touched them. Mrs. Miralai became alarmed. "Maybe the boy's not feeling well." A ray of hope flashed in my mind. "I have always been sickly," I said, unsure whether Mrs. Miralai was concerned about my well-being or this was her way of intimating to her husband that I would be unsuitable for the sacrifice.

"Bah, sick. He's healthy as a young calf."

The word *calf* fell into my heart like a lump of ice. What knowledge I had of the Bible was the little studying we had done in school of the creation of the world, of Moses in the bulrushes and Pharaoh's daughter and the Evangel as read by the priest in church. But somewhere within this scant knowledge was the remembered detail of the sacrifice of the "fatted calf."

Later in the living room Mrs. Miralai brought Turkish coffee and three tiny glasses filled with an amber liquid. Raising his glass, my host fastened his eyes on me and said, "To your health, my young friend, and a long life to you." My mind seized on the last words and a flicker of hope trembled in me. Had my host divined my fears, and was this meant to reassure me?

The liquor was sweetish and tasted of pear.

"Our young guest must be tired," said Mrs. Miralai. "He had no appetite for supper. Maybe he'd like to go to bed."

"I'll show him to his room," said my host.

None of the houses in Kastoria had plumbing, and Miralai first led me through a narrow corridor dimly lit by a kerosene lamp to show me where the privy was. Then he lighted the way up a short flight of narrow stone steps to another corridor at the end of which was the bedroom. Here from the flame of his own candle he lit the wick of another candle stuck in a silver stick on a white marbletop table on which were also a copper ewer filled with water and a porcelain basin.

Miralai put his hand on my shoulder. "Feel at home here. Sleep well," he said and left the room.

There was a single window grilled with two vertical and two horizontal iron bars, and through one of the squares I looked down on a succession of moonlit tiled roofs descending in terraces to the very edge of the lake. I tried to catch sounds, but all was stillness. Not even the bark of a dog could be heard. There was something strange and remote about the scene, especially the body of water glistening in the moonlight. I was within less than a day's journey from home, and yet I felt as if I were in some remote land among strange people.

I lay on the bed and in the silence listened to the sighing of the candle on the marble table. Occasionally the candle would sputter and a tear of melted wax would drip down the stem. I never before knew how alive an inanimate thing could be. Burning and giving light and sighing, the candle was like another living being in the room. And I looked at it, at the quiver of its yellow petallike flame, and listened to it and dreamed that it was trying to say something to me with its sighs and gentle purrs. I then began to think of my mother and of how she would suffer over my having vanished from the living world. Until this moment I had forgotten about the little medallion of St. Christopher Grandfather had given me, and now I took it out and studied the figure. The youthful saint with staff in hand waded across a stream carrying a child on his shoulders. As I held the medallion in my hand I began to pray, but a silent, wordless prayer, for I never knew how to pray with words, except to promise a saint to light a candle before his icon or to put a coin there if he would help me find a lost animal or help me get rid of a cold. While I was thus praying with my heart I heard footsteps in the corridor. After what seemed minutes but could have been only seconds there was a gentle knock on my door, and before I could say a word the door opened and Miralai's tall figure stood in the doorway. He was wearing some kind of loose robe that reached to his ankles and a black skull cap, and with the candle casting its yellow light on his ascetic face with the tapered oily beard he looked the arch-priest of the scriptures ready for the ceremonial.

"Our bedroom is directly under and we can see the light of your window reflected on the roof below. We know you are awake, and Mrs. Miralai is much worried about you. You didn't eat your supper and now you cannot sleep. I know it is hard to sleep away from home in a strange house and a strange bed, but a merchant, you understand, a merchant's got to get used to sleeping in all kinds of places. A merchant is a man of the world, free of fears and superstitions. Besides, you are our guest, and it saddens us that you are not at ease in our home, that you are disturbed. I knew something was preying on your mind, some fear, and I was hoping it would vanish, but now it is keeping you awake and ourselves too." Miralai gave a long sigh, and his deep-set eyes became suffused with a warm glow and he seemed to struggle to find words to be saying what was on his mind.

"Mrs. Miralai is very unhappy and she suffers. And I myself am aggrieved, but I do not feel offended and am not angry with you,

86

because it is not your fault. Now please banish this fear from your mind. There is no truth in it. It is an old lie made up to justify the persecutions and pogroms of my people. Go to sleep now and sleep well. I'll wake you in the morning when it is time to go to the bazaar."

When Miralai wakened me in the morning the sun was streaming through the window, causing the grilled pattern to be duplicated on the floor.

At the same place where it had dropped us the night before the carriage was now waiting for us. Its top was down, and the pleasant morning sun shone warmly on us as we rode toward the market-place. We had had a good breakfast, and as we left the house Mrs. Miralai had embraced me and said how pleased she was I had been their guest and to come stay with them whenever I came to the city. A sense of shame mingled with guilt was upon me, and I stammered something about having been a sulky guest, and she said, "You were tired and alone away from home for the first time. It will be different next time."

In the year that followed before I, too, at age thirteen, joined the universal migration to the New World I was guest at the Miralais' several times. I always brought them walnuts and honey from the country and once a load of firewood, an item scarce and expensive in Kastoria. After Mrs. Miralai's sumptuous and delicious dinners, while she sat near us tending to her embroidering or crocheting, Miralai and I played backgammon, sipped liqueur, and talked, not about calicos, muslins and velvets, but about America, and not Gurkin's America of roundhouses, warehouses, and packing-houses.

Nine years later, after a summer on the Burlington railroad in Wyoming, I stopped in Chicago on my way to school at Valparaiso University, in Indiana. I walked into a clothing store on South Halstead Street to buy a new suit. The man who came to wait on me wore no caftan but a handsome gray worsted suit, and he was clean-shaven, no mustache, no reddish tapered beard. There was instant recognition despite the years and the change in appearance. Miralai embraced me like a son.

"Is Mrs. Miralai here?" I asked.

"She is upstairs. I will call her."

I had dinner with the Miralais and spent the night at their spacious apartment above the store.

8

It was now ten years since Gurkin had discovered America. By this time (1911) there was hardly a household in the village that did not have a son, a brother or a father in America. There were more menfolk in the New World than in the village. Youngsters my own age—I was now in my thirteenth year—joined fathers or older brothers in the new country. It was not an *emigration* in the true sense but a kind of *migratoriness,* motivated by the opportunity to *earn.* The earning period might be two or three years and then back to the village for a spell of affluence. Emigration as such did not start until after the end of World War I, when some of the *migrants* decided to become *immigrants* and began to send for their families, or, if bachelors, to return to the village to marry and hurry back to America.

My father had resented the fascination with America. It upset the old life. It was draining Macedonia of its manhood and weakened the struggle for freedom and autonomy. He was a factotum in the village for years, and it went against his grain for his son to be "carrying iron on his back and dig coal" in America. And so he figured that by giving me more and more responsibility in his varied trading activities he would break the spell. After school hours and during vacations I tended store and made trips to Kastoria to do the buying. As a further involvement in his business he promised to take me on his next trip to Prilep, the historic town three days' journey to the northeast. Prilep was the medieval capital of legendary King Marko, the Slav giant hero about whose incredible physical prowess the South Slav bards have created a wealth of epics. In our schoolbooks I had read some of the shorter ballads, and I wanted to see the ruins of King Marko's towering castles and the monasteries on the hillside above the town. I also knew a good deal about King Marko and his superhuman strength from Grand-father, who, like a blind bard, could narrate, and sometimes recite, some of the better-known epics.

For days before the journey my mother fussed with preparations. She packed two small bags with provisions and made me wear my new jacket and knee britches. I wore knee-high stockings with blue and green horizontal stripes and a green cap with a shiny visor. We traveled on foot, each carrying a bag slung over our shoulders. Once out of the village we took the road that led through the narrow valley toward the mountain passes beyond which lay the wider world I was to see. When we were a couple of hours on the road we reached high wooded places where there were no villages. Except for an occasional shepherd's hut there seemed to be little trace of man's activity.

Then we came to the top of the mountain, naked of trees, and saw beyond in the distance the biggest stretch of open level land I had ever seen. Though the broad plain was bounded by mountains the mountains were so far away they looked like clouds on the far horizon. My father said Prilep was at the northern edge of the plain. Our travel across this plain was full of discoveries and surprises and a couple of adventures that might have ended in tragedy had not the good Lord been watching over us.

After leaving the city of Florina behind we struck out across the plain. The road we took followed a river that did not dash and tumble like our Bistra but meandered placidly like a sluggish canal amidst droopy willows. Not only the river but everything else here was bigger. We came to a grist mill that was a wonder to behold. The water sluiced through wooden troughs into four iron-hooped tubes of great sizes. My father explained that it was a four-stone mill, the water from the tubes driving four separate millstones that ground flour simultaneously.

Here and there on the road we met strange folk in costumes the like of which I had never seen. At one place we met a caravan of mules and horses driven by Vlach muleteers in white frocks with black braid. Their animals were laden with goatskins of olive oil from Elbassan and Valona, with sacks of rice and pulverized red pepper from Kochani, with tobacco from Drama and Kavala, and with salt and sugar from unknown cities to the north. The brass bells at the throats of the pack animals chimed as the caravan panted under its heavy load. To a white mule that tarried by the roadside one of the Vlachs screeched excitedly in a language I did not understand. Many were the nationalities that inhabited Macedonia. Only later, in America, I learned of a mixed vegetable salad called

Macedoine, the variety of vegetables alluding to the diversity of peoples native to my own native land.

Though the river meandered across the plain, making loops and bends, the road seldom deviated from it, crossing it and recrossing it over arched stone bridges some of which, my father said, were built by the Romans. The river seemed anxious to touch on all the villages scattered about the plain. It would flow straight on for a distance, and then it would make an elbow and flow to some village hidden somewhere amidst groves of trees, above which would rise a whitewashed church cupola or a slender minaret with a stork's nest on its balcony. There were more storks here than in our mountain valley. They would wheel above us and light on a tree or in a marsh. They never screeched or squealed or whooped or made any other kind of bird sound, but they could make a rattle like carpenters by clattering their beaks. From the folk tales we children believed that the storks were human beings who spent their winters in warmer climates and turned to birds by immersing themselves in a certain spring. In the fall when they returned to their homeland after raising their young in our land they bathed in the same spring to turn human again.

It was a day's journey from Florina to Bitola, called Monastir by the Turks. Next to Salonika this was the largest city in Macedonia in those days, provincial capital and military center. The city seemed vast to me, with mosques and government buildings. Turkish army officers in dark-blue uniforms and scarlet fezzes, their sabers jingling on the cobblestones, strutted in all their pride and mastery of our country. (What I did not then consider was that it was their country, too, for many of them were born in Macedonia, and for all I knew I might have then seen Kemal Atatürk himself, the father of modern Turkey, who was born in Salonika and at this very time was an officer in Bitola.) On the terraces of coffeehouses sat *agas,* beys and effendis in voluminous *abas* of varicolored cloths, on their heads pumpkinlike turbans. Sedate, dignified, conscious of their mastery of the country, they conversed in low tones, with slow, weaving gestures, and puffed at long *chibouks* or gurgled narghiles as they sucked at the bulbous mouthpieces. I had never dreamed there were cities like Bitola. It made Kastoria and Florina seem like villages, and I was elated that it was a Macedonian city but sad that it was the seat of Ottoman dominion.

That night, at the inn, though I was tired from the journey, it was a long time before I could fall asleep. My whole being was stirred. I had seen so much that I was like an animal let loose in a rich pasture.

On our further journey to Prilep, instead of walking as in the past

90

two days, we hired horses, two excellent mounts, gentle but spirited, brown as walnuts. My father reassured their owner (a friend
of his) that we would take good care of the animals. As we rode
out of the city we came upon a Moslem cemetery, the first one I
ever saw. The graves were topped with turban-shaped marble head-
stones. On all four sides the cemetery was bordered by rows of tall
cypresses, slender, tapered, dark and mournful trees that I also saw
for the first time and forever after, whether seen in Florida or
California, reminded me of this cemetery seen in my boyhood.

The plain widened even more, although in the distance, in a kind
of misty haze, one could see the mountains on the other side of
which, my father said, was the Vardar, Macedonia's mother river
that came down from the Shar Mountain and, after flowing through
Skopje, Veles, and other small towns, emptied into the Aegean
below Salonika. We passed through villages, saw still more different costumes, oxen and horses bigger than I had ever seen, carts
with huge wheels and painted spokes, plows made of steel drawn
by horses.

I had enjoyed the journey on foot, but now, mounted, I felt my
being enlarging and a sense of elation come over me, a feeling that
I was a hero galloping to some distant region to save an imprisoned
maiden. I flicked the reins so that my steed would cock his head and
cavort, so that the fringe of beads and tassels would dance across
his forehead. And my feeling of bigness and elation must have
communicated itself to the animal, for he pranced and cantered
lightly. I took deep breaths, threw my shoulders back, and let my
body drift along with the horse's rhythmic patter. How I pitied my
playmates back in the village! Would they ever see what I was
seeing?

My father told me the names of the villages we passed and the
names of villages lying in the distance and visible from the road.
Many, many years have passed since then, and I have traveled the
world, but still I remember the names of those villages: Orizari,
Topoltchani, Srbtsi, Berantsi, Ushi.

The last place was not a village but an inn, perched on a knoll
that bulged athwart the plain like those ancient burial mounds one
sees in Thrace. The inn itself was a low building shaped like a
horseshoe with a well in the center of the yard. The walls were
mud-brick and the roof pantiled, the eaves overhanging to make a
kind of shaded veranda where travelers could refresh themselves
with food and drink and still enjoy the view of the broad plain and
the misty mountains that bounded it to the west.

We hitched our horses to posts near the well and hung their
nosebags but gave them no water. No one had to tell me that you

did not water sweaty, overheated horses. Even I myself would not drink cold water from a well or spring if I were tired and sweating.

The innkeeper was a Vlach, as most innkeepers in Macedonia were. He wore his national costume—white woolen frock, like Grandfather's, flaring at the bottom, black woolen sash, knee-length stockings, a tasselless white fez, and the hobnailed, brocaded, red-leather *opinitsi,* with yellow pompoms blooming from the spoutlike toes. He brought my father a measure of *rakia* and me a greenish bottle of *gazoza* that you opened by "popping" a glass ball that sealed the bottle in its neck.

There were two other guests at the inn—Albanians of the Gheghi tribe, recognizable by their tight ankle-length britches, loop-braided at the hips and knees, and by their short, sleeveless and buttonless Skanderbeg jackets with fringes of black yarn at the backs like floor mops. Their breasts were diagonally crossed with cartridges, and the filigreed horn handles of their scimitars protruded from their leather girdles in which they kept tobacco, steel and tinder, knives, and other needed things. Propped against the wall within reach were their silver-inlaid, long-barreled *Martinki.*

Dressed alike, the two Gheghi were not members of any uniformed body; they were dressed in their tribal costume. Their fellow nationals, the Toski, who dwelled in the south and close to us, affected the Grecian balletlike skirts, white tights, tasseled fezzes, and the gondola-shaped *tsaruhia.*

When my father and I had dismounted, the two Gheghi had observed us for an instant and had continued with their lunch. They ate in silence, and when they did converse it was in low tones. My father understood Albanian and could have caught what they were saying if he could have heard their words.

With our food the Vlach brought my father a small tankard of wine. The Gheghi had no wine, from which we concluded that they were Moslems. Some Gheghi, of the Mirditi tribe, are Roman Catholic. But Ghegh or Tosk, if an Albanian was a Mohammedan, he was feared by us Christians. Lean, dark men with hooked noses and mustaches twisted upward, our two Gheghi paid scant attention to us. My father, busy with his lunch and the jug of wine, did not seem disquieted, although I once caught an angled glance of his at the Gheghi, which reminded me of the way I looked at vicious dogs that didn't bark. I am not sure I can make this clear: Some times a thought would dart through my mind, a kind of prescience or presentiment, that something untoward would happen. If I thought no more of it, more often than not the thing *would* happen, but if, on the other hand, soon afterward I recollected that such a thought had crossed my mind, this rethinking, or back-take, would have the effect of canceling the premonition. The thought now flashed through my mind that the Gheghi would take our horses.

Just then the Gheghi knocked on the table for the innkeeper. They paid for what they had eaten, picked up their *Martinki,* slung their beaded *vurgits* (skinbags) over their shoulders, and in the gait characteristic of others of their nation strutted toward the posts where our horses were hitched. I say strutted, but this word doesn't adequately describe the walk of an Albanian of those days. Like his speech, an Albanian's walk was "declamatory," an expression of national pride and individual braggadocio. In such roosterlike or peacocklike strut the Gheghi now propelled themselves in the direction of our horses.

Without unhitching the horses the Gheghi took down our bags and hung their own onto the saddles. They did this slowly, casually, without speaking to each other or casting a look in our direction.

My father stood up. Calmly, in their own tongue, he called out to the Gheghi to leave our horses alone. They paid no heed to him but went on about the business of taking down the nosebags and getting ready to mount.

Then my heart sank. My father strode over and without a word took down the Gheghi's skinbags. An icy fear clutched at my heart, and I looked invokingly at the innkeeper, who stood on the terrace watching, his hands at his breast like a person at prayer. I read compassion in his face but realized how helpless he was. I could see that he was astonished at my father's brashness. How could an unarmed Christian, in this lonely way station on the highroad, dare to defy two armed Gheghi? The bravest and cruelest people from Durazzo to Istanbul, the Gheghi were descendants of Christians who soon after the Ottoman conquest had embraced Islam and had grown powerful at the expense of their brethren who had clung to the faith. We regarded the Gheghi as Turks, making no distinction between religion and nationality, all Moslems being Turks to us. But Turks, real Turks, had feelings. Touched by entreaty or by the sight of suffering, they sometimes gave way to human compassion. A defenseless Christian village would sooner be visited by the black plague than by a band of Gheghi. They were like flint and tinder, haughty and arrogant when at peace, merciless when on the warpath.

A new fear seized me. My father and I carried on our person the money for the oxen we were to buy—ten gold pieces (napoleons) wrapped in a piece of wax cloth I carried in my bosom next my skin, like a good-luck charm. And ten *liras* (Turkish pounds) were in a pocket in the lining of my father's vest. The Gheghi might search us and take our money. A worse fear was that the Gheghi might kill my father. They could shoot him or stab him with impunity. I upbraided myself for these thoughts and quickly tried to "unthink" them.

God be praised! The two Gheghi were amused rather than infuriated by my father's rashness. They watched him as a two-headed monster might watch a child tinker with something it cannot harm. When my father, having taken down their bags, put ours back on again, the Gheghi burst out in laughter. Even their laughter was different from ours. It was rhythmic, pompous, declamatory, like their speech and their walk. Their laughter was saying, "Hey, hey, what a foolish man!" Or perhaps "Hey, hey, what a brave man!"

It may have been the latter. Perhaps in admiration of my father's courage, a quality held in high esteem by Albanians, the Gheghi did not shoot or stab my father and did not rob us. Without bothering to take down our bags again and with theirs slung over their shoulders, they flung themselves onto the saddles and galloped away across the plain toward the foothills to the west.

Relieved now that no harm had come to my father and that we were not robbed, I still felt wretched about the horses. Whatever profit we might make on the oxen we would be buying would not suffice to pay for the horses. Reporting the incident to the authorities in Prilep would be a mere formality. Where was King Marko now to redress this wrong! Our only hope was the offices of IMRO —the national revolutionary organization.

How quickly one's mood changes! Was it only a short while ago that I was galloping to the rescue of maidens in distress? How naïve, how preposterous that seemed now! The sunny plain and my own heart darkened as I looked at my father's face. I wanted to say something to him, but I did not know what or how. If only we would turn around and go back to our village! I had no wish now to journey to Prilep or to any other place but home. But my father's footsteps turned toward Prilep.

Again the road stretched like a width of white carpet on the plain. It narrowed in the distance and merged with the horizon. We came to a creek, and here we cut cudgels from a thicket of willows on the bank. Willow wood doesn't make the best kind of walking stick, not like dogwood or hawthorn, but having a stick in your hand on a high road after a misfortune helps the spirit. By and by something heartening crept into me and a firmness came into my step; some of the grayness lifted from the plain and from my own horizon. We crossed the Tsrna River near a village nestling in some low foothills to the west, but to the east the plain spread out as far as the eye could see and through it meandered the Tsrna until somewhere in the blue haze it crossed the Mariovo Mountains to empty into the matriarch of Macedonian rivers—the mighty Vardar.

We traveled on, sometimes walking abreast and sometimes one ahead of the other. At times, as we trudged on, this larger and more expansive world filling my mind, I would forget about the horses, but the moment I looked at my father's face I would remember. Ahead of us now, in the distance, in the shimmering sunlight, the plain seemed to bulge athwart the road like a camel's hump. It seemed to me as if we were reaching the confines of the plain and that we would be entering not mountains but a region of hills and hollows. But when we did reach the hump and crossed it more of the plain stretched before us, not as broad and extensive but still quite large and surrounded by mountains except on the side where we entered. And now we struck across this smaller Prilep plain with the city itself several hours away and Mount Babuna looming behind it. When the last rays of the sun cast a fiery glow on the mountain and twilight shadows descended, my father, sensing my uneasiness at the murk and the approaching night, said we would not be able to reach Prilep and would spend the night in Allentzi, a nearby village where, he said, he had a friend. He asked me if I was hungry.

Allentzi lay in the bosom of a mound with two open arms reaching halfway down toward the high road and embracing an amphitheater of meadows pockmarked with haycocks. A path issued from the village and ran like a ribbon down the middle of the embrasure, joining the road at a point where, from a slab of masonry, a bronze beak spouted water into a mossy stone trough. In a meadow near the spring a lone peasant was swinging a scythe against a swath of tall grass. A mare and her young grazed nearby. Silently we walked toward this lone mower and stood aside so as not to be in the way of the swinging blade. When the man stopped to whet the blade my father said good evening. The man turned, regarded us for a moment, and pulled the whetstone from his girdle, where it was stuck like a dagger. The tempered steel whined as the tongue-shaped stone licked its edge. The man had started sharpening the scythe at the heel, and as the stone kept lapping toward the tapering end there came a moan as of pain from the steel. Finally the man stuck the whetstone back into his girdle and again bent his body to the strip of unmowed grass.

There was something patriarchal about the old mower. He must have been in his seventies, of medium height but stout, with long gray sickle-shaped mustaches, a ruddy and rather full face for a hard-working peasant. He seemed disinclined to talk, and though we stayed with him, keeping out of the compass of the scythe, he never turned his eyes from the curved line the scythe followed as it ate away the flowery grass. My father asked one or two questions, and the man replied without interrupting his work. But when my

95

father asked about his friend Strahil, the man stopped and looked at us for the first time. He held the scythe with the blade up like a standard.

"He's not here. He moved to another village."

"We had hoped to spend the night with him."

"Well, as I say, he's not here. They all moved away."

"We had counted on spending the night at Strahil's," my father repeated, hinting for the man to offer the hospitality of his own home. The man said nothing. He brandished the sharpened instrument against the uncut stand of grass. Serpentlike, the scythe coiled before my eyes. Man and scythe worked in unison. The man's arms turned, his body half rotated, the whining blade flashed like lightning, and the grass toppled at his feet with a sigh. The man's breath whistled through his nostrils and blended with the wrathful hissing of the scythe, which kept gobbling bundles of grass and belching them out in heaps.

My eyes wandered over the plain. A gauzelike violet mist veiled the peaks of Babuna above Prilep, and dusk was prowling over the earth. Then my eyes went to the little village stuck like a brooch in the bosom of the sphinxlike hill.

It might have been the murkiness of the plain, it might have been the churlishness of the man with the scythe, or thoughts of our own warm fireside, or of the Gheghi and the horses, or all of these together, but I burst into tears, sobbing and shaking. I was ashamed and I tried to choke the sobs, but the more I tried the more uncontrollably they burst out from my mouth and nostrils. The mare lifted her muzzle from the grass and looked at me with her big compassionate eyes. Her young held his head high and gave a shrill neigh.

My father spoke to me very gently. "Stop crying," he pleaded. "Why must you cry? Is that the kind of trader you're going to be? And you're not alone. You are not in a strange land. You are in your own country, with your father beside you. Are you not ashamed? Come now, stop crying. Let's go to the spring to wash your face."

At the spring I cupped my hands and dipped them in the stone trough and splashed my face and eyes with the cool water. It is good for eyes that burn from weeping to be bathed with cool water from a spring.

As soon as I was able to speak again without sobbing I wanted to ask where we were going to sleep, but I recalled my father's words and held back my question. The old man finished the strip and locked his scythe by folding the blade against the snath and securing it with an iron ring. He was now tying bundles of the

96

freshly mowed hay to the sides of the mare's pack saddle. He did not say a word to us, nor did we to him, and though it was embarrassing we stood by, watching him tie the bundles of grass as though that would relieve the tension. The colt pranced and nudged its mother's flank.

Now the man, with surprising agility for his age, flung himself onto the saddle, his legs straddling the bundles of hay. With the locked scythe held across his lap like a rifle, he clucked to the mare and the animal nickered and shambled on. The colt jumped a few times, rent the air with its strident neigh, and scampered after its mother.

My father and I followed. The man was riding slowly, perhaps because of the colt, and we could keep close to him without effort. We did not speak. To my relief, the mare would snort and rattle her lips. The colt would suddenly stop as if it had bethought itself of something and then whinny and lope ahead to catch up with its mother.

For a moment I felt heartened by thought of the earth, the ground on which we walked. This same earth extended in a solid mass to our village, and the smell of the fresh-mown hay soothed my fears. The moon, too, now that night was falling, suddenly hung in the sky, full and beautiful, familiar and reassuring. But I couldn't completely quiet my mind and kept wondering where we were going to sleep. I knew we were going to this village, but supposing no door opened to us and, if one did open, it immediately shut in our faces. What if all the inhabitants of this village turned out to be surly like this unfriendly mower? What if they loose their dogs on us?

On either side the path was bowered with bushes, and in the phosphorescence of the moonlight they looked as if they were silvered or rimmed with hoarfrost. We followed the rider like ghosts in the moonlight, neither speaking nor being spoken to.

The path now tunneled between hedgerows, skirted some wattle-fenced gardens and presently emerged before a cluster of low, thatched-roofed, mud-brick houses. We crossed a rill that sang softly in the moonlight, climbed a slight elevation, and entered the village. Here the man dismounted and led his mare through an alley into a broad courtyard, in the center of which rose a lone threshing post.

My father and I stood a few feet from the man, and in the moonlight I quietly took in the surroundings. At the far side of the yard was the house. It looked like a barracks, with a single door in the middle and small windows on either side. Elsewhere the yard was enclosed by sheds, granaries, corn cribs, stables, some built of mud-brick, some of unplastered wattles. In the open sheds horses and donkeys were munching fresh grass and oxen with bulging flanks ruminated and groaned with satisfaction. The heavy breathing and grunting of the animals, the pleasurable sounds they made tended to ameliorate somewhat the man's coldness and inhospitableness. A kind of human warmth and sympathy breathed out from the animals and reached out to us. Also two friendly dogs rushed over and sniffed at us without barking, two shaggy, woolly beasts, nudging us with their moist chins and wagging their tails. We stood still, neither speaking to the dogs nor reaching down to pet them.

Some children ran out of the door, shouting, happy their grandfather had returned from the meadow. They clung to him as he tied the mare to the threshing post and gave her one of the bundles of grass, and then still with the children about him he hobbled toward the house door, whose wings stood open like sentinels.

The old man entered the house of which he was master; my father and I, uninvited strangers, also entered it. I was not now frightened, but something inside me winced and then hardened. I did not know what it was, but it was something real, something alive, and it curled itself into a ball in my stomach, the way a hedgehog does when you touch it with a stick.

Before us, as we advanced, a fire burned in a huge fireplace facing the door. The fireplace did not recede into the wall but extended like a canopy out into the room proper, an arrangement that made it possible for more people to sit around the fireside and also gave more room and access for the cooking and baking that was done there.

The room itself was immense, with straw mats and coarse hempen blankets only partly covering the floor, which was the earth itself, or rather clay mixed with chaff packed down and beaten to tile-hardness and polished from repeated sweepings. The walls were lined with cupboards, pantries, flour chests, kneading troughs, vats, wooden, copper, and earthen utensils and other receptacles of various shapes and sizes.

The room had no ceiling. Hand-hewn beams, rafters, purlined plates were all exposed, or partly exposed, for from the ceiling joists hung skins of animals, festoons of last year's unshelled corn, garlands of dry onions and dry red peppers, slabs of jerky, loops of sausages, bracelets of garlic. Laid across the joists were crooked beech branches sometime to be fashioned into plows, dogwood saplings already bent for oxbows, and other pieces of wood eventually to be shaped into ax helves, snaths, spokes, felloes, vat staves, wagon tongues and ricks, and a dozen other things vital to a peasant household.

But this was no ordinary household, rather one of those South Slav *zadrugas,* or family cooperatives, where for generations nothing was divided and brothers and cousins and nephews lived and worked together as a single family unit. This household was planted solidly in the earth, and there were more than a score of adult people in the house; and one knew that all of them, from birth, had been wedded to the soil, to field and meadow, as everyone before them had been and as all those who would come after them would be unless some future whim of nature or of man would change the pattern of this life. Womenfolk busied themselves about the spacious interior, attending to various chores, with children (there were enough to fill a one-room schoolhouse) clinging to their aprons or hovering about them.

When my father and I crossed the threshold of this human hive we said good evening, to no one in particular, and no one acknowledged the good will we brought in. The fireplace is the center and heart of a peasant house, and you are not in the house proper until you have seated yourself at the fireside. And my father headed for the hearthside, knowing intuitively that it would be more embarrassing for us to remain in the periphery of the room, like dogs or hired hands, than presumptuously to establish our status as guests by taking our places by the fire. And the friendly fire proffered to us its warm hospitality, the logs crackled and blazed into flames, the embers glowed with bright welcome. There was no hearth or hearthstone as such; the earthen floor itself was the hearth. A broad-bellied crock or pot, big as one of Ali Baba's jars, purred in the live ashes at the edge of the fire. Drops of steaming liquid escaping from around the lid sizzled down the bulging sides and spurted on the smoldering embers, causing tiny explosions that threw puffs of ashes around the bottom of the pot.

Sitting cross-legged on the floor, my father took out his *tobakera,* tore a leaf of cigarette paper, and deftly rolled himself a cigarette. Then came the moment I was expecting. Never did a man make himself a cigarette without afterward offering his *tobakera* to any other man who might be present. Nor was the tobacco box handed over casually. It was done ceremonially, with a deferential inclination of the torso, as if not mere tobacco but respect and friendship were being proffered. The recipient, in accepting the honor, would, in addition to bowing slightly, touch his chest with the left hand, a symbolic gesture of thankfulness. This charming custom was Turkish but was adopted by the Christians, as were many of the conqueror's other amenities.

What caused me concern now was not that my father would not offer his *tobakera* to our host—I knew he would—but whether the host would accept it. He might spurn the offer, which would mean that he was still not reconciled to our enforced guesthood, still considering us impudent intruders, like stray dogs or cats that attach themselves to you and follow you home.

When my father had rolled his cigarette he clicked shut the tobacco box and then with just the proper deferential gesture placed it in our host's lap. A hand was being extended, and it might be touched in reconcilement or spurned as a brazen gesture. For a tense moment, during which I felt as if the timbers beneath the roof with all that was on them would come crashing down on us, the *tobakera* remained in our host's lap. Then I let out a deep sigh when he reached for it, opened it, and started to roll himself a cigarette.

Some women now began to set up low long tables for supper, placing on them broken loaves of corn-and-rye bread and wooden spoons and pushing children aside who were taking their places before the elders had done so. Presently the whole populous family had seated itself at the long supper tables. There wasn't a chair in the room. Everybody sat on the floor.

My father and I, unspoken to by anyone since we walked into the house, and now uninvited to share supper, kept to our places by the fireside like two punished children. Hard as this was for me, I was glad that my father did not carry our obtrusiveness to the extremity of sitting down to share another's food unasked. It was one thing to walk into one's house uninvited when you have no place to sleep but quite another to sit at his supper table unbidden. I would rather have gone hungry for days than to have done that.

Yet I was troubled by the deliberate coldness of our reluctant host. To sit down at meal and not to ask others present, be they friends or strangers, to share with you what God gave was a sin among my people. The old man's rejection of us now became a threatening hostility, something tangible and menacing.

I stole glances at the tables. Youngsters and adults were lined up there like celebrants at a free board at a monastery on a saint's feast day. The meal was simple, bread and buttermilk. One broke a morsel from a chunk of bread and mixed it in the mouth with a spoonful of buttermilk dipped from the nearest bowl. Dozens of spoons shuttled between bowls and mouths. The mothers not objecting, some of the children dunked their chunks of bread in the common bowls and, after gnawing and gumming at them, like puppies at bones, brought them back to the bowls for further dunking. A child plunged his bare hand in the bowl and then screamed when his mother struck his wrist with her spoon.

One of the women had large, dark, sunken eyes that bespoke much sorrow. She was the last to sit at table, but first she went to a cupboard and took out an earthen bowl. This she filled with buttermilk from a firkin and placed the bowl before us, propping two wooden spoons against its brim. She then brought us two large chunks of the coarse dark bread and put them on a piece of cheese-cloth that she spread on the floor. Was she told to do this, or would she incur the displeasure of the patriarch? I wondered.

Almost immediately after the table was put away and the crumbs swept, the members of this multitudinous family, without bothering to take off their socks or outer garments, lay down on bedding spread in the very places where they had eaten supper. The old man slept in the patriarchal chimney corner where he had sat before supper. My father and I, after gazing for a while at the dying fire, also laid our heads on a rough straw-stuffed pillow and covered ourselves with a blanket, pillow and blanket brought to us by the same kindly woman who had given us our supper.

The next morning, rubbing my eyes, I woke up to the fact that I was not at home. The experience of the evening before sprang to my mind. For a moment I thought it had been a dream, and then I looked at our host sitting in the same place he had occupied during the evening and in which he had slept. A new fire was glowing in the fireplace, and the old man was preparing his morning Turkish coffee. Elsewhere in the room men and women were fastening up rawhide sandals, taking turns at pouring water from ewers to wash their faces and were soon off to yoke oxen, cinch pack saddles to horses and donkeys, hitch wagons. No breakfast was eaten. Food was packed in bags and baskets and carried with them. The children already had been handed their breakfast—chunks of cornbread and cheese to nibble at as they ran out into the yard, some to play, others to go along to lend a hand in the field work.

The same woman who had given us supper now came over with a pan and ewer and a towel on her arm and poured water for us to wash our hands and faces. We thanked her ceremoniously when we had dried our faces on the coarse, napless but clean towel.

I knew my father's passion for Turkish coffee and was pleased to see two *finjans* by the fire. When the coffee was ready—and it had been brewed with scarcely less care than my father would have bestowed on it—the old man filled both cups. He offered the first cup to my father, but he did not say *poveli,* precious Slavic word of hospitality. My father accepted the offer Turkish fashion by placing the flat of his hand against his chest and bowing slightly. Both men started to sip, barely touching the cups with their lips as they blew on the syrupy liquid.

Now we rose to go, and my father reached out to shake our host's hand, which was grudgingly given, and to thank him for his "hospitality." I had been taught from childhood by my mother to kiss rather than to shake the hands of old people, and so, bending over, I kissed the hand of the man in whose house we had slept but whose name we did not know. On a sudden impulse I took out from my pocket my little notebook with the thin pencil fastened to its spine and asked the man his name, ready to write it down.

"Ah, now," he grumbled, "what would you be wanting my name for? No, I won't have my name written down."

"We were your guests, Grandfather, and we don't even know your name. Some day we may repay you for your goodness." I meant no irony in saying this. I felt guilty that we had so brazenly inflicted our guesthood on the man and was in fact grateful for his patience with us.

"We slept under your roof, and we ate your bread. I'd like to remember your name for your kindness."

"Well, it's Milan Belavoda."

I wrote in my notebook: *Milan Belavoda, village of Allentzi, district of Prilep.*

At the door, as we were leaving, the same woman who had been so thoughtful before and who apparently was assigned to household chores instead of field work handed me a few small buns, which she called *bumbulinia,* a word that intrigued me. I put these in my pocket and later tried to eat one on the road but found it unappetizing. I placed them on a rock wall by the roadside, thinking that birds or other creatures might find them more palatable.

What a difference daylight makes in one's mood! Why is it that night, darkness, in a strange place fills one with fears and apprehensions? The sun now came up from behind the peaks of Babuna and gilded the whole plain. The dew on the grass and wheat glistened like quicksilver. Here and there in the fields and meadows peasants were already at work. Storks sailed in the air or stalked in the meadows looking for frogs and snakes. Little brooks trickled amidst the grass and bushes, chanting a hushed, joyous song in the all too brief ritual of nature when spring imperceptibly ripens into summer.

My father and I walked amidst this festival, oblivious of the extraordinary incidents of our journey. Except that we were on foot, that same feeling of exuberance and high adventure that I experienced before the incident with the Gheghi was upon me. When I thought of my childish fears and the way I had wept I could feel myself reddening with shame.

When we reached the outskirts of Prilep and the high road became an avenue lined on either side with rows of Lombardy poplars, the ruins of King Marko's castles loomed to the left on the

102

hillside. Soon we entered the town, my father leading the way to an old inn in the center of town near the ancient clock tower, a landmark that I was not to see again until forty years later when my wife and I were guests of the new Yugoslav Macedonian republic. The innkeeper, a stout man with a ruddy complexion, shook my father's hand cordially and acknowledged my presence with a remark about the son's following in the father's footsteps.

"What will it be," he then asked my father, "brandy or coffee or both?"

"Both," said my father.

With the coffee and brandy the innkeeper brought hot milk and a cheese turnover for me.

"But how is it you are so early? You couldn't have started from Bitola this morning."

"Oh, no! We left Bitola yesterday morning and planned to be here last night, but at Ushi two Gheghi ran away with our horses. We then traveled on foot and spent the night at Allentzi. I did not know Strahil no longer lives there. I had hoped we would spend the night at his house."

"In whose house did you spend the night?"

"It wasn't a house; it was a dozen houses under one roof. We met an old man down by the road, near the spring. He was mowing. And we followed him home, uninvited. We had to sleep somewhere. He told us Strahil no longer lived in Allentzi."

A serious and meditative look came over the innkeeper's cheerful countenance.

"What was the old man's name?"

"It was Milan Belavoda," I replied. "I've got it written here in my notebook."

The innkeeper moved his head chidingly from side to side, as does a father who's just been told of some perilous exploit on the part of his children. He motioned my father to follow him into another room, where they remained for some time while I drank my milk and ate the turnover.

My father told me nothing of what he and the innkeeper had talked about, and I knew better than to ask, since Macedonia was one vast network of revolutionary cells and secrets and one just didn't ask questions. But in my young mind the suspicion germinated that my father's frequent trips to these parts were not entirely mercantile. Not until much later, when I was getting ready for the longest journey of my life, a pilgrimage that would last my whole lifetime, I learned of the second peril of that trip to Prilep. I was going through my school notes and papers and I came across the little notebook in which I had written, *Milan Belavoda, village of*

Allentzi, district of Prilep. Notebook in hand, I went to my father. "Do you remember the name of that old man in Allentzi where we spent the night?"

"My son," he said, "I never told you how close we were to losing our lives that night. My friend Strahil had not moved away as the old man had said. He was killed, and Belavoda had caused his death. Belavoda was a traitor, an informer. Strahil had become chief of a *komitadji* band. One night he slipped in his house to see his family. A henchman of Belavoda's saw him. The old man himself rode to Prilep in the night and returned with a troop of *souvari.* The *souvari* surrounded the house and began firing. To save his family from certain death Strahil opened the door and was cut down by bullets."

We were both silent for a moment. "You knew Belavoda had caused Strahil's death when we slept in his house?"

"How could I? The innkeeper in Prilep told me. But I did suspect something, some ill feeling or enmity when I mentioned Strahil's name. That's why I didn't ask any more questions about my friend or bring up his name again."

"Then why did we go to his house?"

"We had to . . . because . . . well, it was night and we had to sleep somewhere."

"Was it because of me, because I cried?"

Instead of answering my question he said, "Not long after we slept in the traitor's house he was found dead, stabbed, by the road where we came on him."

I didn't ask who had killed him or how my father had learned of it. In those conspiratorial days in Macedonia even a young fellow had to be discreet about asking too many questions.

104

9

The spell of the New World was too strong to be broken by mercantile trips to Kastoria and Prilep. My father continued to sneer contemptuously at the *Amerikantzi,* strutting about the village in their fineries, fingering gold watch chains and flashing gold teeth.

"You've let these jackasses turn your head with their American trappings. What do you know about America? And what do you think they do there? They dig coal and carry iron on their backs, that's what, and they then come here to parade like *lordas* for a few months."

And then my mother died. On a raw, damp day in March, while washing clothes at the riverbank, she caught a cold that in her winter-worn body turned into pneumonia, followed by a stroke that paralyzed one side of her body, and in three weeks she was gone. I was then in my thirteenth year, and her death came over me like an eclipse. It was as if nature herself had died. Her passing caused a great void in my heart, and for the first time in my life I experienced the tragedy and finality of death. The thought that I would never again see her face, hear the sound of her voice, or feel the palm of her hand on my forehead caused a sinking in my stomach. For many days after her death the days turned into nights for me, and months later, while crossing the ocean, I would cry in my berth in the middle of the night.

Like all women in the village, and most men, my mother was illiterate, but she had an innate, intuitive intelligence. And she was the *ekonom,* the real husbandman of our household, not my father, except for the vineyards, which he tended and cultivated with loving care. Our fields and meadows would have grown to brush or been hired out to others to till and hay were it not for my mother. She sowed and seeded and planted and hoed and reaped and baked the bread and cooked. She godmothered the animals at mating and midwifed them at foaling, calving, and lambing. As soon as I was able, when not "seeing" for Grandfather, I assisted her in some of these chores.

She was not handsome, but no mother is unhandsome to her offspring. She was of medium height, with a strong, square body and a face that would have been attractive had it been planted on a man's body. I inherited from her my love of nature, a passion for the land and all the things that grow on it.

People called my mother Mitra, the diminutive for Demetra, which was her given name. None of us knew anything about mythology, so we were ignorant that she bore the name of the goddess of grain, harvest, and general bountifulness. And she was a worthy daughter of that earth goddess, happiest when she promoted life, when she planted a seed today to reap an ear two or three months hence. Her green fingers had converted the grounds back of the house into an enchanting place. Wherever a thing grew, it grew there because she had chosen the spot for it and her hands cared for it. All the growing things, it seemed to me, vied for her affection. She could bring back to vigorous life a fading plant by merely touching it. And like a good mother who notices the flush or pallor on her child's cheek and instinctively presses a sensitive palm to the forehead, she would bend over a plant to pick off a bug, pinch a blighted leaf, or gather some dirt around a stem that wasn't getting enough nourishment. She loved each growing thing as though it had sprung from her own womb.

Through my many lives the memories of my mother, instead of dimming, have grown brighter. Most of these memories are bound up with nature, with planting, seeding and sowing, cultivating, harvesting, threshing, and with the matings and birthings of animals —in short, with the cycle of life itself. I recall most vividly a scene at which my mother was playing midwife to a yearling goat laboring to give birth to her first kid. Lying on her side on a thin bed of straw in the open sheepfold behind our haybarn, the creature panted and foamed at the mouth. Now and then a moan of pain issued from the stirrings of its trembling body. Though it was still winter, the day was warm with a pale, springlike sun. As the flock fed, the intermittent tinkling of the bells at the goats' throats added a note of cheerfulness to the sunlit air. But this did nothing to ease the pain of the poor mother in labor. The ewes kept jostling one another, some of the more greedy ones hustling from one hay bundle to another, poking and nudging their snouts to the discomfiture of their more timid and less avaricious sisters. Occasionally a goat, trying to usurp feed by bucking a ewe, drew a reproving shout from my mother. A dozen lambs, none older than two weeks, their pelts napped with soft curly wool, wiggled amidst the fleecy sheep. Occasionally a mother, intent on feeding, would turn abruptly and give her little one an admonitory jolt with her busy snout; others would shimmy their rumps and stomp their hoofs to make it hard for the persistent youngsters to keep hold of the slippery nipples. One of the lambs was wearing two sets of pelts, its own and, over it, that of another who had died. We had skinned the dead one and wrapped its pelt around this lamb—a twin—and got it to suckle the lambless ewe, but the ewe wouldn't be fooled, scent or no scent. She would buck vigorously, and the little one would reel on its spindly legs and topple to the ground with a shrill blare. My mother would leave the laboring goat and gather the rejected lamb in her arms, addressing reprimands to the ugly and uncharitable ewe and shower sugary appellations on the snow-white creature in her arms. She would cuddle it and bring its moist chin to her face and kiss the tattoolike black spot in the center of its forehead. At last she would set the creature on the ground with a kindly, measured stroke on its behind. The lamb, finding it hard to steady itself, its thin legs trembling, its white curly trunk shivering, would fill the sunny air with a shrill plaint. And Mother would return to the yearling goat that lay on her side, her legs drawn in and her throat arched out.

"I wish I could do something to help you, you poor dear," my mother said. Something stirred inside the goat, and this something pressed the forelegs closer to the chest and drew in the hind legs, folding them against the distended stomach. The eyes dilated to mirror the pain of the struggling body.

A lull came after the spasm, except for the stomach, which worked like a bellows. Presently the animal was seized by another convulsion during which breathing seemed to cease completely. The head tossed and the chin burrowed in the straw bedding. Instead of the piteous look in them, the eyes were now expressionless, like glazed marbles. During the paroxysms all the breath of the body seemed forced to the lump at the groins.

My mother's palm rubbed gently at the goat's twitching flank. The other goats, munching hay, looked with compassion on their laboring sister. Those that had already been freed of their like burden gave an occasional comforting bleat; the others watched sad-eyed. The little ones wagged their tails and wiggled their behinds as they pumped at the udders. Every so often a ewe would bring its nose to the suckling, sniffing to make sure it was her own and not another's.

The laboring goat seemed like a dying animal. At moments her wide-open eyes lost their opaqueness and became suffused with a light that reflected the pain of the body. They looked imploringly at my mother, as if she were the goddess of whatever phenomenon was taking place and it was in her power to lessen the suffering.

"Come now, be a brave little mother. It's always hard the first time." Despite the animal's suffering and her eagerness to ease the pain, there was exultation on my mother's face.

A restless force rolled through the goat, causing swellings like hoops across the stomach. My mother gently massaged the flank, feeling the life that was being desperately propelled into the world.

"It's nearly over, little sister. It's coming now."

Two small pink hoofs clasped about a tiny chin coated with slimy membrane now showed. The goat's whole body strained to the point of bursting; the legs trembled; the thigh muscles twitched; the breathing seemed to reverse itself.

It took several propulsive coils to release the head and the fore-hoofs. Then my mother's deft hands took over, and the note of relief was sounded in the goat's moans.

My mother's fingertips tenderly rubbed the kid's chin, and the tiny jaws opened to utter a faint but clear cry of joy, a greeting to the world of light. Then ascertaining its sex, my mother placed the kid before the goat. "Here, it's a buck, the brat."

Exhausted from the labor, the goat lay on its side, its head resting on the straw. Yet the moment her firstborn was placed before her, her chin reached out and nudged it. Then the goat mustered strength to pull herself up on her haunches. Her tongue began to lick the slimy membrane on the kid's head, then on the shoulders, then the back, and as the sun fell warmly on the cleaned spots curls of fawn-colored wool glistened in the sunlight like gold braid.

Presently the newborn began to wiggle and squirm as though some spring inside it had been released. Its legs stretched, its tiny hoofs scraped the straw, and the next moment it was on its feet, swaying and tottering, the whole of it trembling and jiggling like a mechanical toy. It seemed as if it were all made of detachable parts and the parts would fly apart, but the spring inside kept them together. Louder and more joyous became the kid's bleating.

Once, when I was about eight or nine and beginning to have some notion about the birds and the bees, my mother had me go along with her while she took a heifer to a bull in the pasture. She led the sleek maidenish creature by a length of rope. I paced behind with a withe ready to apply it to the young thing's rump if she balked. But the heifer trotted on gaily and primly, shaking her virgin body and smartly flicking her tail.

When we reached the pasture some oxen that grazed there lifted their heads and gazed longingly at the young offering. Oxen are eunuchs, but eunuch or not, who can read what's in an ox's head when he looks at a heifer? We once had altered a cat, but every now and then he would disappear for days to return all scratches and weary.

To my mother the servicing of a cow was no different from planting a pepper plant or an onion seed in the ground. And I grew up instinctively to look on animals copulating as something as natural as cornstalks earing, silking, and tasseling. It was the way of nature and of life. If a cow wasn't *held* (and *holding* a cow was the expression used for *breeding* a cow) there would be no milk and no calf to butcher or to grow into an ox.

The bull stopped cropping grass and took a serious and interested look at the young cow. He lowered his head and flicked his tail and then advanced a few steps toward the victim, stopping suddenly as if uncertain. My mother maneuvered the heifer to what she regarded as an accommodating position and stroked the creature's back and spoke comforting words to it as though it were a frightened young bride being reassured on the eve of defloration. She asked me to go in back of the bull and steer him toward the cow. From a distance I waved the withe, but the bull needed no coaxing. As he advanced, his hoofs slowly and ponderously treaded the grass. The muscular buttocks twitched and his dewlap flapped like a sail. As he sniffed the ground gusts of breath issued from his nostrils. One of the grazing oxen lifted his head from the grass, lowed nostalgically, and again turned to his prosaic grass-cropping.

Suddenly the bull grew bolder and took a few more steps. Sensing his nearness, the cow mooed plaintively and tugged at the rope. The bull lowered his massive head and rubbed his chin on the grass, his hoofs scraping. And then the huge body reared itself on the powerful hind legs and landed its forehoofs on the cow's back, causing the poor creature to bend and stagger. My mother dug her heels in the ground and bolstered herself against the cow's chest. "There, there now, steady dear." She acted like a big sister to the heifer, initiating her to the mystery of procreation. The bull's huge body was like a bellows that some invisible force kept at work, while the heifer quivered under the crushing weight, her legs trembling and her back arching inward. Still she did not collapse, helped by Mother but helped more by some inner force not unlike that which kept the bull from crushing her under its own weight.

I was not a bit embarrassed, but I felt kind of sorry for both beasts that they should go through all that to produce a calf that might end up on the butcher's block.

After my mother's burial, my father waited six weeks and then mounted the mule and rode down the valley, going from village to village, looking for another wife. He returned with a much younger wife, a widow plump and smooth and bright as an apple. But she brought with her two little boys and a girl.

It was now a new family and a new household, and my father had second thoughts about my going to America.

PART
TWO

To lose the earth you know,
for greater knowing;

To lose the life you have,
for greater life;

To leave the friends you loved,
for greater loving;

To find a land more kind than home,
more large than earth.

—THOMAS WOLFE

1

The villagers called us *strangers*—their own people, brothers, sons, fathers—strangers! That was because we were going to a strange land. I was the youngest ever to leave the village for America. We started out on a Friday because that was considered a lucky day. No one ever set off for America on a Saturday or a Tuesday. Tuesday especially was a most unlucky day.

There were five of us this time. At other times as many as fifteen and even more would set out for America on a single day. But whether five or fifteen, the days on which the *strangers* started out on the long journey were like holidays. Half the village folk, with flasks of brandy, decanters of wine, baskets of fruit, would come out to bid the "strangers" godspeed. It was like a religious procession. There was much sadness, tears, fear of unknown places to be traversed, mountains, tunnels, great rivers to be crossed, and then the vast ocean, days on end with no land in sight.

The path twisted up the scrub-oaked mountain side, the village nestling down in a kind of notch where the two river branches came together to form the limpid Bistra. Old men and women supporting themselves on cudgels trudged up, stopped a moment now and then to accept a tipple of brandy or wine. They would not turn back till we had reached the high plateau, the traditional place of parting. This treeless area, carpeted with silky, tufted low grass had taken on shrinelike attributes though there was no wayside chapel on it. There should have been one, dedicated to St. Christopher, the patron of travelers, or to Christopher Columbus himself. The place had been hallowed by many partings, by tears and prayers, hopes and yearnings, heartaches of those left behind, hopes and dreams of those departing. It had become a symbol of America, of anxieties and uncertainties. When people in the villages down in the valley thought of America they first thought of this naked saddle of the mountain, the point at which America swallowed their dear ones.

Here we now stood on the naked rim and looked northward across a broad plain. Far out in the distance, hardly perceptible in the blue haze, other mountains bordered the plain, and far beyond them, immeasurably far, farther than the mind could comprehend, was the ocean larger than the land, and on the other side of it AMERICA, the strange, unbelievable new country. And here began the ritual of parting, a scene of embraces, of quiet weeping turned into sobbing and whimpering, of a mother's blessing and a father's admonition, of a son's pledges, a peasant-husband's wordless promise of devotion, a peasant-wife's shy, implicit, unspoken vow of fidelity—a scene of an end and a beginning, of the old and the new, of parting and rejoining.

All the way up to the top of the mountain my father had fumed and uttered curses against Gurkin for having discovered America. He had done everything he could, short of using the rod, to break the spell. None of his stratagems had worked. America had reached across the spaces and had invaded my being. I became impossible, irritable, went about moping, refused to do any work, in the fields or in the store; nor would I go to the cities to do the buying. At long last the truth sank into my father's head that there was no cure for the malady except perhaps a dose of the serum that had caused it. He finally yielded to my importunings and went over to talk to Gurkin, who had made a second journey to America and was now preparing to start on his third. Gurkin offered to look after me until we got to St. Louis, where I had an uncle, husband of my father's only sister.

"All right," said my father, "you may go, but I give you warning not to write to me for money to come back with. Nobody ever sends money to America. I'll give you enough for the passage and a little extra, and I wish for nothing more from America than what I give you."

At parting, upbraiding himself for having given in to my youthful impulses, he urged me not to stay long in America. "Do not hunger for much. Remember the fable of the dog who leaped into the pond after the bone that was but a reflection of the one he held in his jaws. Return to our land. All things grow best in their own soil."

Women embraced me as though I were their own, perhaps to make up for my mother, who did not live to see her son start out for America. Since I was too young for the brandy bottle, they stuffed walnuts in my pockets. Men gave me coins—copper *metaliks*, silver *piasters*—tiny symbols of the money I would be earning in America. They first rubbed the coins against their beards for luck, meaning that I should earn as much money in America as there were hairs on their beards, a custom borrowed from the merchants in the cities.

Young women wept quietly, their cheeks flushed and their eyes red from the weeping and, likely, from thoughts of their husbands in America. It was hard for these young brides. Even I, young as I was, could sense that. One of them was Vanna, my cousin Todor's bride. Three years before, she had married Todor, a tall, lean, handsome fellow who had just returned from America garbed in the glamour and splendor of that fabulous new country. It seemed that none of the girls in our village was beautiful enough for him to marry, and he had to go to other districts to search for a bride. It was Vanna's face that at first had been the focus of my boyhood fascination, but by now, three years later, I had awakened to the attractions of other parts of the female body. Vanna's big brown eyes and handsome peasant face, which had caused the first turmoil in my heart and made me forget America for a while, still charmed me, but my eyes now shyly would alight on a bodice compressing two bulging hillocks and would stray lower to take measure of more expansive areas.

Vanna came over and took my hand and kissed me, wetting my cheeks with her tears and swathing me with her warm breath. It was a cousinly kiss to her, but it sent tremors through my body.

"Please tell my Todor not to stay longer than two years. He promised not to stay more than two years."

Todor had gone back to America a year after he married Vanna, and even if he came back in a year it still would be an eternity to Vanna, to her full ripe body, like a melon in a sunny patch that would burst from overripeness unless gathered. Vanna held my hand in hers, and we walked together as if she were an older sister. She kept holding my right hand, the hand that would shake cousin Todor's hand in America, and she kept on crying quietly, not sobbing or sniffling, just a moist, subdued weeping, her eyes full of warmth and liquid light. Her hand kept its tender hold of mine, as if she were attempting to transfuse some of her feeling for me to pass it on to Todor when I would shake his hand in America. Ah, but momentarily I forgot my excitement of going, and my fourteen years arose in me, wakened and bestirred, and I longed to keep that feeling for myself, and in that brief moment I relived those days of three years before when she captured the heart of the eleven-year-old boy and cast over him a spell even more overpowering than America's. I saw the entourage of six or seven *svatbari* escorting cousin Todor on his quest for a bride more beautiful than any that could be found in our village. The cavalcade was led by a *bairaktar*, who held aloft a pole on which fluttered, like a sheet of flame, a dappled red bandanna, crowned by an apple wreathed in flowers. The riders, with flowers stuck above their ears, rode out to the tune of a droning bagpipe and a wedding song. My eyes veiled with envy as I watched them disappear between the rows of spiry poplars that flanked the road to the north of the village.

"How far will they go?" I asked my mother.

"Only across the Tsrna. For your bride we shall cross the Vardar." My mother always said that I would bring a bride from beyond the Vardar. In our village the women bore more boys than girls. Some believed it was the water. At least one out of four bridegrooms had to look for his bride in some other village. But cousin Todor went farther than anyone else.

Five days passed, and still there was no sign of the return of the *svatbari*. In this time they could have crossed the Tsrna and returned. Maybe that river had flooded its banks and they had to ride far up to find a shallow place. But in our valley it had not rained. When it rained did it not rain all over the world at the same time? No, they must have gone beyond the Vardar. I was jealous of cousin Todor even before I saw the face of his bride.

Most of that fifth day I watched from the balcony of our house for signs of the wedding guests. Not until noon on the sixth day did the wind from the north bring detached squeals of the bagpipe and snatches of a wedding song. And then, in due time, out of the canopy of willows and poplars that lined the road there emerged the gay cavalcade. A rider tore himself from the group and galloped ahead. A red kerchief mottled with yellow dots was tied to the man's right ear; his *kalpak* bloomed with flowers; a pair of knee-length woolen socks of a pattern before unseen in our village dangled at his breast like a decoration, a gift to him from the bride. From the round, leather-bound wooden flask the man spilled some wine on the ground and from his mouth the words "Long live the bride and the groom. May fortune always smile on them." Then he turned his mount and galloped back to rejoin his wedding companions.

Because of the bride the *svatbari* rode slowly into the village. The apple at the top of the flagpole had shrunk; the flowers that wreathed it had faded; and the horses, the motley blankets over the saddles, the men's boots, were besmirched with the murky waters of the Vardar. Man-fashion astride a white mare, her feet in stirrups, the bride rode into Todor's courtyard. In contrast to the horses and mules bestrode by the men, the mare bore no trace of the muddy roads and roily rivers. Before reaching the village the men must have rubbed off the mud from the mare's legs.

116

The bride's face could not be clearly seen because of a spangled veil over it, but I knew in my heart that that face was of surpassing beauty, because everything else about the bride tended to confirm it. She sat on her mount with the grace and poise of a folk-tale princess. Though she rode man-fashion rather than sidesaddle, her voluminous skirt, in sweeping folds of intricate embroidery, covered her ankles and left exposed only her slippers, of red and yellow leather trimmed in gold and silver brocade. Locked in the stirrups, they looked like some fantastic tropical birds caught in traps. The bride's narrow waist was girded with a beaded belt buckled by hand-wrought, saucer-sized silver clasps. Her body above the waist, with its high bust tightly held in the bodice as in a cuirass, gave ample suggestion of the below-the-waist contours and proportions.

Todor rode immediately behind his bride. Despite his air of shyness, he looked like a hero returning from distant conquests and bringing home a princess as his prize. In the dooryard the grooms helped the bride alight. My heart fluttered lest some precious part of her be exposed, but the men were experienced in helping women dismount and handled the bride like a precious vase, the merest scratch on which might mar its beauty and impair its value. It was a wonder to me that they managed to set her feet on the ground without putting a hand where they shouldn't have. So lightly, so gently, so deftly they set her down that it seemed they hardly touched her.

Todor's mother, herself now dressed in the bridal costume of another generation, came out into the courtyard to meet her only son's bride. Three times Vanna bowed before her mother-in-law and three times she kissed her hand through the veil. Then the mother reached up and slowly lifted the veil to see the face of this daughter-in-law from beyond the Vardar. At that moment I felt as if I were lifted in a golden chariot and carried away to a new, remote, and unreal world. She stood erect and radiant in her picturesque costume, but it was her face and her face alone, with its large brown eyes, that caught my heart and blinded me like a strong sun. As I kept gazing at her in a kind of trance, I was too confused and smitten to know whether I was merely enchanted by her glowing beauty or filled with envy.

The wedding was on the following Sunday, but I would not attend it. "Of course you will," my mother argued. "It's your own cousin's wedding. What if Todor refused to come to your wedding?" She shook my shoulder as if to rouse me from my trance and with both hands turned my face toward her. For what seemed a whole minute she kept staring at me without speaking. What she

117

saw or read in my face I couldn't tell, but she said, "You don't have to go if you don't want to."

I stayed home, but I saw more of the wedding than anyone who was there. Not a single detail of the long ceremony escaped my mind's eye. From the balcony where I sat I could not see Todor's courtyard, but I saw everything that went on there. From the roll of drums and the ululations of clarinets and fifes as well as from the songs of the bridesmaids I knew when they were shaving the groom, when they made him kiss the bread loaf with the salt on top of it, and when they made him drink from the wineglass. From the music I followed every step of the wedding, knew exactly when the priest transposed the tinsel crowns on the heads of the newlyweds. I knew when my cousin slipped the wedding ring on Vanna's finger. When they took the bride "to water" I saw her standing on the bank of the river and saw Todor drinking from her slipper.

When it was all over and they were dancing and feasting I heard my mother's voice behind me.

"Are you well?"

"Yes."

She put her cool palm on my forehead. "Your forehead's hot. You're feverish." She soaked a kerchief in cold water, tied it around my forehead, and made me go to bed. My body shivered under the blanket, as if I had been seized by the ague. I might not have felt like that if my mother hadn't insisted I was ill.

Every wonder for three days, the biggest one for seven. The village soon recovered from the wonder of so distant and so beautiful a bride. Nothing could change the life of the village. Though a thousand beautiful brides had come to adorn it, still oxen had to be yoked and the plowshares buried in the soil. The sheep had to be sheared and the wool washed at the stream, carded, spun, and woven into cloth on the handlooms; the earth's fruit had to be gathered and stowed away; the winter wood had to be stacked under the broad eaves of the houses; a hundred different chores had to be done. Even my cousin Todor, whose soul and heart must have been possessed by the treasure that enriched his house, rewedded himself to the soil soon after the old priest had wedded him to Vanna.

Would that it were so with me! I alone remained impervious to the witchery of the soil. About the house and in the store I attended to such tasks as I was supposed to, but I did it with the vagueness and lethargy of an old man rather than with the spirit and liveliness of a boy. My father was too preoccupied with his manifold interests to notice that a new enchantment had displaced America from my mind. If he did notice my strange behavior he must have attributed it to my daydreams of America. It was different with my mother. She knew a new spell had been cast over me. And womanlike and motherlike she had her own remedy for my condition.

Some weeks after the wedding my mother told me that Todor had taken his mother to the doctor in the city and Vanna would be alone and I must go and spend the night with her. In the weeks after the wedding I saw Vanna frequently. I saw her going down to the village green to fill her jugs at the fountain; I saw her coming from the vineyard with a basket of glinting grapes balanced on her head; I saw her many times, but I never spoke a word to her, though I yearned to tell her how beautiful she was. And now I would be spending a whole night with her. The prospect of spending the night with her began to take possession of me, and my whole body quivered with excitement.

That night there was tension at the supper table, and I surmised that my mother had told my father about my having to spend the night with Vanna and that he had disapproved. All through the meal no word passed between my parents. My father wiped his mouth with the napkin and in the same motion stroked his mustaches. He then broke another morsel of bread and his spoon sallied forth. My mother kept looking before her and quietly chewed at her food. I dipped my own spoon in the bowl and bit at my chunk of bread. The spoons, as they journeyed from bowl to mouth, seemed to me to be engaged in a mute argument about my having to spend the night with my cousin Todor's bride.

At last my mother put away the spoons and the empty bowls. She removed the low round table and swept the crumbs later to be given to the chickens. The chickens were never fed except for crumbs and tares and scraps; mostly they scrabbled in the weeds or in the barns in winter. I sat down next to Grandfather in his corner of the hearthside and watched my father go through the ritual of brewing his Turkish coffee. When I was younger he would give me his emptied *finjan* with the thick residue of bitter-sweet grains at the bottom, which I scooped out with my finger and ate like candy. Now that I was eleven this indulgence was neither offered nor desired. I still enjoyed the exotic aroma of the coffee, which we bought green in the bean and roasted over the fire in a little drum with a long handle. I generally attended to this chore, as well as to grinding the coffee afterward in the long cylindrical brass coffee grinder. My father now attended to it himself. To prevent scorching, every now and then he would pull the roaster away from the fire and shake it. He did that now so vigorously that the popping beans inside seemed to fortify his disapproval of my having to spend the night with Vanna. Even when later he was pulverizing

119

the coffee in the mill you could feel anger in his movements, as if he were grinding not coffee but my mother's reasons for making the arrangement. What those reasons were and why my father objected I could not tell. All I thought was that Vanna would be afraid to sleep alone in the house.

My father put two heaping teaspoonfuls of the finely ground coffee and two lumps of sugar in the coffeemaker, a long-handled copper vessel shaped like an hourglass. He filled it with water and stuck it in the embers. The hearth was an old discarded millstone set about three or four inches below the level of the floor and bordered on the floorside by a semicircle of bricks set edgewise and level with the floor. My father was fussy about his coffee and brewed it with concentration, as if he were concocting some mysterious alchemic potion. He kept his eyes on the forming brown froth slowly swelling up, and just as it would threaten to spume over the brim he would snatch the pot away and blow at it. When the head would subside, he again would stick the pot in the live ashes to make the cream rise again, only to pull the pot away before any of the precious "top" was lost. Three times he repeated the process, each time in the nick of time to prevent the seething "top" from overflowing.

Something like that was going on in my own being. A strange feeling would rise up in me to fill me with excitement over the prospect of spending the night with Vanna, only to be followed by an unknown fear or shyness that would blow a cold breath on it and cause it to shrink within me.

My father poured the thick, syrupy liquid in two porcelain *finjans* set on the hearthstone. The pouring was a ritual in itself. He did not fill one cup and then another but alternately emptied the contents a little at a time so as to distribute evenly the precious cream, for Turkish coffee without a "top" is like beer without a head. He then pushed one cup toward me to hand to Grandfather, while he, with the coffee before him untouched, opened his *tobakera,* a silver affair with Arabic scrolls on it, and rolled himself a cigarette. He lit the cigarette with a live coal clamped up with the fire tongs and lifted the coffee cup. He did not *drink* the coffee; the demitasse was too little for that. The contents could be emptied in two gulps, and there was no enjoyment in that. He *aerated,* or vaporized, the black liquid with much hissing noise, his lips barely touching the brim of the porcelain. Usually he allowed nothing to interfere with the enjoyment of his after-dinner smoke and coffee—no anger, no upset of any kind. But in the sibilant "music" that now accompanied the "drinking" of the coffee there was anger.

At last he spoke, and after the long interval of oppressive silence

120

his voice sounded like an explosion. "Eleven-year-olds jumping fences! Why couldn't one of the neighbor girls spend the night with her? Why must *he* go?"

My mother made no reply. She went on with her work as if he had not spoken. Grandfather, startled, knocked the ashes from his pipe on the hearthstone and repacked his pipe. "Where is he supposed to go?" he asked.

"He's being sent to spend the night with Todor's bride. Todor is in the city with his mother. So our hero will guard the princess from the dragon." He blew at the amber mouthpiece of his long *chibook,* and the glowing stub at the other end dropped in the fireplace like a bullet. He rolled himself another cigarette, twisted one end of it into the holder, lit it, and filled his lungs with smoke. Filaments of blue smoke spun out of his nostrils like yarn.

He turned to me with sarcasm in his voice. "Well, why don't you go? It is already dark, and she is alone, waiting for you."

"You better go now," said my mother quietly but firmly.

Outside the pale-yellow lights of kerosene lamps glimmered at windows and voices could be heard. A child screamed; a mother's scolding voice screeched in the night; a dog barked somewhere in the upper quarter of the village; a mule whinnied in some shed. My heart throbbed and my whole body trembled with anticipation. Vague, unclear ideas and notions hovered in my mind. Why *did* my mother send me to sleep with Vanna? Did Vanna ask, did she know how I felt, or was this my mother's idea? Were mothers capable of reading what was in their children's hearts? Had she sensed by her maternal intuition how completely my innocent young heart had been captivated by cousin Todor's beautiful bride? Or did she believe that I had become the victim of some powerful witchery? A few days before, while she was talking with a neighbor woman, I overheard the woman use the word *hexed.* Could they have been talking about me?

When I got to Vanna's courtyard my whole body began to tremble. What would I say to her? The thought that she was waiting for me enveloped me in a warm, sunny feeling. Even the scene of the priest wedding her to Todor, which now sprang in my mind, did not dampen my elation.

As I made ready to knock at the door a sudden fear that the sound might rouse the neighbors stayed my hand. Heads would thrust out of windows, voices would giggle, the whole village would soon know. So instead of knocking I pawed and scratched at the door like a dog asking to be let in. Presently I heard the soft patter of pantofles coming from inside and then a sweet voice saying, "Is it you, Little Cousin?" It was the first time I had heard her voice, and

121

the sweetness of it, together with the bitter note of the "little" with the "cousin," was absorbed by my body.

"It's me," I whispered, my voice sounding conspiratorial in the darkness. The door drew inward, bowing like a lackey to make way for my entry. For a moment I stood at the threshold not knowing what to say.

"I've been waiting for you." Her words anointed me like a benediction. She was waiting for me! Alone, in the night, in her house! The petallike flame of the torch she held fluttered as though it understood, and I quickly entered and closed the door.

The house was as familiar to me as our own, and I could find my way in the dark, but she lighted my way to the kitchen. In those days in Macedonian villages the kitchen was the center of family life, serving as sitting room and dining room and often, especially in winter, as bedroom. Even in cities people slept on the floor on blankets spread on rugs. Only wealthy merchants like my friend Miralai enjoyed the luxury of beds. There were no chairs either. People sat cross-legged around the fireplace where all the cooking was done, or reclined against walls lined with straw-packed cushions.

I sat down by the fireplace, which also gave me its warm welcome, as all fireplaces do. "A house without a fireplace," Grandfather often said, "is like a church without an altar or a man without a soul." My eyes scanned the room as though I hadn't been in it a hundred times. Objects that I had never noticed or been aware of now stared at me as if they had come in with me, like pets, and had taken their appointed places as I had mine. On the wall facing me a glass kerosene lamp held in a gilt tinsel frame cast its weak light over the interior. The yellow petallike flame winked knowingly, and my abashed eyes quickly shifted to less animate objects, to the row of cupboards, the kneading trough in the center of them, the wooden and earthen receptacles of various shapes on the shelves, only to come to rest on the silver-framed icon of the household's patron saint. I had paid scarce notice to this icon before, but now something about it, something magnetic or supernatural, kept my eyes fastened to it. I noticed that the silver frame was not square or rectangular but formed an arch, a halo, around the saint's head. The left hand held against the chest a big book with gem-studded leather binding. Under the book the right hand was pressed against the chest, except that the first two fingers, long and slender, were extended out and pointed directly at me. At the same time the saint's large, deep-set Byzantine eyes, brooding and remonstrant, were fixed on me. The whole visage, ascetic, compassionate, and stern at the same time, seemed to be directing at me a benign reproach or rebuke. And a sudden uneasy feeling made

122

me turn my eyes to the fire, whose cheery welcome was more in keeping with my visit.

My eyes also sought out Vanna, who had been busying herself about the kitchen, and my eyes caught her just as she was reaching for something on a shelf. As her body strained up my eyes quickly ran over it and as quickly fell to my lap when she turned. There they stayed lowered but furtively followed her movements, lingering on her when, with her back to me, she stooped to open a cupboard. She wore no stockings, and she padded about the floor in slippered bare feet. Whenever she stooped over the hem at the back of her skirt went up to reveal the calves of her legs. I was at the age now when a girl's legs began to play an important role in my appraisal of her attractiveness. It was Vanna's beautiful face that at first had caused the obsession, and now her shapely legs fortified the enchantment. She left the room for a few minutes to return with a jug of wine and a bowl of cracked but unshelled walnuts, which she put on a tray at the edge of the hearth. In sitting down by the fireside she crossed her legs but covered them so deftly with her skirt and apron that not even the slippers were visible.

I had not yet said a word to her. Neither had she spoken except at the door. To dispel any notion that I was shy or ill at ease, I looked straight at her, ready to say something, but when my eyes met hers a strange, vague sensation stirred in some deep, unfamiliar part of my body. I was speechless.

She came to my rescue. "You were so good to come, little cousin." She smiled, and her smile caused such confusion to sweep over me that, without being asked, I reached into the bowl and took a walnut. With both thumbs I chipped the broken shell and tossed the fragments into the fire. They smoked an instant, like incense, fizzed, then burst into flame and quickly died out, reduced to ashes.

"Why don't you talk to me, little cousin? You didn't want to come, did you? Your mother *made* you come."

Instead of replying I took another walnut and fumbled at the shell with my fingers. I couldn't remember eating the kernels I had just shelled. I must have swallowed them half chewed.

Vanna edged closer to me without rising. She sort of sidled gracefully to be closer. She looked at me caressingly, her big brown eyes warm and liquid. The nearness of her magnified her charm, and to hide my excitement and confusion I took still another walnut and nearly punctured my thumb on a bit of sharp shell.

"Was it a pair of socks I brought you as my wedding gift?"

Something like an eddy swirled in the depth of my being. Without looking at her I now heard myself say, "You gave socks to my father."

"Ah, then I brought no gift for you. I am sorry, little cousin."

123

She reached out with a consoling hand and stroked my hair. Then fleetingly her fingers prowled in my hair, and as she withdrew them they touched my cheek lingeringly. A tremor went through me and my eyes welled with tears, but I forced the tears back and this sent a streak, like a hot wire, tingling through my nostrils.

"Then I shall knit you a sweater like the one I am knitting for my Todor."

The fire, which had been burning quietly, soundlessly, except for an occasional cough or sniffle, came back to life. It now crackled and whistled, a mocking kind of whistle.

"You're a handsome boy, little cousin. I am so glad you are my Todor's kin."

Little cousin! My Todor! The words bored into my heart like a toothache.

"But you're not drinking wine. Does your father allow you to drink wine?"

"My father lets me do anything I like. I go to the cities to buy for the store all by myself."

"Of course. How old are you?"

"I am eleven."

"My, but you are big for your age. You'll soon be looking for a bride. Will you go far, like your cousin Todor?"

The log in the fire made a noise like an old man clearing his throat, and a spark leaped out to expire the instant it touched the hearthstone. Presently the log made a kind of buzzing, razzing sound, and I reached for the poker but the log quieted before I could poke it.

Now Vanna rose and took down a basket from a niche in the wall beside the saint. Again she sat next to me but facing me. She took a hank of yarn from the basket and held it out toward me. "This is for Todor's sweater. Will you help me wind it?"

Knowing my function in the operation, I extended my arms and she looped the skein on my wrists. She hardly touched me doing this. To do this she had to lean toward me, and her eyes and face and breath enveloped me.

Strands of yarn unreeled from around my wrists, slipped and spun, twirled before my eyes and twined on the forming ball in her hands. I raised or lowered my forearms to accommodate the unwinding yarn and keep it from snagging. But every now and then the yarn would get snarled and Vanna would lean over close to me to untangle it. Her nimble fingers would pick at the strands and smooth and straighten them, and presently her hand would begin to weave in the air and furl the yarn around the growing ball. Her

124

closeness to me and her breath cast a mist on me, and I felt as if I were being tossed in the air like that ball of yarn enmeshed in quantities of yarn.

"Your hair is not really black, little cousin. It's more brown than black. Don't you think my Todor will look handsome in this deep-red sweater?"

A sudden weakness came over me, and my arms dropped involuntarily in my lap, the band of yarn still on them but loose.

"Tell me, do you think I am beautiful?" When I didn't answer she said, "Oh, so you don't think I am beautiful." Her hand left the ball and reached over to lift my chin. "Well, my Todor thinks I am beautiful."

Again I held up my arms, and the reel stretched on my wrists and the ball rotated in the air, the yarn unfurling from my wrists and spinning about the ball. But now with every strand that unwound from around my wrists and spooled on the ball I felt a little lighter and a little freer. Some kind of wooliness that lay over me like fog began to shed away, and in the clarity a vague thought sprang up about my mother's reasons for sending me to spend the night with Vanna.

The lone surviving log in the fire let out a final somnolent sigh. The glowing embers that had given me their warm welcome when I came into the room had turned into ashes. On the wall the flame of the kerosene lamp seemed wilted, flickering a pale, strained light over the room. In the iconostasis the patron saint was absorbed in meditation. And the last strand of yarn fell from my wrists and trailed toward Vanna, crawling before my eyes like a snake's tail disappearing into a hole.

"You must be getting tired, little cousin. It's past your bedtime. I'll make your bed on this side. My Todor and I sleep on the other side."

The thought of whether I would sleep with her under the same cover had been with me from the moment my mother had told me I would spend the night with her. A dozen times I saw myself blissfully lying in her arms, her loving hands stroking my head, her warm lips touching my cheek. And as many times I imagined myself crouched like a dog by the door to guard her as the dragon guards the folk-tale princess imprisoned in the rocky cave.

Vanna covered me with a blanket and kissed me good night on the forehead and said how good I was to come and how grateful "my Todor" would be that she didn't have to spend the night alone. I turned my face to the wall and fell asleep almost instantly. When I awoke the next morning it took me a minute or two to realize that I was not in our own house. Somewhere deep within me there was sadness, but at the same time my heart felt free, as though it had been a bird in a cage and had suddenly been let out.

2

Although Gurkin was supposed to look after me, my guardian, friend and companion on the voyage, and afterward in America, was a simple shepherd named Nichola. Like myself, he was making his first trip to America, and if I were the youngster of the group, he was the oldest. He had been a shepherd since boyhood, a real hillman, and should never have left his sheep and the highland pastures. Yet for him, too, the magic of America and the lure of gold was too much. America had found him in the Macedonian hills and had cast its spell over his simple heart and mind. After four decades of a serene pastoral life he abandoned his bleating companions to brave continents and *okeans* in order to enrich himself. There was about him a refreshing simplicity and naïveté, a natural goodness, a rustic ingenuousness that endeared him to me. This gentle man needed as much guidance and looking after as did I, the mere boy in the group. Six feet tall, straight as a poplar, bony and sinewy, and, unlike most of us, fair of complexion, blond hair turning gray, albinolike bushy brows, there was something serene and majestic about Nichola. Yet removed from his element, from his bucolic environment, he seemed divested of his strength and self-confidence. He looked dwarfed and confused by the strange places through which we passed. In Salonika he discarded the white woolen frock he always wore and encased himself, as in a strait-jacket, in pantaloons and jacket. He looked comical; the others laughed at him, which further diminished his person. At times he felt he had made a mistake and was seized by a nostalgic mood for the hill pastures where he was king and for his flock of sheep and goats. He once said to me "I wish the *pampour* [steamship] on which Gurkin crossed had sunk and he had never found America." Then quickly he added, "I don't really mean that."

I had thought that Gurkin would be picking the way for us through Europe like a scout following a trail in a forest, but we were always on trains and frequently changing trains and always were met by agents of the steamship company, who led us about from one railway station to another or quartered us overnight and sometimes for a day or two in places where we were boarded free and slept in dormitories as in barracks. We didn't know what countries we were passing through or what were the languages we heard spoken, but fortunately the agents were either Croats, Czechs, or Poles who spoke languages akin to our Bulgarian speech, and we managed. In the cities where we stayed I sometimes ventured out from our quarters for short walks in little squares or parks and saw for the first time fountains and statues with twisting intertwined naked male and female human bodies of bronze or marble and in one place saw a little fountain with the water pouring from the erect penis of a naked boy. I had been through the sixth grade in school and was the only "educated" member of the group, but I never dreamed that such things existed.

Sometimes the agents rode with us on the train for great distances and did not turn back until they had delivered us into the care of other representatives of the line. They pinned red buttons with white stars on our coat lapels so that it was easy for the agents to pick us out as we stepped off the trains in what seemed to me vast railway stations. In this way we jogged along for days and nights on what we didn't know at the time were slow trains and circuitous routes, changing trains frequently. In one town on a river (many years later on my travels through Europe I came to this town and recognized it as Basel and the river the Rhine) we stayed for two days, and while walking about we saw in a window pickled pigs' feet and our mouths drooled but we didn't speak the language and didn't have the right kind of money.

After some days of such meandering about Europe we came to a place called Cherbourg, and here we waited for the boat for six days, lodged and boarded by the steamship company in an immense building where we found scores of other emigrants, some of whom had waited for a week or two to be put on board a ship. It seemed to me that the whole world had discovered America at the same time that Gurkin did and was in a hurry to get there. Slavic languages predominated, and we made friends with fellow Bulgarians. Even though it cost nothing for board and lodging we were all anxious to get to America before the proverbial gold in the streets was picked up by others.

"Patience," said Gurkin, "patience! We'll get there, awright, awright." The "awright," spoken in the original tongue, sounded more reassuring to me than the "patience."

We were landfolk and frightened of the sea. Crossing the *okean* we dreaded more than the uncertainty of the strange new world to which we were bound and the proverbial hostility of the immigration inspectors at the "Island." Ellis Island in those days was known to millions of immigrants merely as the "Island," and it was a word that filled us with forebodings. It was one of the principal hazards of the journey to America, for it was here, after making the long journey, that people were denied entrance into the promised land and were turned back. Three emigrants from my own village had been refused admission, and I remembered their return to the village. In contrast to the glory of the returned "Americans," these unfortunates presented a pathetic sight. They had mortgaged fields or vineyards for money for their passage, money that could be paid back only with earnings in America. Here in Cherbourg I heard stories of people who had jumped into the ocean rather than return to their villages to face eviction from their homes.

I don't know which we feared more, the immigration inspectors or the ocean. The ship we crossed on, a tough little White Star liner aptly called the *Oceanic,* filled us with awe and wonder, for on the very first day out at sea she began a struggle with the elements that lasted for days. The ocean heaved its bosom into great towering mounds that burst into white-crested ridges and rolled high and menacing toward the brave ship. Not having seen anything like it, some of us landlubbers expected to be swallowed by the ocean ship and all in spite of reassurances from Gurkin and others who had crossed the ocean. The sturdy *Oceanic* squeaked and trembled in every rib and sinew of her frame, breasted and scaled the rising seas, dipping her prow into the ocean and rearing up like a bull. At times she seemed to come to a dead stop, but when I looked down her side to the churning waters below I could detect her motion.

The storm lasted for four days, and the angry ocean gave in, tamed and defeated by the indomitable little ship. Calmly and proudly now she glided over the smooth waters. We came up on deck to enjoy the smooth seas and the sun. We were proud of the little ship and grateful to it. My friend Nichola was overcome with admiration, leaning on the rail and watching the ship glide smoothly over the friendly ocean. There was no life of any kind, no birds in the air, nothing but the vastness of the sea blending with the sky in a blue mist somewhere at the end of the world.

"You think a French *pampour* could have done it, eh?"

"I can't say, Uncle Nichola."

"I think the Englisi have outdeviled the Frangi, what do you say?"

"I think when it comes to sailing the seas the English have it all over the French. They say that the sun never sets on English soil."

"Does it read like that in the books?"

"Yes. The English are supposed to be the masters of all the oceans."

"What about the Americans?"

"I don't know, Uncle Nichola."

"But you'll read about it. If it's in the books you'll find out. You've got four eyes, you've got learning." Nichola had the illiterate person's awe of learning. He felt lost not only because he could not read or write but he could not tell figures; he could not look at a watch or clock and tell what time it was. He was helpless and he depended on me, the way my grandfather had depended on my "seeing" for him. It was pathetic to see this strong man, removed from his element, become so helpless and depending for help on a mere boy. How would he manage in America? How would he find his way about? Why did he leave his mountains? He was strong; ordinary people looked like pygmies beside him. Long and thick were his mustaches; his straw-colored eyebrows drooped over his gray eyes like tufts of hemp. His arms branched out from his tall angular body like branches of an oak.

"Don't you be worrying about writing and such things, Uncle Nichola. I'll write your letters for you and look after everything."

It was fitting that the first sign we saw of the New World should be a bright light gleaming in the distance. For the last two days we saw birds flying about and seaweed floating on the water, harbingers of the nearness of America, but this light that glowed brightly and then expired and then lit up again was a semaphore signaling the new land's welcome to us. It was around nine o'clock in the evening, and some of us were on the small steerage deck at the prow of the ship surrounded by the darkness when suddenly the light blinked. I fastened my eyes on this light of my future and kept them there till they welled with tears from the strain.

There was commotion among the passengers. Animated conversation in a dozen languages indicated the excitement over the sight of the New World, even if it was only a light that went on and off. Nichola stood beside me saying little, happy in his silence that the dreadful *okean* had at last been crossed. The ship glided smoothly through the darkness, and in a little while other lights began to leap out of the darkness, but instead of blinking these lights stayed on and grew larger and multiplied until they became so numerous that it was easier to believe the ship was sailing against a starry sky than against land. We still were on the water and had seen no land, but America was revealing herself to us in dazzling brilliance.

We passed the first rotating light and left it behind us and the ship came to a stop, but Nichola and I stood on deck for a long time gazing in wonder at the illuminated world around us. There was a sustained roar, or din, as though something were stirring in the bowels of the earth. Steamboats groaned with plaintive, mysterious voices; now and then what sounded like distant, muffled thunder reached us. We wondered what it was like in the midst of the myriad lights, wondered also what was behind those lights and whether we would be able to find our way in this luminous new land and what would happen to us. As I wondered about myself I also wondered about Nichola, this simple man so helpless despite his strength. The more I peered into those dazzling lights illuminating the sky the more I thought how naïve and simple-minded Gurkin's stories must have been compared to the actual wonders that were before us. And I was thrilled and happy now that I was at the gate to the hoped-for land but also frightened and apprehensive as to what would happen to us. I could not then foresee that to some of us, to me especially, *America would happen.*

It was near midnight when Nichola and I finally went below to that cloying ship smell that sickened me more than the rolling and pitching of the ship itself. I crawled into my bunk and the ship still seemed to sway, a sensation that persisted for some time after we landed. I was so excited that my whole body throbbed, and I kept seeing those myriad lights. It was a long time before I fell asleep.

The next morning I was one of the first on deck. The *Oceanic* seemed to have sailed into a kind of lake, for all around it sprawled the New World. Directly in front, rising out of the water's edge, was a cluster of buildings rearing up in serried terraces. Some of them had flat tops, others were surmounted by slender towers, and the whole agglomeration reminded me of prints I had seen of Jerusalem, but much magnified, and I imagined I was looking at a colossal cathedral or monastery with many turrets, cupolas, steeples, and belfries buttressed by innumerable chapels and sanctuaries.

To the left on an island there loomed a colossal statue in human form, with its right arm uplifted like the single branch of a gigantic tree. I had seen statuary in little squares and parks of European cities where we waited for trains but nothing to compare with the colossus here at the door to the new land. Somehow it occurred to me that such a statue placed here at the threshold of America must have some special significance connected with the dreams and hopes of the tides of immigrants struggling to reach this golden gateway to a new life. As the vessel passed closer to it, the statue loomed even larger than it appeared from the distance, and I now perceived that the upraised arm held in its hand a balcony or pavilion shaped like a torch. Nichola was by my side, and he too gazed in wonder. "Maybe it's an American saint, the giver of gold."

We were all on deck with hungry eyes and avid minds, marveling and wondering, with the fears of the immigration inspectors hovering about us like pestiferous flies. Gurkin was ever polite and kind to me, having promised my father to look after me, but also, I suspected, because of my schooling and literateness, so that when I asked him about the statue he shook his head at me admonishingly. "Now I can't believe you don't know what that statue is, and you been to the first class in school. What do they teach in school anyway? The whole world knows that's Cristoforo Columbo. I suppose you don't even know who that was."

"Yes, I know. He got to America before you did."

When I rejoined Nichola he was talking to Budak, a tall, lanky Croat who had been a sergeant in the Austro-Hungarian army. He too had been in America before but did not pretend to know as much about it as Gurkin.

"It's Christopher Columbo, Uncle Nichola."

"What's Cristofor Columbo?"

"The statue!"

"If you listen to Gurkin he'll tell you it's Abdul Hamid. If it wasn't for Budak here I wouldn't believe this is America if only because Gurkin says it is. I don't believe Gurkin; I don't believe anything he says. Budak here just told me it's liberty."

"No, not liberty," corrected Budak. He spoke in Croatian but tried to make it sound like Bulgarian. "It's a *monument* to liberty."

Nichola scowled and scratched his neck. His bushy brows almost covered his eyes. The word *monument* he associated with *tombstones,* and this association with a monument to liberty caused some confusion in his simple, pastoral mind.

"A *monument!* You mean like they put on the graves?"

"Yes . . . Well . . . not exactly. You see, the figure is a woman, a goddess, a goddess of freedom. The statue means freedom. It says welcome here, this is a free country, you will be free here. The figure stands for it, like a patron saint, a saint protector. It says to you when you are admitted here that you will be a free man."

The word *admitted* wakened in Nichola the fear of the immigration inspectors. "You mean once you get past the *Island?"*

"Yes, that's right. Then you are free to become a citizen, it takes five years. And then you can vote to elect public officials. And if you are smart and save your money you can run for office yourself."

This was too much for Nichola, too much in fact for the rest of us. All we knew was that all public officials, judges, and tax collectors were appointed by the sultan.

132

"You mean you can vote here to choose the sultan?"

"There are no sultans here."

"Then who rules?"

"Nobody. There are no *rulers* here. The people *rule*. They elect a President, but he doesn't rule; he just governs."

Nichola scratched his head. His eyes narrowed.

"Can he be elected President?" Nichola pointed at me in all seriousness. "He's smart. He's got four eyes."

Budak laughed heartily and patted my shoulder. "He looks sharp. If he goes to school and to the university maybe he can be elected a Senator. To be President you have to be born in America."

The boat now entered a narrow passage, tall buildings on the right, high banks on the left, with rows of houses and high factory chimneys belching columns of smoke. All kinds of small boats, ferries, tugboats, barges, tankers, freighters, excursion boats, none of which I could name at the time, weaved in and out, braying like bulls, calling and answering, almost colliding but never doing so. It was the first vision of America, frightening, confusing, exciting. This was Nevi York.

Presently Gurkin joined us, and Budak instantly turned on him with vehemence in his voice. "You never once admit you don't know a thing. Cristofor Columbo! Can't you say you don't know? Must you misinform people?"

"That's what everybody says it is."

"What everybody? Who said so? Now listen, Gurkin, I've been inside that statue, all the way up, up through the arm to the torch in the hand, see. And I know what that statue is, and everybody else does, and I have read the writing at the bottom. It's a poem about us, written by one of us immigrants, all about us, the poor, the unknowing, the ignorant, the frightened, the scared, the confused. It says come, 'I lift my lamp beside the golden door.'"

Gurkin blushed and twisted his mustaches to hide his embarrassment. He looked sheepish. "Somebody told me it was Columbo."

"You say the statue is hollow inside?" I asked.

"Yes. They lift you up in an *elevator* part way."

"An *elevator?*"

"That's the room that goes up and down on ropes and stops wherever you want to stop," Gurkin put in. "Then you walk up the rest of the way," added Budak. "You start walking where the arm is raised up from the body. The stairway's in the arm. You walk inside the arm step by step, up to the torch. The torch is really a balcony, and you can stand in the torch and see New York and the harbor and far beyond."

133

There was a look of concern on Nichola's face, which I attributed to anxiety over the impending ordeal at the Island. He was like a blind man whose sense of touch and hearing became acute to compensate for the blindness. He made up for his lack of education and worldly contact by whetting his instincts and developing his innate intelligence to a kind of natural canniness and peasant shrewdness. He was now bothered about the statue's being hollow and said so.

"Well, what's wrong with that?" Budak wondered.

"It stands for freedom, don't it? And it's hollow!"

We did not pursue the subject of the hollowness of the symbol of liberty, as the *Oceanic* had now gone some distance up the narrow passage that somebody said was a river called the Hudson and a couple of spunky little boats came puffing alongside her and began to maneuver her toward the pier. Groaning and hiccuping, the tugboats heaved their padded sides against the vessel and trembled as they gently pushed her toward her berth. They reminded me of ants dragging bumblebees twenty times their weight.

We were not disembarked at the pier but were transferred onto a ferry and taken directly to the Island, where the ferry disgorged us and we formed queues extending from the landing itself all the way to the main entrance. Mostly Slavs and Jews, brown-eyed, almond-eyed, dreamy-eyed, some bearded, some mustachioed, all in rumpled jackets and pants, capped by headgear as diverse as ourselves, carrying bundles or valises made of straw or cardboard, raw human fodder for the capacious intestines of America. With dreams in our eyes and fright in our hearts, we draggled along toward what we regarded as an inevitable purgatory before the gates of heaven would open to us.

One hand clutching my valise and the other my papers, I entered the building where future Americans and begetters and progenitors of generations of future Americans, of professors and senators and presidents of corporations and of the United States, of builders of bridges and skyscrapers and amenders and enlargers and enrichers of a new nation and a new human culture, kept shuffling along like puppets on a conveyor belt, cringing and bewildered under the scrutiny of the brown-uniformed gatekeepers of the promised land, gatekeepers who themselves or their fathers had in like manner cowed at these very gates. I sidled through narrow, railed-in stalls, then in single file up a stairway into an immense hall with a glass roof supported by round pylons, lamps hanging from the roof, and narrow institutional windows as high as the walls themselves. Different inspectors, without detaining us, went through the inspection routine. One would pass his fingers through the hair; another

134

would turn up the eyelids with a metallic instrument, quickly, mechanically, before one realized what was happening; still another would examine the hands, looking at the palms and the wrists and rubbing the skin. If an immigrant stopped, confused, befuddled, and held up the line, he was shoved ahead unceremoniously. On the backs of some the inspectors made white chalk marks as though they were pieces of baggage, and they did this so deftly that the ones so marked were unaware of it. Farther on the chalk marks were either wiped off by other inspectors or the man was drawn aside to worry and bemoan his fate.

Nichola was immediately ahead of me, tall, gaunt, and ungainly. He kept turning his head to see if I was following.

After winding through several corridors, being pushed this way and that like dummies, with the floor still swaying beneath (for the sensation of the ship's rocking still persisted), Nichola and I came into a vast hall lined with benches all the way to the far side, at which other inspectors, some in uniforms and some in civilian clothes, were seated at desks interrogating immigrants. These inspectors did not hurry; they took their time questioning the would-be Americans. We had been standing and moving along in line for a long time, and it was a relief to sit down and put our bundles and valises on the floor. We had thought all the inspecting was over, but here we were now in this vast hall filled with immigrants seated on benches. Nichola gave a deep sigh, for we could see we now faced a different kind of inspection, an inspection of the mind, not just the hands, the eyes, the skin, the way you walked, the way you lifted up your arms.

"You have nothing to worry about, little one," Nichola comforted me. "You know reading and writing and how to tell what the clock says, and you can do figures on paper not like me scratching on a piece of wood how much milk the sheep gave. It's me that's got to worry, me that's got eyes but cannot see. A man needs two pair of eyes, one to see with and another to read with, like yourself. That's what learning does to you, gives you an extra pair of eyes."

"Don't be afraid, Uncle Nichola. I'll tell the inspectors we are together, and I'll be doing all the writing and figuring for both of us."

We sidled along on the bench, pushing our luggage, such as it was, with our feet, and other immigrants behind us filled the benches. There never seemed to be an end to people coming to America. There must have been other boats arriving at the same time we did.

"What's your name?" asked the one in civilian clothes of the two men at the inspection desk. The language in which he addressed

Nichola was a basic Slavic intelligible to us, as well as to Croats, Serbs, Poles, Czechs, Ukrainians, etc. Nichola's eyes brightened and his face opened in an innocent smile at the sound of familiar words in this forbidding place.

"His name's written in the passport," I hastened to inform the inspector.

"You keep quiet and sit down. We'll come to you next."

The other inspector, the one in uniform, sitting down at the desk, was a huge man, with a rubber-tire neck and bulging middle that seemed to confirm the notion that Americans were orbicular. He reminded me of bloated Turkish tax collectors and other officials that sometimes came to the village. I thought it silly for the Slav-speaking one to be asking Nichola for his name when he was looking at his passport where Nichola's name was written in Turkish as well as Latin characters.

"How do you call yourself?"

"Nichola Zlatin."

"How old are you?" Again I was tempted to tell the inspector that in the passport there was written the day, month, and year in which Nichola was born, but I refrained from doing so in fear of antagonizing him and thus hurt our chances of being accepted in America.

"Forty-seven," replied Nichola.

"And you are going where?"

"To Santo Louis."

"Have you any kin there?"

"Yes, my brother-in-law." And Nichola handed him an envelope with the name and the address in East St. Louis of his relative.

All through the questioning the seated inspector did not say a word. Apparently he did not speak any of the Slavic languages, but he seemed to know what was being asked and what the answers were.

"How much money have you?"

Nichola fished out his moneybag from his bosom and laid the money on the desk, all of twenty-seven dollars, converted into American currency by the steamship agent at Cherbourg.

"Do you read and write?"

I forgot the rebuff and said quickly, rising to my feet, "Whatever reading and writing's to be done for him I'll do it myself. I've been to the first class in school."

This time the man did not shout at me to be quiet; he just stared at me until I could feel myself shrivel in my skin and I sat back on the bench.

"Can you read and write?"

Nichola looked at me imploringly and then at the man and then nodded his head. Even though with us in sign language nodding the head up and down meant *no* and shaking it from side to side meant *yes,* all contrary to American sign language, the inspector understood and said, "But you can count, can you not?"

"Count?" Nichola stood confused and his eyes again searched for me, but realizing I was not to speak in his behalf, he looked at the inspector. "You mean one . . . two . . . three . . . ?"

"Yes."

"I used to count my sheep in the old country. That's hard. It's hard to count sheep."

"How high can you count?"

"High . . . er . . . I've counted up to three hundred and fifty. I've never had more sheep than that in my flock."

"Fine. Now count downward from twenty-one to thirteen."

My heart ached for my friend. He stood there wan and forlorn, his long arms hanging at his sides, an expression of utmost helplessness on his countenance.

Thinking perhaps that Nichola did not understand him, the inspector (he really was an interpreter) couched his question as close to the Bulgarian language as he could. "You say you *can* count. Very well, start at twenty-one, but go down instead of up, and stop counting when you come to thirteen. Do you understand?"

Again Nichola looked at me with troubled eyes partially fringed by straw-colored brows. Why did these inspectors have to torture my friend like this? Why was *counting* so important? Nichola wasn't going to be a bookkeeper in America. He would be working in the mines or shovel coal or clean engines. And why this counting backward?

Haltingly, cautiously, as though he were fording a stream backward and fearful he might stumble over a slippery stone, Nichola began counting. "Twenty-one—" he took a breath and swallowed —"twenty . . . er . . . nineteen . . . eighteen . . ." He stopped at thirteen with a deep sigh and wiped the sweat off his forehead with the back of his hand.

"Good enough. Go along. And good luck to you."

A big weight lifted from my heart. I had forgotten about my own ordeal in worrying over Nichola, who now picked up his bundle and crossed to the other side. It was only a few steps, but it was a stride across vast spaces. It was a crossing from one world to another, from one life to another, from fright to courage, from despair to hope. And all this was held in the hand of one man. Maybe it wasn't so. Maybe this one man, or these two men, did not have all that power, the power to cast a human being from light into darkness, but we did not know that. Nichola stood by the railing on the other side waiting for me, but a guard told him to move along and pointed to a door toward which other immigrants were headed, with happy faces and sprightly step.

"It's written on the passport! Of course it's written on the passport. Where else would it be written? *Your* name, too, is written on the passport, but we have to ask, understand. How do we know it's *your* passport? How old are you?"

"Sixteen."

"How old are you now, not two or three years hence?"

"I am sixteen now. It says so on the passport."

"We know what it says on the passport. You can have anything written in the passport in those Balkan countries."

"I am sixteen, even if I don't look it."

The two men exchanged a few words in English. The fat man seemed amused. His little eyes blinked, and a friendly smirk caused one side of his mouth to slant upward.

"How much money have you?"

I showed him the twenty-three dollars I had.

"Who gave you the money?"

"My father."

"Then your father is not in this country."

"No, I am going to live with my uncle in St. Louis."

"Is this uncle your father's brother?"

"He is married to my father's sister."

"Is this uncle working?"

"He works at the Terminal."

"How do you know?"

"He wrote to us. He knows I am coming. Here is his name and address."

The two men held a brief conversation in English. The fat man looked at me, his eyes mere slits behind folds of flesh. He said something to me in English, and I looked at the other man for a translation of what the fat man said, but he did not translate. He handed me my passport. "All right, you may go. You are now in America. And don't be so smart."

I ran for the door into which Nichola had disappeared. He was waiting for me just inside the door, in a large room filled with immigrants who had passed the inspection. There were cheers and joy in this spacious room, and a babel of languages, and smiles, and hand-shaking—rich ore for the capacious crucible, for the giant melting pot.

"Them inspectors! Can you count? What do they think we are? Count backwards. Jackasses."

"It wasn't so bad, Uncle Nichola. Wasn't as bad as we feared it would be."

"Anyway, we are in America now. Or are we? Aren't we still on the Island?"

"Yes, Uncle Nichola, but the Island is in America."

"Wouldn't it be something if they turned Gurkin back?"

But Gurkin and the others came striding in at intervals, one at a time, all smiles and giggles. We heard of how some were detained, possibly for further examination, possibly to be turned back, but none of us suffered that, and there was general rejoicing. Even Nichola and Gurkin shook hands.

For us it was all over. But was it? For presently a man in a khaki uniform came along and asked to see our papers, the places in America to which we were going, names, addresses. After he examined the papers he tied tags to the lapels of our coats. We were mystified about this until Gurkin once again contributed his knowledge. On the tag was written the city to which one was going and the train he was to be put on. This was because many people, Gurkin explained, not knowing the language or anything about America, took the wrong train and found themselves hundreds of miles from their destinations. Gurkin spoke of it with approbation, but Nichola insisted that it was undignified to treat human beings like that, labeling us as though we were pieces of baggage. Now that the terrifying inspectors were behind us and we were in America, Nichola availed himself of the freedom of speech. At least they didn't brand us, said Nichola, like sheep.

In the midst of this another man, again in uniform, also asked to see our papers, but this one demanded money, fifty cents from each of us. Some of us demurred, fearing that we poor immigrants were being bilked by some unscrupulous American disguised as an official in uniform.

"It's for telegrams to Santo Louis to tell them we have arrived and have passed inspection."

"Hei! hei!" exclaimed Nichola. "Here we have just barely set foot in America and already we are doing business with the telegram companies."

Still another man, this one in a white jacket, came wheeling a small hand truck loaded with square paper boxes. To everyone of us he handed a box without saying a word and stuck up his index finger. Gurkin forked out a dollar before you could say amen, that being the signal for the rest of us to do likewise.

"What's it for now?" Nichola demanded. "We came here to earn money and they are taking from us what we brought from the old

139

country." But feeling the weight of the box, he said, "It's most likely food for our journey to Santo Louis."

"Of course it's food, and you'll need it on the train. Don't open it here," Gurkin counseled.

Nichola opened his moneybag for the man to help himself to a dollar.

Shortly after we were ferried to a railroad station on the shore opposite the big city and were put on a train. It was the Wabash, said Gurkin. He pronounced it "Vabash."

The coaches, unlike those in Europe with doors along the sides, had entrances at either end, and then you walked through an aisle with double seats on either side.

"This looks like first class. We must be in the wrong car," said Nichola, observing the luxurious plush seats. We were used to the hard wooden benches on the European trains.

"There's no classes here. Everybody pays the same and everybody rides the same way," explained Gurkin, innocent of Pullmans.

Nichola and I sat together, myself near the window. "I like this," said Nichola. "I guess maybe this is a good country. Them inspectors!" We opened the dollar paper boxes and were delighted on discovering the wisdom of that arbitrary sale. We explored the contents with the anticipation of children and thanked the Americans for their foresight and generosity. The cartons were packed with food, sufficient to last us the two days and nights on the trains to St. Louis. We were like children unwrapping Christmas presents and were rewarded with many surprises. Out of neat tissue-paper wrappings emerged slices of white bread enclosing slices of yellow cheese, ham, salami, bologna. We had never seen anything like that —slices of cheese and sausages between slices of bread.

"They're sandwiches," said Gurkin.

Nichola would have preferred a loaf of bread and hunks of cheese and a sausage you could bite into as you would a cucumber, but he was pleased nonetheless. He twisted a cheese sandwich into a roll and stuffed half of it into his mouth. He rummaged deeper into the carton and was rewarded with a variety of delicacies. I do not know to this day whether these food boxes were a profitable business on the part of some enterprising caterer or were the undertaking of some philanthropic women's organization, for the price we paid was nominal. There were oranges, apples, pieces of cake, an apple pie neatly fitted in a paper plate. Blissfully Nichola regarded the pie, never before having seen this typical product of the American kitchen, which was to become an important component of our new diet. We ate the pie without a fork, the way we ate the sandwiches. Toward the bottom of the box we came upon some

140

strange-looking things that looked like thin cucumbers with smooth yellow skins. Nichola stared at one and then with a twinkle in his eye he held it out toward Gurkin. Gurkin gave his mustache a twist to hide his blush and informed Nichola and the rest of us that they were bananas, an inexpensive, nourishing fruit that was to become an indispensable item of the lunchbox.

But I was hungrier for the sight of America than for the food, and I kept my face to the window to watch the new country unfold before my eyes. The train sped past flat country dotted with factories with high smokestacks. In our school we used the Cyrillic alphabet, but in my last year in school we had studied French and I was able to read writings in the Latin alphabet without knowing what they meant. I thought of Grandfather, who could not see, but here I was with eyes to see but not knowing what I was seeing. I was a blind man with good vision, seeing things and not knowing what they were.

Nichola nudged me and pointed to a little bag of peanuts in my lap, which a lad with a tray strapped to his waist had placed in the lap of every one of us. "Don't touch it," warned Nichola. "They don't give things here for nothing. The fellow will soon be back to collect for it." The peanuts reposed innocently in our laps. I kept looking out the window at America, the country flying back as the train roared ahead, the locomotive blasting prolonged, piercing whistles, unlike the timid toots of European trains.

The peanut man came by again, but instead of picking up the little bags, as we expected, he deposited larger ones in our laps.

"Maybe it's a gift from the railroad company. What do you think?"

"They are probably samples, Uncle Nichola."

Gurkin couldn't help us this time. He was as baffled as we were.

Presently the young man came back and without saying a word picked up the larger packages but did not touch the smaller ones. Nichola scratched his neck and inclined his head inquisitively. What could be the meaning of this? "I think the little one's a sample and the big one was for sale. But who knows? There may be a catch in this somewhere. He is not doing this just for exercise. Better not touch it yet."

In a little while the young man came around again and dropped chocolate bars in our laps but did not pick up the peanut samples. Thereafter he went up and down the aisle and spoke words that we did not understand, but he placed no more objects in our laps. Finally he picked up the chocolate bars.

The train roared ahead across interminable stretches of country. It rumbled over iron bridges spanning lazy, swelling rivers the names of which we did not know. It stopped at small and big stations and clattered through large and small cities the names of which Gurkin did not know either. We reached mountain regions where the train snaked through narrow valleys and bored through tunnels again to come into open country for long stretches of undulating, hilly land. The cities through which we passed were for the most part shut from view by warehouses, factories, countless passenger and freight cars parked in interminable sidings, and by dilapidated brick or frame houses with their grimy backs toward the tracks. All I knew was that we were in America, but where exactly and what regions we were traversing none of us knew. At night sometimes we passed through cities or the outskirts of cities or it may have been just industrial areas where the sky was red and the atmosphere ablaze from the flames that leaped out of windows, smokestacks, or other openings of what, for all we knew, must have been foundries and steel mills. The flames cast coppery reflections on glistening, slimy rivers on which floated squat, bulgy steamships and long barges towed by tugs.

"*Ei, ei,* little one, what have we come to? Why didn't Gurkin and the others say something of this America?"

"It can't be all like this, Uncle Nichola."

And it wasn't. On the second morning the sun shone on endless stretches of flat open farmland with here and there clusters of trees. I wondered about the land itself, the magnitude of America, the cities, the mountains, the iron bridges that spanned the broad rivers, the people who built the gleaming white farmhouses and the cupolaed cathedrallike red barns with the adjoining round towers painted the same deep-red color. I wondered even more how Gurkin and the others who preceded us had ever found their way through this endless land. All this stunned us—the expanse, the cities, the mountains, the rivers, the disklike land rolling away interminably without a ridge or hillock to interrupt the view. The people, too, those we saw at stations where the train stopped—the conductors and other trainmen who changed at intervals even though we did not change except once in a big city that Gurkin said was Chinchinnati—were a constant source of wonder and amazement. Well-fed people these, well dressed and lighter of complexion and nearly all, young and old, with shaven lips.

"My God, they all look like grandmothers, and they aren't ashamed either," said Nichola. In the old country a pair of well-groomed mustaches was a prize possession. Men there swore by their mustaches, and when they did that they were believed as if they had sworn by their lives. Nobody ever shaved one's head, and if one had, there would have been nothing shameful about it; but

142

the mustaches, one would no more dream of shaving his mustaches than a woman would of shearing her hair. In fact a woman caught in an act of infidelity would be publicly disgraced by an enforced shearing of her hair.

"How much farther is it to Santo Louis?" Nichola inquired of Gurkin. "Is Santo Louis at the end of America? Or is there no end to this America?"

"If we keep on going for months we'd be back home," said Gurkin.

"Without turning back?"

"Without turning back."

"What do you think? Do you think that could be?" Nichola's voice and eyes were full of distrust.

"I think that's possible, Uncle Nichola. We may not strike exactly home, but we would be near."

"Does it say so in the books?"

"Yes."

"But why, how?"

"Because the earth is round, like a ball, and if you start at one point and keep on going and going you will come to where you started from, or nearby."

Nichola shook his head in wonderment. I could see he just could not believe it.

Sympathizing with my friend, I myself suffered because of my own ignorance. I didn't know where we were, what the names were of the cities through which we passed, the names of the rivers and the mountains, how much farther it was to St. Louis, where St. Louis was, at the far end of America or in the center of it. I would know this land, I would know its cities and its hamlets and the rivers and the mountains and where the rivers started from and where they emptied and what their names were; I would know the lakes, too, and the names of all the states, and I would learn the language the people spoke and in which the books and the newspapers were written and maybe, too, I myself would write books in that language; and I would get to know these people and become one of them, and more than that, I would know not only the living but the dead ones. I would go back into the history of this nation and learn who the founders were; I would not go back to Macedonia and be a subject of the bloody Abdul Hamid or any other sultan. And the train pierced the air with its steam whistle and the car wheels clattered on the rails and a lot of America rolled back and more of it opened up ahead. I would embrace this land, I would master the language and would find out who wrote its books, who made its laws, who its poets and philosophers were. I would be a part of this

143

country, of this nation, even if no more than a pebble or a grain of sand. My birthplace is a province of the Ottoman Empire, and that is not my country. America is a country meant for people like me, especially people like me with a birthplace and a mother tongue but without a country, without a native government, a subject people ruled by foreign tyrants and autocrats. I would adopt this country and this nation, or this country and this nation would adopt me so I would be an integral part of this land. Even as the train rolled ahead I could feel the land enter my being, the broad swelling rivers flowing through me, the horizons ever retreating and never closing in, never confining the land. The land itself was not confined with delimiting rock walls or hedges into tiny fields, only the horizon or a riverbank fringed with old willows interrupting the view. The land was not worn out and divided and subdivided into rock-walled enclosures, the towns or villages on it wide apart and hugging the land, sighted from the train and detected only because of steeples or those immense metallic globes mounted on steel towers. Who built these tracks and these trains? How was it that once we had passed the hurdles of the Island nobody asked to see our passports, no gendarmes or soldiers walked up and down the aisle to glare at us?

3

After two days and a night we came to the biggest river we had yet seen, the mighty Mississippi, and the longest bridge, at the other end of which was St. Louis. With our odd-shaped old country valises and bundles we marched down Market Street, Gurkin leading the way. This was the first American street we had set foot on and it lived up to expectations. It was lit up with *elektrichestvo*. The light of the street lamps fell on us; the people on the sidewalks stared at us. I wished Gurkin would turn into a less lighted street, but he marched on, unaware of my sensitiveness and apparently indifferent to our being exposed to the stares of the passersby.

A trolley clanged impatiently to a horse-drawn wagon limping along in front of it. We trudged on for some fifteen blocks and came to Broadway, the city's principal business street at that time. Here we turned south and trudged for three or four blocks until we were stopped by two bars with red lamps hanging from them. We set down our burdens to rest our arms and waited for the bars to open. Presently we heard a bell ringing and then with a kind of volcanic groan a locomotive came blasting through the darkness, its big round eye blinding us for a moment. Boxcars, flatcars, gondola-shaped coal cars rolled past us and plunged ahead into the darkness. When the last car with its two blinking red lights disappeared and the barriers were lifted we turned east and followed the track over which the train had just passed. We walked in the track for three blocks and came to Second Street, the Bulgarian immigrant colony in St. Louis. The Mississippi was only a block away, but view of it was impeded by elevated railway tracks. Second Street on both sides for a block north of Poplar and a block south was lined with coffeehouses, poolrooms, restaurants, bakery shops, saloons, grocery stores, a bookstore, all operated by Bulgarians from Macedonia. All this I was yet to learn, but now we walked a block south on Second Street to Plum Street, a short street that started at the river and ended blind at Fourth Street. It was a dark, dreary street, lit only by weak lights reflected from the two-story brick houses with stoops, on some of which sat lone women, wrapped in shawls and silent as ghosts. From a saloon on the opposite corner came the sounds of a player piano making a feeble effort to dispel the gloom. Halfway up the block, on the north side, Gurkin and I came to No. 27, my uncle's address. Nichola had gone into the coffeehouse with the others. I was not to see my friend again for many weeks. His brother-in-law, who had been warned of his coming by that telegram from the "Island," was waiting for him to take him back across the river to East St. Louis.

"Well, this is where your uncle lives," said Gurkin. "On the top floor. You go through the hall to the yard in back and up the stairs to the balcony."

The hallway had no doors in front or rear. The wooden stairway led to a decklike porch, and the only entrance to the flat was from the porch. I was halfway up the creaky stairway when I heard familiar native words. The door was open, and a cousin of mine named Andro rushed over and took my valise and embraced me. It was a two-room flat, half-lighted by a kerosene lamp hanging on the wall. My uncle was not in and I was told that he worked nights. There were six men in the flat now. They all worked *daytime,* as they put it, sharing six cots with a like number of men who worked *nighttime.* All the twelve men occupying the two-room flat were from my own village. The iron cots, placed lengthwise along the walls in the farther room overlooking the street, were never given a rest or an airing. There were no bed sheets, and the blankets and comfortables were so grimy with the coal dust, oil and grease from the roundhouses that they looked like tarpaulins. For a week I had to sleep on the floor, as my uncle's bed was slept in by one of the six men working days. Fortunately one of them was to leave for the old country within the week, and my uncle had arranged for me to take his place as one of the twelve occupants of the flat. And this was no easy matter. Living here was like living in a *zadruga,* or cooperative, presided over with seignorial authority by a middle-aged man named Shano who had to be consulted about everything. The flat had the reputation as the best-managed quarters in the colony and the one most difficult to become a resident of. Thanks to my uncle, I was to have the privilege of living in this exclusive establishment.

There was no running water or sink or drain in the kitchen, and water had to be brought up in buckets from a tap in the yard at the foot of the stairway and the dishes washed in pans on the porch. The

146

whole arrangement, or pattern of living here, had something transitory or impermanent about it. It was more like being "on location," a kind of on-the-job indoor camping, the object being to work long hours and live as inexpensively as possible in order to return to the old country with as much money as possible. The rent was six dollars a month, or fifty cents per month per occupant. Board, which included two meals a day, never exceeded four dollars a month per occupant. Pork chops were seven cents a pound; a round loaf of bread baked by Macedonians nearby was a nickel; a quart can of draft beer to carry from Fritz's saloon at the corner was also a nickel. Pay at the roundhouses was ten cents an hour, or one dollar and twenty cents a day or night, Sundays included.

As I say, the only entrance to the flat was from the porch, and the room it opened on was kitchen and living room. In the center of this room reposed a large round table, shiny with the drippings of many greasy stews and stained with the soot of kettles. Near it was a coal stove, a piece of junk crouching on four bandy legs that terminated into cat's-paws gripping the floor. The stove was not cylindrical like the stoves I was familiar with but squat and bulgy. It sat there "scrooching," like old women in marketplaces with trays in their laps selling herbs. The stove had a door, but it also had two openings at the top, now covered with lids. Farther out, close to the wall, there was another stove, a two-burner kerosene stove for heating water or cooking stews in hot weather.

In a corner, near a heap of coal on the floor (not in a bin), a galvanized oilcan aimed its beaklike spout to a place on the wall where twelve white coffee mugs hung by their handles on tenpenny nails driven into the wall. The cups were arranged in two horizontal parallel rows and appeared to me like twelve white pigeons in flight from the oilcan-hawk that was making ready to soar after them. To one side of the cups, as though to lend reality to my fancy, was the only cheerful object in the grim interior. It was a Coca-Cola calendar, a color print of lush green meadows, tall trees, a blue sky, and in the foreground a goddesslike young woman sipping the brown beverage with the aid of a straw. After glancing over kettles and pans hanging on the walls with their sooty bottoms facing the room, or the wooden shelf on which the dishes were stacked, my eyes time and again reverted to the calendar on the wall.

My study of the depressing interior was interrupted by something that was said about me. One of the men said bluntly that my coming to America was a mistake. "He's too young, *brei*, too young. It will be hard for him to get a job. In another year or two, maybe, he should have come." It was Shano, the flat's major-domo, who made this pronouncement.

The time was December, and there was fire in the truncated

147

potbellied stove. One of the men removed a lid and placed over the opening a coffeepot, which he filled with a dipper from the pail on the floor. Then from a cupboard he brought out a round loaf of white bread and some white cheese and black olives and put them on the table.

"Are jobs scarce?" I asked timidly.

"Oh, there's jobs for them that's able and willing to work," snarled Shano. There was a note of bitterness or injury in his voice. "America! America!" he grumbled. "Here it is. Why aren't they working? Why do they sloth and sour in the coffeehouses preaching *tsutsulismo* and *kummunismo.*" I had no idea what the strange words meant and was unable to divine whether the remarks were meant for my benefit or whether this was a grudge against America.

"All I can make out is the *kummunisti* and *tsutsulisti* want to take from the rich their money and possessions and divide them." Then Shano looked straight at me as if he were instructing me and exclaimed, "And who do you suppose is the *bash-tsutsulist* [head Socialist]? Well, it's Mango, the same that was a hod carrier for me in the old country. Now he sits for hours in the coffeehouses and babbles *tsutsulismo.* You should hear him. 'Exploitation!' 'Means of production.' 'The fruit of our labor!' 'A new day has dawned!' He mouths words he doesn't understand. This new day should open his eyes and give him some light so the *tembel* [loafer] can see beyond his dirty nose. 'Intelligentsia,' they call themselves. Hod carriers and pig herders suddenly turned into 'intelligentsia,' whatever that means. They refuse to work for the rich for a dollar and a half a day when they produce twenty. They don't know how to hit a nail on the head or lay a brick straight."

The strong aroma of the coffee mingled with Shano's vehemence. The man who attended to the making of the coffee took cups from their nails on the wall and set them on the table. He poured the coffee through a strainer, filling each cup to the brim. No one helped him; all the rest sat around to be waited on by this one man. I was soon to learn that the six men did the kitchen chores in rotation, each doing the cooking, serving, dishwashing every sixth day. This arrangement prevailed also among the day occupants of the flat, and I myself fell into it, combining my day with that of my uncle, who did the cooking and left everything else to me.

While we ate white bread and cheese, washing it down with black coffee, some other countrymen from neighboring flats dropped in. I studied them with avid eyes. All of them looked as if they had been playing mummers and hadn't done a good job of washing away the lampblack. They were sooty, stained like the table and

148

everything else in the place. The hard economy they practiced, the bad diet, mostly starch, had imprinted themselves on their faces. All of them wore blue work shirts with pockets at the breasts in which those who smoked kept little sacks of tobacco. From the mouths of the tobacco sacks, which had the picture of a bull on them, dangled strings with a paper medallion at the end. To me the medallion appeared like an order, like a badge of Americanism, of which the wearer seemed to be conscious, for as he moved his torso the medallion swayed, and this swaying, or the effect of it, was not lost to the wearer. I could almost hear the men say to me, as I observed every gesture and every expression on the face, "Ah, well, this is nothing, only a trifle. There's things and things we know. You are a greenhorn."

I was in America now, and my young mind and my eyes missed nothing. The making of a cigarette was a ritual I observed closely. A man would take the little sack with the picture of the bull from the shirt pocket, open it dexterously, bite the string, and let the sack dangle at his breast. Then he would peel off a cigarette paper, pinch the paper between the thumb and forefinger, and with the right hand shake a quantity of the loose tobacco from the sack, measuring it like an apothecary measuring powdered medicine. Holding the unrolled cigarette, the man, still biting one end of the string, would draw away the sack until it closed, and then he would replace the sack in the pocket in such a way that the medallion would remain outside to dangle at the breast. When all this was performed, both hands would engage in the rolling of the cigarette, which, though done exactly as in the old country, still seemed to have acquired certain American manipulations.

All of these people I knew, some well, some not so well. I knew their families and their relations in the old country. They had been through the initiation ritual in America, and they were not over-looking the opportunity of playing the sophisticates. In speech, in posturing, in gestures, in saying "yes" instead of *"da,"* "no" instead of *"né,"* in wagging the head sidewise for "no" and moving it up and down for "yes," in all sorts of other mannerisms of speech and body, they bespoke America. At least it so appeared to me at the time.

149

4

My uncle Tanas immediately assumed a protective, paternal attitude toward me. On the day following my arrival he lost some sleep to take me to a secondhand store in South Broadway to buy me work clothes. For a few dollars we bought blue overalls, a denim jacket, a blue shirt, a turtleneck cotton sweater, a black canvas cap with a shiny visor, a pair of work shoes, and cotton gloves and socks. And I was now ready to look for the job that Shano said it would be hard for me to find. Nearly all of my villagers worked in roundhouses. The roundhouses near the Union Station, which at that time was the pride of America, were the largest in St. Louis and were exclusively in the hands of immigrants from my village. Working here was known as working at the Terminal, and the Terminal was a sort of caravanserai where railroads that used the Union Station "stabled" their locomotives. Here the engines were fire-knocked, wiped, repaired, refueled, and otherwise put in shape for their new trips. For years, passing jobs from one to another (as one would leave for the old country and another would arrive), erstwhile plowmen and shepherds, or craftsmen who abandoned their crafts for better pay in America, cleaned the noses of groaning locomotives, emptied carloads of ashes from their cylindrical bellies, stuffed their yawning jaws with coal, filled their tanks with water. The peasants fondled the mechanical monsters as though they were oxen that helped them plow their fields. And the jobs at the Terminal were at a premium, as hard to get as pashaships in the Ottoman Empire. Frank, the foreman, a vile-tempered Irishman who cursed the hell out of the "goddam Dagos," was the most important personage in America. He took bribes for the coveted jobs he handed out.

My uncle did not work at the Terminal but in a roundhouse on

150

the eastern, the Illinois, bank of the Mississippi. The shop was directly across Plum Street, which ran down to the river a block and a half from the flat. Morning and evening my uncle crossed the river on the Poplar Street ferry. He was on the job twelve hours and was paid twelve cents an hour. In a year of nights, Sunday nights included, this came to quite a sum if the share of the rent at the flat was fifty cents for the month and the share for the bread and the groceries never more than four dollars. In two years this kind of hard work and hard economy made it possible for one to go back to the old country and live there like a vizier. One of Uncle Tanas's favorite sayings was "Live like a miser in America that you may live like a vizier in the old country."

One wasted no time after arrival in America in looking for a job. The first place a newcomer looked for a job, unless one already had been secured for him at the Terminal, was the Carshop. Nearly everybody had worked at the Carshop at one time or another. In a way it was another "Island," a kind of purgatory one had to go through before graduating to higher spheres, like the can factory, or the Sunlight Shoe factory on South Seventh Street. There were many jokes about the Carshop. Those who had worked there and had been lucky enough to be graduated to fire-knocking, engine-wiping, table-turning jobs at the Terminal made fun of the green-horns by asking questions in English to which they themselves supplied the answers.

"Ver you vork?"
"Carshop."
"Ou old you?"
"Carshop."
"Ver you leev?"
"Carshop."

On Monday morning I rose at five o'clock to go to the Carshop. Some young men from my village who worked there while they waited for opportunities to open up at the roundhouses were my guides. We had to start walking at six o'clock; work at the Carshop began at seven. There was a trolley on Broadway that could take one to the Carshop in fifteen or twenty minutes, but it cost a nickel, and we walked the twenty blocks to save that nickel.

I put on my work clothes and wrapped my lunch in newspaper —two fried-egg sandwiches and a banana. The men at the flat said that I looked like a locomotive engineer in my overalls and black canvas cap with the shiny visor. As we started walking down Second Street it was still dark, and I was depressed because Nichola had gone to East St. Louis to work in the packinghouses. We had parted in Paskal's coffeehouse on Second Street. Nichola was confused and

151

worried and acted like a man who had broken his eyeglasses, and I felt bad because I couldn't write his letters to his wife and attend to such other chores as an illiterate person cannot attend to himself. But I too now needed guidance and direction, and one of the young fellows—his name was Daniel but he called himself Dan now— took me under his wing and said not to worry; he would try to get me into the shop and talk to the foreman because they might reject me at the employment office on account of my age.

Men in working clothes with lunch pails or lunch packages issued from dark, dreary houses along Second Street or from the side streets, and we all trooped down the middle of the street, as there were no tramways here and no other traffic except an occasional horse-drawn wagon delivering milk or bread.

Dawn was breaking by the time we reached the plant. Streams of workers discharged by the Broadway trolleys poured into the gate and were swallowed by the complex of shops. Long sheds of corrugated steel or iron, their pitched roofs surmounted by tall smokestacks guyed by wires, extended for blocks along the bank of the Mississippi. A sign over the gate read AMERICAN CAR AND FOUNDRY. There was no Carshop sign.

Dan handed our lunch packages to our friends, and we detached ourselves from the mass of workers that poured like a dark river into the wide gate.

"You just follow me," said Dan.

We crawled under freight cars, squeezed between piles of lumber, climbed over rows of axles and wheels, clambered over wire fences, and finally through a side door, opened to us from the inside by one of our fellows, we entered an immense barnlike shed. I felt as though I had been transported into a nether region and began to yearn for the grimy flat on Plum Street, which in contrast to all this took on the attributes of a comforting home.

"You just stay here and wait," said Dan. He busied himself with his task, although the seven-o'clock whistle had not yet blown.

The whole plant hovered with activity preliminary to beginning operations at seven. From one end to the other of the long shed ran tracks on which stood skeletons of freight cars in process of construction. In the lanes, between the tracks, at intervals along the whole length, were small ovens with their mouths opening onto the tracks. Young men in tattered clothing and bare arms shoveled rivets into these ovens. With long iron tongs they stirred the rivets, causing sparks to sputter about the mouths of the ovens. Hammermen and their helpers were climbing over the half-completed cars and putting on their goggles. People stirred throughout, testing tools, putting on mittens, girding themselves, as though once work

152

started there would not be time to tie one's shoestrings. The rivet-boys stood at the mouths of the roaring ovens, tongs in hands, like sentinels at the entrances of some infernal caves. Everybody seemed to be conscious of the few remaining minutes before the whistle. Workers looked at their watches, did things it would be too late to do afterward, like making certain their goggles were wiped or their fly buttons were securely fastened. Once the whistle blew, I thought, normal life would be suspended until the end of the day.

When the whistle sounded the whole crowded interior plunged into instantaneous operation, as though a single machine had been set in motion. Beneath the peaked roof cranes moved on iron beams, dangling pieces of steel and setting them down on the car skeletons, where they were fitted into their appointed places and riveted by the goggled hammermen. The rivet-boys thrust their tongs into the flaming jaws of the ovens, clamped white-hot rivets, and tossed them onto the cars. They picked the rivets with amazing speed and tossed them with such dexterity, with such unfailing precision, that rarely did a rivet, flashing like the tail of a falling star in the tortured air, fall but at its intended place, where a man clasped it with a pair of pincers and fitted it in a hole for the air hammer to pound the other end of it into a button.

The rattling hammers made a deafening racket. I held my palms to my ears to keep my eardrums from bursting. No one spoke; all communication was carried on by signs. With their fingers the hammermen indicated to the rivet-boys the sizes of rivets they wished tossed out to them. Human beings were deprived of their God-given voices; demoniac noise, generated and sustained by human energy, had subjugated man.

There was no cessation. Wheels and axles came rolling in, and as they were pushed ahead, the cranes thrust their monstrous arms and placed on them beams and girders and braces that were riveted at various points on the way. When certain operations were performed before one oven, the skeleton was pushed on by man power to the next oven and the next, until the axles and wheels introduced at one end of the shop left the other as boxcars ready for the carpenters and painters.

No one paid any attention to me. Once only Dan, who tended the nearby furnace, patted me on the shoulder between thrusts of the tongs into the flames. I stood there clutching my lunch package and gazing at the infernal scene. In my overalls and jacket, my secondhand shoes, the cotton mittens on my hands, the black canvas cap with the shiny visor pulled over my forehead, I must have looked like a miniature model of a working man.

But I was still capable of thoughts, thoughts of how my friends

153

earned one dollar a day, how they rose at five o'clock in the morning, walked the twenty blocks to the shop, and then for ten hours reached with the tongs into the flames for that dollar.

Why had not Gurkin said anything about this? Why hadn't the others after him spoken of it? Was the whole thing a deception? All those legends about America? Was this how money was earned in the New World?

I began to visualize hours of the inferno, days of it, weeks, months! And I became seized with terror. I felt as though life had ended for me. There stretched before me an endless chain of hellish days. I saw myself reaching with the tongs into the flames, thousands, millions of times, to pull out enough pennies to take me back to the old country.

Then something strange happened. I suddenly found myself in the street, outside the shop, just as I was, with my lunch package under my arm. To this day I do not know how I got out, whether I miraculously retraced my way through the jungle of iron and lumber in the yards or whether I found my way out through the gate. Nor do I know what exactly caused me to run out of the place.

I stood in the street and my first sensation was one of relief and triumph, as though I had escaped from some terrible danger. I still was terror-struck, however, and I instinctively hurried up Second Street. I was halfway up, near the Gashouse, before I was really myself again. Here I stopped, turned off into an empty lot, and sat down on a heap of earth. I was overcome with a sense of self-pity and burst into tears.

The sun was up now, and I was warm in my cotton sweater and denim jacket. I felt lonely and dejected. It never occurred to me to attribute my action to my youth or to the fact that I had all too rapidly been thrown from an idyllic Balkan scene into an industrial jungle. I felt only that my father had been right, that the whole thing was a mistake. But it was too late now; I must go through this to earn enough money to pay for my trip back. For an instant I considered the possibility of walking back to the Carshop, but the vision of it caused me to shudder and filled me with fright.

I rose and walked a few more blocks north on Second Street. It occurred to me that the night shift at the flat did not go to sleep until about ten o'clock, and as I did not wish to be questioned, I turned east and came to the bank of the Mississippi. I had heard from the returned "Americans" that the Mississippi flowed upward, and I had imagined a river rushing up a hill. But the river was so calm and unruffled it was hard to detect in which direction it flowed. I fastened my eyes on a floating log and by watching its motion perceived the current, which was in the direction of the Carshop.

I sat on a log on the cobbled bank and looked at the great river spread before me in all its calm majesty. On the smooth yellowish surface floated ferries and barges, the latter laden with crates and boxes. Across from me, on the Illinois side, engines puffed huge fleeces of pale-blue smoke. Somewhere there where those engines coughed was the roundhouse in which my uncle worked. Farther on, to the north, smokestacks rose above the flat land. That was East St. Louis. There Nichola worked. Then all at once the scene took on a more familiar aspect, and I felt somewhat comforted.

The heaviness that had filled me gradually lifted, and a sense of intimacy with the scene, an element of friendliness, began to warm my heart. A barge heaped with crates and packing cases and towed by a fussing little tug caused a ripple in the river's surface and a wave splashed gently at the cobbled bank where I sat. From the bend to the south appeared a ship white as a dove and rearing high like a tower. The ship came serenely on, with an air of repose and dignity, and yet with jauntiness and bravado, like a romantic actor walking across the stage in a comic opera. If the ship had had a hat, I thought, it would have cocked it. There was something about the bravery of ships that I had understood when the courageous *Oceanic* had battled the waves of the Atlantic. The way that vessel had fought the elements and driven ahead through mounting waters was a miracle to us, who had never before seen a steamboat. I rose and returned to the flat. My uncle and the rest were asleep. I was careful not to wake them. I ate my lunch and went to Paskal's coffeehouse.

5

The tomato splashed at the nape of my neck. And it was rotten. The juice of it felt cold and clammy on my skin. I turned around quickly, and I saw a young face, younger than mine, leering at me from one of the doorless hallways that opened directly onto the sidewalk. My hand itched for a stone, and it could aim a stone well, but there were no stones here on a city pavement, so instead my hand went to my neck and wiped the mess there.

A man going in the opposite direction stared at me and made me conscious of the invectives in my own tongue bursting from my mouth like firecrackers. With clamped jaws and gnashed teeth I tried to suppress the tears. My eyes and nostrils smarted as if they were peppered, and I gulped some of the wrath that threatened to spill out in tears.

Crossing over to the next block, I became aware that my arm was pressing too hard against the lunch package, and I relaxed the pressure lest it should mash the two fried eggs and the banana neatly wrapped in newspaper and tied with string. The eggs, fried on both sides (an American way), were ensconced by slices of bread to make "sandwiches." Until I came to America I had never eaten eggs, or anything else, flattened like that between slices of bread —white bread.

As I kept walking I was on my guard, glancing back over my shoulder. I was like a dog that has wandered into a strange neighborhood. The sky was clear and the sun had risen above the flatness across the Mississippi River. There was a haze in the air, and black smoke was rising from the tall chimneys of the barnlike factories that flanked the nearby bank of the great river. The deep, prolonged siren of a steamboat was like a hand pulling at my heartstrings. The stench of a chemical plant across the street almost stopped my breathing. This was an utterly, radically different world I was in. Even the smells were different. I had never smelled such smells before.

I did not know where this world began and where it ended, where the center of it was, or if there was a center. I could find my way from the house where I lived to the can factory where I had found a job and to which I was now going. But where the house and the can factory were in relation to the rest of St. Louis I didn't know, or where St. Louis was in relation to other places in America, or what the other places were. I had no idea where America began and where it ended, what mountains rose athwart it, and what rivers ran across its face. On Sundays, and sometimes in the evenings before it got dark, I went down to the bank of the Mississippi to look at the mighty stream. But where it came from and where it went I didn't know.

I walked down the bleak street and my heart was full of sadness. The tears still welled in my eyes, and I did not know whether they were tears of lingering anger or of loneliness and remoteness. The can factory was still five or six blocks away.

Blocks! Already I knew the difference between a "block" and a "street." Ever since I set foot on American soil I had been asking questions. I was like a person learning a complicated trade, to whom some things have to be explained and some deduced by himself. And I was learning fast, from what was told me by the older immigrants and from intuition. I would find out about that tomato, too. Already I was beginning to perceive the wherefore of it. But I would ask Lambo just the same. Maybe Lambo, a young man from my own village, had had a like experience.

At the next corner I waited for a beer wagon to pass. The beer kegs piled high reminded me of the picture card some "American" had sent to the village. The picture showed a real American drinking beer from a keg balanced on his stomach, which was bigger than the keg and was a pictorial proof of the bounty that was supposed to be in America.

When the six horses, big as haystacks, with heads like tree stumps, their hoofs pounding on the cobbles, had hauled away their load of beer, I resumed my walk. The tomato still hurt. The rottenness of it hurt. If it had been a stone it would have hurt less. Vaguely I suspected that it was not just a youngster's prank, that there was a more profound reason for it. A new wave of anger surged through me, and again I had to clench my teeth and tense my face muscles to choke the tears that welled up.

I examined my clothing. Everything I had on was American—the blue overalls, the brown shoes that buttoned on the side, with their toes bulging up like fists, the jacket, the cap, the blue shirt with the breast pockets and attached collar. And look at the words I already knew—"sporty," "stylish," "block," "bluff," "two bits." They were not merely American words I had learned; they were new concepts to me. I knew nothing equivalent in my own language. I was not merely learning a new language; I was learning new things through the language, a new life. My free hand went into my coat pocket and fingered there the little metal hook I used to button my shoes with. I had acquired the knack of passing the hook through the buttonhole, catching hold of the button and with a deft twist causing it to pass through the hole. I looked at the single row of buttons, like beads, down the side of the shoe. I was not certain whether the shoes were "stylish," since I had seen some of the "sports" in Andon's coffeehouse wear shoes that laced.

Already my head was beginning to buzz like a hive with American words, and some of these words I could put together to make sentences. Listen:

"Vat kind peeple yoo?" I had learned that on the train that had brought me from New York to St. Louis.

"Vat yoo nem?" I looked around to see if anybody could hear me. Two black men were walking toward me, but they were a block away.

"Ao ol yoo?"

One of the two black men was laughing but not at me. He was just laughing, a deep, roaring laugh like thunder. On his trouser leg there was a slit that came up to the knee. The trouser leg flapped like a shirt. The man struck his thigh with the flat of his hand, and laughter poured out from his mouth like a torrent from a cavernous rock. The two black men passed on without even noticing me, so absorbed were they in whatever it was that had caused the one man to laugh so heartily.

At the entrance to the factory—a four-story brick building—I stopped to wait for Lambo. My eyes scanned the faces, looking for one with dissimilar sides, an upturned nose, and a broad but low forehead. A lame Greek youth who spoke English like an American and operated the punching machine next to me said, "Good morning." As he swung his lame foot on the steps he looked back and said, "Who you waiting for?" I did not answer, but in repeating the words to myself, as best I could, I had to contort my mouth, and the result sounded to me like half barking.

Then I saw the upturned nose sniffing the morning air. "Say, Lambo, a sanababetch hit me with a tomato."

Lambo's black canvas cap with its shiny visor was pushed back so that the mop of curly black hair could be seen straining down the

158

forehead to reach the eyebrows. The small eyes gleamed, and the right side of the face drew up. The other side seemed to be in a reverie. The words, like a pig's grunt, came from the nostrils. "Yeah, and a rotten one, wasn't it? A rotten one! Right in the neck, eh? But wait till you get an egg, a stinking one."

"Why?"

Both sides of the face grinned, causing a distortion. "Because you're a *Dago,* that's why!"

Lambo went downstairs to the galvanizing department. I climbed the two flights of stairs to the third floor, where the punching machines stood in rows like people at their morning prayer, with arms folded and heads bowed. An electric bulb in a wire cage, like an image lamp, hung before every machine.

When the whistle blew the whole floor went into instant action. The axles and the pulleys began to whir; the belts slapped at the wheels. I put my foot on the machine's treadle and my right hand started to feed the punch. So long as I kept my foot on the treadle the punch went up and down automatically, piercing holes in the pieces of metal and bending them so that they looked like ears. As the punch rose the pieces catapulted down a chute into a tub at the back. All I had to do was stand by with foot on the treadle and feed the machine.

My whole body was tuned to the machine's tempo and worked with a cadence begotten of the machine. At times I was oblivious of the machine and of my own function, which I could now perform with eyes closed. I would grab a handful of the flat metal pieces and my right hand would flip them into the mold beneath the punch one at a time. If I missed and the punch fell down unprovided for, nothing happened. I knew that, and my movements were casual and confident, but on the day I started work, when the foreman—by actual demonstration—had shown me how to operate the punch, I had thought that if the punch did not fall on a piece of metal something dreadful would happen, the machine would break down, or an explosion would occur. As the foreman, after demonstrating for several minutes, had stepped aside and I put my foot on the treadle, I began to work faster than the punch. What with watching for my fingers, and fearing the punch might fall down on an empty mold, I slipped in a piece before the preceding one had been cleared. The punch came down on both pieces, jamming them together. The machine rumbled and shook.

"Slower," said the foreman. "Take it easy. Watch me." He flipped the pieces casually, like tossing peanuts to a monkey. "See? No hurry." He stepped aside, watched me for several minutes, and walked away.

159

In a few days I was as good as the foreman. But the not knowing, not knowing the language, not knowing where I was in St. Louis and where St. Louis was in America, extended to the work I was doing. There was nothing intricate or difficult or important about the work. The machine did the work. I didn't even have to count the pieces the machine punched in an hour, or in a day, or in a week. The machine itself counted them, a meter at the top clicking numbers as the punch fell.

Toward the end of each day a man came along to check the number on the meter. At the end of the first week another man came by and asked me my name. He handed me a little envelope with my name written in pencil at the top of it. I opened the envelope and found eight dollars and three shiny quarters. I took this to be my pay. I had expected someone to come along with a bag of money and hand out to me what was coming to me. Instead, a man carried a tray strapped to his shoulders, and in it the envelopes were neatly arranged.

I liked very much the idea of the envelope. It was the first money I had earned in America, or anywhere, and it was a lot of money. With this much money I could buy a horse or a team of oxen in the old country.

At the end of another week the same man came by and handed me another envelope. This one contained nine dollars and some change. I deduced from this—I had to deduce a lot of things—that there was a connection between my pay and the number of pieces I had fed into the machine. And so my ken widened by yet another concept: *piecework*.

But what I still didn't know was what the ear-shaped metal pieces were called, where they came from, where they went, what eventual use they were put to, why I was punching holes in them.

The ten hours I was yoked to the machine, during which I hardly spoke a word and only heard the whirring of the wheels and the unvaried, rhythmic pounding of the machines, was a suspension of life, a kind of dehumanization. Of course it was bound up with the pay envelope. That little brown envelope represented six days of insulation from life. And it seemed to me I was paid not so much for doing any hard work—for it was not hard work—as for not living. In the old country work was a part of living. Work and life were inextricably bound up. There was a union between the doer and the thing done. When you pruned the vines you knew why you had to do it, and you could see the sap running from the eye of the slashed vine like tears from a human eye. When you swung the scythe in the meadow you heard the grass sigh as it fell in swaths at your feet. The scythe itself hissed like a snake as it devoured the

160

flowery grass. Whatever you did in the old country you understood. And there was an affinity between living and work, between the sweat of your brow and the tears of the vine, between your own breath and the earth's exhalation.

During the lunch hour on this day I sat on a window ledge munching my egg sandwich and "reading" the American newspaper in which the sandwiches had been wrapped. On little flat hand trucks, on window ledges, on sheets of tin, in corners, workers ate their lunches in silence. The machines were silent, the wheels and belts and axles at rest. I pored over the paper, staring at words of which I knew neither the meaning nor the pronunciation. The gulf between spelling and pronunciation was so wide I failed to recognize words I already knew by sound. Still I "read."

In four paragraphs of laborious reading I made out three words. This thrilled me. I felt as if the three words were the photographs of people I knew personally. And this tiniest ray of light, this spider-thread connection with the vast unknown that surrounded me, made me feel less alone. I kept poring over words, saying them in my mind over and over again, when I was startled by Lambo's voice.

"What's in the paper?" Lambo's words thrummed at his nostrils like the sounds of a guitar.

"Oh . . . er . . . I was just looking at the pictures."

Lambo's overalls and shirt were spangled with silver, dried to the fabric. "Come on down," he said. "I'll show you how I galvanize."

In the basement we walked between pillars of empty pails, fitted one into the other, bottoms up, and came to some huge caldrons along a wall, in which molten metal, the color of silver, bubbled and blistered continuously. With a pair of tongs Lambo clamped a pail and dipped it into one of the caldrons. When he pulled it out the bluish metal was no more and the whole pail glistened in its silver coating.

"That's all there's to it," said Lambo. "Now it's galvanized." He put the pail on a rack to dry.

I looked at the pail for several seconds and suddenly reached out to touch it, but remembering in time that it must be hot, I drew back my hand. "Look," I cried to Lambo, "this is what I punch!" I pointed to the ears at the top of the pail where the bale would go. "I punch the holes in them." I said this as if I had made an astonishing discovery.

"Didn't you know that?"

"No! We have pails like these at the flat, but I never noticed the ears on them. Just think, Lambo, I do that. I punch the holes. I help make these pails."

"Jiminy, the way you talk for just punching holes! What of it?"

"But now I know what I'm doing. I know why I punch the holes."

"It's still punching holes. What's so wonderful about punching holes?"

"All right, all right, it's nothing."

"Of course it's nothing. It's just holes."

But as I retraced my way between the pillars of pails I could see only the ears and the holes in the ears.

The six-o'clock whistle put an end to the whirring of the wheels and axles and the slapping of belts. The machines stood in silent rows. With my jacket over my arm I was walking up Second Street on my way home, but I kept feeding the machine with imaginary bucket ears. My body was tuned to the tempo of the machine, whose metallic clatter kept going in my brain. Crossing over into the block where in the morning I had been struck with the tomato, I began to smart under a fresh wave of anger, and my eyes went to the hallway whence the tomato had come. There was no one there now.

Just before reaching Plum Street I stopped for a minute to look in the window of an Assyrian coffeehouse. The narghile, the trays of baklava and Turkish delights, and the little copper coffeepots and tiny blue porcelain cups with gilt edges advertised a different world inside, a miniature Oriental world set up here to comfort the immigrants who spent their days in the factories.

Plum Street was alive with little black bodies in flowery dresses or patchy shirts and trousers playing ball in the street or skipping ropes. Older folk sat on the stoops or on benches or wooden boxes against the walls of the houses. The peculiar odor of the race, something new to me, permeated the warm air. Although now I had lived in their midst for some weeks and had seen them every day, I was still fascinated by their strangeness. I had always associated black-skinned people with folk tales, and this notion was still not entirely dissipated from my mind. The Negroes still seemed to belong to some world wholly unlike this one. A gigantic black woman was seated on a bench with her skirt about her like a tent. Clinging to her skirt, like an ornament, was a little girl of perhaps five or six, her kinky hair plaited in two braids that stuck out hornlike above her ears. As I passed by, a naked little arm, black as ebony, reached out and touched my coat. "Hello, mistuh man." The words were not words as such but sounds made by a musical instrument. With her large, wide-open eyes, perfect white teeth, thick lips, and chocolate skin so smooth it looked lacquered, the little girl seemed unearthly. The mother's black hand stroked the glistening hair.

"What yuh name, mistuh man?" the little mouth crooned.

One of the strange things about black people was that they spoke American. Somehow American and these black and brown folk did not go together. I had expected them to speak a language of their own, a black language, perhaps, as unlike American as they were from the Americans. That they were themselves Americans never occurred to me.

"My name's Alma Jane!" The great eyes blinked shyly and opened wider and brighter. The fleshy arms, naked from the shoulder, rubbed the flowers on the motley cotton dress, and the whole little body swayed coquettishly.

After the tomato I felt something dissolving within me and warming my heart. For a brief moment I wanted desperately to kneel down on the sidewalk and stretch out my arms to gather in this little folk-tale creature that seemed the most human and alive thing I had seen since I had left my village in the Balkans. "Goodbye, Alaama Jane," I said, waving.

A few houses up the street my eyes went to a first-floor window from which a middle-aged woman usually leaned out. She was there now, her bare arms folded in front of her and supporting her bosoms, partly exposed for such passersby as looked thither of their own free will and for such as did so at her own prompting. I had never rested my eyes on her long enough to know exactly what she looked like, but whether she was at the window or not I always smelled the perfume that exuded from the window. I had heard her tap at the windowpane or beckon to others, but never to me or to my uncle whenever I was with him. Catching me glancing at her now, she gave me an indifferent smile, and I quickly averted my eyes.

At the top landing now, I stood on the porch that extended the width of the house and looked down on the maze of backyards enclosed by the rears of houses and separated one from the other by board fences. Within them were piles of rusty tin cans, bottomless tubs and buckets, discarded stoves, and all kinds of other junk and refuse. In various corners stood the outhouses, like hen coops, and over all was a network of clotheslines. Nothing like this backyard scene had ever been part of my imaginings of America. In fact it contradicted the fantastic tales of the New World told by the returned "Americans"—those Columbuses of my village who had gone away in peasant garb and had returned decked out in fineries to fire the imaginations of some, like myself, and fill the hearts of others with discontent.

I entered the empty flat. My uncle and the other day occupants had already gone to the roundhouses, whence the nighttimers had not yet returned. I went over to the kerosene stove and lifted the lid from the pot there. The aroma had already told me it was lamb and cabbage stew for supper. I struck a match and lit the stove. The flame began to sputter, and soon the heat from it accentuated the odor of the cooked cabbage. That kerosene stove was the only item in the flat that came within the category of conveniences as described by the returned "Americans." The first night I spent in this flat I had looked in vain for the *elektrichestvo,* which would light a room by the mere pressing of a button and which you couldn't blow out no matter how hard you blew.

I sat down and removed my shoes and socks to air my feet, hot and aching from ten hours of stepping on the machine's pedal. My eyes wandered over the drab interior and alighted on a singular cheerful object, a new colorful grocery calendar with a beautiful girl gazing dreamily into nothingness and clutching to her heart a torn envelope, from which protruded the corner of a letter. At the bottom of the calendar were the words *absence makes the heart grow fonder.* I read the words many times, mispronouncing them, and recited them to myself, but *makes* was the only word I knew.

I heard the others coming up, their footsteps sounding heavy on the creaking steps. Presently they clumped in one at a time, their bodies drooped with labor. All five of them returned from the Terminal unwashed, just as they had worked, in their dirty overalls and jackets and the black canvas caps with the imitation patent-leather visors. There was something ghostly about them, their faces black with the coal dust and soot and grease, their teeth and the whites of their eyes glowing unnaturally. (They reminded me of the mummers on New Year's Eve who went from house to house in the village to stage a little play.) To dissolve the grime from their hands and faces they used a coarse slate-gray soap called Lava. The admixture of smoke, soot, coal dust, and grease had graven itself in the wrinkles, in the crow's-feet, in the seams of the foreheads and necks, and in the pores of the skin. Their eyelids were perpetually blackened, and around the eyes they seemed to have mascara, which made their eyes appear larger than they were and gave them a startled, cadaverous appearance.

Stephan, the oldest of the group, took his seat at the table and said, "Whose turn is it to go for beer?" He knew it was Kosta's, since he looked straight at him. Kosta, the youngest after me, was about twenty and had been in America more than a year. At first he had worked at the Carshop, later in a shoe factory, and now at the Terminal. Kosta took five beer buckets from a shelf and started out for Fritz's saloon at the corner.

"Tell that fat Swaba to fill them up with beer, not foam," Stephan grumbled.

I put on the table six spoons and sliced two loaves of white bread. That set the table. In the center of the table was a large white bowl into which Lazar, a tall, lean, dark man, poured the stew. Lazar had been a pack-saddle maker who had forsaken this ancient trade for the promise of America. He looked the ghostliest of the lot and seemed to drip with grease. He always complained of the grease at the Terminal.

To make up for the daytimers' cooking our suppers, we nighttimers did the housework, what there was of it. We swept the flat, filled the water pails at the tap down in the yard, washed the stewpot, and did other minor chores in the two-room flat. All those working at the Terminal shared not only beds but jobs as well. They worked twelve-hour shifts, one man taking up where another left off. There being no Sunday or holidays off, the two shifts were never at the flat at the same time. Though they lived together, they never saw one another at the flat but only at their jobs. My own presence on Sundays was no disturbance to this arrangement, since I ate my supper with my own crew, same as on a working day. And there was no conflict as to the bed, which I shared with my uncle, he occupying it in the daytime and I at night.

Kosta returned with the beer, and immediately everyone took his place at the table. Six spoons commenced journeys from bowl to mouth. Each spoon gathered shreds of cabbage and liquid from the common bowl and darted for the open mouth like a bird for its nest. Juice dribbled on the bare wooden table. A half slice of bread became a morsel; two spoonfuls of stew washed it down. No one spoke, everyone being intent on the business at hand. The six spoons plunged from six directions into the bowl. As they rummaged in the bowl for chunks of meat, they appeared to me like storks' beaks clamping frogs in the ponds. The spoons deposited the pieces of meat on slices of bread on the table, whence the fingers retrieved them and carried them on the second lap of the trip to the mouth. Every now and then the spoons were set on the board, and the hands would reach for the beer buckets on the floor. Holding the bucket with both hands, one swished down the beer with relish, wiping the foam with the back of the hand afterward.

The building trembled intermittently, the tremors being caused by the freight trains in the Poplar Street track, which bounded the block to the north, and by the passenger trains on the elevated tracks half a block south. The noise of the engines drowned the noise of the clattering spoons, which sometimes collided in the common bowl. The whistles of the passenger engines were as familiar to these Terminal workers as their own voices. They often made remarks about the engines as if they were real people. When now

165

a passenger train thundered past and split the air with its neigh, Lazar exclaimed, "Eee . . . there goes that Vandalia. The *putana*. Klement's waiting to knock her fire out."

Nobody acknowledged Lazar's remark, not by so much as a nod of a head or a gesture with a spoon.

Kosta was the first to rise. "I've got to hurry," he announced. "The bathhouse closes at ten."

I stood up, remembering the tomato. "I'll come too, Kosta."

Kosta tried to sidetrack the suggestion. "But I'm going with Vangel and Mirko."

"What of it? They don't own the bathhouse. It's public."

"All right, all right."

It was still daylight outdoors. A group of black boys had formed a ring in the street and were shooting dice for pennies. One of them tilted up his chin and rattled his thick lips like a colt. He blew at the dice, kissed them, spat on them, and then rolled them on the pavement.

Kosta looked angry. He acted like a big brother who had been forced to take along his younger brother.

Vangel and Mirko waited near their house at the corner of Third and Plum, in front of Fritz's saloon, from which the music of a player piano scattered ineffectual gaiety on the sidewalk. Vangel and Mirko wore their jackets over blue overalls, faded from too many washings. The peaks of their caps were pulled low over their foreheads, but the caps themselves were way back on their heads. Seeing me with Kosta, they muttered something through their teeth and started ahead.

The four of us, walking in pairs, turned south into Fourth Street. A few blocks down, Fourth Street lost itself into Broadway, like a smaller river joining a bigger one. On Broadway it was much livelier. There was a trolley line here and shops lined the street, mostly secondhand shops, with old suits dangling above the sidewalk, the pants stretched down like scarecrows. On benches against the walls were rows of made-over shoes, glossed to look like new. Better ones could be seen in glass cases or in the windows.

The public bath was on South Seventh Street, a red-brick building with wide cement steps facing a little park and playground. Vangel and Mirko walked in as though they owned the place. Inside, I followed Kosta through a corridor paved with green tiles, on either side of which were the shower baths, partitioned off like stalls. From the far end of the corridor came the voices of youngsters and the sounds of splashings in a pool. Kosta stopped before the first unoccupied shower and said, "You take this." He showed me how to turn on the water.

The water filtered through a sieve or strainer at the top, pattering dense drops on my shoulders and back. This was better than in the village, where sometimes during a downpour following a heat spell I would run out into the rain with other boys to play and sing. Here I could make it rain harder, or lighter, or cooler, or warmer. And I could throw out my chest and catch the rain on it. And for nothing. They really ought to charge a nickel, though. It was worth it. Funny, this America! It clumps you on the neck with a ripe tomato or a rotten egg and then gives you a free bath.

Without my having touched the taps the water turned hotter, and I jumped out of its path like a cat rebounding from something it had been playing with and discovering it could bite. For a minute I stood aside, then I put out my hand to test the water and it was all right. I went back in, standing still under the water, my arms down, my eyes closed. A thousand thin, gentle, tapering fingers patted my back and shoulders and kneaded my flesh. Hey, what a pleasure! The wonderful sensation penetrated into my body. Once again I arched my chest, and the sheaf of water drummed at it. It was wonderful, and it was all for nothing, absolutely for nothing. Ah, the pleasures there must be here in America in places where they charged.

To soap myself again, I shut off the water from an innate sense of economy. No use wasting hot water just because you don't pay. I was liberal with the soap, rubbing plenty of it all over my body. As I worked the lather something strange happened to me. For the first time in months, since long before I had left the village, I heard myself singing. The moment I became aware of it, however, I stopped, fearing I might be violating some rules. But the singing went on inside me. It was an old-country song about a nightingale that was so enamored of its song and sang so passionately its heart burst from its song.

"Hey, you ready?" Kosta was at the door.

"Wait for me, will you, Kosta?"

"We'll be outside. Hurry up."

Quickly I washed away the soap, dried myself, and put on the clean shirt I had brought along. No use taking a bath and putting sweaty clothes right back on.

I went through the corridor on wings, my whole body charged with new strength and vibrancy. I had an urge to soar out into space, and I felt clean, clean in my soul, clean in my voice. I felt so good I longed to embrace something, something clean and light and full of life, that felt the way I did.

"Just 'cause it's free you didn't have to stay there forever!"

This Kosta was an annoying fellow. He called himself Gus. And he started calling me Stan. He always had too much to say. In the next breath, however, he said, "To your health."

"And to yours!" I returned the benediction. Taking a bath certainly called for salutation. At the flat we all congratulated one another for such lesser rituals as a haircut.

It was dark now. On Broadway the street lamps were lit.

"It sure feels good after a bath," said Kosta.

Vangel and Mirko were walking ahead and talking in whispers. "What's the matter with them?"

Kosta shrugged. "Nothing I can see."

"You think there's people who come here every day?"

"Come where?"

"To the baths."

"Sure. And some go places where you pay."

"Pay! Why pay when it's free?"

"Listen. You don't know nothing." A trolley clanged to a wagon to get out of its tracks. "Them places where you pay you get more'n a bath."

"What more?"

"You get rubbed with creams and perfumes. Massaged all over. You lay on a bench. It feels so good you faint with the pleasure that comes to you."

"Who wants to faint?"

"A man died from the pleasure that came to him." His washed ears stuck out under the cap, the hair around them still damp.

"You been to places like that?"

"No, but I heard about 'em."

"You believe in that? About the perfuming and massaging?"

"Sure Mike."

I waited till we crossed to the next block and then I said, "It must cost a lot. To go to those places."

"Two dollars."

"Two dollars!"

"Yeah, but that's not the whole of it. There's more."

"For two dollars there ought to be more."

"There's more, all right."

"What more?"

"They trim your toenails."

"That don't seem so special. What pleasure can come to you from somebody trimming your toenails?"

"You ask too many questions. Besides, you don't understand nohow."

"What's there to understand?"

Vangel and Mirko had slowed down, and Kosta and I, engrossed

168

in our conversation, had passed them without saying a word to them.

On Fourth Street the lampposts were wider apart and it was darker than on Broadway.

"I'll tell you about it some other time," Kosta said.

"Tell me what?"

"About what you get in them places where you pay two dollars."

We walked in silence for half a block. Vangel and Mirko were a whole block behind us.

"Guess I'll tell you now anyway," Kosta said. "Un'erstand now, I never seen it with my own eyes and it never's been done to me. But it's women what does it to you."

"Does what?"

"The rubbin' and the massagin'."

"You believe that?"

"Sure."

A black going in the opposite direction was talking to himself. Listening to his unintelligible words, I had the feeling that the black was denying the truth of what Kosta was saying.

"What kind of women can they be?"

"Beautiful women. The most beautiful women that can be."

"And you're naked when they massage you?"

" 'Course. They're naked too."

My throat contracted. I swallowed and moistened my lips. "I'd be ashamed. I couldn't enjoy it."

"Listen, it feels so good a man died from the pleasure which came to him."

"You said that. But I don't believe it. People don't die from pleasure. People die from pain."

"No use telling you about such things."

"But everybody knows you die from pain. From pleasure . . . well, pleasure makes you laugh."

"All right. When somebody tickles you, you laugh, don't you?"

"Yeah."

"Why you laugh? Eh, why?"

"Because . . . well . . . because it tickles."

"Because it tickles! Of course because it tickles. But if somebody kept tickling you and you laughed and laughed and he didn't stop tickling you you'd die from laughing. You know that?"

"It seems like it can happen."

" 'Course it can. This man I been telling you about. Listen. He heard about them massagin' places and he begged some people to take him there. Un'erstand? Well, they did. And what happens? Two women comes to him and says to him if he pay four dollars

169

they'd both together at the same time with four hands make double pleasure come to him. One woman rubbin' here, the other massagin' there. The pleasure come to him too strong and too sweet. Next thing he wasn't breathing. It was too much for him. But it's wonderful to die like that. I hope I die like that when my time comes."

This Kosta sure was a smart fellow, making a thing like that sound like it could be true.

A birdlike sound from one of the low brick houses made our heads turn in that direction. From a dimly lit window on the first floor a woman was beckoning.

A few houses down, Kosta, who was walking on the inside, was almost tripped. A woman standing on the lowest step of a stoop flung her leg out before him. "Show you a good time, honey," she said in throaty English.

At the corner we stopped. Looking back down Fourth Street, we saw a man go into the house with the woman we had just passed but could see neither Vangel nor Mirko in the semidarkness. "What happened to them?" I asked.

"Oh, they're all right. Listen. I gotta go somewhere. If they're still up at the flat you say I stopped for a Coca-Cola with Vangel and Mirko. Un'stand?"

"All right."

Alone, I walked faster, looked straight ahead, not averting my head when I heard tapping on windowpanes or whisperings from hallways.

At the corner of Third the half doors of Fritz's saloon swung outward and a man came reeling into the street. The man stumbled at the curb, steadied himself, and whirled back, still on his feet. Facing the door that had disgorged him, he muttered some angry words and shook his fist. Then his arms waved and he started for the door, lunging toward it like a dazed wrestler. The wings of the half door swung inward as he dove in. A moment later he came staggering back to the sidewalk to the accompaniment of music from the player piano inside.

I hurried through the dark hallway and up the two flights of stairs. In the flat the kerosene lamp on the wall was turned low, casting a pale, flickering light over the interior. Next to the lamp hung the new calendar with the upper half taken up by the picture of the girl with bare arms and shoulders and the bunch of red roses at her bosom. My eyes alighted for a moment on the picture and then turned away guiltily.

Leaving the lamp still lit for Kosta, I tiptoed into the other room. The men lay uncovered on their iron cots. In their soiled union suits

170

they looked like dead rebels stripped of their outer clothing by the soldiers who had killed them.

I took off my shirt and trousers and went to bed in my clean underwear. It was too hot for the blanket and I lay uncovered, like the rest, who were sound asleep. But I couldn't go to sleep. I kept hearing low, raucous voices and throaty whisperings from dark hallways and dimly lit windows. When Kosta returned I was still awake and I wished I hadn't been, for then I wouldn't have smelled the heavy, cloying perfume that clung to him.

6

At the flat I fell into the routine as established and enforced by Shano the major-domo and by my uncle. Like the rest, I had to practice the severest economy. My life outside the flat was circumscribed. I walked to the factory and back, and I spent as much time as I could at Paskal's coffeehouse on Second Street, though my uncle frowned on this. It was the first step toward a deviation from the strict pattern of work-and-save that he and Shano prescribed. The coffeehouse was the breeding ground for unorthodox social ideas and an inducement to laziness. Here on Sundays meetings were held at which Socialist and Communist agitators denounced the exploitative capitalistic system and aired their doctrines about the reconstruction of the world. Although he lacked a systematic education, Paskal was the intellectual leader of the colony. He catered to the select among the immigrants and never stooped to engaging belly dancers, as did some other coffeehouses. Those who enjoyed this form of entertainment could go to the Greek coffeehouses on South Sixth Street. Paskal's knowledge of politics embraced the international scene. On Sundays and holidays immigrants came from Madison, Granite City, Alton, and even from as far as St. Charles, for the sole purpose of rubbing shoulders with the intelligentsia and of listening to Paskal discourse on politics and diplomacy. This was a treat for them, a bright moment in their otherwise monotonous, labor-laden existence.

Before his American days Paskal was a building contractor in Sofia. In the course of his business there he had come in contact with important people, had even dined with a minister of state, though this was doubted by many of his patrons. He was the only one who could read the American newspapers and inform the immigrants of what was going on in the world of politics, a subject of profound interest even to the most ignorant Balkan peasant. Paskal not only read what was in the papers but analyzed the news as well. And he was well aware of his unique position as disseminator of news and political oracle. He regarded his proprietorship of the coffeehouse as something beneath his dignity, something that the exigency of America had forced on him. It never occurred to me to wonder why he had come to America, for in those days I thought coming to America was a natural and inevitable thing, but now I believe there must have been some special reason for his having become a coffeehouse proprietor in St. Louis if he had been a man of consequence in the capital of Bulgaria.

Paskal read the *Post-Dispatch* and the *Globe-Democrat,* translating as he went along. He used words I had never encountered in the schoolbooks, such words as *status quo, condominium, protocol, pogrom, ukase.* I used to sit near him and marvel at the knowledge that was in his head. To know English as he did was an achievement, but to read it from the paper directly into Bulgarian, as though it were written in Bulgarian, seemed like magic. I sat at his feet, as at the feet of an oracle, and drank from his knowledge.

Once a week Paskal went to the Bank of Commerce on North Broadway to transact business for himself and for some of his patrons. On these occasions he wore his double-breasted blue serge suit and the black derby, which everybody called a *bômbé.* It was the only one in the colony; no one else would have dared to wear anything like that for fear of ridicule. But one who had a head with as much knowledge in it as Paskal's could put on it a *bômbé* without fear of ridicule. When I looked at him dressed for the bank trip (it was before I had found a job) I believed all the stories about his having hobnobbed with cabinet ministers. Often I hoped that he would ask me to accompany him on one of those trips uptown. He never did, and I began to suspect that perhaps he paid visits to places other than the bank, places to which he could not take me.

It was Sunday and I was now on my way to Paskal's. I would also go down to the riverbank to look at the great river. Often I would sit there on the bank on a drift log and gaze at the Mississippi. Out in the street I came on Alma Jane. In a bright, warm Sunday dress she looked like a flowerpot in bloom.

" 'Ello, mistuh man." To say that, little Alma Jane had to take a candy rooster impaled on a stick out of her mouth. The rooster was as red as Alma Jane's tongue.

"Good morning, Alaama Jane. You pretty." I may not have had the courage to utter a whole sentence in English to anyone but Alma Jane. The little girl shook the rooster at me admonishingly. "I tol' yuh, not Alaama. Alma."

173

"Oh, awright, Alma, awright." I gave her a nickel.

Clutching the coin in her palm, her great eyes smiling, she started for the Assyrian candymaker on the opposite corner.

Walking toward the coffeehouse, I examined my trousers. They did not have the crease I had seen on the sports' trousers, but they were "stylish." Baggy at the hips, they narrowed at the ankles and had broad cuffs. I wished I could see the knot in my necktie, which was a green knitted one, with horizontal stripes. Already I knew how to tie a good knot. One of these days I'd buy myself a blue silk tie with white dots on it, like Paskal's, and learn to tie it sidewise, like wings at my throat.

I took off my blue flannel cap and looked at the lining. I had done that many times because I liked the green silk lining, with the golden crown and the words *Supreme Quality* stamped on it. "Soopraymay Kooaleetee" I read, certain I was not pronouncing correctly. From my limited experience I had found out the vast difference between English spelling and pronunciation. The first time I saw a ten-cent piece I read the words on it, *Ohnay Deemay.* I knew better now. *Fai dallars,* not *feevay dole-ars!* Every new word I learned I repeated to myself a hundred times. The language was slowly taking hold of me like an infectious song. It kept vibrating in my subconscious. Words I had heard but didn't know the meaning of hummed in my mind.

Every time I went to the coffeehouse I learned something new. It was true that the people who patronized the place were not Americans. They were my own people. But all of them had been in America longer than I, some of them for many years. And they allknew a thing or two. They interlarded our tongue with English words and phrases, some of which were thrown in whole, without any change, like *datsol, surenuff, 'course.* Others were nationalized: *wipam enginia; feelam bad; workam na carshopo; drinkam Coca-Cola.* At the coffeehouse people spoke of other cities, where they had friends and relatives, from whom they received letters. Butte, Detrovitch, Milvoki, Indianapolis, Kalamazoo, Kokomo. Where were these places? How did Macedonian peasants ever find these places?

As was usual on Sundays the coffeehouse was crowded. People sat at the marble-topped tables, on chairs with legs and backs of twisted iron. They drank sodas and smoked cigars. There were people who had come over from across the Mississippi, from Granite City, Madison, East St. Louis, where they worked in steel mills, in foundries, in packinghouses, in aluminum factories.

I sat at one of the tables. A man whom I remembered from the village as Naoum but whom everybody now called Numan happened to be "treating."

174

"Have something. I am treating." I ordered a Celery Cola and listened to the conversation. Unfamiliar words, strange names poured from the mouths of these familiar people grown different. One of them was a molder, another a chipper, still another a coremaker. All of them had been plowmen in the old country. One young fellow was a busboy and still another a bellhop in a hotel. These two seemed to be in a class by themselves.

All of them gathered here on Sundays to exchange news, to discourse on politics, on things intellectual and sociological. They spoke of things I vaguely understood. But I listened intently, devouring the new words. A young man with a shock of black hair and pockets stuffed with newspapers was saying something about production, distribution, exploitation. What did it all mean? Where did these people learn such words?

Paskal, the proprietor, went from table to table, beaming at them. He patted me on the shoulder. There were other coffeehouses along Second Street, but they all had the stigma of poolrooms. The Balkan as run by Paskal was a high-class establishment. Here, too, there was a pool table, but it did not occupy the center of the floor. It was in a kind of alcove. For reasons of business, Paskal made you understand, he put up with a single pool table. It was the coffeehouse proper that was the main thing with him. And he took pride in the fact that his coffeehouse was the rendezvous for the intelligentsia. Still Paskal did not discourage the patronage of simple folk, provided they came like "gents" and not in overalls and in shirt sleeves. If someone did commit such an error, he was not requested to leave. The learned Paskal had a way of looking at him that made a repetition of the indiscretion quite improbable.

Paskal did the same with those who tried to get familiar with the girl who served the drinks. You could look at the girl and enjoy giving your order to her. But that was all. She was there to attract business, and she was for everybody. For the colony was a man's world, and it was a fine thing to have a pretty girl wipe the table and swish her skirt by you. Many gave repeat orders just for the pleasure of having the girl come over and look at them and say in her sweet voice, "What do you wish to drink?" And she always smiled.

On Sundays Paskal was in his element. He went from table to table bestowing compliments on his patrons. He was a shrewd man, and he had many clever ways of sponsoring customs and initiating practices that would redound to his profit. To bring people into the coffeehouse was one thing; to make them order liberally was another. And Paskal fostered the habit of "treating" by flattering those who indulged in it. He would sit at their table and accept

175

them as his equals, which was no small honor. The light in which he viewed the behavior of people carried weight with everybody. People wanted to be in his good graces so as not to be spoken of disparagingly by Paskal, who had a bitter tongue and could make up stinging epithets. If Paskal despised you and called you "professor" you could be certain you were regarded as a simpleton, but if he called you a "simpleton" or a "wooden philosopher," that meant you had some intelligence.

Quickly I grasped these things. My eyes took in things avidly, and my hungry mind was ever preoccupied with the thousand different things in this new world to which I had come. Though some of the new things were not American, or new, I identified them with America because it was here I first encountered them.

Take "treating," for example. And Paskal made it clear by his attitude that treating was modern, progressive, civilized, and, therefore, typically American. Conscious of this, the "treaters" were something to behold. They blushed as those whom they treated lifted their glasses and bowed in their direction in acknowledgment of the friendly gesture. Until the next round of drinks they were in the spotlight, and they left all conversation to the others or to Paskal if he happened to be at the table. And Paskal in his own ingenious way managed to turn the conversation to the celebrity of the moment and pay tribute to his progressivism. He was never at a loss for a compliment.

Because of my age I did not have to treat, but I well understood that if any of the older men were at a table where treating was in rotation and they did not fall into line they'd remember it with shame for many a day. So one treat begot another, and Paskal, the begetter of it, acting as host, master of ceremonies, moral and social arbitrator, political commentator, and news purveyor, with his eyes on the patrons and his ears tuned to the ring of the cash register, went about from table to table with the benign air of a visiting bishop.

Those old-fashioned, "backward" immigrants like my uncle, who never spent a nickel without first, or afterward, thinking of it in terms of its equivalent in old-country coin, Paskal had dubbed the "pharisees." The others, the show-off treaters, the spenders, he called "sports." I came to know that those who deserved the latter appellation were in step with the place and the times; that, as much as possible, they were living and behaving like Americans. They worked to earn money with which to enjoy life, to have a good time, to wear good clothes. They were contemptuous of the pharisees and their preachment of tight economy. In other words, being a sport meant more than merely being a good spender and a good liver; it also meant, in a way, being an American. To the pharisees it was just a fancy word for *bum*.

Even at this early stage I suspected that the sports were not really Americanized but, being bewitched by the idea, played at being Americans. For one thing, was it really American to spend everything you earned? The sports did that. Unlike the pharisees, who cut one another's hair, washed their own clothes, kept house on a cooperative basis, the sports lived in furnished rooms, which was the height of extravagance, ate their meals in the restaurants, sent their wash to the laundry, and went to the barbershops to have their hair trimmed.

I could spot a sport on sight. They all dressed "stylish," spoke English among themselves, and hummed American songs. They carried American newspapers, folded up to fit into the coat pocket. It was obvious that this was for effect, since some of them, I knew well, couldn't read our own language, let alone English.

Yet I was intrigued by the ways of the sports. To observe them was a thing of fascination. I had known most of them as plowboys and shepherd boys and as just plain village youths. Now they looked and behaved as if they had never seen a village. They put on all kinds of airs and even changed their names. Vasil became "Bill," Dimiter, "James," Sotir, "Sam," Kosta, "Gus." They also had given one another descriptive American nicknames— "Shorty," "Baldy," "Slim," "Hi there, Fatty!" Every gesture, every movement they made, the way they smoked, the way they laughed even, curling up their lips to show their gold teeth, bespoke America. They smoked ready-made cigarettes. When they went up on Broadway or Sixth Street they never took anyone along who was not a sport, who might, by his mustaches, by not wearing a collar and tie, or by speaking his own language in the street, give them away as not being Americans.

The sports played pool. Somehow I understood that pool was a gentleman's game, not a game for peasants. To play pool with all the trimmings, the preenings, and posturings was an achievement and an eloquent proof of one's removal from the world of the pharisees into that of the sports.

I was so taken in by the sight of erstwhile plowmen playing pool that no matter how interesting the conversations at the table, if there was a pool game going on I would rather be there to watch it. And now when two sports rose to play, I followed immediately and perched myself on one of the high stools ranged along the wall.

Both players were similarly dressed, like twins, in dark-green suits, brown shoes, and both wore gray felt hats pulled low over their foreheads. It was the thing to do for cronies to buy similar suits, hats, ties, shoes. One of the two had been the village cattle herder. I could see him right now standing in the village green and yelling at the top of his lungs, to be heard all over the village, "Hey, drive out the cattle, drive out!" His father had mortgaged the house, two fields, and a vineyard for the money needed for his fare to America. Now he held a billiard cue, scepterlike, instead of the cattle staff. And he twirled the cue in his hand like a spindle.

They started the game. The balls clacked and rolled smoothly over the soft green felt. Some of them hit the cushions and zigzagged, and some slipped into the pockets. Though knowing a good deal about the game from previous observations, I was occasionally puzzled, as when a ball that had dropped into a pocket was sometimes retrieved and "spotted" back on the table instead of being put on the rack to be included in the score. I asked about this and it was explained to me, but the explanation was a mixture of English and Bulgarian and I couldn't get the point.

It seemed to me that shooting a ball into a pocket was very easy. When I tried it I found out how difficult it really was. But just now that seemed merely the excuse for a lot of posturing. For instance, the player always kept one button of his coat fastened at the waist. Just before striking the ball he would unfasten the button, pull up one trouser leg, and give the hat an upward poke with the thumb. Immediately after the shot, the coat was rebuttoned and the hat brim pulled back to its former low position on the forehead. Then there was the ritual of chalking the cue, which was done leisurely and sort of absent-mindedly. Everything—from the very moment the players selected their cues, squinting at them to make sure they were not warped, and sizing them up for length—was done leisurely.

As the players paced around the table, their shoes went *skrtz* . . . *skrtz*. And the *skrtz-skrtz* of the shoes seemed to go with the game. Both players smoked cigars, which, again, appeared to be an integral part of the game. Without the cigars, somehow the game would have been incomplete. Once in a while—and this was a signal that the impending shot was important—the player would relieve himself of the cigar by balancing it on the border of the table, the lit end outward. The first thing he did directly after the shot was to pick up the cigar and take a few puffs at it, blowing the smoke at the ceiling.

I observed the spectacle with tremendous interest until my attention was drawn away by the entrance into the coffeehouse of a remarkable person. This person bore likeness to a youth named Mitko who had left the village four or five years before I did. The resemblance to that youth was something like the resemblance of

178

a finished portrait in colors to an artist's preliminary sketch. If this was Mitko, thought I, then his was the most amazing transformation America had wrought on one of my countrymen. Everything about this person glowed and glittered. His gait was so proud, so arrogant. As he directed his footsteps toward an unoccupied table, he looked about disdainfully and he greeted no one, and no one greeted him.

When he reached the table he pulled out a brown handkerchief from the breast pocket on the left side of his coat and dusted the seat of the chair before sitting down. He replaced the handkerchief in the pocket in such a way that one corner of it remained flying. As soon as he sat down he pulled at the knees of his trousers and with his thumb and forefinger sharpened the creases of the trouser legs.

Observing all this from a distance, I gave up my high seat by the pool table and sat nearer so as to study the person at close range. It must be Mitko, I thought to myself. But why is it nobody speaks to him? If I had seen him in the street, I reflected, I'd have thought he was an American for certain. For it was incredible what America had done to Mitko, if this were Mitko. Everything about him had realized itself to its fullest potentialities, at least externally. All the dreams of America people had in the old country had been realized in this person.

He wore a brown suit with very pronounced gray stripes and a double-breasted vest with two rows of brown buttons down the front. His necktie was also brown, as were his socks, which showed below the trouser cuffs. You could see that the necktie was of the softest silk, and it had flowers woven in or printed on it. Just below the thick knot there was stuck a pin, shaped like a horseshoe, with diamonds, or what looked like diamonds (you could never be sure in America), where the nails should be. Across the buttonhole on the lapel of his coat there was a gold bar from which depended a gold chain, which I surmised must be attached to a watch in the breast pocket. This was the right side pocket, not the one from which the corner of the handkerchief spread out like the wing of a bird.

I couldn't keep my eyes off the man. Twice I had to avert them because he caught me staring and I didn't wish to give the impression that I was dazzled or anything like that. The third time I got caught I did not avert my eyes but sort of smiled, because I thought I had seen a light of recognition in the man's eyes. I was quickly rebuked when he fished out the watch from his pocket and brandished it before his eyes. It must have been a watch without a cover, for he didn't click it open to look at it. He slipped it back into the

179

pocket, and then with one finger flicked away an imaginary speck of dust from his knee. Again he tugged at the knee of one trouser leg.

The more I observed him the less he appeared to be Mitko. I remembered Mitko as a skinny, awkward youth, with spindly legs and scrawny neck. In summertime he used to hire out as the village's swineherd; in winter he drove a donkey packed with firewood. The man here looked as if he had never seen a pig or a donkey and never done a stroke of work in his life. His neck was smooth and round like the fatted necks of the Americans, and his complexion looked as if he had been fed on milk and honey and white bread all his life and had had a daily massage. I recalled Mitko's mother, too, recalled her as I had last seen her in the village only a few days before I had set off for America. A dark, small woman, her caked heels thumping naked on the ground, she shuffled on, the hem of her rough, homespun skirt flapping at her dung-smudged ankles. Was she the mother of this man sitting here like a prince from a fairy tale?

Paskal, who had been busy flattering guests elsewhere, finally came over to the man's table. He shook hands with him and said in English, "How do you do, William?" William! Could that be the American equivalent of Mitko, as Gus was of Kosta and Tony of Andon? Paskal sat down.

Presently the serving girl came to take their orders. She smiled to William as she wiped the table. She always wiped the table whether it needed wiping or not. Since the order was for cigars, the girl brought over a whole box. She offered it first to William, who took two, and then to Paskal, who took one. William flung a fifty-cent piece on the table. From his vest pocket he took out a little implement that looked like a combination knife and scissors, and with it he clipped one end of the cigar. This end he lighted. The other cigar he put in his right vest pocket, next to his fountain pen.

Paskal thanked William for the treat by raising his own cigar as if it were a drink, and, smiling broadly, he put the unlighted cigar on the table in front of him, later to replace it in the box for resale. Paskal made fun of the pharisees for reckoning nickels in terms of old-country valuta, but whenever somebody treated him he always took a cigar, which he later put back in the box. And no nickel cigars for him either. Paskal was particular about what he didn't smoke.

It was either to detract attention from his not lighting the cigar or to promote another "treat" from William that Paskal now took notice of me and asked me to sit at their table. Then I was certain it was Mitko, because Paskal wouldn't be asking me to join them if the man were an American.

"I knew you were Mitko the moment I saw you," I said, smiling, and proffered my hand. "You sure have changed, though. I was beginning to doubt . . ." My proffered hand had remained ungrasped. Mitko rolled his cigar in his hand and tapped it with one finger in order to shake away ashes that had not yet formed. I withdrew my spurned hand and put it in my pocket.

"His name's William now," Paskal explained. "And he doesn't speak Bulgarian." Paskal tugged at my arm. "Sit down, sit down. Have a Coca-Cola on the house."

"I'll have a Celery Cola."

"Good. Anything you like."

The two men conversed in English. Though I understood little of what was said, I listened as if every word were spoken for my benefit. I understood more of Paskal's English than of Mitko's, but Mitko did most of the talking. And it was such a talk as I had never before heard. By now I could tell that people who seemed to speak English freely spoke it not at all. They fished for words with hooks and held the words before their mouths squirming and shivering. Some words, like birds just released from cages and not yet aware of their release, beat their wings in confusion.

Mitko's talk was fluent and facile. I couldn't tell yet if it was really good English, but there was no mistaking the fluency and freedom of it. It all sounded to me as if Mitko didn't talk to express himself but to hear himself talk, that his English was not a medium for the expression of thoughts and ideas but an end in itself, like a song.

I observed every movement of his mouth; my ears missed not a sound, not the slightest intonation. Some syllables brimmed out from the nostrils, others seemed to roll at the throat, and still others were detonated from deep down in the diaphragm. The lips continually twisted and puckered, now forming a round orifice through which flutelike sounds lilted out, now closing in such a way that a word blistered from the corner of the mouth and distended like a soap bubble. Those words I understood plopped out like eggs from hens. And all the time it was Mitko.

When he rose to go he shook hands with Paskal but ignored me. Then he strutted out.

"He didn't say a word to anyone else here," I said to Paskal.

"He doesn't know anyone here. He's an American."

"He's Mitko. You know he's Mitko."

"He was Mitko. He's William now."

"Is he ashamed of himself? I mean of Mitko that was?"

"He never thinks of Mitko. He never was Mitko. He's always been William. He never knew these people. He's an American, and he's always been William."

"Has he got a good job like the Americans? Is he a boss?"

"I don't know what he does or where he lives. He comes here two or three times a year. Kosta and Argyr once saw him at Sixth and Olive dressed in overalls and carrying a pail and some window-washing equipment. They said hello to him, but he said to them, 'Shut up, you goddam lousy Dagos!' "

"He didn't throw any rotten tomatoes at them?"

"No. Nor eggs either."

"Wonder why he comes here at all."

"Who knows? Maybe he gets lonesome sometimes."

"For Mitko?"

Paskal laughed.

7

My uncle was angry. I knew that because he took off his cap, blew at it, and put it back on his head. He had never done that before. It was a black cap, with a button on top. Like everybody else in the flat, he wore his cap indoors. Some of the men slept with their caps on.

"I don't want to work at the Terminal," I said again with much emphasis.

"I don't either, but didn't we come here to work?"

"But I *am* working."

"You'll be making more money at the Terminal, and the work's not hard. We nap a good deal when there are no engines to be worked on."

My uncle had taken a fatherly attitude toward me from the moment I had arrived in America. He had no children of his own, and he treated me as if I were his own son. Even though I was now past my fourteenth birthday, a childhood habit persisted and I sometimes wet my bed. Needless to say I was ashamed and embarrassed, but it was downright maddening and even unsanitary because a few hours after I had left the bed my uncle had to sleep in it. Whenever this happened I would stand the mattress on edge against the wall to get it aired. My uncle never complained, never even gave any intimation by word or otherwise that he was aware of it. I recall this uncle with affection. He was a kind, gentle, tolerant, soft-spoken man. But he belonged to the category of immigrants whom Paskal had dubbed the pharisees.

"Twelve hours a day, with no Sundays or holidays off," I complained. "When am I going to learn English? There won't be any time to go anywhere."

"Go where?" He paused a minute and then added, "To the coffeehouse I suppose."

183

The thought sprang up in my young mind that the motive behind this job at the Terminal was not the extra earnings but the extra days and hours there that would leave no time for visits to the coffeehouses and the poolrooms and who knows what other places my uncle had in mind. I suspected there must have been some correspondence between him and my father for him to take such a paternalistic attitude toward me.

I was sitting directly across from him at the table but was not looking at him. The table was clumsy and ponderous. Its round top rested on a central pillar that ramified into the three huge paws that clawed the floor. Like everything else, like the walls, like the faces of the people who lived in the flat, the surface of the table had lost its original color and had acquired a coating compounded of dust and stew drippings, soot, and grease from frying pans and from the Terminal.

My eyes were on the opposite wall, which sometime in the dim past must have been a light green but which now was almost black where the finish had not blistered and flaked. Over spots where the plaster had peeled off there were pasted pictures clipped from newspapers and old commercial calendars.

"And what good is English to you?" There was a plea in my uncle's voice, a note of helplessness. We were alone in the flat. All the other day occupants of the flat, save one, had gone on to the coffeehouse as soon as the early Sunday dinner was over. The one still about was Klement, nighttime fire knocker at the Union Terminal. He was out on the back porch washing a pair of overalls in a galvanized washtub.

"Who'll pay you money for English? We didn't come here to learn English. We're here to work and save and go back home to live like human beings, as God meant we should live. Are you listening to me?" Again his hand reached for the cap but only touched it.

"Why can't we live here like human beings?" My eyes now were on a full-page rotogravure portrait of William Howard Taft, who was no longer President but whose mighty front and remarkable mustaches continued to hide the crumbling plaster. Taft fitted my notion of an American in every way except the mustaches. A frying pan with its sooty bottom hung on a nail directly under Taft's portrait, like the pendulum to a clock.

"Because we don't belong here," my uncle said. "How can we live decent lives here? Here we are . . . well, here we are something like the gypsies in our own country, who come and go. The Americans think of us as we think of the gypsies. The sooner we go back, the better. You'll be earning twice as much at the Terminal. The hours are long, but wiping engines is not such a hard chore. Besides, I've already given Frank the ten dollars. I thought you'd be glad to work at the Terminal. Everybody is. People who work at the Carshop wait months for a chance to work at the Terminal."

"What did you give Frank ten dollars for?"

"For the job. Nobody gets a job at the Terminal without giving Frank at least ten dollars. For some jobs you give more. Lambo had to give twenty dollars for the turntable job. It pays a cent more an hour than fire knocking, and it's much easier."

"When am I to start there?"

"In a week."

Klement had hung his overalls on a rope above the porch and returned to the room. He was not a big man, but the whole of him was like the knot on a tree, and so was his character. He had something to say about everything and had pronounced opinions regarding my own future in America. I disliked him and I was glad he worked nights.

"A *bumba*, a *bumba*, that's what he'll become," Klement said. "You take my word for it. I could tell you that the moment he got here. The way he spends time in the coffeehouse! And who knows what other places he goes?"

"All right, Klement, all right," my uncle said.

Klement buttoned his shirt sleeves and put on his coat. "You listen to what I'm telling you. Take him out on a photograph because by and by you won't be seeing him."

Then Klement left for the coffeehouse, to which Sunday visits were as regular as churchgoing in the village. The men cut short their sleep in order to spend a couple of hours at Paskal's. It was the only diversion in the otherwise routine existence, if it were not itself part of the routine.

"I hear you go to the coffeehouse in the evenings," said my uncle.

"Some evenings. I learn things there."

"What things? Things it won't do you any good to learn and be better off if you didn't know. Who goes on weekdays to the coffeehouse? Only the loafers, the *bumbi*, to make Paskal rich. Paskal knows how to flatter them and milk their nickels."

The coffeehouse indeed was what worried him. If he could get me to work at the Terminal there wouldn't be any time for the coffeehouse, habitual attendance at which was the first step away from the straight and narrow path of work-and-save, away from the old country toward the temptations of America. To be sure, the coffeehouse was anything but America. In fact, it was very much the old country. But it opened the door to America. Not that my uncle

185

had anything against America. In truth, he had an awesome respect for the America that printed the dollar bills and gave you a piece of paper that you sent across the ocean to the old country, where it was converted into gold coins. He knew the America that had built the locomotives, and the big St. Louis Terminal was mighty, but what had he, or I, or the *bumbi,* to do with that America?

"Yes, there's decent people in America." His voice was calm and even, as if he were not arguing but just thinking aloud. "There's people here who live good lives. Who have homes and wives and children. They were born here. This is their country. The *bumbi* have nothing to do with those Americans. The *bumbi* know only the gamblers and the bad women who take their money and give them diseases and . . ." He suddenly checked himself, apparently becoming aware that he was giving voice to something that he had believed he was merely thinking.

"The Americans will never give us the easy jobs." His voice changed, some warmth and animation coming into it. "It'll be coal shoveling, engine wiping for us. You don't want to do that forever, do you? You can't strike roots here. You'll always be a stranger here."

I stirred in my chair, hoping this would make him rise so we might go to the coffeehouse together for the regular Sunday visit. But he still had things to say.

"The *bumbi* think they're Americans because they learn a little English like parrots. How can they be Americans? Until yesterday they herded sheep and poked oxen and wore pigskin sandals. Because now they wear silk shirts and neckties and brown shoes and pantaloons and have gold on their teeth, does that make them Americans? Clothes don't make Americans. You can put on the finest clothes you can buy on Sixth Street and still under them you'd be what you always were. A silver saddle doesn't make a stallion out of a donkey. Americans! They! Americans! Until they came here they were lucky to eat cornbread and to sleep on straw mats on the ground. Now that they tasted white bread they want to eat in the restaurants. And to live on *foornish* and go to the theatricals, the electricals, and the live ones. Now I can understand how it might be amusing to go to an electrical once and see photographs that move, but to go to a live show like the Standard where I hear women who have no shame come out without clothes on! That's bad!"

"It only costs a nickel at the electricals."

"It's not the money. A nickel. All right, a dime. Though I always like to remember that a dime saved here is ten dimes in the old country. It's what you see that takes your mind away from the things

186

you came here for. It don't matter how we live here. Nobody in our village will ask you how many times you went to the theatricals or how many English words you know. How many gold napoleons you brought with you is what counts. Live like a miser in America that you may live like a vizier in your own country." He sat there in his chair with his head slightly tilted over his shoulder. There was a suppressed cry in his voice.

I felt sorry for my uncle. As soon as I had arrived in St. Louis I had noticed the change in him. A lean, wiry man with a small-featured face, but strong, there had always been about him a tough, tempered strength. Two years in America with the tight routine of travail and thrift had dwarfed him. He seemed stripped of his patriarchal authority and innate dignity. He looked weak and help-less.

"Aren't we going to the coffeehouse? It's getting late," I said at last and rose.

"I don't think I'll come."

I started, with my hands in my trousers pockets. At the door I stopped and looked back but turned again and walked across the porch toward the stairway.

I could see my uncle sitting motionless in his chair, just as I had left him, with his head still inclined over his right shoulder. I knew he was listening to my footsteps as I was descending the steps. I knew he felt terribly alone. Maybe I'd never come back; maybe I'd go to live "on foornish" somewhere on the West Side. Maybe Klement was right.

My uncle should never have come to America. But he too had become a victim of the Americamania that had possessed the people in all the villages. Dollars, pantaloons, neckties, silk shirts, pencils that needed no sharpening, and pens that wrote without being dipped in inkwells had acted like magic, had disturbed the lives of thousands of people. Good people who crossed themselves at meal-time, fathers and husbands, clean people. God-fearing people. America put greed in their hearts and cleverness in their minds. He saw the deception, but it was too late. He saw the dreadful things America had done to young men who had left the village with healthy bodies and clean minds. Look at them now! The blight's on them. He would go back to his own world, where he was a man, and he would build houses again.

Yes, houses! It seemed like a dream now, the engine wiper building houses. They were small houses, but they had windows and doors and some of them had balconies overlooking little courts paved with flagstones. He built these houses for people to live in, to live like human beings, like God meant for them to live. The houses had cupboards in them and kneading troughs and weaving looms and fireplaces. What's a house without a fireplace? A church without an altar. A man without a soul.

He would be a *Maistor* again and build houses, my uncle would. People would honor him and call him *Maistor.* He could lay bricks and stones and fit window frames into walls, rig up roofs and do all kinds of carpentering. His trousers might have been patched in the old country, but his soul was intact. Here the pants must not be patched, even though the body be fouled by disease and the soul moldering.

My uncle was here only with his body. His mind, his heart, his whole being were back in the homeland where life had meaning for him, where life was rooted in decency and dignity. The man he worked for there was his host and not his boss. That was because he was building him a house to live in, or a barrel to keep his wine in, or a wedding chest for his daughter. He could sit down with him for a glass of brandy or a cup of Turkish coffee. This America was boring into his life like a worm into the core of an apple, hollowing out the soundness, the meaning.

I am sitting at a table at Paskal's watching a game of cards when I feel a hand on my shoulder. I look up and it's my friend Nichola. I leap to my feet and embrace my friend with filial affection.

"Ai, ai, little one . . . but you've grown. Not such a little one any more. Let's sit at another table by ourselves. Let's do that."

We picked a table in a corner where we could be by ourselves. "Now what will you drink? I am treating. You order for both of us."

I ordered two Celery Colas.

"Every day I thought of you, every day. I wanted to come, but I can't by myself and nobody would come with me, everybody busy. I didn't worry about you, though. He's got four eyes, I said to myself; he's got learning. Besides, I knew you were working. Is your job a light one? They wouldn't give a heavy one to one like you who knows how to read and write proper."

"It's not hard, Uncle Nichola. I cut little pieces of leather with a small die and a hammer made of resin. You see these little pieces on the back of the shoes? That's what I cut."

"But I heard you were working in a factory where they make buckets."

"Yes, I was, but I quit. Risto Saroff—you know him—he works at the Sunlight Shoe Factory and he got me the job there. It pays more. I cut these pieces on a wooden block, cut thousands of them. I cut them from other small pieces, from odds and ends. They don't waste anything. There's men there who cut bigger pieces for the sides and the uppers and the toes of the shoes. And what do you think they make? From fifteen to twenty dollars a week!"

"Hey, hey! For just doing that, just cutting leather. But couldn't they give you a writing job, where you would be sitting at a desk and write?"

"I couldn't do that, Uncle Nichola. I don't know yet how to write in English."

"Oh, you mean they write different. Isn't all writing the same? There are different writings!"

"Hundreds, maybe more."

"Well, then, you'll soon learn how to do it their way. You will."

Nichola's voice sounded weak. It had a scared note in it. He looked tired, too, and seemed smaller to me now, shrunk. He had always been lean and bony, but now he looked haggard. His once ruddy complexion had turned gray.

"Have you been feeling well, Uncle Nichola? Has everything been all right?"

"Oh, yes, I feel good."

"And how's your job—heavy?"

"Oh, I don't mind that. It's kind of heavy, but I don't mind that. It's not because of that I gave it up."

"You quit your job?"

"Yes. No more of that for me. We're going to Montana to work on the Great Nordern. That's a railway, Slavko says—Slavko's the man who signs people up. I signed up already—he says the Great Nordern treats people the best of any railway. Slavko's now in Granite City signing up people to make up the gang. That's what he calls it, a gang. I signed up already and I told Slavko about you. He said it's all right. Sure, he said, the boy can be water boy. That's what he said."

"Water boy?"

"Yes, all you do is carry a pail with water and let people drink. You get paid same as everybody else. I asked about that."

"I'd like to go with you, Uncle Nichola, but I can't. I am all right here. They just added a dollar to my pay at the shoe factory."

"But you'll make more in Montana. Thirteen cents an hour, ten hours a day, six days a week. No rent to pay. Besides, there's grass and trees there and mountains. That's what everybody says that's been there. Just think, to drink water that comes out of the earth, just like in the old country. Slavko says you can even get eggs from real hens."

"Eggs from real hens?"

"Sure. Didn't you know the eggs here are not from hens?"

189

I kept a straight face so as not to offend my friend by reflecting on his ignorance. He sensed, however, that I was not convinced, and after a sip of his soft drink he added, "A man in East St. Louis told me he worked in a factory where they made chickens by machines, thousands of them."

I hesitated, not knowing exactly how to go about it. "That's true, Uncle Nichola, the chickens are hatched by machines, but the eggs are real, laid by real hens. They put natural hen-laid eggs in the machine and the machine hatches the chicks. They call it *artificial* hatching. We can ask Paskal if you like."

"Paskal, Paskal! How could he know more than you? But you say they are *artificial*. Doesn't that mean they are not real?"

"It does. But the hens are *not* artificial, nor the chicks. The *hatching* is artificial. After all, what does the brooding hen do but lie over the eggs to keep them warm till they hatch? Well, in this case the machine—an *incubator*, they call it—takes the place of the hen and supplies the heat, just like the hen. The machine *is* the hen." I shouldn't have said the last sentence. It bothered Nichola. He shook his head.

"That's just it," he said. "The machine is the hen. What next? If you say so it must be so. Besides, what do I know? I am only a shepherd. But I tell you this. There's things here that have got me all mixed up. You got to have four eyes, like yourself, to figure 'em out. Now I ask you. Would you eat meat if you knew it was from a dead animal?"

"I would not."

"Good! But that's what you been doing ever since you been here. I know it because I do it every day."

"Do what?"

"I make cattle die. Now I know this. Nobody told me about this. I've been hitting steers on the head with a hammer and I've watched them die, thousands of them. Just like that. Now you wouldn't eat the meat of cattle when the throats hadn't been cut, would you?"

"Of course not. Don't you cut their throats? Don't you bleed them?"

"That's just what I am telling you. One whack with the hammer and the steer's dead. Then it's skinned and cut up and you eat the meat."

"Do they die from one stroke?"

"Yes! But you got to know where to hit. There's a spot on the forehead, between the horns. That's where you hit. If you miss, there's trouble. I seldom miss."

"Let's have another drink, Uncle Nichola. I'm treating this time. Let's have coffee."

190

"All right, Little One. Here I am still calling you Little One. I suppose I'll always call you that. You don't mind?"

"Mind! No matter how big I grow you may always call me Little One. About your job, did you quit because of the way you make the beasts die?"

"Well, maybe. I don't like to make critters die like that. It's different when you cut their throats and let the blood flow, the way it's always been done. I don't know why they had to give me such a job. It must be because I am strong."

"Can't you get a different job?"

"What's the use? We are going to this Montana. You will come too. You must."

"I can't, Uncle Nichola. It's not the pay. I must stay here for other reasons. My Uncle Tanas is not feeling well, and I have just started going to school to study the language. I go three nights a week. And Paskal here is helping me."

"Paskal! How could he be helping you when you know more than he does? Well, if you will not go, then I will not go. But I don't like what I am doing."

8

Every morning at five o'clock the rooster crowed. It was Lazar's job to wind it up in the evening before turning in. And Lazar regularly did, though he had no need of its crowing, rising as he did before the metallic ring sounded through the flat to wake the others.

When I opened my eyes the light was on in the kitchen and the strong aroma of brewing coffee was in my nostrils. Lazar's heavy work shoes clumped on the floor. I sat up in bed and reached for my overalls. Again I became conscious of that emptiness inside me, that void in my stomach, or in my heart, or wherever it was inside me. Ever since I started work at the Terminal I went to bed with that hollowness and rose with it. The sleep never filled it up. All vitality, all energy had gone from down there up to the mind, perhaps to keep those engines moving. For my mind was filled with the vastness of the Terminal—the tracks, the water tanks on the trestles, the smoldering ash pits, the coal chutes, the roundhouses, the engines, the turntables, the rows upon rows of freight and passenger cars. There was the same confusion in this *mental* terminal as in the real one and the same order in the confusion. The engines, as they ran in all directions, clattering over frogs and switch points, seemed headed for inevitable collision but never collided. Just when it appeared they'd crash head on, one of them took a direction away from the other.

I hated the terminals—the one in the mind and the real one. Every evening I went to bed half determined not to rise in the morning to go back to the Terminal. Yet I always rose with the "rooster's" crow and had my breakfast with the five others. It wasn't only because my uncle wanted me to work at the Terminal or that I was making three dollars a week more than at the shoe factory. It was the ethics or morality of the flat. No one quit a job

192

unless it was to go to another, one with higher pay, or to go back to the old country.

And so something outside me propelled me into this routine existence. Nothing varied, not even the breakfasts. Coffee and bread every morning. The coffee was boiled and was black and bitter. At first I could not swallow it. "Put plenty of sugar in it," advised the others. "Sugar's cheap here and you don't have to pinch it." So I put three teaspoonfuls of sugar into a cup of coffee. The coffee was always boiling hot, and I learned from the others how to cool it in the drinking by blowing at it in reverse. You barely touched the coffee with your lips. The reverse blowing sucked it into the mouth through an invisible siphon, and there it mixed with the bread.

The bread was white. Back home, when my father would go to the city to market, he always brought white city bread. I would hold a piece of it in one hand and a chunk of homemade corn and rye bread in the other and bite at them alternately—generously of the home bread, economically of the other, as if one were bread and the other cheese.

At five-thirty we would be on our way. All six of us trooped together like convicts, our caps on and the lunch packages under our arms. We walked on in pairs, I with Kosta. This Kosta put on airs, because instead of wiping engines he roasted sand in the sand house and fed the sand to the engines through a spout that he pulled down with a rope. He said the engines used the sand to stop and on upgrades to give the wheels traction. Without the sand, he said, the engines couldn't stop, as if stopping were the most important thing the engines did. He ribbed me every time he got the chance. "You can't become a *bumba* now," he would drone. "You're too busy wiping engines to become a *bumba* now."

"Grease, grease for him now," echoed Lazar in his tinny voice. "What a life to sit in the coffeehouse to sip Celery Cola. The girl bends down to wipe the table and she smiles at you. Her arms smooth and white and plump."

A block away from the flat we would enter Poplar Street. The railway track in the street led straight into the Terminal, losing itself there in the maze of yards like a brook in a lake. We followed the track, stepping over the ties, the cinders crunching under the soles of our work shoes. Low brick and frame buildings with fronts blackened by the smoke from the engines flanked the track. The flimsy curtains on some windows were like black veils, hiding the wretchedness inside and advertising it.

No danger here of being run over by a train. Only freight trains used the track, and the engines were very slow, dragging endless rows of cars—boxcars, flatcars, gondolas, coal cars. From blocks away we could hear an engine's groan. As it came nearer it heaved and panted. We could wait till it was half a rail behind us before we jumped out of its path. Long after the engine had passed ahead, the cars rolled along, block after block, squeaking and creaking, the wheels jangling on the joints. Each car wheeled along as though propelled by independent power. It seemed unbelievable that an engine that had passed full minutes ago still exerted pulling power away out here, blocks behind.

We tramped along in the middle of the track quite unconcerned about the trains. "The corn's all in the granaries," Turpen would say. "And the grapes are fermenting in the vats. Red peppers are all strung up, drying on the walls. Next year, with God's will, we'll roast a whole lamb on a spit, out in the open. One more year, ah . . ." Every morning Turpen talked to himself like that about the homeland.

"Suppose there's no old country to go back to," I suddenly cried out. "Suppose this is life forever, until you die. Suppose you never get out of this track, like the trains!"

"Listen to him now. He thinks he's reading the Psalter."

"Yeah, it sure don't pay to send boys to school," Lazar agreed. "Give 'em schooling and they want things what's not meant for them. Schooling opens the eyes but not for the right things to see. He thinks he's too good for wiping engines."

"How nice it is to sit in the coffeehouse and drink *krimsodas* and look at the girl," Turpen said.

"Or maybe go to the electricals and look at women in moving photographs."

"Or to the live one, eh?" Lazar said. "You been to one yet? Wait till he sees a live one!"

"Ah, he'll be a *bigbumba* yet," Kosta chuckled. "One of these days he'll go to a show that's live and electrical at the same time. Wait till the *sanavagan* gets a taste of that kind of honey."

"Then he'll be running there every day like a dog to a butcher," Lazar whinnied.

"And then he'll get stung," said Turpen. "That kind of honey is sweet for a minute and then bitter for months. Them *putanas* sting like wasps. Look at Luben, still walking with his legs wide apart like he was on stilts."

Turpen's remark silenced everyone. The rest of the way no one spoke a word, as if everyone was trying to hide a sting.

My job was the commonest there was in the bewildering world of the locomotives. With waste soaked in oil I wiped the big, vatlike bodies of the engines. First I wiped the tops, polishing the bells and the sandboxes; then I climbed down and rubbed the bulging sides; finally I wiped the rust and the mud from the wheels, from the spokes and the hubs. When I got finished with one engine I moved on to another. I could tell the engines had performed great feats, for they were smudged with mud and dust and looked grimy and sweaty. They all had been to far places, carrying freight and passengers.

And now, like tired horses brought to their stables, they seemed conscious of the difficult tasks they had performed and expected homage from everybody. Resting over the ash pits, they sneezed and snorted and looked authoritative, especially the ones that took out and brought in the passenger trains, like the Vandalia. When they moved from place to place in the yards they glided on leisurely, their huge wheels turning slowly, their pistons shuttling.

People were not important at the Terminal—not even the engineers, machinists, pipers, boilermakers, conductors, brakemen, switchmen, yardmasters, dispatchers. This was the locomotive's world, and everybody was subservient to the locomotives. Here they returned from their long journeys; from here, cleaned and polished, they set out on their new trips. If they needed more than refueling and wiping, they were taken into the roundhouses. Their huge bellies were emptied of the smoldering coals, and the machinists and boilermakers crawled into the yawning fireboxes and started hammering. Then Turpen started new fires in them, and it took a long time to get their steam up so they could be moved.

When the engineers came they behaved like priests performing ceremonials before supernatural beings. From cans with long beaks they squirted oil into valves, tightened bolts, and with waste, which they carried in the hip pockets of their overalls, they rubbed mechanical parts it was not my duty to attend to. To me it seemed that the engineers were fondling the locomotives, patting them and curry-combing them the way people do trustworthy horses. The engineers could well enough do that, for they would presently climb onto the cab, pull the bell rope, and glide away to the station shed to pick up a long row of cars filled with passengers and haul them across the wide Mississippi or westward through the plains and forests that stretched away forever.

There was no skill in what I myself was doing, and the hours were long and wearying. They were, in fact, no longer hours as such but pennies, those copper coins with Abraham Lincoln on them. Lincoln's picture hung in a prominent place in Paskal's coffeehouse, ensconced on the walls by a strange company of *haiduks* and *komitadjis*. His face had the lean, suffering, graven features of a

195

Macedonian mountaineer's face. The gentleness and compassion emanating from the deep-set eyes made me think of Lincoln as the grandfather of all the troubled and unhappy children of the world.

I worked an hour, and a little pile of pennies lay snugly in my pocket. The day divided itself into twelve such piles. That was the day. Yet as I climbed from engine to engine amidst the stifling, smoke-laden air of the Terminal I dreamed of time that was not money, of minutes that did not mint themselves into pennies. The penny became to me a symbol of bondage. It robbed me of my freedom and chained me to the Terminal. And on that score I wished that Lincoln's compassionate image were not on the face of the pennies. For I had heard that Lincoln had freed the black people, Alma Jane's people. I did not wish my "bondage" to convert itself into "Lincolns." And still I knew that money was freedom. Like freedom itself it had to be earned with sweat. So maybe it was all right after all that Lincoln's image was on the pennies. Maybe! Who knows? Paskal might know.

The Terminal blotted out the days and left little of the nights. With its locomotives it controlled all of life. It was the point of departure and return, not alone for the engines but for me, too. My own existence began and ended at the Terminal. Twelve hours there, the hour it took to make the trip back and forth, and the chores at the flat, left no time for anything else. In weeks I had been able just once, before twilight one evening, to sit on the bank of the Mississippi and watch the great river go on its way. I relived that half hour many times over in my mind while my hands kept busy wiping engines. It helped sometimes to forget the hours as piles of pennies and live them, at least in fancy, as free hours.

One day as I rubbed the top of an engine I was seeing the river's swelling current. Contemplation of the river restored in me a sense of movement, of freedom to be had. The great river had life, boundless, surging life that flowed across America. I still did not know where the Mississippi came from and where it went, but it must come a long way. No short river could be this wide, said I, sitting on the bank of the great river while my hands were wiping and polishing a rusty spot. This engine, resting between chores, was alive under me. It expelled vapors from its valves while I massaged and rubbed its cylindrical body. I worked steadily, uniformly, rubbing the grease-soaked waste over the metal. The engine purred under my strokes.

The unskilled, common kind of work at least did not chain my mind, only my body. I was free to go to the river, to sit on the bank and look at it. I sat on a washed-up log on the bank and watched the great river flow before my eyes. I heard nothing of the racket

196

of the Terminal. I was deaf to the continuous clanging of bells, to the constant hammering of the boilermakers and the machinists, to the thunderous noise of coal as it tumbled down the chutes. I heard only the deep, expansive, elemental breathing of the Mississippi as it flowed before my dream-filled eyes. The river was as wide as the sea, with its current scarcely perceptible. Yet the current must be swift, for when I gazed at one spot too long I got dizzy, and the river rushed up to me ready to engulf me and carry me along. I then shifted my eyes to another spot to avoid being borne along by the current. I looked across to the far bank, which was overgrown with scrub and bushes, and looked beyond the rim of growth into the flatness where smoke spiraled in the hazy air. I knew out there was another state—Illinois—as I knew that where I sat it was Missouri. But beyond that I knew nothing. And I yearned for knowledge, of the land and the river, which was never twice the same river.

My eyes went to a barge in midstream. The barge was loaded with crates and bales of cotton and was hauled upstream by a spunky towboat that fussed and hiccuped as if in protest against the heavy load. Behind it the river churned, a foamy gash in the brown expanse. My eyes left the towboat and the barge and turned to the two ferries that shuttled continually between the banks and which at this moment met in midstream and greeted each other with short toots of their sirens. They looked like giant red tortoises as they plied over the muddy water. A passenger ship heaved into sight from the bend to the north, and this ship sailed serenely on like a fairy-tale castle with white towers. She was broad and boastful and free, and she bragged to me about the many towns she knew. She blew her whistle, which had a calm and deep sound, unlike the ranting neighs of the locomotives. There was gaiety in her bell, too, which now rang on her tower like a village bell on the eve of a holiday. The happy ship glided on without effort, not fussing or groaning. Again she sounded her deep-toned whistle, inviting me to come aboard to view from her tower the river towns past which she sailed, to see the plains, which rolled out from the banks of the river.

And it was just at that moment that another whistle, a shrill, screaming whistle, yanked me away from the riverbank with such a sharp sting that, like a person violently wakened from a deep sleep, I swayed on top of the engine. My feet scraped on the slippery metal and my arms twirled in an effort to steady my body. But the engine shivered beneath me and the coal chute in the distance rushed toward me with its tower. The next instant I was flat on my stomach and gliding down the engine's side, my hands trying vainly to grasp the bare metal. My feet knocked at the pipes

197

and wheels and then I was on the ground. The engine snorted like a vicious mule that had just thrown its rider.

I must have cried out in the falling, or else the engineer from the cab must have seen me tumble down.

"What happened, kid?" he asked. "Lost your balance?" He leaned over me. "Did you get hurt?"

"No hurt, no," I panted. But a sharp pain was stabbing at my right forearm. My left hand went involuntarily to the stab and pressed there. The pain grew fiercer, a hundred hornets stinging. "It hurt," I admitted, holding my arm.

The engineer quickly ripped the sleeve. Seeing reddened, steam-scalded flesh, he hurried to the cab and returned with the oilcan. Squirting oil on the arm, the engineer cursed.

The whole arm now was aflame like a firebrand. I began to moan.

The foreman and two brakemen also came over. They talked with the engineer. They talked calmly; their voices sounded cold and dispassionate.

"He musta had his arm right over the whistle when I blew it," said the engineer.

"Nasty business, steam burn," said one of the brakemen.

"We'll take you to the doctor, kid," said the foreman.

"Goddam it. How was I to know he had his arm over the whistle?"

Through the pain that scraped at the nerves and coursed like a thousand toothaches all the way down to the heels, the self-admonition kept recurring. "I shouldn't have gone to the river."

There was a narrow pause in the pain, like a pause in respiration. "But nobody can know I wasn't on the job when it happened," I whispered.

"What'd you say, fella? Come on. We'll take you to the doctor now."

The nurse held my hand in hers. Clasped in the whiteness and softness of her hand, mine looked like a bunch of grease-soaked waste held in a glove of satin.

With wads of cotton the nurse's other hand gently wiped the lubricating oil from the scalded forearm. She was so close to me her breath at my cheek was like a breeze on a sultry summer day. The pain was always there, but for whole seconds at a time I forgot the pain because of the nurse.

"Why do you wanna be working in that horrid place for, honey? Lucky you got away with just a burn. You oughta see some of the accidents that come from there." There was a reproving tone in her voice, but I could perceive the sweetness and compassion in it. She was like a big sister chiding a young brother for having gotten into mischief.

She tossed the soiled cotton pellets into the basket and drew out clean pads from a packet on the table. She dipped these into a bowl of clear liquid and dabbed the scalded flesh. And she continued punctuating her movements with sisterly admonitions, which I tried to interpret, from the sound and intonation of her voice, with the intuition of a pet animal listening to its mistress's good-natured rebukes.

For a fleeting instant the moistened cotton caused the flame to flare up more violently over the arm. She engaged both her hands in the bandaging. Her smooth, tapering fingers spun nimbly, kneading the gauze like dough.

When the arm was swaddled she made a loop from another roll of cloth, put the loop over my neck, and slung the bandaged arm into it. She stood up. There was a momentary stillness in the pain. Then, realizing she was through, I rose, embarrassed for having dirtied the place with my clumsy work shoes and soiled overalls. Everything was so clean and white and polished here. And she in her white uniform and hat was like a goddess of cleanliness. The arm rested comfortably in the sling. The fire still burned, but it was a fire covered with ashes, with an occasional subdued crackle in it.

"You come again in two days."

The arm smarted in one spot. A sputtering charcoal there had succeeded in shooting up a tiny flame through the ashes.

"What are you staring at me for? Don't you understand?"

"Yeah. Day after tomorrow I come."

"No. Not day after tomorrow. Two . . . days . . . after . . . tomorrow." The words came out one at a time, reluctant to leave the mouth. They lingered on the red lips.

"Whatever makes you people come to this country when you don't even know how to talk?"

"I un'stand. I come Friday."

"Friday. That's right. I shoulda told you that in the first place. You're not so dumb at that. Not with those eyes. They don't miss a thing."

I walked out, perplexed that nobody asked for money. Maybe they would take it out of my wages.

9

Again I was tasting free time. Now time wasn't money. But I had learned the basic truth that time was a precious thing and must not be wasted. I savored my free time now as connoisseurs savor the bouquets of wine. And this made free time even more precious than the Terminal time at so much per hour. Of course, time by itself was nothing. It was only valuable in terms of yourself, your body, and your mind. And my mind, not stupefied by the long hours of labor, became alert, eager, and still more hungry for knowledge of the New World, especially for the language, the window through which this unknown world was revealing itself to me.

Now look at Paskal. He spent hours reading the *Post-Dispatch* and the *Globe-Democrat,* and he was not wasting time. That Paskal turned out to be, in my free time, an entirely different person. He was as apathetic toward his business on weekdays as he was mercenary on Sundays. On weekdays the atmosphere and clientele of the coffeehouse were different, too. The Sunday commercialism was supplanted by an intellectual, almost genteel atmosphere. The serving girl, busy taking orders on Sundays, on Monday morning assumed an ornamental role. She sat at one of the marble-topped tables and read the funny papers. If someone knocked for a drink she would rise, pick up the inevitable wiping cloth, and propel her supple body in the direction whence the knock came.

She was a young girl of Polish extraction, with gray eyes and a fair complexion. Paskal had chosen her with due consideration for his patrons' taste in women, which was on the fleshy side. As she walked, all the girl's mobility came from the hips and the shoulders. And she took her time wiping the tables, rewarding the customers by bending at proper angles. That, indeed, was the reason for the strict rule that she must wipe the table whether it needed wiping or not.

The girl did all that quite innocently, with the natural inclinations of a woman and not because of any training, for Paskal never hired girls that had experience in the Greek coffeehouses in South Sixth Street. As a rule such girls were cheats and were spoiled by the Greeks. They might be innocent enough when they started, but if they stayed on the job sooner or later the Greeks corrupted them, turned them, with their offers of money and gifts, into semi-prostitutes. Such girls continued to work in the coffeehouses not so much for the pay they got, which was small, as for the contacts they made. Many a Greek immigrant, becoming infatuated with one of these girls, would squander his hard-earned money, to be dropped cold as soon as the money gave out.

As the girl at Paskal's did not report for work until eleven o'clock, if an early patron, like myself, wished a drink before that time he had to go back of the counter and help himself. For Paskal, sipping his Turkish coffee, had his nose buried in the pages of the *Post-Dispatch* and would not disturb himself for a measly nickel. Paskal's blue serge trousers were shiny at the seat, but he put on a clean white shirt every day, and his shoes were always polished. What little hair he still had was combed neatly back, and the skin on his face was smooth and polished as if it had been rubbed with pumice stone. Paskal had a round, full face. His head was large and spherical and full of knowledge. Day after day I sat by Paskal, drinking from his great knowledge. He was a born teacher.

"When you learn to read the newspapers," he said, "read the editorials."

"What are editorials?"

Paskal showed me the editorial page. "It's here where the editors comment. Elsewhere in the paper it's news, no comment, no opinion, only what happens. Here on this page you get what the editors think and believe. Here things are analyzed and interpreted, and the writing itself, the *style,* is superior."

"There is *style* in writing, like in clothes?"

Paskal laughed. "Well, in a way. I can't explain it to you. But you'll learn it by yourself." I listened to him read the American papers directly into our own language, as if they had been written in it. And the words Paskal used—*kultura, tsivilizatsia, strategia.* I never knew that our language had such words in it. They were as strange to me as English itself.

I learned many things from Paskal. My mind was astir like a beehive ready to swarm. Thoughts and ideas, bits of knowledge, facts, rays of imagination hovered and darted in my mind like industrious worker bees waiting for the queen to set off on a new adventure. A world, unseen but concrete, was taking shape in my mind. If only I could absorb in my own head as much knowledge as was in Paskal's. Knowledge of *politika,* of *diplomatsia,* and the language, the English language.

Paskal and I were third or fourth cousins, but I did not remember him from the old country. Before I was born he, as a youth, had left the village, first going to Rumania, then to Bulgaria and finally to America. In the capitals of the aforementioned Balkan countries he had amassed quite a fortune as a building contractor. Having lost it all in a brick-manufacturing venture in Salonika, Paskal had joined the stream of emigrants to America. Arriving in St. Louis, he had worked for six or seven months at the Terminal and had then started the coffeehouse, a business which, though beneath his previous accomplishments and his present intellectual level, he did not regard as beneath his dignity.

Paskal's coffeehouse became a kind of school for me and Paskal himself my mentor and guide. It was as delightful and stimulating to be in the coffeehouse as it was dull, sweaty, and stupefying in the Terminal. The intellectuals who worked at odd jobs, or as waiters at clubs, or who were taking it easy between jobs, sat around discussing politics or social and labor questions, or played cards and backgammon. They talked in such an elevated style ("style" was becoming part of my vocabulary) that such expressions as "class struggle," "predatory capitalism," "proprietary interests" were bandied about by people who had no clear notion of their meaning.

Around the corner and half a block up was the flat. But a space as wide as the Atlantic Ocean divided the world of the flat from the weekday world of the coffeehouse. The flat constricted life, narrowed it down to pennies, black coffee and white bread, lunches wrapped in newspaper, talk of the jobs, of Frank, the Terminal foreman, who took bribes and seemed to be more important than President Wilson, of the trains and the engines, which were invested with human attributes, like personalities, and were talked about in detail. All this tightness of spirit, this miserliness, this airlessness of life, this moldiness of the mind Paskal expressed in the single word *pharisaism.*

Paskal had nicknames for his individual customers too. There was a fellow who had worked for seventeen years in the diamond mines in the Transvaal, South Africa, and who spoke English somewhat differently from the way the sports spoke it. It was incredible to me that a Macedonian could have been to a place called the Transvaal, South Africa. Paskal had dubbed this man the "Philologian" because of his preoccupation with words. This man carried an immense book with him, a bigger book than I had ever seen, and he would sit at a table and study this book for hours.

The Philologian never smoked or drank and sustained life largely on bread and cultured sour milk, which a Bulgarian made in a little shop a block down the street. It was said he followed this regimen not so much for reasons of economy as for some stomach ailment he suffered.

He could tell how a word came into being and trace its meanings through time as you would the story of a man or the history of a nation. He could tell whether the word was "obsolete" or "archaic" or "modern" and whether it could be used in ordinary speech or only in poetry. If he heard an unusual word, or even an ordinary word that he knew something unusual about, he would look up from his big book and start talking about the word as if it were some human being concerning whom he knew things that nobody else did. Since few people listened to him, he found in me a ready and eager audience, and he would address his remarks to me even though they were meant for everybody else to hear.

"Do you know what Mississippi means? Of course you don't. Well, I'll tell you." He took off his glasses, and his great filmy eyes became suffused with a warm light.

"Capricious! Ah, yes, yes, capricious. Now you just heard that there individual [to the Philologian, men were individuals or sometimes digits or entities] use the word *capricious*. Does he know its real signification and its subtle connotations? Of course not. How could he? But you, you are possessed of the capacity to become an erudite individual. You hold knowledge in high esteem, and your mind's thirsty for it. When I tell you that *capricious* derives from *capra,* which is Italian for that fickle, four-footed horned and bearded animal known to us as a goat, then to you a capricious individual will be a goatlike individual, which is to say a fickle and unreliable individual who jumps from one thing to another without reason or logic, the same as a goat, scraping at a bush, rushes to another bush, even though the bush at which it was scraping still had foliage to be scraped."

The Philologian wiped his glasses with his dirty handkerchief and was about to put them on and return to his great book when Paskal used the word *diplomat.*

"Ah, yes, diplomat, diplomat! Now you just heard my friend Paskal use that word. He of course knows what it means, but do you, my young and worthy disciple? Of course you don't. You are not an etymologist yet. An etymologist, of course, is a word scientist. To an etymologist words are not mere words; to him they are living individuals whose histories he explores. Now as to diplomacy. It derives from the Greek, and the first syllable, *diplo,* means 'double,' while the last, *mati,* signifies 'eyes.' Now, then, a diplomat is a man with two sets of eyes. That is to say, according

203

to the letter, a diplomat has double sight, one for the surface of things and one for what is not on the surface but on the underside. Ordinary people, with one pair of eyes, see only on the surface; a diplomat sees on both sides at the same time, before the thing is turned upside down."

"What about Mississippi?"

"Ah, yes, yes, Mississippi! You have a consecutive mind. Yes, Mississippi. The name is Indian and it signifies 'Father of Waters.' Just ruminate over that a little. Father of Waters! Now, are you zealous after more knowledge?"

"Tell me about Dago."

"Dago! Uh hum! I see! Somebody has *catapulted* at you that disagreeable *epithet.*"

"No. But somebody has *catapulted* at me a rotten tomato."

"A tomato! Uh hum. I see. A tomato. It's the same thing. The tomato is the concrete, tangible, palpable form of the insulting appellation. To have been the target of such a pulpy *missile* is *tantamount* to having been *stigmatized* a Dago without the epithet having been orally enunciated against you."

"I understand. But why Dago?"

"Ah, yes, yes. You have a logical and consecutive mind. Dago! Do you know what 'day' means in English?"

"Yes."

"And 'go'?"

"Yes."

The Philologian scratched his chin. "There's your origin. Day-go. The day is gone."

"Then why is it an insult?"

"Ah, that. Oh, yes . . . Well, you see . . . when the first Italian immigrants came to this country they were then, as now, remunerated for their labor by the day. When a laborious day came to an end and there was another dollar added to the pay, they would say 'Dago,' meaning that the day is gone. And so they were called Dagos."

All such bits of knowledge, whatever their source and whether real or fancied (years later I found out how fanciful was the Philologian's version of the origin of "Dago"), I fed to my hungry mind. From Paskal I learned things that transcended America, things about the world, about life itself. A teacher at heart, he loved to share his accumulation of knowledge. Paskal's familiarity with America was not real and intimate, rather an academic one, and his knowledge of the English language was largely book knowledge. But of all the people I had so far met in the colony, Paskal was the only one of large dimensions. He had had no extensive schooling,

204

and he was not well read in literature; but he had a truly wonderful mind, and I always had the feeling that his proprietorship of the coffeehouse was as temporary as his onetime job at the Terminal, that it was a steppingstone to something else. Perhaps because he was a self-educated man, he worshiped formal education, and he advised me to undertake a systematic study of the English language.

On Sundays and holidays Paskal would not sit at the table and indulge in prolonged discourses, but on weekdays he would sit with me for hours and share with me his wisdom and great knowledge of the world. To show my gratitude I did occasional errands for him and even helped him in the coffeehouse, especially in the evenings after the girl went home. Sometimes during the dinner hour, when Paskal went to the restaurant up the street for his meal and he wished someone he trusted to be on hand so the girl wouldn't be putting the nickels in her pocket instead of in the cash register, I would stay in the coffeehouse.

"Little cousin," said Paskal, "you came to America at the right age. Right now is the time for you to begin the study of the language methodically. Through the language you will grasp America, and through your grasp of America you can view the world as a reflection in a mirror. But you must not learn English like a parrot. You must learn it scientifically.

"First of all, before it is too late, you must learn how to spell every word you already know. Unlike in our own language, spelling in English is an important factor. Every new word you add to your vocabulary you must learn how to pronounce and how to spell. Otherwise the words would be mere sounds and when you see them in the newspapers or on the billboards or in books or anywhere else you would not recognize them. If you don't start doing that now, later on when you begin reading and writing you will have to learn many things all over again. You must now begin to learn to read, write, and pronounce, all in one operation.

"Learning English is, in a sense, like learning how to play music. Some people, like the gypsies, play without notes; others play from notes. Those that play from notes can look at music and hear the melody. Those that don't are like parrots; they must hear. I don't mean to minimize the importance of spoken English. You're young, and it is possible for you to learn to speak English fluently, but I wish to impress upon you the importance of English as it is written, for you see more English than you hear. English is spread all over, like rugs, like tapestries. It is embroidered on packages, scrawled on windows, it dances on electric signs, on the screens of motion pictures, and of course in the newspapers and in books.

"Behind all this embroidery of language is America, like a stage behind a curtain, and you never can see America, as you cannot see the drama on the stage, unless the curtain is lifted. Before your eyes and America itself stands the language, and that is the curtain. Don't try to unravel this complicated language embroidery all at once. Take small bits at a time, unstitch them as you would unstitch a piece of embroidery, learn how the stitches were strung together. Then take another, and soon you will find that these tiny patterns repeat themselves, and then you will know them instantly on sight, and you will not have to take them apart to find out how they were formed. Start now, work hard, and I will help you."

I did not have to go far to realize the soundness of Paskal's advice. Uptown, where I ventured when I was not imbibing knowledge, I would suddenly find myself in a strange and incomprehensible world. The curtain was there before my eyes, and I did not know what was going on behind that curtain.

Whenever I ventured away from the known world of the colony I did so with the curiosity of a cat exploring the grounds of a new home, and I was cautious. I almost sniffed as I went along, making mental notes of larger buildings and other landmarks to guide me back to the base at Second and Plum. Alone, in the daytime, in free time, in unmeasured hours, I would walk the streets of St. Louis. Leaving behind me the sooty, dilapidated houses in which my people lived, surrounded by warehouses, freight houses, factories, and shops, I would come upon Broadway, which was the avenue that led to the uptown world, to a whirlpool of people that puzzled me with their apparent idleness. They hurried along or ambled leisurely, entering shops and turning corners, feeling at home and confident. They all seemed fortunate in their knowledge of the city, of the language, of America. They knew where they were and where they were going, and no matter where they went or how far they went, they still knew their way back! They looked clean and well dressed, and there was something about them that set them apart from the people in the colony.

As I walked I would keep close to the buildings or close to the curb, unconsciously shifting about to make way for people going in the opposite direction. It never occurred to me that others might make way for me. My footsteps fell on the pavement lightly, as though I feared I might wake or otherwise disturb the master of these premises, where I was trespassing.

I could not overcome the feeling that when I was not on Second Street I was not on my own ground. For however much my knowledge of the city widened, the colony on Second Street remained the center, and I felt drawn to the cluster of brick houses there tenanted by my people. Returning there was, in a sense, like returning to the old country, a temporary and somewhat modified old country transplanted on American soil. Already I could detect something impermanent about the colony. There life was as at a campsite. The flats were not homes; they were just temporary quarters, and the people living in them marked time till their return to the real old country.

And so I walked along uptown. Though I felt a transgressor here, I wished to be like everybody else, to be undistinguishable from the rest of the people. But dressed in the secondhand suit from Morgan Street, I could see myself plainly for the immigrant I was.

A tall young man, wearing a gray suit, with the coat slitted in two places in the back, was just ahead of me. As he stepped on, the apron between the slits flapped gently, like a fan. At regular intervals the young man's right hand went into his coat pocket and took out a peanut. The hand cracked the peanut as it carried it to the mouth, where the teeth and the lips shelled out the kernel. The hand flicked away the shell fragments into the street near the curb. The young man did not bother to see where the shells fell.

I envied him. He must have bought the peanuts without even being aware that he was buying peanuts; he must just have stopped at some corner where a man was selling them and handed the man a nickel without saying a word and taken the bag, and he did not look into the bag, or feel its weight, to see whether he was getting a good nickel's worth.

I followed in the young man's footsteps and watched his every movement, as a faithful dog watches those of a master. He did not turn aside to make way for people walking against him. He just seemed to be unaware of their being there. And they made way for him.

That's the way to walk in a city street! When one walked like that, others would make way.

The long legs shifted along slowly, regularly. The trouser cuffs rotated about the ankles, then stopped suspended as the trouser leg momentarily draped itself on the calf. The gray felt hat fitted snugly on the proud head. Even the haircut had something poised about it. The hair was trimmed rather than cut, and it bunched at the nape of the neck into a kind of clump. The sports had their hair clipped high in back, raw and severe, accentuating the broadness and roundness of the neck. This young man's neck was lean and muscular, without being scrawny, and his hair neat and trim and full, without giving him the look of a freshly shorn ewe.

All the time he ate his peanuts with the ease and unconsciousness of breathing. What a way to eat peanuts! To eat peanuts like that in the streets you must not think of it. You must not think even that you are in the street, that you are walking. You must be oblivious of the people and of your own self. And above all, you must not think of the nickel you spent for the peanuts. The young man was not eating peanuts because he was hungry. With him it was a diversion.

It was not the peanuts, after all, or the way the young man ate them. Anyone, if he put his mind to it, could do that. The point of it was that to eat peanuts that way was proof that the peanuts were not important to you. It was proof that a nickel spent for peanuts —which you did not know you were eating and which when eaten you did not know you had eaten—was as nothing to you. It was proof that the nickel spent was not an amalgamation of twenty minutes of engine wiping.

Besides, the young man eating peanuts like that maybe would eat a whole lobster the same way. I had seen a lobster in a window, a monstrous red thing that Kosta said was full of delicious white meat under the shell. It was tastier, Kosta had said, than the meat of partridges or of any fowl or fish he had ever eaten. But to eat one, Kosta had said, he had to pay one dollar. Six hours of engine wiping for one lobster!

And, who could tell, the young man might have bought that fine suit without thinking about it. He most likely just walked into a store in that casual, proud way and said, "Wrap this suit up for me." Maybe he had half a dozen suits like that. Who knows? Such things were possible. Didn't some of the sports have two suits?

With full awareness I threw my shoulders back and deliberately held myself erect. Suddenly a tide of fearlessness coursed through my body. I wished it had been possible to see just how the single slit at the back of my coat opened and closed as I walked along, whether the tails separated by the slit flapped rhythmically as I stepped, and whether my trouser legs played gracefully around the ankles. For my footstep had a firmness in it now. I was not afraid of disturbing some imaginary master here. Ah, this is the way to walk! I did not watch out for others to make way for them.

I walked for two blocks without making way for anyone. I bumped into no one and no one bumped into me, though others didn't make way for me either. It was a revelation to me that it was possible to walk with such ease in the midst of so many pedestrians.

At Broadway and Washington Avenue, parked close to the curb a few paces away from the corner, I spied a peanut cart. Smoke spun out in gray filaments from the tin pipe above the oven in which the peanuts were roasting. Those already roasted were packed in brown bags and kept warm in a glass compartment.

I took out a nickel. Just a nickel. Just some metal minted into a round coin with a buffalo on one side of it and the head of an Indian on the other. No, it was not twenty minutes of engine wiping. It was just a nickel. It was nothing, nothing. I handed it to the man without saying a word, without even pointing to the peanuts.

The man handed me a bag of peanuts. The paper was still warm, and I put the bag in my pocket. I did not look into it or feel its weight. I resumed my walk, my new fearless walk.

My hand went into the pocket and took out one peanut, just one. The fingers snapped in the air, cracking the shell. They brought the peanut to the mouth. The lips and teeth extracted the kernel with some difficulty, and the hand tossed out the shells into the street not far from the curb. The next minute I spat out the half-chewed kernel. A foul taste in my mouth told me the peanut must have been stale or wormy. It's better to look at them before you put them in your mouth.

Nevertheless, I ate the next peanut in the same way. I walked slowly, ambling along. At regular intervals my hand reached into the pocket, the fingers snapped in the air, the teeth and lips, assisted by the fingers, picked out the kernels. So I went on, repeating the process.

But I knew it. I was doing it on purpose, not unconsciously. I tried to think of other things.

The street door of a tall, massive building kept turning. Its vanes disgorged people as they revolved outward and swallowed others as they revolved inward. This was a time-saving door. People poured out of it and into it and the doorway was never opened and closed. It was always open and it was always closed.

Farther down, behind a huge window, a girl dressed like a nurse in a white skirt and cap was pouring batter onto a flat iron plate. In still another window an Indian, dressed in skins and feathers and beads, lay flat on his back. His stomach rose and fell, rose and fell, as if he were breathing. I had stood by the window several times before to watch, and I had concluded that he was not a real live Indian, and what appeared like breathing was nothing but a concealed bellows. I stopped still in the middle of the sidewalk and stared at my hands, both of them shelling peanuts. My mouth was full, chewing. In the few minutes that I had forgotten about the peanuts I had reverted to my old habit.

10

The nighttime Terminal workers were getting ready for their regular Sunday-morning visit to the coffeehouse. The day before there was mail from the old country, and there they would hear news from others who had got letters. Letters from the old country came in bunches. Sometimes letters written a week or ten days apart would come in the same mail.

In yesterday's mail one of the men, Damian, had received two letters, both written by his fourteen-year-old son. Knowledge of reading and writing being one of the deep mysteries to Damian, the letters were read to him by Klement, who had never been a day to school but who, through superhuman efforts, had penetrated the mystery that Damian had failed to do. But Damian had at least succeeded in learning the ciphers, and so he was now able to tell numbers at sight up to about a thousand, and he could read the time on the face of a watch or a clock and could weigh things on scales, provided the scales were simple and he did not have to bother with fractions.

One of Damian's letters had been written after the feast of the Blessed Mother, and in it the fourteen-year-old boy had told how he and his mother had missed Damian on that important holiday. As Klement held the paper and slowly read the words, Damian shook his head in wonderment that words his boy had put on that piece of paper back home had traveled across so much land and water to be read to him here in St. Louis. Damian was proud of his boy.

"All the time we were thinking of you out there in faraway America," Klement read, punctuating every word with a long pause. Some words gave him trouble, and of these he repeated such syllables as he could make out until the word finally would dawn on him and he would pronounce it with gusto, as if he had jumped a hurdle or pulled a chestnut from the fire. Before proceeding to the next word, he would say the preceding one several times over, so as to limber up, as it were, before plunging ahead in total darkness.

"We had a fine feast—" Klement extracted the words from the paper—"and we drank a pitcherful of wine from the small barrel of last year's vintage, which we are saving for you. We did this in your honor. For we missed you very much. Mother sighed and said, 'Ah, my son, we ate and we drank, now if only your father were here!' " Klement stopped to collect his breath. And he was ready to resume his great efforts when a peal of laughter interrupted him. He looked up, puzzled, wondering if he had misread something. Damian, too, directed his small eyes from face to face. The eyes looked at every face and returned to the one whence the laughter had come. It was Trayko's face, the grin still on it. All faces save this guilty one were straight and somber. With his bewildered look Damian asked of every innocent face the same question: "Why did he laugh? What's so laughable about my wife and son missing me?"

In some face, or in all of them, Damian must have read the answer. For then his own face turned crimson and his hand snatched the letter from Klement. He put the letter in his pocket and walked out to the porch to be by himself.

The grin on Trayko's face etched itself deeper; his mouth opened and from it came the words in a drooling voice: "Ah, my son, we ate and we drank, and now if only your father were here! Heh, heh!"

My uncle snatched his cap and blew at it fiercely. The grin on Trayko's face faded away, and he rose silently and put on a freshly laundered blue shirt. Still silent, he started for the coffeehouse with Klement and Kozma. Presently Damian returned from the porch and went into the sleeping room, to which he closed the door.

"Are you coming to the coffeehouse?" my uncle asked me.

"No. I'm going down by the river."

"All right."

"I'd rather watch the boats."

"Your arm's all right now, isn't it?"

"Oh yes, it doesn't hurt at all. Just itches a little."

"That's the healing. Then you'll be coming back to work. You know every day you stay away you lose money."

"It doesn't make much difference. I'm not wasting my time."

"You're not! I suppose you're getting paid for sitting in the coffeehouse with those bums!"

"I'm not going to the coffeehouse now, am I?"

211

"That's only because it's Sunday and there's some decent, self-respecting people there now. You'd rather be there on weekdays with the loafers. How can you sit around doing nothing? Is that what you wanted to come here for?"

"I didn't come here to wipe engines."

"You can't drive the engines! And you can't be a brakeman or a fireman."

"The Terminal isn't the only place where there's a job."

"For us if it's not the Terminal it's the Carshop or the foundries. It's all the same."

"I am not going back to the Terminal."

For a full minute my uncle sat silent. Without another word he rose and quietly walked out of the room.

My uncle was right as regards the coffeehouse on Sunday. I did not wish to go there and listen to the pharisees. Paskal would be too busy promoting treats, and the intellectuals stayed away too. So I walked down to the bank of the river, my favorite place when I was not at the coffeehouse. The stifling heat of summer was displaced by balmy October days. It was still warm though not stifling. Back over the city hung a blue haze, and here by the river it was brighter, the sun falling gently on the bank and its rays casting glistening sheets on the placid-appearing but swiftly moving water.

The river was like a spiritual bath. Its expanse, its movement, its depth and breadth gave range to the mind. And it sang of the bigness of America, murmuring the magic names of the far places I had heard of in the coffeehouse. I sat there and let my dreams flow on with the mighty stream.

But the great river had something forbidding and awe-inspiring, something as mysterious and unfathomable as its depth. To me rivers have lives of their own, lives far more mysterious and ramifying than the lives of great men. And it was a matter of constant wonder that the Americans had succeeded in spanning the river with iron bridges.

I wondered, too, if it had been necessary when the foundations of the bridges were built to propitiate the river-god with the sacrifice of a human life. In the stone bridges that arched over rivers in the old country there were immured, alive, human beings. On a clear moonlit night, especially during harvest, people claimed they heard the voices of the people who long ago had to be sacrificed so that these bridges might stand to form a link between worlds on opposite banks of the rivers.

Sitting there on the bank, I was thinking of this old river legend told me by my blind grandfather when some chatter suddenly

212

brought me back to the Mississippi. Looking back, I saw a group of blacks, at least a score of them—men, women, and children—coming toward the river. They looked like some huge live bouquet, their happy chatter and laughter its perfume spraying the air. Some great invisible hand was carrying this bouquet toward the river as an offering to it.

Perhaps because my mind had been preoccupied with the old-country folk tales and legends, the approaching black people appeared to me exactly as I had fancied them before I had seen them in America. To the riverbank, so close to the streets, and yet so far away, they lent further enchantment, and again I was sitting on the bank of a wide, wide stream in some storied land, peopled by black folk in motley costumes, people full of carefree laughter and gaiety.

Little boys and girls traipsed along, their naked legs and arms black as ebony or brown as coffee. Some clung to their mothers' flowered skirts, like incredibly large blossoms hanging to mother plants. One of these little creatures fell away from her mother's skirt and came close to me. Two wide yellow eyes I had seen in another dream smiled up at me; a voice I likewise thought I had heard in that dream called out to me, "Hello, mistuh man."

It was Alma Jane's voice ringing out like a little silver bell. Hands clutching at my own, she began to tug at me.

"Come on, mistuh man."

Two other youngsters, a boy and a girl, also stopped. With smiling eyes and faces but without their hands, they too pulled at me, helping Alma Jane. "Come, mistuh," they said.

"Come on along, young fella," a deep voice boomed out from the midst of the bouquet.

"Sure, come!" said the river.

Alma Jane led me by the hand. I was now part of the offering, and I approached the river in a spirit of worship and sacrifice. At the water's edge the group ranged itself before the river as before an altar. The mirth and noise stopped, except for some young voices that were finally shushed by older ones.

I stood in silent reverence before the stream. A little wave, alert and eager, splashed to within a few inches of my feet. In retreating the wave left a stick of wood bleached like a bone. The next little wave leaped farther out and gathered the stick back into the stream.

A tall black in a long black coat and striped trousers detached himself from the group and waded into the stream until the water reached to his knees and the tail of his coat floated on it. He then stopped and turned, facing the gathering. He was completely bald on top, and his hair at the temples was silver gray. The sun, as it fell on his shiny dome and silver temples, glittered to cause a kind

213

of halo. The black man stood knee-deep in the water, his eyes on the people. He was silent. He stood there as if waiting for the river to soak through his being before he would speak. His arms, which were so long that the water, when it swelled up, lapped at the fingers, hung at his sides.

The man was beardless, and his clothes were not like the clothes priests wore in the old country, but having sensed a religious motif in the scene, I surmised that the man was a priest. The scene, in fact, reminded me of the Epiphany ceremony, during which the village priest threw the silver cross into the river and men plunged into the icy water to retrieve it.

The preacher's arms slowly lifted and opened out as if to embrace his people on the bank. "Bruthern and sistren!" The man's voice had something of the depth of the river in it. The words were familiar to me, though I had never heard them pronounced exactly like that.

"Bruthern and sistren!" The voice rose in volume and sonority. "The Lord God Jehovah . . ." The rest was unfamiliar. The words came out from the big mouth like iridescent bubbles blown by the river through the man. They floated and expanded in the sun-steeped air, and as they collided they burst and spilled over the heads of the people.

"Bruthern and sistren." Again the familiar words, and then again the rush of radiant bubbles. The water swirled at the man's knees. He grew perceptibly in stature, as if his body, like some fast-growing plant, imbibed vitality from the river. His voice enlarged too. The silvery bubbles grew to balloonlike proportions.

In a little while, at least in my eyes, the man grew to twice his size. He did, in a way, appear superhuman, as if he had not come here with this pious group but was of the river and had emerged from it to welcome the group.

The rumble of a train on the elevated track back of us drowned the preacher's voice for a moment, only to make it sound more sonorous as the noise died away. On the opposite bank unseen engines, their speed perceivable from the moving pillars of smoke above the bushes and trees, could be heard coughing and groaning. The two barn-red ferries, idle on Sundays, lay moored to the landing like giant tortoises asleep in the water. The river's main current went swiftly on, indifferent to the pious group. But wavelets, curious and inquisitive like pups, came nosing toward the bank, lapped and sniffed at ankles and hurried on, not to be left behind.

The river man's words now rolled out in cadences. It made no difference that I did not understand. I fell under the spell just as much as the black folk did, for this was no language addressed to the intelligence; this was the river talking through the man. The tall

214

angular body became fluid and rhythmical. Engulfed by the sounds that flowed through it, it swayed to their rhythm. Out of the depth of the river came the sounds, musical and moving. The arms spread out and beat like wings in the air; the mouth opened wider to let out the torrential music of the river.

"Bruthern and sistren . . . the Lord God Jehovah!" The music came in waves, advancing and receding, the same over and over again. The man's body swayed with its own music.

"The Lord God Jehovah!"

"A . . . men!" a voice from the group responded passionately.

"Bruthern and sistern!" beat the refrain.

"Yes, Lord!" A thin, high-pitched voice pierced the air. It was a woman's voice, which sounded like an engine's shrill whistle to the preacher's enginelike roar, and the preacher's voice gained momentum exactly as an engine starting out and picking up speed, except that when the preacher's voice reached its highest pitch it started all over again, as an engine would if it stopped and started, stopped and started. All the while the preacher's arms shuttled pistonlike, faster and faster, as the engine gathered speed.

With a start I became aware of my own body swaying to the rhythm of the river man's voice. Likewise I noticed that other bodies moved with the tempo of his voice and movements. The whole cluster stirred like a bush in the wind. And out of this stirring rose a humming noise, like an undertone of the preacher's own voice. Yet at times this humming swelled up like a tide and threatened to drown the preacher's voice, which in turn boomed louder, rising like a wave above the swelling tide.

The preacher stepped farther back into the stream, and the water swirled above his knees, lapped at his waist. The same water billowed out toward the bank and splashed at feet now sidling in. Then the water glided up, hiding ankles, trouser legs, hems of skirts. The whole group, except the children, waded in.

"In the River Jordan!" bellowed the preacher.

"Yes, Lord! Lord, O Lord!"

Water trickled in my brown shoes, went up my trouser legs.

"John the Baptist!"

"A . . . men!"

Arms shook above heads; fingers trembled in the sunlit air; voices quavered. The river went swiftly on.

Two black men seized a woman in a white robe and walked her deeper into the water.

"In the River Jordan . . ." The four arms pushed the white-clad figure into the water. The submerged body kicked and tossed, churning foam on the eddying surface.

"Hallelujah!"

215

The four arms fished out the body, still squirming and tossing like a hooked shark. It was a fat round body, to which the cloth stuck, tight at the breasts, wrinkled at the waist, tight again at the hips. The four arms half dragged and half carried the body to the bank.

Other men seized another white-robed woman and walked her to where the preacher stood in the water.

"In the River Jordan . . ."

"Hallelujah!"

"Hallelujah!" My voice echoed with the rest.

"Lord, O Lord! Yes, Lord!"

The Mississippi–River Jordan churned and eddied on the spot where it swallowed the woman. Presently it disgorged the head, sleek and shining, then the shoulders, then the firm breasts. The body was young, slender, contourless. It pranced and twisted in the arms that held it, slipping through them like an eel. To prevent its gliding through, the four hands kneaded the torso and the hips. When the breasts threatened to spill out like dough, the fingers kneaded them in. I found myself lending a hand from where I stood, my own body straining up at whichever point the borne body sagged, my hands quick to mold back the supple flesh wherever the other hands were slow to reach. In this way, from a distance, I helped carry the body to a dry spot on the bank.

Then my eyes went back to where the preacher stood in the water, and I saw there still another woman being ducked into the river. When she was pulled out I saw that she was old, gaunt, bony, her arms dangling as if lifeless. And I turned again to see what was happening to the young body with the skullcap breasts.

It was at that instant the sound of "Hallelujah" blasted so close to my ears that I closed my eyes to keep my eardrums from bursting. And then I felt a viselike grip on my burned arm, and I shouted, as if that would save me from whatever was happening to me. When I opened my eyes the river, the whole wide river, was rushing upon me. The preacher's voice was booming over my head, "In the River Jordan . . ." The rest was muffled by water gurgling at my ears. I was completely submerged.

A few minutes later I stood on the bank, my clothes dripping. I tried to wring the water from my jacket, but that caused wrinkles, so I let the water drip.

The black folk were now all out of the river. Again in a group they started to retrace their way up the bank. The preacher stopped by me and said something and smiled and gave me his hand, a black, sinewy hand with big knuckles. I took it.

Alma Jane smiled. "Mistuh man, him bim baptized too." With her people she disappeared up the street.

216

Not wishing to return to the flat until I was completely dry, I took off my jacket and spread it on a log. Then I remembered my pocketbook with eleven dollars in it, one five and six singles. Finding the water had not penetrated the leather, I let out a sigh of relief.

For a long time I sat there in the warming sun. The river flowed on calm and unruffled. It did not awe me much now. I had been baptized in it. But what had I been baptized? What? I wondered if my religion had been changed, without my knowing. No, it couldn't be that. The black people were Christians. There was the Hallelujah! and the Lord Jehovah and the River Jordan. Maybe I had been baptized an American! Was the Mississippi the great font into which black men, white men, men from all climes were baptized Americans?

11

The nurse removed the river-stained bandage from my forearm. With wads of cotton she sponged and wiped off the streaks of salve. Then she rose, and my eyes followed her across the floor. From the ball of brown hair at the nape of the neck, the eyes shifted lower where the white skirt fitted snugly to the hips, jerking along with them as if it were part of the anatomy. At first I had been charmed by the face, by the delicately textured complexion, but on subsequent visits I observed her figure.

It was some years since I had stopped classifying women as beautiful or ugly according to their faces. I must have been ten when quite suddenly I transferred my attention from the faces to the ankles. For me the ankles held the key to the shaping of the whole body.

I could not see the nurse's ankles, for her shoes buttoned high and the hem of the skirt came too low. But in reverse process, from the bust, from the waistline, from the hips, I envisioned the ankles with a sculptor's knowledge of anatomy. And they were perfect. I let out a forced cough to hide my thoughts.

The doctor looked closely at my arm, bending it up to examine the underside, where the burn had been most severe. He dropped the arm in my lap and took a card from the nurse at which he glanced cursorily and then scribbled something on it. He then went away.

"You're all right now," the nurse said. "As good as new. You don't have to come any more. Keep your sleeve rolled up and let air get on your arm." Her upper lip twitched a bit in the corner.

"Not come no more, eh?"

"No more. And don't you go have any more accidents now."

My mind raced after her words for the meaning like a cat leaping

218

over the grass to catch a mouse before it disappeared into a hole.

She was so good! As a boy I had always envied boys of my own age who had older sisters to knit them socks and sweaters. I wanted to do wonderful things for the nurse, like buying her a silk dress.

My eyes tried to be good, too. They did not stray from her face. The right corner of her mouth, where the glistening silky nap on the upper lip was more pronounced than elsewhere, went up a little, causing the nostril on the same side to dilate. She did this often, and it always gave her face a characteristic winsome expression that produced in me a swaying sensation. But now it went deeper through me, like a warning of an approaching dizziness.

"What are you staring at me for?" She looked at me reprovingly. But the tone of anger in her voice was unconvincing, like the pretended anger of a mistress chiding her pet animal.

Disappointment must have been written on my face, for the next instant she said, "Aren't you glad you don't have to come any more?"

Maybe she was telling me to go. Why was I sitting there anyway? She was all through with me for good. She was putting the scissors, the cotton, the little vials in a glass case.

I rose abruptly and made as if to rush out but suddenly checked myself and stood there hesitantly. They still hadn't asked for money. I had already got my last pay, and they hadn't taken out anything for fees. The nurse's back was turned to me. My eyes, involuntarily, went up from her ankles to her hips.

I waited for her to turn so she might at least see me go, for I was still uncertain as to whether I was supposed to go. There might be something more. Besides, it just didn't seem right for me to walk out like that and never see her again.

When she faced me I nodded, and then I began to move awkwardly, at an angle, toward the door. Before I got to it the door swung open and a man with a bandaged head walked in. He was a big, husky fellow, whom I immediately took to be a brakeman, for he strode into the room as if it were a caboose.

"Hi, beautiful!" He waved at the nurse. As easy as that, like swinging a lantern to the engines.

"Sit down," she said coldly.

"Okay, beautiful! You're the boss." The man slumped down in a chair.

And then it was to me she turned her beautiful eyes. "You wait a minute," she said.

"What's ailing the little Wop?" asked the man.

"Mind your own business."

"Okay, beautiful."

219

"Smarty pants!"

The words *smart* and *pants* were already in my vocabulary, but put together they conveyed no meaning, unless it was that the man's trousers were stylish, which they weren't.

"Come along with me," she said to me in the same angry voice she had used to the brakeman.

I followed her out into the corridor and down to the far end of it into another office. To a little bald man who was sitting at a desk nearest the door the nurse gave the card the doctor had signed. She then turned and without saying goodbye or any other word walked out. She did not smile at me, did not nod at me, did not even glance at me. She left me there as if I were a piece of baggage identified by the card she had handed to the man at the desk.

I felt crushed. I would never see her again. And she left me there just like that, without a word, without a sign, and after bandaging my arm five different times and being so good and kind. All that big-sister talk, too! If she had at least been contemptuous and resentful, the way she had been with the brakeman. But no, she did not even deem me worthy of that much. She just left me there, the article to which the card referred, a suitcase, deposited on the floor.

But why had she brought me in here? Was it here where they collected the fees? The five times she had bandaged my arm were no doubt recorded on the card. So much per bandaging. Now I would have to pay. All that sweetness until it came time to pay!

The man had been going through a filing cabinet against the wall. Now he returned to his desk, bringing back with him a bunch of papers, to which he secured the card with a metal clip.

"What is your name?" The man pronounced the words slowly and distinctly, pausing between each two words. He did not say, "Watchyr nem?"

I told him my name.

To the next question I shook my head. Long before this I had learned to shake my head sidewise for a "no" instead of up and down as we did in our village. The man continued to speak slowly and distinctly. He had a gold front tooth in the upper row, and the gold tooth tried to interpret for me. It said the man was asking for money. I shook my head more firmly, hoping thus, through pretended ignorance, to bring the matter to a close. The man might construe the shaking of my head as a sign that I had no money with which to pay.

Then I thought it wasn't right not to pay. After the way they had healed my arm. And I had an impulse to open my pocketbook so that the man might help himself to whatever the charges were. A stronger impulse to cling to my money checked the other. The thing to have done, had I thought of it in time, would have been to remove all but two or three dollars from the pocketbook and then open it to settle up with whatever remained. But now the man might take all my money. I kept shaking my head.

Finally the man wrote something on a piece of paper and gave it to me. I stared at the paper a moment, put it in my pocket, and walked out of the office.

That Paskal was a wizard. He merely glanced at the writing I brought to him and instantly knew what it was about. Had it been printed, like the newspapers, like the signs on windows and posters, I might have made out a word or two. But it was scribbled in pencil, and I couldn't decipher a single word. Everything was plain to Paskal.

"Yeah, just as I thought. It's from the claim agent. He wants you to go back and bring an interpreter along."

"What's a claim agent?"

"He's the man who'll fix things so you won't sue the Terminal."

"Sue? You mean go to court? What for?"

"For burning your arm."

"Do you go to court here if you burn your arm?"

Paskal smiled. "You burned your arm while at work. Your arm is healed, but you lost time from work and suffered pain. Besides, how do you know your arm's as good as it ever was? Six months from now it may hurt you."

"And supposing it does. What has the Terminal got to do with it? I burned my arm."

"No, you didn't. The engine did. The engine belongs to the company. The engineer, too. That's the company, the engine, the engineer, you. You are the company when you work for the company. If you injured somebody, it's the company that does it; if somebody injures you, it's the company that does it. And the company has to pay."

"Pay?"

"Pay damages. For time lost. For possible disability."

"I won't sue the company."

"Then you'll sign for nothing."

"Do I have to sign?"

"You have to sign papers renouncing all claims against the Terminal."

"I'll do that."

"Don't be a pharisee! The least they'd do is pay you for the two weeks you lost."

"You mean they'll pay me for the time I was not working?"

221

"You should get more. I'll go with you to interpret. We may settle for a hundred dollars."

"What about the doctoring?"

"They do that for nothing. They have to do that. Suppose they hadn't and suppose an infection had set in and, God forbid, you had lost your arm. Then they'd have to pay for the whole arm—thousands of dollars."

"They pay here for arms?"

"I think the law is two thousand dollars for an arm. I am not sure. For a finger I think the law is two hundred dollars. Depending on which finger it is. Some fingers are more than others. For a leg I think the law is five thousand dollars."

"It's all according to the law?"

"Of course. It's not the company's *magnanimity.*"

Magnanimity! I made a mental note of that word.

"Suppose you lose an arm while you're not on the job. Who pays?"

"Nobody. Unless you're insured. If you're insured no matter when or how it happens the insurance company pays."

"Would the insurance company insure an arm?"

"They'd insure anything. A woman—she is a French actress—has her legs insured for one million dollars."

"But if you're not insured and you weren't on the job when the accident happened, nobody pays."

"Nobody."

"Well, I wasn't on the job when it happened. I was there, of course, on top of the engine, wiping, but my mind wasn't there."

"What's that got to do with it? Your mind could have been in the old country, or here in the coffeehouse, or a thousand other places. Your arm was there wiping, and your arm got burned. Not your mind. And Uncle Sam compels the company to compensate you."

"Who's he? Who's Uncle Sam?"

Paskal smiled, and then after a moment's reflection he said, "I think you better ask the Philologian to explain to you who and what Uncle Sam is."

"But you know who he is?"

"He's not a person. He is . . . well, he's an idea."

"He's an uncle, you said."

Again Paskal smiled indulgently. "You know, I myself should very much like to hear the Philologian explain the meaning and origin of Uncle Sam. I would indeed. Until you asked me I had never thought about it. This is an instance such as when adults learn from children. Not that you are a child, but your newness here in

222

America, your fresh impressions and reactions, your curiosity are like a child's. And that's wonderful. I wish I had come to this country at your age. I believe I would have been as eager and curious as you are. And who knows, today I might not be brewing coffee for the sports and the pharisees!"

"You won't be doing that for long, I think."

"Who knows? As for Uncle Sam, I can tell you about him, of course, but I think it would be better if you found out for yourself. For you will eventually. Then you may say that Paskal was all wrong about Uncle Sam!"

"Tell me anyway."

"There's no such living person. Not as a single individual anyway. Still he exists, collectively—which is to say, he is the entire people of America. In that sense he is an idea. Or, you might say, a spirit. He's a *symbol.* That's more like it. He is the symbol of the American nation. He is the American nation. Let me put it this way: Supposing I were telling you a folk tale, and each character in this folk tale was a country, a nation. France would be a woman, a tall, beautiful woman, and her name would be Marianne. Russia would be Grandfather Ivan. You know him. England would be a stout, strong, stubborn, thick-necked man who goes by the name of John Bull. America—that would be Uncle Sam."

"Let's have a drink, Paskal," I said. "I'll treat."

Paskal smiled. He knew from my entranced countenance that I understood even better than he hoped.

"Shall we have coffee?"

"May as well."

"Maybe you'd like a cigar instead."

"No."

I knocked on the table for the girl, and when she came I ordered two coffees—after she had wiped the table.

"I had never thought of Uncle Sam in terms of interpreting him," Paskal continued. "I had always thought of him as America itself, the entire American people. And that's what he is. But just now it occurs to me to wonder why he is an *uncle.* Why not just Sam, like Marianne for France? Or Sam Jones, like John Bull, or Grandfather Sam, like Grandfather Ivan. Why Uncle Sam?"

The girl brought two steaming little cups of coffee and set them on the table gently.

"This girl's become an expert at making Turkish coffee," said Paskal as he raised his cup and took a long draft of the thick, syrupy liquid. He then lit a cigarette.

"What does Uncle Sam look like?" I asked.

"He's tall and stern-looking, with hard-set jaws and a long, tapering beard. He wears a stovepipe hat with stars and stripes on it. Sometimes his trousers and his coat have stars and stripes on them."

"Oh, I know him. I've seen pictures of him!"

"You no doubt have."

"You said you wondered why he is an *uncle.*"

"I am wondering right now. Now I don't know anything about the origin of Uncle Sam, but it occurs to me that whoever evolved the idea of an Uncle rather than a Father or Grandfather Sam hit the nail on the head. Now you take fatherhood, or grandfatherhood, they both imply blood relationship, don't they? Unclehood is broader and can take in children of other bloods. You don't have to be related by blood to somebody for him to be your uncle."

"Like my Uncle Tanas," I said.

"That's right," said Paskal.

"America is made up of the children of all the nations and Uncle Sam can be the uncle of all."

If time at the Terminal stamped itself into pennies, time at the coffeehouse with Paskal minted itself into gold coins.

"Now I think I've said a good deal about Uncle Sam. And I shouldn't be surprised if you, not so much because of what I said but because of your young and impressionable mind, have a better notion than I of who and what Uncle Sam is."

"I think I know who and what Uncle Sam is," I said.

Paskal sighed. "As for myself, I regret that I didn't come to this country a generation ago. For Uncle Sam is not so fond of making nephews of men his own age. Like most uncles he is a stern and opinionated old man. He believes in his ways, and he believes his ways are the right ways. And so he is fond of children and youths who grow up to love him and love his ways and become devoted to his beliefs and ideas. To such he bequeaths his great legacy, spiritual and material. For them he can trust. Well, I guess we better say no more about Uncle Sam. Wouldn't you like to hear what the Philologian has to say about him?"

"I'd rather we didn't ask him. Let's leave it exactly the way you put it."

"Good. Tomorrow, then, we go to the claim agent together."

"And Uncle Sam goes with us."

"That's right. That's absolutely right."

The next day I walked up Broadway with the omniscient proprietor of the Balkan. He was dressed like a steamship agent or maybe like a banker. You couldn't tell in a thousand years that he ran a coffeehouse. He wore a double-breasted blue serge suit, with four buttons in each row. As we walked up Broadway toward Market, my heart swelled with admiration for Paskal. There was something about him, about the way his black patent-leather shoes stepped on the sidewalk, about the way he set the *bômbé* on his big head—full of knowledge that it was—about the way he carried his stoutish body that said you could be born in Macedonia or Portugal or Rumania, and you could still be quite at home here in America.

At Market Street we took the trolley going to the Union Station. I handed the conductor a dime and raised two fingers, indicating I was paying both fares. The conductor tugged at a rope and the trolley bucked ahead like a stubborn mule. The trolley behaved as if it owned the whole street. It was impatient of other vehicles, banging its gong alarmingly to automobiles or horse-drawn carriages that dared to ride its tracks. At times when it was all clear ahead, the trolley raced, swaying and diving, causing me a kind of seasickness.

"You let me do all the talking," said Paskal.

"As if I could do any talking myself."

"I mean you leave everything to me."

Paskal must have been to the claim agent's before, because he knew exactly where to go.

The bald man was there, bent over his desk. Glancing at us, he not only recognized me but must have remembered my name, for he rose and went over to the filing cabinets. He seemed to know exactly where the papers were, in which drawer, as he didn't search for them but pulled them out promptly, all clipped together. He motioned us to follow him, and we walked behind him down an aisle flanked by desks at which men pored over piles of papers.

We came to a corner where a room was formed by frosted-glass partitions. The door, too, was of the same glass, and across it, in black letters, it said ELMER PETER CLIFTON. The Peter in the sign gave me the clue that it was a name, not a statement, and my surmise was substantiated when the man who was leading us used the expression "Mr. Clifton" in speaking to the girl who sat at a desk near the door. The man gave the girl the papers and walked back. The girl rose, raised her blouse a bit at both shoulders, and picked up the bunch of papers. Then she opened the glass door, pushing ELMER PETER CLIFTON against my face.

The "Peter" was spelled exactly as in my own language. It was a good name. I had always liked the name because I had two cousins so named and liked them both. The "Elmer" made no particular impression on me, except that I wondered whether it was pronounced Ale-mare or Il-mir. For some unaccountable reason "Clifton" struck me as very funny. American names with which I was familiar so far were short names like Sam, Mike, Frank, Tony, Steve, Jack, and big names like Washington, Lincoln, Roccafalla.

But Clifton fell in neither category. It sounded soft and pulpy, as if there might be something flatulent about it.

ELMER PETER CLIFTON was drawn away, and Paskal and I entered the private office. In a corner sat Mr. Clifton. We took the two chairs at either end of the desk, and the three of us formed a triangle.

Mr. Clifton fitted his name to perfection. A man in his forties, he was soft, blubbery, his face round and the skin smooth and of a sickly pallor. The only sound thing about him was his hair, which was thick and curly. His pudgy fingers crackled the papers, and the gray eyes began to shift from the papers to Paskal's black *bômbé,* which he had set on the table.

Four cigars stuck up from one of Mr. Clifton's vest pockets. There was something bright and heroic about the cigars in their gold wrappings and red bands. They tried to contradict my impression of Mr. Clifton. One cigar stuck its head a little higher than the others, and this one was the most animated, arguing in Mr. Clifton's favor. At one moment it was on the verge of scoring a point in his favor, when suddenly Mr. Clifton's right hand detached itself from the papers and the sausage fingers clamped the cigar and proffered it to Paskal. Without a word, but with a determined movement of the hand, which cleaved the air in front of him, Paskal showed how incorruptible he was. The sausages then tore the red band, stripped the gold foil, and stuck the cigar between Mr. Clifton's blisterlike lips. As he lit it the cigar cried gently.

Paskal's *bômbé* on the desk was defiant, as if it were his emblem of authority, like the messpots of the janissaries. There was nothing cringing about Paskal. The conversation between him and the claim agent was too rapid and fluent for me to follow in any connected sense. Occasionally, in the darkness of the speech, a known word would flash like a firefly, giving a little light. I understood more words spoken by Paskal than by the claim agent. The latter talked with the cigar in his mouth and his words sounded like gurgling and sputtering.

Then all at once, out of Paskal's mouth, came the intelligible words "One hundred dollars."

The agent closed his eyes and shook his head. When he reopened his eyes he took the cigar from his mouth and set it in an ashtray. A flow of words pattered on the table. Some syllables rolled away by themselves, like pebbles, and spelled out, "Fifty dollars."

Now I knew what was asked and what was offered. Still I turned to Paskal. "What does he say?"

"He offers fifty." Paskal sifted the Bulgarian words through his teeth, as if fearing the American might understand.

"It's all right. Let's take it."

Instead of communicating that to the agent, he reached for his bowler. "Let's go."

"But fifty is enough. It's twice as much as I would have made if I had been working."

"All right," he said resignedly. "It's your money."

Then I heard him say "Sixty" to the agent. And the agent agreed to that.

Out in the street I offered Paskal ten dollars for his trouble.

"I couldn't take that even from a pharisee," he said.

"It really belongs to you. I had settled for fifty."

"I couldn't take a penny." And he wouldn't.

12

In my inside coat pocket the money was like a charm. It radiated warmth and energy through my body; it made me feel strong and powerful and free. I had heard a story about some man in the old country who could, on a bet, jump across a wide stream. The point of the story had always been somewhat vague to me until now. The man jumped the stream on every bet until one day a shrewd old peasant, noticing a string around the man's neck, assumed that a little icon or talisman was tied to it that gave the man secret strength. So he bet the man double the usual sum, provided that he jumped after first removing what he wore around his neck. The man agreed and removed the string. Hanging to it was no icon or amulet or talisman but a moneybag made of cotton cloth dipped in beeswax. The bag was heavy, and the sound of gold tinkled as the man dropped the bag into the custody of another man's hands. Then he stepped back away from the bank to allow himself a good run and gain momentum. He started running slowly, gathering force as he neared the bank, reaching which he jumped—and landed in the middle of the stream. When he paid his bet and passed his head through the loop of string and shoved the moneybag into his bosom next to his bare skin, he thought he would try again, just for the fun of it. This time, as always before, he landed on the opposite bank.

The six goldbacks plus my savings gave me some such secret power now as I walked uptown. Some blocks north of Market I stopped in front of a clothing store to look at some suits in the window. In a high mirror running through the middle of the window I caught sight of a full reflection of myself, and I was startled. For a moment I wondered if there was some trick to the mirror to make people look shabby so as to get them to buy new suits. Or perhaps the mirror itself was honest, and it was the newness and stylishness of the suits in the window that made my own look so drab. I began to notice all kinds of things that were wrong with my suit. The lapels of the coat curled at the edges instead of lying flat and smooth. The trousers were too short, revealing part of the socks; the sleeves, too, were short, leaving at least two or three inches of shirt sleeve exposed. I blushed at my appearance, and the next instant I was in the store, having accomplished the bold step in a kind of trance. Once inside a wave of shyness swept over me. Several clerks stood by like vultures waiting for customers. One of them made for me. The others did not move, as though there were among them a tacit understanding as to whose was to be the next prey.

The clerk, dressed though he was in a style calculated to uphold the reputation of the store, suddenly appeared to me like any cloth merchant in the old-country marketplaces, except that he spoke to me in English—at least so I thought.

I tried on the jackets of several suits until I put on a brown one that, the salesman said, was a perfect fit and the last word in stylishness. The sleeves were just the right length. The trousers were a trifle long, but the salesman advised against shortening them. The suit was of such fine cloth it would last me for years. "In six months you'll grow to the pants," said the clerk. "For now wear suspenders." Quickly he fastened a pair of suspenders to the buttons at the back of the trousers, strapped them over my shoulders like a harness, and buttoned them to the front of the trousers.

"Magnificent!" he exclaimed. "Special was it made for you! You can't buy such a suit at Famous and Barr. In this suit you can go anywhere and you will be proud." He stepped back a few feet, clasped his hands, and shook his head adoringly from side to side.

"On Broadway everybody will think a sport you are."

I said, as well as I could, that I didn't want to be a sport.

"All right. He don't want to be no sport! Who said a sport he must be? Who? This is a free country. Nothing you have to be in this country which you don't want to be. Did I say you have to be a sport? Did I? I said people will think a sport you are. Did I say wrong? A compliment it is for people to think a sport you are."

"How much?" I asked.

"Yesterday twenty dollars it was. This morning we reduced it to fourteen dollars and ninety-nine cents."

"Too much."

"Too much! About suits you know? What you know about suits? Such kind of suit did you ever buy before? Tell me. You I'm asking!"

229

"Too much."

"You can afford maybe a cheap suit, eh? Like the one you got on? How much do you want to pay?"

"Seven dollars."

"Take off the suit! You think in a store on South Broadway you are, or on Morgan Street, maybe?"

I turned toward the privacy of the booth to make the change. The salesman stayed with me.

"Such a suit! And such a fit!" He took me by the arm. "You can afford twelve dollars?"

"No."

"Wait a minute. You don't take off the suit! I will see the boss."

He walked away and soon returned with the boss. The boss examined the suit, felt the cloth, and swayed his head in admiration of the fine material. The two held a brief conference and the manager left.

"I told him you'll bring other customers to our store," said the salesman. "And he says the suit you can buy for nine ninety-nine."

"All right. I buy the suit."

"He'll buy the suit! Listen to him now! He'll buy the suit. For nine ninety-nine? The suit'll buy you."

The man reached up to touch my cap. He made a grimace as if he had swallowed vinegar. "Ach, a cap mit a suit like this!" he grieved. Again he reached up and this time removed the cap, looking inside it, no doubt to ascertain the size. Having done that, he went straight to the shelves where the hats were and took out a soft brown hat, cleaved the crown with his hands, pressed dimples on either side of it, turned down the brim in front, and set the hat on my head. Then he stepped back to show his admiration by swaying his head and making groans.

"How much?"

"For you, two-fifty."

"My cap good enough."

"Mit a cap you can't wear this suit."

"No."

"I tell you what I'm going to do for you. A crime it is to wear a cap mit this suit. I will give you the hat for two dollars."

"No."

"You want people should look at you and know that you are an immigrant? You want that should be? Or you want you should walk in any street and feel as good as anybody, or maybe better. Which? Only two dollars will make the difference. How can you go out of here wearing the cap mit this suit? You will wear the suit, isn't it?"

"Yes."

230

"Mit that cap?"

"Yes."

The man put the palms of his hands flat against his ears. For a second he stood like that, then, taking down his hands, he said with finality, "All right. Take the hat for nothing. I will not let that suit be worn mit a cap. I will give you the hat."

"I no want for nothing. I got money to buy."

"Your money we don't want. You should be satisfied we want."

"All right. I take hat. And I pay. That's all!"

"He says that's all. Listen to him now. He got a suit from which there's no better. He got a hat. And he's got suspenders. But he'll wear an old blue shirt to spoil everything. And he says that's all."

"I got other shirt."

"What kind shirt you got? What kind? A blue shirt? Or a white one with blue stripes maybe? It's a brown shirt of silk you need. Everything should be brown. To match the suit."

"No shirt."

Broadway was the same street. The buildings in it were the same. The people, though not exactly the same people, were not any different from the people of an hour ago. And yet everything was different, because I was different. The buildings had dwindled in size; the streets had narrowed.

I caught a glimpse of myself reflected in a store window. I had to look again to make sure it was myself I had seen the first time. Some miracle had happened. While everything else—street, buildings, people—had undergone a shrinkage, I alone had gained in stature. I felt big, tall.

The brown hat with its cleft and dimpled crown and downturned brim sat on my head at a rakish angle, inclining toward the right ear, which it touched, almost.

I couldn't keep my eyes from the store windows, where I viewed the dreamlike reflection of myself. The trouser legs hung straight down to the ankles, not a whorl or wrinkle on them, the crease sharp. The new suit gave the body a new vitality and held it straight and proud. In a suit like that a body couldn't stoop or slouch. I felt good. There was a spring in my step.

And then suddenly as I looked into a store window I saw reflected, beside the body in the new American suit and hat, a peasant boy wearing jacket and breeches of homespun cloth dyed in alder bark and walnut hulls. The boy's long woolen socks met the breeches at the knees, and his feet were encased in pigskin sandals. On his head he wore a saucer-shaped hat with loops of green and yellow embroidery.

231

"Go away, don't follow me!" The proud boy in the American suit tried to push away the boy in the homespun breeches.

"Stop putting on airs. Who do you think you are? You think you're an American because you've got on a new American suit and hat? Let me hear you speak English. And where do you think you're going all dressed up like that? To the flat on Plum Street? I dare you to. I dare you to walk in there and face your uncle and the others in this new suit and hat!"

In the next window there was a clock and it pointed at four. Fifteen minutes would bring me to the flat. The men there never left till five-thirty. I would stay out until they had gone to work, and I had been thinking of doing that now, but the peasant boy had challenged me.

"Why should I stay away? Why? Sooner or later they'll see my new suit. Why shouldn't I walk in now dressed in my new suit? It's *my* suit. I bought it with my own money, money Uncle Sam made the Terminal give me."

I knew exactly how the pharisees would feel about the new suit. But there was a bigness in me now, a spirit of defiance. The pharisees never bought new suits except when they started back for the old country, so as to dazzle the stay-at-homes and give the impression that that was how they dressed in America.

Yes, I would walk right into the flat in my new suit. Let them say what they liked. What had they to do with my life that I should try to live it according to their standards? As for my uncle, I had no wish to cause him needless embarrassment or hardship, but if he was governed by pharisaical notions and tried to impose them on me, it couldn't be helped. I will go straight to the flat dressed in my new American suit. Let them say what they like. I will keep quiet. Now, I am who I am. And I just bought myself a new suit of clothes, my first new American suit. I bought it with my own money, which was given to me by America, because of the law here. I'll wear my suit whenever I like and wherever I like. I'm wearing it now, and I'm going straight to the flat because I pay rent at the flat and can go in and out when I please, dressed as I please.

As I climbed the steps toward the porch I heard the clatter of the spoons. And then six pairs of astonished eyes glared unbelievingly at the apparition at the door; and six spoons, some filled and some empty, wherever they happened to be in their journeyings from bowl to mouth, remained suspended in mid-air. Only Klement's mouth continued to chew absently; all others were frozen as if by sudden paralysis. Klement gulped down the half-chewed food and attempted to speak, but he found himself voiceless, like a stork.

My footsteps as I walked in were cries of derision and defiance. "Shut up, shut up," the footfalls on the floor kept repeating.

The first move at the table was made by my uncle. He reached down to the floor to pick up the beer bucket. Holding the can in one hand, he stroked his mustaches with the back of the other, and then, placing both palms against the sides of the can, he tipped it. He did not lower the can until every drop of the amber liquid had been drained. He put the empty bucket back on the floor, wiped the froth at his lips and mustaches with a palm, and pulled out the old Turkish watch. He glanced at it, clicked the cover, and dropped the watch back into the lower vest pocket. Then he laid his hands on his lap and sat there with his head inclined over his right shoulder. His cap, which he wore at all times, lay on his head like a frightened cat. The others resumed their meal in a silence broken by occasional inane remarks.

I walked into the bedroom and proceeded to unwrap the flat box containing my old suit. I wasn't going to wear my new suit around the flat. When I had changed, I folded the new suit carefully so as to keep its press and laid it out flat in the box, which I shoved under the bed. Then I lay on the cot to wait for the others to leave for the Terminal. But the next instant I swung my legs and sat up in the bed. My uncle was standing by the bed with a yellow envelope in his hand. It was a telegram from Ellis Island. My father was on the way to St. Louis. The telegram was addressed to my uncle, not to me.

13

There must have been some correspondence between my uncle and my father that I knew nothing about. My uncle now announced that he would be returning to the old country, and it seemed that it had all been arranged for my father to inherit his job at the roundhouse and his place at the flat. It was inconceivable to me that my father should join the stream of immigrants to America, he who had derided it and ridiculed the returned *Amerikantzi,* sneered at their fineries and belittled everything about them or what they represented. Could it be that he had come because of me, that my uncle had written that I was on the way to being swallowed by the alluring bypaths of the new country and that he would never see me again? I just couldn't believe that America had cast its powerful spell over him as it had over the millions. He should never have come here; he was an anachronism in America. And he could not have come at a worse time for me, when I was not working. There was no more convincing proof that one was on the way to perdition than not to be working when there were jobs around.

The day after my father's arrival he and my uncle and myself, the three of us as was proper, went to Paskal's. My uncle did the treating. For a newcomer a visit to the coffeehouse was like an initiation. Thereafter he might, or might not, drop in for a brief visit and a treat, but on his arrival it was like taking communion after a fast or visiting a monastery after recovery from an illness.

On his last night at the roundhouse my uncle took Father along to familiarize him with the crossing on the ferry and with his job and to introduce him to the boss. I went along so that my father would not be alone on his return. The big river and I were old friends, but it had never occurred to me to take a ride on the ferry. It cost only a nickel.

My uncle showed us the sandhouse, a shack of corrugated sheet iron where he roasted the sand in a huge cylindrical stove and fed it to the locomotives through a swinging overhead pipe. He had to clamber up the sides of the engines to the sandbox at the top near the steam whistle. My father looked lost and confused in this complicated world of ash pits, coal chutes, turntables, groaning locomotives, blowing sparks, and puffs of steam.

On our return to the ferry landing my father and I were silent. It just didn't seem real to me that he should be walking on this path along the eastern bank of the Mississippi. We walked along like two ghosts in the twilight, in a strange world, with engine noises in the distance and the river lapping at the bank. A pink mist lay over the city across the river. What was my father doing here in this strange and alien world? We did not talk, but a lot was being said in our silence; an inaudible, unuttered dialogue was going on between us. I resented his coming, but I was determined his presence in America would have no effect on my future, on my dreams, or the kind of life I would be striving to fashion for myself in the new country. It would be better to talk instead of to walk in this pregnant silence, to say what was in our minds and hearts, as father to son and son to father, to give voice to the suppressed thoughts.

In the nearly a year and a half that I had not seen him he had changed physically. It was not old age; he was forty-seven years old. But he had lost weight, his body had shrunk some, his face had lost its firmness, and the color had paled. I was carrying on the silent dialogue, kept asking him questions, to which I myself supplied the answers. Why did he come here? Why? Did he suffer some reverses in his minor trading activities? Did he finally succumb to the lure of gold in America, like those whom he mocked and taunted? If he came here because of me, then why was he not glad to see me? Why did he not talk to me? Why did he not put a father's hand on my shoulder? Was he displeased and angry because I had given up my job at the Terminal? Well, then, I would tell him because I did not dream of coming to America to waste my youth in the ash pits of the roundhouses. I would tell him that I would soon be starting to work as a busboy in a fancy restaurant on the sixth floor of Famous and Barr, the largest department store in St. Louis; that I would be working only four hours a day, from ten to two in the middle of the day and no Sundays; that I would be making more than at the Terminal and get a free lunch to boot; that I would not be wearing greasy overalls but a white jacket freshly laundered and pressed every day and that my face and hands would not be grimed with coal dust and stained with my own sweat and the oily sweat of the engines. I would have time, too—yes, time—to study the language

235

and to learn where exactly I was in America and where I was going and how I was to get there.

My father could not peer into my mind or into my heart in order to plumb the depth of my desires, my longing to comprehend this land, to embrace this nation of many peoples. Who made this nation? Why were millions of people, speaking different languages, pouring into this land, striving to make new lives for themselves?

I was now in my fifteenth year. I had been in America almost two years and was beginning to untangle some of the intricacies of the language and to glimpse, in my mind's eye, the shape and contour of the land. They were only gleanings, there were vast areas of darkness, unrevealed, uncomprehended, but my mind was in ferment, growing faster than my body. It was expanding, reaching out, hungry for knowledge, not for mathematics, geometry, physics or any of the other sciences but for the language and for the land and the people, for the meaning and essence of this nation, its history, its traditions, its idioms. I had not come here as a migrant worker, a mere wage earner, but to be of this land, of this nation. I had no clear notion as to how I would go about achieving this, except that I must master the language, not just its grammar and syntax and lexicography but its nativeness, its idiom, the "you speak my language" kind of language, and the process would reveal itself to me as it had to millions before me.

The red-painted ferry plowed through the muddy water like an immense tortoise. The river meant nothing to my father; it was nothing to him that he was amidstream of the living artery of this continent, that he was on the waters of this mighty river, crossing the breadth of America and gathering unto itself a dozen other great rivers before branching like the spread-out fingers of a hand to empty into the sea.

We walked up Poplar and turned south on Second Street. Paskal's was on the west side of the block. I asked my father if he would like to stop at Paskal's for a while. He said no, not angrily, just a flat no. I said I would go by myself. He took my hand and said, "Please don't go. I want to talk to you." We went back to the flat, and he told me that two months after I had set out on my journey to America his wife had left him. One day, without saying a word to him, she took her three children and returned to her own village.

14

The head busboy at the restaurant was a Macedonian, a friend of Paskal's, which was how I got the job. "It's light work," Paskal had said, "and short hours. Just what you want." And he was right.

How different it was to be walking to work dressed in my new suit, in a clean white shirt and necktie, patent leather shoes, and a felt hat instead of the black cap with the shiny visor, to walk up Broadway and Market Street and then up Sixth Street to the very heart of the business district and there enter the big department store like any customer and ride up in the elevator to the sixth floor and then past displays of dining tables, cabinets, cupboards, stuffed chairs and sofas and then oil paintings in gilt frames and past huge urns out of which grew dwarf trees with tiny oranges on them and plants with broad leaves tough as rubber, and then into the restaurant itself, the brightest, most cheerful, most festive place, with gleaming white tablecloths, neatly folded napkins like tricorn hats, shiny silver, china vases blooming with fresh posies.

Hanging chandeliers, as in a church, cast soft light over the diners, mostly women carrying packages, which they placed on the floor beside the chairs. The waiters, in black trousers and trim red waistcoats, weaved in and out carrying balanced on one arm large trays loaded with dishes.

In my white jacket, my hair sleeked with some sticky stuff the head busboy made me put on, I maneuvered my little hand truck around the tables and picked up the dirty dishes and trundled them to the kitchens and to the dishwashers. I scrupulously left on the tables the dimes or quarters left by the customers. They were for the waiters, most of whom were Greeks. Occasionally one of them would slip me a quarter for paying closer attention to his tables. Once an elderly woman, in a big hat with two huge feathers, had sat down at a table that had just been vacated and not yet cleared of the dishes. She called to me and asked me to clean up. There was a quarter on the table that I left untouched. Noticing that, she opened her purse and rummaged in it and came out with a nickel pinched between her thumb and forefinger and offered it to me. I don't know what made me do so, but I swung the little truck and trotted away without taking the coin. The very next moment a sense of remorse swept over me and I almost turned back to say "I am sorry" but did not do so.

The most important thing to me about this job was that I was among people—Americans—and not among engines. There was no factory whistle piercing the air and causing a tremor in your heart. The drone and chatter at the tables, even if I understood little of it, was more like a symphony to me. Words that I knew, over-hearing them, leaped out like the familiar notes of a song, or like old friends, to greet me. For the first time, though I was not a part of it, I was in a completely American environment. The contrast between this cleanness and brightness, between well-dressed, beautiful people paying eighty-five cents for lunch, and the dreary roundhouses and factories and the ten-cents lunches wrapped in newspaper was painful to me. I envied the young men who came in to lunch with their wives or sweethearts, and I yearned for the day when I, too, might be able to walk into this restaurant as a guest with my wife on my arm. That day did come, alas, when I was no longer young. Half a century later my American-born wife and I were conducted by a hostess to a table that had just been vacated and the dishes had not been removed. She hailed a busboy. He was about the same age as I when I performed this same chore half a century before. He had thick brown hair that came low over his forehead and lively, gleaming brown eyes. His face was lean, sharp, sensitive. My wife asked him if he was a Macedonian. No, he was born in Yanina, in the Epirus. I told him I had written a biography of Ali Pasha, the Lion of Yanina. He either didn't understand what I was saying or he wasn't impressed. Then I told him that I had been a busboy here fifty years before. His face and eyes lit up, and he pointed to the badge and white ribbon with gold lettering on my jacket's lapel. I explained that I was a Vermont state senator and that I was attending the annual meeting of the National Legislative Conference and had brought my wife to lunch here where I used to be a busboy. Neither I nor my wife could tell how much of it he believed or how much of it he understood.

My father thought little of my work at the restaurant, in spite of the short hours, or perhaps because of it. He did not disparage it

238

but intimated that it was undignified work for one brought up in a tradition that a man must never help with the dishes or with other kitchen chores. It was different doing your share of the cooking and dishwashing at the flat. That was more like camping, being on a job to earn money. But he did not try to assert himself, to impose paternal authority over me. There were no arguments between us, though in various ways, mostly through silences, he let it be understood that he disapproved of my unorthodox ways and that he suffered because of it. I believe what repressed him was the fear that I might leave the flat and go to live on *foornish.* And so he let things slide along, trying to make the best of what he regarded as a very bad situation. And I continued to live in the flat, where Shano was the patriarch, for my father's sake. I slept there and had early dinner with the nighttime workers. The pharisees would permit no one to live in their midst unless one fitted into their pattern of life and subscribed to their notions. They put up with me only because of my father, with whom they sympathized. And while resenting their sympathy, he was nevertheless grateful to them for tolerating me in their quarters. At least this way I still dwelt under the same roof with him. Besides, I was hardly ever in the place except to sleep and take one meal. Lately I had begun to attend English classes three times a week at a public school on the north side. And I spent much time studying English in a quiet corner of Paskal's coffeehouse, with the Philologian very eager to share his lexicographic knowledge with me.

Neither was my father pleased with this. He grumbled as he did about some books I bought at a Bulgarian bookstore–coffeehouse in the colony. One of these books, a handbook for the study of the English language with texts in both languages, was written by an American missionary named Thompson who must have spent many years in Bulgaria to have mastered the language of that country. Called *A Method for Studying the English Language,* this book proved of immense value to me. From it I not only enlarged my vocabulary but also obtained a rudimentary knowledge of the principles of English grammar. Later, in Montana, somehow I came into possession of an English grammar by George Lyman Kittredge. It was providential that this particular book should fall into my hands. Only years later I learned that the author was a celebrated Shakespearean scholar and teacher, and his grammar was one of the best ever written. Also at this Bulgarian bookstore I purchased, at the Philologian's suggestion, an Anglo-Bulgarian and a Bulgarian-English dictionary, two pioneering works by a fellow Macedonian, a Yale graduate, who at this time was a lecturer at the University of Sofia and a correspondent for the Chicago *Daily News.* Along with the Philologian's oral didactics, these two dictionaries, harbingers of big Websters, Oxfords, and others yet to come, were my first introduction to the fascinating study of linguistics. I treasured them and pored over them, little suspecting that in ten years I would succeed their compiler as the Balkan correspondent of the Chicago *Daily News.*

The language became an obsession with me, words and phrases humming and twanging, seeking to be orchestrated into sentences. Sometimes a word would keep repeating itself, insisting that it be pronounced correctly, pursuing me like a pestiferous fly or bee. Paskal was as much interested in my progress as I was myself. He seemed to take some pride in my strivings. He regarded himself as my tutor and adviser, and that pleased him. In me he probably was seeing something that he in his youth had dreamed of accomplishing but never had, ending up as a coffeehouse proprietor in an immigrant colony. He counseled that as soon as I learned a new word I must also learn how to spell it. Otherwise, he said, the words would be mere sounds and there would be confusion. "You must learn to read, write, and speak English in one operation. Just like music. Some people—the gypsies, for instance—play without notes; others play with notes. Those that play with notes can look at music and hear the melody. Those that don't are like parrots; they must hear. Hearing is important; it helps your pronunciation, but in English spelling is even more important. You see more English than you hear, for English is spread all over. It is on packages, on windows, on signs, on the screen in motion pictures, on everything and everywhere, and of course in newspapers, magazines, and books. And behind it all is America."

And Paskal was right. I looked around and there was the language embroidered everywhere. Bit by bit I began to unstitch this complicated embroidery. I took tiny patterns apart, learned how they were put together. Then to my delight these patterns repeated themselves so that I didn't have to take them apart again, since I knew exactly how they were stitched. Some I could not understand; after I had unraveled them I could not knit them together again. I puzzled over them. *Would that I could. Contrary and notwithstanding. Be that as it may.* Paskal said no grammatical rules applied here; these were idiomatic expressions, peculiarities of the language. *Idiomatic!*

The night school I now attended was in the neighborhood of a free public bath that did not close until ten. At least once a week, after a two-hour lesson in English, I treated myself to a bath. I needed no one to guide me about now. I could walk in the streets in the daytime or at nighttime, and I knew where I was, even if I ventured into unexplored parts of the city. I could always orient myself back to Broadway or to Market Street and thence to the colony on Second Street. I had money in my pocket, good clothes, and Uncle Sam saw to it that I got free instruction in his language and a free bath whenever I desired. The money was not given to me by the Terminal because of the Terminal's "magnanimity" (Paskal's word) but because Uncle Sam said so. Like St. Peter in heaven, who had a register in which were recorded the sins and virtues of every human being on earth, Uncle Sam had such a book of all the people in his land. And I had been in that book before I had ever heard of Uncle Sam.

But there was one thing I could not attribute to Uncle Sam or discuss with Paskal or with my father. The journey at night from the school to the coffeehouse was difficult. I had to pass some dark streets where whisperings from dim doorways, gentle tappings on windowpanes, and other forms of beckonings were hurdles in my path, especially on those nights when I had taken a bath. I would keep going, my eyes straight ahead, but it was like going past a cemetery at night, with my whole being alert for sounds and apparitions.

To avoid this section, one evening I went out of my way, intending to return by going down Broadway and then down Poplar Street. But I had not gone far when, instead of looking straight ahead, my eyes began to go to doorways and windows in search of mysterious shadows that were not there. My ears listened intently for familiar calls. Then an unaccountable disappointment seized me, and I turned in my tracks and went back over the usual route, where my eyes darted to the low, dingy houses, glimpsing a silhouette in a darkened window with its shade halfway down, my body trembling to the sibilant sounds issuing thence, like the calls some birds make. A low, oozing voice, charged with the substance offered and pregnant with its promise of revelation, chased after me. A bolder creature flung a leg in my pathway, and as I hurried away I heard her angry mutterings, like those of an aggressive street beggar whose pleas are ignored.

Having passed the place, I walked on undisturbed, except by myself, for the thing was still there with me. There was an incompleteness in my wakened body, a new hunger that made other things inadequate. The money in my pocket, my growing knowledge of the language, my expanding perspective of America would become unimportant. This thing with its urgency overshadowed them.

It was not an American phenomenon, like sandwiches or "crackerjack" or like frying eggs on both sides; yet I was aware that America had made it acute by making it available in the streets. And though this thing was far more overpowering than any other physical desire, I couldn't satisfy it with the inconsequence and casualness with which I had bought the bag of peanuts or a package of crackerjack. Something put it in the category of shame and danger. I remembered Kosta's allusions to a show that was live and electrical at the same time, and my father's guarded warnings, and Turpen's saying that you couldn't visit a flour mill without getting flour on your cap. There was more to it than the mere fear or danger of it. Something innate, something deep-seated and obscure, made you feel that a bath couldn't wash it away or a doctor cure it.

Returning from school to the coffeehouse one evening, I saw a new face there, or rather an old and familiar face rendered new by America. It was Vasil, whom I had not seen for four or five years but whom I instantly recognized. He rose promptly and with a broad smile on his weather-tanned face shook my hand vigorously.

"I was waiting for you," said Vasil. "Paskal's been telling me you're already teaching him English."

"Get yourself a drink before you sit down," Paskal said.

"I suppose you thought I wouldn't recognize you," I said to Vasil, returning from behind the counter with a bottle of pop. And maybe I wouldn't have if I hadn't seen a photograph of you just before I left the old country. Where did you come from?"

"I've been here only a couple of hours, and I came from Denver, by way of Chicago."

"On the Burlington, eh?"

"How'd you know that?"

"I used to work at the Terminal."

"He doesn't work there any more, though," Paskal said. "He's a bum like the rest of us. He only works four hours a day as a busboy uptown at Famous and Barr. But he still lives with the pharisees."

"You'd like the West." Vasil nodded significantly. "Once you go there you'll never want to go back to the old country."

"No West for him. And no old country, either," Paskal objected. "He'll be a professor, a real one."

I had seen other immigrants who had returned from the West, but none had about him the air of bigness and expansiveness that exuded from Vasil's person. This was manifest in the way he talked, in the way he was dressed, and in the aura of strength and self-confidence. There was about him none of the immigrant's constraint and shyness. His poise and self-assurance were derived from an expanse of earth and sky. He seemed to have a stake in the ground on which he stood.

There was nothing unusual about Vasil's dark-green suit, but his hat, shirt, necktie, and belt bespoke a different America from that with which I, so far, had a passing acquaintance. Tipped back on his well-shaped head, itself set on a long, lean neck, was a broad-brimmed cream-colored felt hat, with its crown not cleaved in the middle and dimpled on two sides but rising like a cone and pressed in on three sides. Instead of a ribbon this hat had a narrow strap of brown leather, with an ornamental design on it like a frieze. His shirt was wool flannel and of approximately the same color as the hat. Tied to his neck in a knot and flowing from the throat was a black ribbon about an inch wide. The brown belt was a replica of the hatband, except that it was wider and had a large embossed silver buckle. When Vasil had stood to greet me I had noticed that the belt girded him below the waistline, just above the hipbones, on which the trousers seemed to hang loosely without support from the belt. This gave Vasil the appearance of a lean, healthy hound, and with his weathered and open countenance, his free and easy speech, his apparent pride in his Western attire he was a living advertisement of an America as different from the Terminal, the can factory, the flat, the sports as St. Louis itself was different from the village where Vasil and I were born.

In the weeks that followed the America that Vasil breathed began to insinuate itself into my blood and bones like leaven into dough. Between us two, despite the four or five years difference in our ages, there began a companionship that lasted as long as Vasil's brief life. The bond between us was America and its language. Vasil loved America with his whole soul. Through this association my perspective on America broadened and deepened.

Paskal's America was of the mind, gathered from the pages of the *Post-Dispatch* and the *Globe-Democrat;* Vasil's was an intimate, eye-witness America. He had worked in the copper mines in Butte, had harvested wheat in the Dakotas, had dug pipe lines in Texas and Oklahoma, had picked oranges in Los Angeles County. In Portland, Denver, Omaha, and other distant places Vasil had washed dishes for a meal. With a dollar in his pocket, or no dollar at all, he had ridden freights or jumped passenger trains across the length of states. He knew all the railways of the Southwest, the Northwest, and the Far West. Names of strange cities, of rivers and mountains rolled from his tongue like shiny pebbles, full of color and a new mystery. And Vasil conjured up for my avid mind and imagination a western America that thrilled me with the power of sorcery.

Holding before my eyes and mind the promise of this new America, Vasil meantime enlarged for me the boundaries of the immediate, the St. Louis America. The first time we went uptown together I noticed that people stared at my friend, but it was a different staring from that directed at the immigrants. They stared at a tall, lean person who swung along, erect and proud, his big hat tipped back, the silver buckle glittering at his waist. Youngsters looked at him with envy in their eyes, and I sensed how to them, too, Vasil must typify an America of their longing.

We stopped at a store on Sixth Street, where Vasil bought himself two white shirts and an ordinary hat with a narrower brim and low crown and some commonplace neckties. Already he shed some of the spell of the Big Horn River, the North Platte, the magic of Utah and Arizona, the iridescence of Shasta Glacier.

We took in movies together—at a nickelodeon on Broadway that Vasil said was operated by two Greeks named Spiro and Charlie Skouras. We went to a vaudeville show at Sixth and Olive, and when we came out I said to Vasil, "Was that a real live show?"

"It was live all right, but there's livelier live ones."

"Did you understand everything that was said?"

"Oh yes. You're bound to miss some things."

I walked along with hands in my pockets and a feeling of frustration. It was not that the show was a disappointment, but it brought home to me the truth of how far away I was from America. I had gone into the theater with no clear notion of what to expect. The first thing we saw on the stage, which was like an altar with all kinds of gilt carvings on either side, was a man, a woman, and a boy simultaneously engaged in putting a menagerie of dogs and cats, some of them in petticoats and bloomers and some with ribbons on their heads, through a series of antics. A dog pedaled a bicycle while the man walked along as a guide; two yellow-haired cats, their forepaws in boxing gloves, were pummeling each other under the boy's prodding, while two other dogs were jumping through a hoop the woman raised higher and higher after each jump.

Presently a dog was lifted up to a rope stretched across the stage between two iron posts. The other dogs and the cats, as well as the audience, watched in breathless silence while the man urged this one dog to negotiate the tightrope. And when it had done so, I was startled by a sudden burst of noise that sounded like the crackle of rifle fire and that caused the dogs on the stage to yelp. I almost leaped out of my seat, and the next instant I felt embarrassed, seeing how the noise was the result of people striking the flats of their hands together.

As the clamor went on, the stage itself was in turns concealed from the audience and revealed to it by the lowering and lifting of a curtain. During the momentary intervals when the stage was visible the three people there were bowing and some of the pups were barking. When finally the hand-clapping subsided, the drop did not go up again. The band then struck a different tune, and suddenly there appeared two men, one at either side of the stage. They walked rapidly toward each other and met at the middle, in front of the drop. One of them then addressed a barrage of English to the other, who seemed bewildered and made frantic but vain efforts to inject a word of his own.

I sat at the edge of the chair, my whole body straining after the running speech. I had never before heard so much English spilled out so fast. My mind, in its eagerness to catch words, ran after the speech but the speech ran faster than my mind's ability to comprehend. Sometimes the speech came to a calculated pause, and the pause was filled with a burst of laughter and hand-clapping.

It seemed to me that the whole audience knew I was there and that I alone understood nothing. And the whole audience laughed at me for my ignorance. Through five or six acts the language ran through my fevered mind like water through a sieve. Not even the presence of Vasil and all that he represented could dispel my gloom. At this moment America seemed remote and impossible to attain.

But once out in the street I felt a surge of relief. As Vasil walked by my side with his proud gait, my mood began to change.

At Market Street, where we turned into Broadway, I said, "I didn't like the animals. There's nothing to understand."

"I like girl shows best, with plenty of dances and songs," said Vasil. "Have you been to the Standard yet?"

"No."

"Would you like to go sometime?"

"Yes."

"I guess they'd let you in there. You're big enough. Do they sell you drinks in the saloons?"

"I haven't been to a saloon yet. Why do you say they may not let me in at the Standard?"

"Well, it's a show for grownups. We ought to try a saloon and see if they'd sell you drinks. Would you like that?"

"Nothing wrong in it?"

"Not unless you get drunk."

"Do you get drunk?"

"Now and then. The last time it was on beer. It's worse than a whiskey drunk. But I spend my money on something else."

"Like what?"

"Women. Have you had a woman yet? I mean been to one yet?"

245

"No."

"Well, that's one place I won't take you."

"Why? Is it bad?"

"It all depends. It's bad if you catch something. And it's bad if you spend all your money on them bitches. Once you start going to them it's hard to stay away. First thing you know you're working for them bitches. Many times I've spent my last buck to go to one. I've been here five years and I got no more money than you have. As fast as I've made it I've spent it. You can't earn money fast enough for that business. In Butte, Montana, I once spent fifty dollars in four days, all the money I had saved in three months. It's wide open in Butte, and there are five hundred registered prostitutes in the town. All kinds of them—Chinese, Japanese, French. Different styles."

"Styles? You mean the different clothes they wear?"

Vasil laughed. For a long time we were silent.

One evening Vasil took me to the Standard, but the "nude" dancing girls wore tights. Only one of them appeared in the nude, but behind some transparent mesh. To us in the twenty-five-cent seats in the second balcony she was a misty form. A man next to us had a pair of binoculars. He lent them to us without our asking, but it was more rewarding without them, since at our distance the girls in their flesh-colored tights at least gave the illusion of nudity. Every time the girls turned their posteriors to us and bucked, the band sounded as if a carload of junk had been dumped.

The music was loud and jerky, or slow and sinuous, depending on the exertions of the girls, who, as they weaved or pranced, were bathed in floods of different lights. As the show progressed the whole interior became pervaded with a kind of miasmic something that cast itself like a spell on the audience, causing some men to utter unashamed animal groans and others, hanging onto their seats, to leer ahead in glazed quietude.

I felt the exhalations creep up on me, working on me like some strange magic, repellent and yet fascinating. Intermittently I thought of what Vasil had said about going to prostitutes. I knew his warnings would be unavailing if I carried the mood of the place outside with me. And then in my mind would spring up the syphilitic figures I had seen in a ten-cent wax museum on Broadway. I felt alternately swayed and irritated, as if my body were a stick of wood being rubbed against another stick and then dampened just when a spark might flash.

When we came outside into the chaste air again I felt the relief of having wakened from a nightmare.

246

PART
THREE

A New Language Is

a New Soul.

—SPANISH PROVERB

1

Returning to the flat one evening, I found my father seated by the table in the kitchen.

"Are you ill, Father?"

He did not stir. He sat there as in a trance, his cap slightly askew.

"Father."

"Yes."

"Is it bad with you?"

"I am not sick. I felt too tired. A night's rest would do me good." He talked in a low voice, perhaps in consideration of the others sleeping in the other room. "Sit down, my son. I want to talk to you." His voice was a mere whisper.

The kerosene lamp on the wall cast a dim light over the interior. The coal stove panted like an overheated animal.

"Is it true," he asked, "that you are going to *linia* to Montana with this Mitko who's signing up people?" He removed his cap and held it in his left hand. With the right hand he touched his forehead, inclined over the shoulder in that characteristic fashion that meant he had resigned himself to something to which his whole will still objected but which it was powerless to alter.

I did not answer immediately. Looking at him sitting there, so helpless, I felt a surge of pity for him. If only he would give vent to his anger! If he would at least try to assert his will! I still would do what I was determined to do. But I would have less pity for him and I would go on to Montana with a lighter heart. I had my own life to live, and I was in America. America was already invading my being, forming my thoughts, channeling my desires. My mind was a loom in which pulleys and treadles wove the complex fabric of the new language. The stirrings in my young mind and in my body were innate and universal. But they were guided by the new sights and proximities, the new climate and environment. The fare that would satisfy these longings of body and outreachings of mind was American. And it was that that my father couldn't alter. That's why he couldn't speak with force and will.

"You would leave me," he said pathetically. "You would go to this remote country without even telling me about it. I had to hear it from others." The thumb and forefinger of his right hand twirled a link of the heavy silver watch chain on his vest. Even in the hottest summer days he wore his vest. The collar of his blue shirt was always buttoned. He never wore a necktie.

"I would have told you before long."

"And do you think it wise, my son, this going to work on the line?"

"Lots of people are going. The shipping fee is five dollars. And they give you a free pass back to St. Louis."

"I know that. But you have to work at least six months to earn a free pass back. And with the kind of people signing up for this gang it will be the wonder of wonders if the gang lasts a month."

"But there are more phari . . . Lots more older people have signed than sports."

"It makes no difference. One hot pepper is enough to spoil the stew. Besides, why must you go to *linia?* Listen, my son, if you don't want to work here in St. Louis, let us then go back to the old country. Now I've worked steadily and I've saved enough for both of us. We don't need much. We can quite well get along without America."

"I don't want to go back to the old country. If I was there now I'd be longing to come to America."

"And is it better to work on the line and live like a gypsy? Is plowing your own soil and living under your own roof worse than carrying steel on the railway?"

"I may carry steel for a while and live like a gypsy a summer or two to save enough money to go to school, maybe go to college. In the old country it's plowing and poking donkeys till you die. There's no use arguing, Father; I've signed up and I am going."

"And if I should forbid you to go?"

"You can't forbid me. This is a free country."

"It's a free country. Yes. That's what the sports say. That's how they excuse their laziness. It's a free country—but that doesn't mean a son should have no respect for his father and go contrary to his father's wishes."

"I am going to Montana."

"And that is final?"

"Yes."

250

"All right then. I shall go, too."

"On the line?"

"Yes."

"But you think it's unwise to go on the line."

"You don't think so yourself. Maybe you are wiser than I. If it's good for you, then it should be good for me, too."

"But it's different with you. You like it better at the round-house."

"No. I never liked it at the roundhouse. I work there because if I don't work there I'd have to have work somewhere else, and one place is as bad as another."

"Your only reason for wanting to go on the line is because I am going."

"Wouldn't that be a good reason?"

"But I am not a child. I can look after myself."

"I know you can, and I am not coming to look after you. I am coming because it may be better to work on the line. If it's good enough for you and a hundred other people it should be good enough for me."

"But I . . . I don't want you to come."

"I don't want you to go either. But you are going. You say this is a free country. Well, if it is free for you it should be free for me, too. I am not going because of you, and I am not going with you. I am going with the gang." He pulled out the watch and clicked it open. It was an old Turkish watch, and he wound it up with the little silver key that hung from the chain like a fob. The watch made sounds like a cricket as the key turned. The numerals on the dial were Arabic ciphers, and the golden lid and case were ornamented with Arabic scrolls. It was a familiar object to me since childhood, but that watch seemed strange to me now and it seemed curious that that old Turkish timepiece should keep time here in America in a different climate and a different civilization. Suppose you took out the movement from the Turkish case and set it in an American case with an open American dial. Who then would know that it was an old Turkish watch? Watches differed only outwardly. Inside there was something common to all of them. I began to muse on how human beings were different only outwardly and inside they all were the same, like the watches, and it was all a matter of adjustment, but I looked at my father's face and the comparison began to grow vague and complex in my mind.

Mitko, the straw boss–interpreter, had set the first of March for the gang's departure for Montana. He had arrived in St. Louis from St. Paul in the beginning of February, sent by the Great Northern

251

to recruit a large gang for the Montana division. With an array of "self-writing" pens and pencils in his vest pockets and a notebook, he went around signing up people.

He was a man of rather imposing appearance, which was augmented by an overcoat and a hat made of the skins of animals. For buttons the overcoat had sticks of polished wood, or it might be pieces of horn, or bone—you couldn't tell, as you couldn't tell whether the coat and hat were made of the skins of bears, buffalo, raccoon, or some other kind of American animal. The buttons, or what were supposed to be buttons, were an inch long, with their ends pointed and polished, and to button them you had to pass them through loops. The hat was black, its fur smooth and glossy, and it was made something like a double hat, for on either side it had extra folds, which were tied at the top and which could be pulled down over the ears to protect them from the cold. It was apparent that Mitko had come from a cold region. With his frosty brows and straw-colored mustaches and a watch fob made of an animal's claw, so extracted from the animal's paw that there was still some gray hair on it, he did bring into the coffeehouse a suggestion of blizzards and snowy fields and forests.

With his prepossessing appearance Mitko inspired confidence in everybody. It was not entirely the prospect of money that made people sign up for the gang. Some of them, especially the younger ones, made as much as two and three dollars a day as chippers and core-makers in the steel mills in Granite City, while the pay on the railroad would be much less. It was more the release, perhaps, from these heavy, sweaty tasks, the getting away from soot and grime and smoke and ashes and grease that made them sign up for Montana. With some it was the distant sorcery of the West, the freedom and mobility, the great regions beyond. They had come five thousand miles from the hearthside to where they were, and they would go still another two thousand miles in their search for America. Perhaps, in a way, they were not unlike the early pioneers who, trekking westward in their covered wagons, passed the fat and fertile lands of Iowa and pushed on farther into Kansas or Nebraska, only to turn back and settle on the good lands they had left behind. Perhaps the same spirit impelled these latter-day pioneers of a different blood and of a different, industrial America.

Mitko did little talking. He made no extravagant promises about wages, living conditions, or special privileges. Answering questions with a kind of Anglo-Saxon curtness and brevity, he said that of all Northwestern railroads the Great Northern was the largest and had the best reputation for "treating good" its employees. He was a goodhearted, good-meaning man, for although he was endangering his own position as straw boss–interpreter he signed up sports and others who could—as the saying goes—buy and sell him when it came to knowledge of the English language, or knowledge of any kind for that matter. He turned no one down, despite warnings from the pharisees. He did not bat an eyelash when Vasil, who had a reputation as an "agitator" and "gang-buster," proffered his five-dollar shipping fee.

Paskal's lunar face radiated elation as the ring of the cash register sang sweet and inebriating songs to him. From various tables came simultaneous knocks for rounds of drinks. Paskal would hurry from behind the little counter, where he filled the orders, to help the girl serve them. Too busy for the usual amenities, such as sitting down at the tables to play up to the "treaters," all Paskal could spare now was the bestowal of an occasional beatific smile.

The girl, on the other hand, did not deviate from her dual role. She did not sidle along in that undulatory, droopy way she affected on quiet days, but she never omitted to wipe the tables between treats. And she took her time doing it, bending low and reaching out unstintingly with her naked arms. She served Turkish coffee, "pops," Turkish delights, cigars, to men in blue shirts and overalls sitting side by side with men in silk shirts, white collars, and silk neckties. The snooty Balkan establishment had gone democratic and proletarian. In the corners and out-of-the-way places were stacked bundles, rolled blankets, suitcases ranging from imitation leather ones just bought in St. Louis to old-country valises of reeds and cane. And there were many musical instruments—banjos, violins, mandolins, clarinets, guitars, distinguishable by the shapes of their cases.

An experienced eye could look at the baggage and tell the composition of the gang, tell that it was made up of sports, intellectuals, pharisees, of men who put crosses before their names as written down by Mitko, and of men who wrote down their names in great flourishes. He could tell that the backbone of the gang were the men in overalls, whose things were rolled in bundles or packed in the old-country valises. The flashy suitcases with the straps and shiny brass clamps, as well as the cases containing the musical instruments, occupied less space. And in that there was ground for optimism, for when a gang "busted up" the busting up was often the result of too strong an ingredient of intellectuality and sportiness and not enough good old-fashioned pharisaism.

Even so, many heads on which rested shapeless, crumpled caps, like moldy splotches of cow dung, shook ominously over Mitko's having accepted so many heads coifed with pearly gray felt hats. There was one man who even wore a *bômbé*, like Paskal's. He had been a waiter in some rich men's club uptown and a student of law at St. Louis University. Wholly for reasons of health—he had large blueish circles at his eyes and a sunken chest—he had joined the gang and had been nicknamed the "Avocat." Already some of the mustachioed gentry began to make jokes about his impending juridical career on the line. The Avocat good-naturedly made himself deaf to these gibes. A little man with a scrawny neck on which stood—precariously, it seemed—a disproportionately large head, he assumed an attitude of philosophical sufferance. His face, though pallid, was of a cherubic aspect, and his eyes stared wide and almost popped out of their sockets. There was about the little Avocat such an appearance of physical frailty and thinness of voice that his choice of the legal profession was incongruous in the eyes of his compatriots, who associated *avokastvo* with bombastic oratory. His membership in the gang was comically pathetic, but no more so than that of the bibliophilic philologian, who was also going and taking with him, to my advantage, his store of knowledge—the big book.

2

Paskal's coffeehouse looked like the waiting room of a railway station. For several days before the departure of the gang for Montana Paskal threw out the window all pretense to intellectualism and the rather exclusive air of his establishment. The place was thronged with people treating liberally as on a holiday. Some, the younger ones, were dressed in blue serge suits and wore neckties. The majority were in freshly laundered overalls and jackets. Nearly all had quit jobs in factories, foundries, the Carshop, packinghouses, even roundhouses, to join the gang. Transportation to Montana was at the expense of the Great Northern, but since that railway did not come to St. Louis, we were to be carried to St. Paul, the eastern terminus of the Great Northern, by the Burlington line.

The gang numbered about a hundred men. There were people of varying degrees of intelligence. There were simple and illiterate folk like my friend Nichola, and there were some who had gone to grammar schools and knew something about the shape of the world and how it was organized. Some had been in America three or four years and spoke a little English; others were greenhorns who had signed up for the gang immediately after their arrival from the old country, and this was to be their first job. But whatever the background of the individual workers, whatever the extent of their education or the lack of it, the gang had a way of leveling them so that no one put on any airs. We were all privates of a single company, except Mitko.

The train glided out of the shed and twisted through the yards, the engine ahead snorting and scenting with its nose. Coal chutes, ash pits, roundhouses, where I had labored, revolved into the background. Some of our people in their greasy overalls stood on the

255

tracks, their mummers' faces grinning as they waved to us. Once I had stood there like that, watching the trains and wishing I were on them to be traveling through America. That seemed remote now, like something from a dimly remembered past. Already things that had happened to me in America were forming a past, a history and a background.

The train roared ahead through open country. The illusion of the earth's moving backward communicated to me a sense of growth, of a widening of the ken. It was a growth nourished by the new climate and the new environment, a growth pushing its young roots into American soil. St. Louis was now the nucleus of an American memory, which would deepen and broaden till it would blot out the old transatlantic memory.

The train rumbled over an iron bridge and the noise drowned the chatter of the Balkanians. I kept my face to the window. A sudden deafening roar, galelike, blasted in my ears and my view was blocked by another passenger train going in the opposite direction. The train on which I was went ahead, carrying me forward into a new life.

But I turned my face from the window and there beside me was my old life. My father was asleep there, the old cap on his head. True, my father was going with me and not I with my father, but the ponderous watch chain at his vest seemed tied to my own neck as much as it was to that old Turkish watch, bulging there in the vest pocket, ticking away the old life. And that wasn't all. I was riding in an American train, going across the heart of America— but as a member of a Balkan community-on-wheels, as one of a hundred people who held their nationality in the palms of their hands, like old coins. In the three coaches, set aside for the gang, the talk, the music, the memories were Balkan. The old country was quarantined here, and I was of it.

Used to sleeping in the daytime, my father dozed. Occasionally he would wake and lean over to the window. For a minute or two his sleepy eyes would gaze listlessly at white farmhouses, cathedral-like red barns with cupolas on their roofs, and circular towers, like campaniles, attached to them. He would shake his bewildered head and close his eyes again. I knew he was unhappy, and it hurt me.

Yet I had only to look out the window at the fields and farmhouses and the clumps of trees rotating backward to regain my sense of separation and forward motion. This was not like the journey from New York to St. Louis, where there was no flicker of familiarity with the scene, and the journey had been as unemotional as a dream. Now the new before me made the strange of yesterday take on the guise of familiarity. The unfolding landscape, with the reactions it evoked, flew backward to pour itself into the store of an American memory, to stitch itself into the tapestry that the loom of the mind was forever weaving. Broad, flat earth rolled away with American prodigality. And my being yearned to be one with it. There was no snow, and the earth was brown. In a hollow, on a swelling of earth or on the flatness itself, clusters of farm buildings, with their immense, cupolaed barns and towerlike silos, looked like feudal domains.

Small towns whirred past. A little depot with the name of the town beneath the gable would revolve away, to be succeeded by a factory chimney spinning after it, then a white church spire, a red-brick schoolhouse with a façade of rectangular windows. And then again rolling, spreading earth, boundless, unhedged.

There was a sudden commotion in the coach. Through the noise of the music and the general clatter a voice had shouted the word *Mississippi!* There was a rush to the other side of the coach. People held playing cards in their hands or musical instruments as they leaned over one another for a view of the familiar river.

I leaped over to the other side.

"Hey, the Mississippi, the Mississippi! There she is, as big as in St. Louis!"

It was my river. My Mississippi. I had been baptized in its paternal waters. I had sat on its bank to watch it flow. I had dreamed of it when I was imprisoned in the Terminal. There it was now, close to me. It had been there, close to me, even when I couldn't see it. It would go by St. Louis; little wavelets would lap at the cobbled bank, only a couple of blocks from Paskal. It bound me with St. Louis and with the place where I was and with wherever I was going. For it flowed through the heart of America. I knew that.

The train was now so close to the river I could see from the window the muddy waters swirling at the gnarled dwarfy trees along the bank. A small island—a clump of trees and brush in midstream—seemed to float along toward St. Louis. On the island shore the bleached, barkless trunks of washed-out trees looked like the skeletons of prehistoric animals excavated by the river.

I kept my face to the window as long as the river could be seen. For a brief moment it became hidden from view by a bluff. Then the bluff melted away and the river reappeared, but the earth drove a wedge between the track and the riverbank. The wedge of earth grew wider and wider until the tree-lined riverbank was a barely perceptible fence in the horizon. Then I went back to my seat on the other side of the aisle. My father was still asleep. He had slept through the excitement and had not seen the Mississippi. Would it have made him feel a little less lost, less bewildered? I thought not.

257

And a sense of guilt squeezed at my heart. He was so out of place.

But for me the land unrolled, spreading itself for my eyes to see. There was more land ahead than had spun back, much more. And it kept unrolling.

Then night fell and the darkness blotted out the land. But I could still see it unroll. In the darkness, under the wheels jangling on the rail joints, was the land, still unfolding. In the darkness somewhere to my right was the Mississippi, flowing on toward St. Louis. All about was the lonely darkness, but in the darkness was the infinity of America. And I didn't mind the darkness.

From the other end of the coach came the strains of a song. It was an old-country song and a familiar one to me. I knew how to sing it and did sing it as a boy, but it sounded strange here, like the song of another people, not mine. The song of the train, of the wheels jangling on the rail joints, of the roll of the earth beneath the wheels, that was more mine. And to that song I listened.

When the train had gone so far into the night that there was as much night in the background as there was in the foreground, the lights in the coach were switched off—all but two, one at either end. Some people wrapped blankets about themselves and tried to sleep, but others were talking, and a single mandolin persisted in its strumming until the dimmed lights had a subduing effect on it, and then it, too, ceased its monotonous drone.

I sat up with my feet resting on the base of the seat in front, the blanket that I shared with my father covering my knees. Having slept most of the day, my father was wide awake. The peak of his cap was pulled low over his forehead to shield his eyes from the single light ahead. He moved fitfully in his seat. Finally I was wakened for good by an icy feeling on the side of my body nearest the window. I rubbed the benumbed shoulder and, turning to the window, saw that a frosty film had rimed the glass. With my fingernail I scraped a small area on the pane and peered through it to see a world mantled in white. From a clear, starlit sky a bright moon was flooding the whiteness with a cold phosphorescent light. Before my eyes was a weird, unreal world, with silhouetted farmhouses asleep in the silvery moonlight. It seemed as if during the night while we were asleep the train had entered a frigid, glacial region.

Through this region the train now traveled faster, leaving the night behind and catching up with the dawn. For as the train flew over the snowy land a leaden grayness came upon the sky. Then the Balkanians stirred in their seats, stretching stiffened limbs and necks and rubbing eyes cobwebbed with the insufficiency of sleep. Some walked up and down the aisle, swaying and wavering as if their legs were not fully awake.

"Where are we?" asked my father.

"I don't know."

He leaned over and looked through the opening I had made on the frosty windowpane. Then he clicked his tongue and in a tone of fatality he said, "Snow!"

The Avocat came by. The circles at his eyes were pronounced in the grayness of the dawn and his eyes appeared unnaturally large. He smiled wanly. "Where are we?" I asked him.

"We can't be far from St. Paul," replied the Avocat.

"How far yet to Montana?" asked my father.

"About a thousand miles."

"A thousand miles!" He took off his cap and stroked it like a cat.

The three Burlington coaches disgorged their Balkan cargo at St. Paul. With valises in hands and bundles on shoulders, we filed out of the old wood-frame Union Station into the little park and walked across it to a limestone building facing the park. In the journey from St. Louis no boundaries had been passed; no uniformed people had come into the coaches to ask for passports or examine the baggage. This was a journey of climate, a passage from the beginnings of spring into midwinter.

"How many miles is it back to St. Louis?" someone asked Vasil.

"About seven hundred."

"And it's still the same country, still America?"

"And a thousand miles beyond and more," Vasil bragged. He was now wearing his broad-brimmed hat and flannel shirt and the flowing black tie. Between him and this wintry town there was an air of comradeship. To my America, which had its nucleus in St. Louis, St. Paul was at the edge. And it was a matter of wonderment to me when I found out that the limestone building that we entered was a combination coffeehouse-restaurant-hotel run by a country-man of ours. In my own way I had felt like a pioneer, making a personal exploration of America, and here in this remote place a Macedonian had preceded me and had established himself.

The place proved too small to accommodate the entire gang, but the proprietor, a man with an innkeeper's tradition in his blood, must have had word of the gang's impending arrival and had made arrangements with other nearby hotels, where some of the men were billeted. It appeared that this Macedonian Magellan had also made arrangements with some stores, to which he directed the men for the purchase of heavy clothing.

Unlike Paskal's coffeehouse, where the departure of a gang for the West, or the return of one, caused a disruption in the otherwise genteel atmosphere, this place, located strategically like an old-country caravanserai on the crossroads of important highways, de-

259

pended for its business on gangs going to and fro and on such floating migratory workers as passed through St. Paul out of season. Nobody stared at us, groups of migratory workers being a common sight here and rousing no interest in the local folk. People even smiled and nodded to us as we walked about in groups, speaking a foreign tongue. We would be here only a few days before going to our destined places on the railroad. Everybody seemed to know that, for St. Paul was the gateway to the Northwest.

"From here on, across the whole Northwest," said Vasil, "through Minnesota, North Dakota, Montana, Oregon, Washington, to the end of America, to the Pacific Ocean, it's the Great Northern. Engines, coaches, stations, yards, freight houses, docks, whole towns and cities are part of the Great Northern empire. St. Paul is the capital and James Hill is the emperor. All power comes from St. Paul. All orders. All checks. Every piece of work done on the line has to be reported to St. Paul. If you pull out a rotten tie at Shelby, or tighten a bolt in Cut Bank, St. Paul must know about it. Once a month, no matter where we are on the line, the pay car will find us."

In one respect St. Paul was very much like St. Louis. One evening Vasil and I went to a vaudeville show and came out at eleven o'clock. The street down which we walked toward the hostelry was illumined by corner lamps, leaving the middle of the blocks in shadow, except for an occasional light blinking below street level to light the way into a cellar café. From the dimness of a store entrance a woman emerged and fell in with us, walking along as if she were in our company. "Show you a good time, fellas," she said.

"No, not now. Thank you." Vasil tried to shake her off.

"I won't hurry you. You can take your time."

"No," said Vasil. "No. Thank you."

She walked to the corner and then dropped behind silently.

"Maybe I should have gone with her," said Vasil. "Come on. Let's go get a beer somewhere."

"My old man's sitting in the coffeehouse eating his heart out."

"Psst." A sound from a doorway hobbled our steps.

"How much?" asked Vasil of the form that etched itself out in the semidarkness.

"Only a buck, honey." The voice was husky, like a voice with a cold in it.

"Is your room far?" asked Vasil.

"Just down a ways," said the rough voice.

"Okay. See you later," said Vasil to me.

"How about him?" the throaty voice demanded.

"He's too young," said Vasil.

"No, he ain't. He's a big fella. Come on, honey."

"You go to hell," growled Vasil and started ahead. "Come on," he said to me. "Goddam bitch. To hell with her."

A couple of blocks down he stopped and said, "Think I'll go back and pick up that other one. One's as good as another. You go along back, eh?"

"Sure."

But I stood there awhile watching Vasil's figure recede up the street. I caught sight of him in the light of the corner lamp and then his big hat melted into the dark.

Just as I suspected, my father was waiting up for me. He sighed with relief on seeing me without Vasil. He was a sad and forlorn figure, bewildered by the remoteness from St. Louis, by the futility of traveling about America, by the payless days. What was the sense of going to Montana, losing days on the way, sitting idle in strange places, when there was plenty of work and good pay in St. Louis?

I bought myself a sheepskin-lined brown canvas coat with metallic clasps like those on my galoshes. Likewise I equipped myself with woolen mittens, warm socks, woolen underwear, and a gray woolen shirt like Vasil's. I began to feel like a Westerner and liked St. Paul with its easy informality. The immigrant here felt less the immigrant and more the settler, the pioneer. People went about bundled up in heavy furs and mackinaws. I saw men and even women in bearskin cloaks, fur caps, and galoshes. Such sights I never saw in St. Louis. Even though I did not precisely know what it was, I perceived a change here, became aware of that peculiar foretaste of the Northwest. Here one could go about carrying a bundle on the shoulder or a sack on the back without embarrassment, without attracting attention. In relation to St. Louis the city had a frontierlike appearance and a welcome informality. Still, as I was to learn, it was the metropolis for millions of people who lived and worked hundreds of miles away.

I took Nichola for a walk through the city. He was afraid to venture alone even though St. Paul did not sprawl over a vast area like St. Louis. To our surprise the Mississippi was here too.

"How do you know it's the Mississippi?"

"It says so on the sign."

The river didn't spread out like a sea, as it did in St. Louis, but was compressed within high narrow banks. The sight of the river made Nichola feel less lost. "Just imagine, little one, it's our old friend. If we dropped something here it would pass under the McKinley Bridge. But how small it is here! Who knows how many other rivers flow in it before it reaches St. Louis? Who knows?"

"The Missouri joins it just above St. Louis, Uncle Nichola."

261

"The Missouri?"

"Yes. That's a long river, the longest river in the world."

"Bigger than the Mississippi?"

"No, not bigger, but longer. The Mississippi has more water in it."

"I see! It's according to the water. And is the Mississippi the biggest river in the world?"

"No. The Amazon is."

I could read disappointment on Nichola's face. "Amazon . . . Amazon . . . What names, what names!"

"It's named after a race of women warriors, Uncle Nichola. The word means 'big.' "

"Yeah, yeah, now that does sound like a big river, the biggest river there is. And is that in America?"

"Yes, but not in *our* America. We are in North America. The Amazon is in South America, in Brazil."

"Brazil. Hey, hey! You know everything. You can be anywhere and you'd know where you are. That's wonderful. To know where you are no matter where you are."

"I don't know much, Uncle Nichola. There's much I have to learn, much."

The town clustered about a hill up which ran the main street, with flour mills down in the hollows and at the top of the hill an imposing building we never approached. It was the state house. Forty-six years later, in 1970, as a Vermont state senator attending a National Legislative Conference, I visited this magnificent building, called on the young and charismatic governor with the Scandinavian name, and attended seminars in its spacious halls. I marveled at the beauty and elegance of the building, at its marble hallways and stairways, its ornate chambers, its murals depicting scenes of pioneer days. I felt a kind of historic pride when told that the building had been constructed in 1903, only eleven years before I had first laid eyes on it from a distance, and at a cost of three million dollars, which now sounded like peanuts but which must have been an enormous sum in those days. The noble capitol was the only remaining landmark of the city I remembered. Gone was the city of pioneering aspect. Halfway between the center of the city and the capitol the hill was transversed by a multilane throughway overpassed by the road leading to the capitol. Main street downtown was transformed. Only an occasional low brick building with peeling paint or scabby bluish whitewash survived as a reminder of 1914 St. Paul. Slim, high-rise apartments and hotels and glittering emporiums lined the old street. I walked up and down the unrecognizable main street. I was myself unrecognizable. I was registered at one of those sumptuous hotels at thirty-two dollars a night and recalled the fifty cents a night I had paid at the "caravanserai." The night before, dining at a fancy restaurant with fellow legislators, the bill was twelve dollars per person. The state of Vermont was paying for it, and I should have been pleased with myself, but a strange sadness dogged my steps, assuaged by pride that my American origins went back to pioneering days.

3

At last Mitko announced that the bunk cars were in the yards and we could start getting them in shape. Whereupon like a flock of sheep we descended on the row of boxcars parked in the yards behind the Union Station. The cars were old and dilapidated, no longer fit for freight traffic and consigned to their last usefulness as housing for track hands.

And it was a good thing that we were soon to leave St. Paul. Some of the sports and intellectuals who had started out with limited funds ran out of money and had to borrow. But since those in a position to lend were mostly of the pharisee category, borrowing was difficult. They would only make good one's meals and lodging and not a penny for "good times." And even this much they lent grudgingly, charging interest in the form of admonition and preachment on the soundness of the good old principles of pharisaism.

There was a scramble for choice of boxcars, though there wasn't much of a choice. So far as I could make out, one boxcar was as good or as bad as another. Several cars were designated for communal use, such as dining cars, a kitchen, a bakery, and a storage car. The bakery was at the end of the row of bunk cars, and next to it was a flatcar with a round wooden tank on it. This was the water car, which was always to remain attached to the bakery in case of fire.

The company carpenters had built eight double-deck bunks in each car, thus making provision for sixteen workers. Only hobo gangs would put up with such an arrangement. The Balkanians refused to be crowded; no more than eight would consent to live in a single car. The workers formed themselves into groups of eight. As soon as they moved in they took out hammers and saws

264

from their valises and sawed off the top berths, using the extra lumber for chairs and tables. They built washstands, coal bins, shelves, and ladders that could be flung out from the thresholds to the ground to afford easier access and exit than did the perpendicular ones nailed by the sides of the doors.

The organization of the commune-on-wheels proceeded with true American efficiency. I could contribute little toward its upbuilding, but I watched with absorption the innumerable details that were attended to by the others. It was like watching a new little world take shape before one's eyes. Beginning from scratch, we had in a few days established a functioning semi-cooperative commune. Food commissars were chosen to attend to the buying of provisions, to keep the books and to apportion the expenditures equally among the members at the end of the month. Unlike the hobo gangs, which were made up entirely of floating migratory workers and were boarded by the company at a fixed rate per day, to be deducted from their pay, we Balkanians boarded ourselves like a single family at less than one-third the rate the company charged the hobos. The company paid the wages of our cook and two flunkies, as well as that of the baker. If the gang was stationed in some isolated place on the line, as it often was, the company provided free passes for one or two of the commissars and paid their wages so that they could go to the nearest large town and buy provisions, which the company carried free of charge. These privileges, I learned in time, had been wrested from the company by gangs of Balkanians in years past and had become traditions, the slightest infraction of which was immediate cause for a strike.

The cook and the two helpers and the baker were chosen from among us. There was some talk about my being assigned to the kitchen, but this was instantly quashed by Nichola, who put his foot down firmly and got Mitko to announce that I was to be the water boy. I was the youngest in the gang.

The three food commissars went to a hardware store and bought kettles, pans, pots, enameled dishes and cups, tinny spoons and knives and forks, and a variety of other kitchenware. From there they went to a wholesale grocery and bought provisions as for a regiment. Trucks drove to the edge of the yards and unloaded sacks of flour, burlap bags of potatoes, quantities of beans and rice and lentils, cases of canned tomatoes and other canned goods, bags of dried onions, and salt and sugar and coffee and pepper and many other foodstuffs. Other trucks came and threw down on the snow-covered ground whole quarters of beef, slabs of bacon, huge butts of ham, all kinds of sausages, tubs of lard, whole skinned lambs. We carried these things into the kitchen and the store car, and it looked

265

to me as though we were preparing for an expedition into some wild country where there was nothing to be had and all food had to be carried with us.

It was amazing to me that none of us paid any money for these outfittings and provisions. Nor did my wonderment diminish when I learned that all was bought on credit against the guaranty of the railway company. For it was something to wonder at. Here we had come riding on the train all the way from St. Louis without paying fare. Then we had moved into homes provided for us by the company free of rent. We now went to the company's storehouses and helped ourselves to kerosene lamps, water pails, brooms, hatchets, and other necessary paraphernalia for our mobile households.

The whole thing seemed to me like play acting. All these grown-up people who had wives and children in the old country appeared to be engaged in some infantile make-believe enterprise that at any moment might burst like a soap bubble.

But the thing worked! Meals were served in the dining cars and the whole commune began to function. This was no play.

As soon as Nichola finished sawing off the top of the two-deck bunk and making himself a little shelf for his things, he proceeded to do the same for me and for my father. My father and I chose adjoining bunks. Vasil took one across from me and Nichola next to him. Among the four on the other side were Kozma and Toma, who had given up jobs in the steel mills in Granite City to join the gang. Kozma was a short, chubby man with a face like a pumpkin. The long black mustaches made his face appear smaller and rounder than it was. One might say that Kozma had no forehead, for his hair reached almost to his brows, themselves thick and black. Beneath them gleamed small, berrylike eyes, dark and treacherous. He was a clever, crafty man, and Nichola disliked him; but even if Nichola had not disliked him he would have resented Kozma's calling me "Little Cousin" and giving everybody the impression he was a relative of mine. Nichola nicknamed him "Hedgehog," because whenever the little man got angry he reminded the shepherd of a hedgehog bristling his quills. "Please don't ask that Hedgehog to do anything for you," he said to me. "We've got to live with him, but that don't mean he can go around making people believe you are his brother's child."

Nichola disliked Kozma, but Kozma's crony, Toma, was Nichola's particular hate. Nichola was a kindly soul and he did not hate without reason. His enmity for Toma was well founded and had its roots in the old country. Toma and Kozma had worked and lived together in Granite City, and certainly Nichola was not going to insist that they should separate now. "We'll just have to put up with them, that's all," he said to me. "And you don't have to pay any attention to them."

Toma was a hunchback with a wedge-shaped face. His nose was like a hatchet. He was smarter than all of us in the bunk put together, and he knew it, which made him unbearable, except to Kozma, whom he continually flattered.

I had known both these men in the old country but had not come in close contact with them. I must say that I did not share Nichola's feelings toward either of them. In fact, I felt that Toma was a better man than his appearance led people to believe. It was true that he looked positively demoniac, with his narrow face, hornlike nose, protruding teeth, and the peak of his hump rising ominously above his shoulders. And there's no denying that his outlook on life had been distorted by his physical deformity.

When Kozma proposed that Toma be one of the three food commissars, I feared Nichola would oppose him strenuously. But Nichola was discreetly silent. Afterward he said to me, "I'm glad they made him commissar. That tick is clever."

It was not until we had lived together for months that I learned the reasons for the suppressed enmity between the two men. It had its beginnings in Toma's unfortunate marriage. I knew that the hunchback had taken a veritable Amazon for a wife, a woman of such stature that it seemed the very earth trembled where she stepped. Toma's bent figure hardly reached to her waist. And that figure was comical enough for such as are prone to regard misfortunes in that light, but that Toma should further deform his life by such a marriage was one of those ironies that are all too common. It was no secret in the village that this gigantic though sterile woman had recourse to other men to quench the passion of her great body. But because I was too young, I had not known that whenever she went up to the mountain for kindling with her mule she always took a direction in which Nichola's flock was grazing.

The wife had thus contributed to a further, spiritual deformity in a man already unfortunate. Toma had become a cynical person, leering at people and making unkind remarks. He never accepted things at their face value but always turned them about, tried to find a handle to the egg, as the saying goes. He made biting remarks about my friend Nichola but couched them in words that he thought Nichola was too stupid to understand. For that matter Nichola did not have to understand them. Anything that Toma said about him he construed as derogatory, whether he understood it or not.

Nichola, however, never gave Toma provocation for a quarrel. His dislike of him was too profound for that. Once he said to me,

"Now you can say what you like, but that tick's got a heart no bigger than a button and his soul spits poison just like a snake. Some day maybe I'll lose my patience and then I'll crush him in my hand just like you would crush a berry."

After a few days of communal organization we were ready to pull out for Montana. At dinner Mitko gave warning that everyone should be in camp by nine, for we might start any time after that hour and he did not like the idea of anyone's being left behind. And indeed shortly after nine in the evening the brakemen showed up, swinging yellow lanterns. They wore heavy woolen jackets, cloth caps with narrow visors, huge mittens. As they moved up and down the row of cars they warned us to draw up the improvised ladders from the doorways.

It was quite some time, however, before the engine made contact with the camp. By that time a good many of us had gone to bed. The engineer seemed unaware that human beings lay sleeping in their bunks, that kerosene lamps, with their glass chimneys fastened by wire loops, were hanging on the walls, that in the kitchen and store car there were foodstuffs in jars and cases of eggs. He approached the camp in no spirit of good will or amity. He bumped against the bunk cars with no consideration for their creaky and dilapidated condition, with the utmost disregard of the fact that they were now human habitations.

I wakened in my bunk when the car shrieked to heaven with pain in its squeaky joints. And I was too dazed to know what had actually happened. But from the unrestrained swearing in which Toma indulged I quickly gathered that man and not earth was responsible for the tremors.

From the time the engine made contact with the camp until we pulled out from the yards we were in an earthquake. Coughing and groaning like a dragon, the engine apparently was unable to make up its mind whether to push or to pull the row of bunks. It kept jogging back and forth, each reverse movement effected with such abruptness that the cars all but leaped from the rails.

I stuck my head out of the little window and looked into the jungle of yards. From doorways and other windows voices bellowed into the night, some angry, some conciliatory. Nichola sat silently on his bunk. He accepted the torment stoically. He asked me not to stick my head too far out. "It may strike something."

Kozma was in the doorway, "hedgehogged," bristling with invectives against the engineer, who proved determined to maneuver the bunks forever through the labyrinthine yards. The whole camp coiled and clanged on frogs and joints. At times it broke in two or three sections, like a snake cut in pieces, each piece quivering with pain and life. Again all sections united and made as though to start for good, only to come to a sudden standstill after a flourish of motion.

Finally the whistle blew shrilly and the engine breezed ahead as if in earnest, the bunks rattling over the rail joints. It appeared now that the commune was on its way at last and the misery was over. But again the thing came to a dead stop with such force that the whole length of the train trembled and shrieked as though a powerful tremor of the earth rather than an engine was the cause of the phenomenon. Men were pitched from their beds onto the floor, water pails spilled, lamp chimneys shattered to pieces. Angry heads stuck out at doorways and windows, and voices polluted the night air with curses against the engine, the engineer, the railway company, and America. It seemed clear to us that if Americans had been occupants of the bunks such things would not have happened. We believed it was the engineer's contempt for the "goddam Dagos" that made him juggle the camp the way he did.

I myself thought of the engine as a kind of mechanical ogre torturing our village-on-wheels much as *lamias* in the folk tales victimized villages until some hero slew them or found the secret source of their strength. In Mitko, the straw boss–interpreter, who stepped down to reason with the crew, I vainly looked for the ballad hero who would accomplish the noble deed.

"Watinell you tink we, peegs? Go easy, villia? Dis ain't no first time I bin moved in bunks!" This was how Mitko addressed the brakemen.

"Aw, go to hell, you goddam lousy Bohunk. You ain't gonna tell us how to make up a train. Get back to yer bunk if you don't wanna be left in the yards."

"Shut up, you sonababeeches chewtobaccos! Wat you tink dis, a stock train?" This was Toma, coming to Mitko's aid from the doorway, where he stood in the dim light more like a portent of evil than a human being.

An empty beer bottle whizzed like a bolt from a doorway and crashed on the rail near one of the brakemen. Before the pieces had scattered in the tracks, other missiles fell noisily about the man. The yellow flame in his lantern described quick arcs in the darkness and an alarming whistle from the engine rent the air. Suddenly a roaring noise like that of an approaching wave issued from the car next the engine and traveled all through the length of the camp. Car after car quickly communicated it to the next, the sound preceding the impact so that people were warned, as thunder warns of the storm, to grip at the beds, hold onto the wall, or otherwise prepare for the tremor. When the violent vibration through the bunks reached the tail end, where the caboose was already attached, the backward wave suddenly reversed with equal violence. The double motion caused a terrific pull at the human intestines, while the poor old bunks creaked in their rickety frames and all but split asunder.

With this last powerful fling the camp leaped ahead. The engine let out ponderous groans, fumed and fulminated like an angry beast. The twenty-odd cars shimmied after it through the yards and out onto the main line.

The journey of a thousand miles from St. Paul to our destination in Montana in those rattling bunk cars was an ordeal that I still remember after so many years. At each division point a new engine with a new crew came to pick us up from some siding in the yards where the last crew dumped us like so much refuse, glad to be rid of us. The camp did not constitute a train by itself but was always attached to a freight train. For some reason I never divined it was anathema to the crews. Some conductors were kinder than others and asked the engineer to go easy on us. But those freight-train engineers were unused to carrying human beings and subjected us to repeated shocks. Some of us bore the torture in silence; others jabbered and cursed angrily.

The chef refused to cook, as he never knew when the stew might spill out over the floor. For four days we had to eat dry stuff. Moreover, we could not have even our cold meals on schedule but only when it suited the crew's convenience.

For days and nights we were shut in those bunk cars, eight people in a single room. In our own car the quiet hostility between Nichola and Toma and the open antagonism between Nichola and Kozma did not make for gaiety. To make things worse, Nichola had bought a violin in St. Paul. He had heard some young fellows on the train from St. Louis play their fiddles and mandolins, and he must have thought that they were as easy to play as the shepherd's flute. While he and I walked the streets of St. Paul Nichola stopped time and time again in front of a music store and gazed at the window where there was on display a veritable museum of musical instruments. It never occurred to me that he contemplated buying any of them until he pointed to a violin in a beautiful leather case and said, "Now I wonder how much they'd ask for that one."

"You mean you wish to buy it, Uncle Nichola?"

"Well . . . and why not? We want music, don't we?"

"But you can't play it, Uncle Nichola. Why not buy a flute?"

"Ugh. A flute! Who wants a flute? I've been playing flutes all my life. Violins give better music. I once heard a man in East St. Louis play a violin. You should have heard him. You can't draw music from a flute like you can from a violin. The music that man played made me think of our mountains. I nearly cried, it was so beautiful!"

"But a violin is hard to play."

"Bah! Hard to play! It can't be hard. If there's music in it and you pass the bow over the strings the music's bound to come out. We won't buy it unless it plays. But maybe they'll ask too much money for it. Maybe it's five dollars. You go ask."

"Let's both go in."

"No, you go alone. I'll wait here."

I went into the store and pointed to the violin in the window. "How much?" I asked.

"Eighty dollars."

"Eight dollars?"

"Eighty. Eighty! We've got others cheaper, as little as four dollars."

I walked out.

"It's eighty dollars, Uncle Nichola."

"You sure?"

"Yes. He's got others for as little as four dollars."

"But do they play?"

"They must."

"My God! Who'd pay eighty dollars for a violin? That's twenty napoleons, gold ones. You can buy a flock of sheep with that. Did he say he'd give us a case with a cheap one?"

"I didn't ask him."

"Let's see. You go in first."

I led the way into the store and did all the talking, such as it was.

In ten minutes we came out with a violin for which we paid seven dollars. Instead of a fine leather case lined with red velvet and opening through the middle like a suitcase we had a canvas one that opened at the base and you shoved the violin into it like a pistol in a holster. But the case had a handle and you could carry it like a suitcase.

"You want to carry it?"

"No, you carry it, Uncle Nichola."

"You can play it any time you like. It belongs to both of us."

We walked down through the park toward the yards. Nichola still could not understand why there should be such a big difference in the prices of violins. All right, this one had a better case, that one was made of better wood, maybe. But wood was wood, after all!

"You sure he said there's violins that cost five thousand dollars?"

"That's what he said."

271

"But who'd buy them? Who'd pay that much money for a violin?"

I shrugged my shoulders.

I had thought that as soon as we got to the bunks Nichola would go to work on the violin. But he shoved it under his bunk and did not touch it until the morning after we left the yards. Perhaps it was the movement of the train that gave him courage; perhaps it was because no one could walk in on him from the outside while the train was rolling; but he "played" only while the train was in motion.

As the camp rolled on through Minnesota, through strange and remote places that made even St. Louis seem like home to us, Nichola for the first time pulled out the violin from under his bunk where it had been since we bought it. Kozma and Toma had not been in the bunk car when we had brought it in and knew nothing about it. It was a complete surprise to them. Considering that they both were eager for opportunities to rib the shepherd, whom they regarded as far beneath their mental level, Nichola had courage to try to coax music out of that instrument in their presence.

The train was rushing on with speed and the ramshackle bunks rattled frightfully. You could not hold a cup of water in your hand without having the water fly out of it. But that did not deter Nichola.

Kozma and Toma sat up in their bunks facing the stove. The moment Nichola fished out the violin they both focused their eyes on him like hawks. I sat in my bunk opposite Nichola, more interested in watching the two men watch Nichola than in what Nichola was going to do to the violin. I was glad that they did not grin or laugh, for I hated the thought of a fight so early in our communal bunk life.

Nichola handled the violin tenderly. He passed his huge palm down the baseboard, fingered the pegs, the bridge, the tailpiece. He picked at the strings with his thumb. Then he rested the broad end of the instrument on his shoulder and took the bow.

I hoped that the noise of the jangling wheels and the creaking of the boxcars as they tossed on their springs would drown whatever "music" Nichola would produce. I hoped in vain.

The moment Nichola passed the bow across the strings the violin cried like a pup. After the initial stroke, which was not a timid one, Nichola stopped and casually turned his eyes toward the two men who, he knew, were watching him intently. Both of them maintained a discreet silence.

Then again Nichola passed the bow over the strings, and again the same canine howl rose. But this time Nichola did not stop with one stroke. He made a counterstroke with a sudden stablike movement, producing a gritty sound that made it seem as though the brakes were being quickly applied to the wheels and the train was coming to an abrupt stop.

This must have outraged Nichola's musical sense. He lowered the violin to his lap and sat there for a moment in a pensive mood. Then he turned to me.

"Would you like to try it?"

"Not just now, Uncle Nichola."

Again he raised the instrument. Up and down went the bow. The howling dog now provoked several other animals into a kind of barnyard contest. I never until then suspected that so many animal cries could come out of a violin. For a long time we were subjected to a series of squeals, grunts, catcalls, cawings, and croakings.

Only when the train stopped did we have a respite from the torturous, fiendish noises that Nichola evoked from the violin. As soon as the train moved we had to listen to it again.

None of us spoke of the violin until the third day. Even then no one mentioned it directly. But Toma told a parable apropos of nothing that I felt certain was meant for Nichola. We were in Minot, North Dakota, not far from the Montana boundary line, switched up in a siding and waiting for the next freight train to pick us up and carry us to Glasgow. As usual, Toma and Kozma sat in their bunks facing the stove and smoking their pipes. Nichola lay in his cot, with his hands folded at his neck, waiting for the camp to move so that he might get busy on the fiddle. I sat near the stove on the wooden stool that Nichola had built for me. Toma began to tell Kozma a story about a man who went to an eye doctor for a pair of *reading* glasses. The doctor fitted the man with glasses, but in a day or two the man went back and said the glasses were no good; he couldn't *read* with them.

"That's just like doctors," Kozma put in spiritedly. "They take your money and they don't do nothing for you. What happened then? Did he give the man another pair of glasses?"

"Yes, he gave him a new pair."

"And didn't charge him extra?"

"No."

"That's hard to believe!"

I thought that was the end of the story, but Toma continued: "Well, what happens? This! In a day or two the man goes back again and says the new glasses are no good either. He can't read with them."

"Is that a fact?"

"Absolutely."

273

"I tell you, you can't trust them doctors!"

"But it wasn't the doctor's fault. He gave him the right glasses."

"He did?"

"Absolutely."

"I don't understand," said Kozma.

"Well, then I'll tell you. The man didn't know how to read. He had heard one could get reading glasses from a doctor and he decided to get a pair to read with."

"Is that a fact?"

"Yes. Lots of people have ideas like that about other things."

Nichola did not respond, but as soon as the camp moved again he took up the violin and began to belabor it with even firmer resolution.

4

A skin-cracking cold gripped the earth. The wind howled over the vast, frozen Montana plain, winnowing flurries of powdery snow and lashing at the old bunks, which were parked at last in a spur off the main line. In front of the camp a red grain elevator loomed dismally above the tracks. Near it, on pillars now sculptured in ice, and with its spout upraised, stood a round watertank, like a huge chandelier with pendent icicles. The grain elevator, the water-tank, and a white telephone booth, standing like a tiny chapel on the embankment, were the only signs of life in this remote flat region.

We sat around the stoves warming our fronts while the cold stung at our backs. We were waiting for the work train from Glasgow to bring tools and track material. All of us looked larger than we were, stuffed in sweaters and wrapped in coats lined with sheepskins, or in Mackinaws.

When the work train arrived at the switch point, Mitko, who had been on the lookout for it, roared out in his deep voice as though in defiance of the cold, *"All out!"*

Encumbered as we were in our heavy wraps, we began tumbling down the ladders like bundles and waddling toward the main track, where the work train had already stopped, the engine groaning and expelling gusts of vapor through its valves.

From the caboose of the work train three important-looking personages stepped down, wearing bearskin cloaks reaching almost to their ankles. Their hands were hidden in huge furry gloves, their feet in fur-lined galoshes, and on their heads they wore black fur hats with ear flaps. They were the first Montana people I saw, and they looked like members of some strange tribe.

As it turned out, one of these men was to be our foreman. He was the smallest of the three, a wiry, ruddy-cheeked Irishman, with a generous sprinkling of freckles and with the tip of his nose slightly upturned. From the way he fussed and fumed it was easy to deduce that the others were his superiors. And so they were, one being the roadmaster and the other the division superintendent, a gigantic bear of a man.

"All right, boys, let's get going now. We've got a lotta steel to lay." The foreman lost no time in getting us started.

A dozen men or so grabbed line bars and climbed onto the work train. It began moving slowly, and the men on it pushed new rails down on the frozen embankment, dumped kegs of spikes, bolts, bunches of fish plates and tie plates, burlaps of tie plugs, and other track material.

Meanwhile, a score of us started to unload implements from the tool car, throwing down clawbars, spikemalls, tongs, line wrenches, adzes, sledgehammers, chisels. Other men piled these up on a push car, which had been brought along by the work train.

Mitko and the Irishman kept running about getting the men started on the track. They chose eight men for the clawbars and immediately put them to work ripping up the old track at the point where the first new rail had been unloaded. These men, four on the inside and four on the outside of the rail, fitted the claws of their bars to the heads of the old spikes and pulled at them with vigor. Most spikes snapped out, but some, having rusted in the tie or grooved in the rail near their crowns, refused to yield. The men had to hang to the bars with both hands and yank down as though they were pulling the teeth of giants. Sometimes a spike, bedded like a dead worm in the wood, yielded only the head, and this so treacherously that the man, losing his balance, staggered down the embankment or landed in the ditch on his back.

Behind the clawbars two line-bar men pushed away the unchained rails, which, despite the rigid cold, coiled like snakes as they slid down the ballast. Other men scraped off the old tie plates, swept the bed of dirt and cinders, and stuck wooden plugs into the holes from which the old spikes had been extracted.

Several elderly men with sharp adzes hewed at the ties, where the teeth of the old plates had grooved into the wood, and then set in the new and larger plates.

In this manner the track bed was prepared for the new steel, which was laid in by the tongmen. Sixteen of them, four pairs at each end of the rail, clamped the jaws of the tongs to the spines of the new rails and carried them like corpses to their destined places in the line.

Behind the tongmen other workers coupled the rails with the fish plates and locked them up with bolts.

276

At last came the spikers, the artillery of track laying, the hardest workers in railroad construction. They both gauged the line and chained the steel to the ties, to the permanent bed. In pairs, each partner swinging away from the other (no two with a like swing could be partners), they brought down their heavy malls on the heads of the spikes, driving them like bullets into the heart of the frozen wood. Now in all this allotment of tasks and coordination of operations into a working unit, which at first functioned somewhat slowly and clumsily but which soon got under way, I did not participate. I stood there wrapped in my sporty sheep-lined coat, my feet in galoshes, my hands in woolen mittens, and a cap pulled over my ears. I was to be the water boy, but nobody asked for water. And who would in such weather?

Watching the process of ripping up the old track and building it anew, I was astounded by its simplicity. I had imagined the construction of a railroad as an intricate engineering process, but before my eyes a gang of Balkan peasants was tearing up the old track and putting down a new one with not an engineer in sight.

I stood there ready for work, getting paid the same as anybody else. I was bothered by the thought that I was not contributing my share of energy to the human machine that scraped off the old worn steel belt and girded the earth with a new and stronger one. Every worker was doing his bit, earning his wages and repaying the company for what seemed to me then unheard-of benefactions. The clawbars wrestled with the old spikes, the tongmen lifted the new steel, the mallmen behind drove the new spikes with powerful blows. Some even began to shed their heavy wraps, for the hard work warmed their bodies. Those assigned to lighter work, like the adzemen and the wrenchmen, were still bundled up in their cumbersome woolens, but all fought with the steel, all forgot the cold, their bodies active. All but me.

I was not conscience-stricken about it. Nor was my sense of justice outraged. I merely felt useless and at odds with myself for not doing my share of the work when I knew that the gang functioned as a unit, as a semi-cooperative commune. I was the water boy, and the gang had a right to a water boy whether anybody cared for a drink or not. But something—perhaps my youth, perhaps my wish to be grown-up like the rest, perhaps the boy in me longing to build bridges—made me want to be an equal member of the commune. I wanted to work, to lay steel. I felt like a little boy with a gang of bigger boys who were playing an exciting game from which he alone was excluded.

I stood there and listened to the orchestration of bars and hammers as they demolished and rebuilt; I listened gloomily to the wind whining ominously across the flat expanse on either side of the line; I listened to the mysterious moaning of the telegraph wires that hung in loops between the poles. Tears trickled down my frozen cheeks and I did not know whether they were from the cold or from the way I felt.

At last Mitko took notice of me. Whiffs of blue breath wafted from his mouth and nose and floated like tiny pieces of finely spun wool.

"Well, now! What kind of a water boy are you anyway? Where's your bucket?" His voice sounded warm and cheerful. "Must I tell you how to put water in a bucket?"

"But it's cold. Who'd drink water in weather like this? Let me do something else."

"Cold or no cold, what if someone asks for a drink?"

I started for the bunks, walking in the middle of the track, padding with my galoshes through the cinders and powdered snow. My cheeks burned with the cold and my eyes teared. Instinctively I struck the palms of my gloved hands to keep them warm, for the cold penetrated through the wool. The metallic sound of the instruments behind me, steel striking steel, rang in my ears. My eyes regarded the new rails, noting their greater length, noting how the new spikes made a pattern, and how some spikes were driven in crooked, their heads twisted, while others were driven in so straight that they looked as though they had hardly been touched by the hammers but merely pressed in by hand. Then my eyes ranged over the prairie, but I couldn't see very far, for the wind whipped the dry snow into fluttering white drapes. Spirals of blue smoke ascended from the stovepipe chimneys of the bunks, kept warm by the coal stoves.

The cook gave me a new galvanized pail with the picture of an elk pasted on it. He also gave me an enameled dipper with a long handle.

"You'll have to fill your bucket from the top," said one of the helpers. "The faucet don't run; it's frozen." He handed me a piece of rope with which to lower the pail.

I climbed onto the flat top of the water car and dropped the pail into it. Having drawn the water, I set the pail on the edge of the car and descended to the ground. Then I reached up and hugged the pail with both arms, but when I tried to set it on the ground in order to get hold of it by the bale, it would not come off my chest. Its ice-glazed surface stuck to my coat like glue. I had to struggle for some minutes in order to separate myself from the bucket without spilling the water over me.

"*Woda . . . Woda . . .*" I called out with a tremor in my voice

278

as I walked up and down the track. Some workers, seeing the congealed water in my pail, asked for a drink just to be funny. In the same spirit I proffered them the frozen pail. They laughed, and I laughed with them, but my heart was sad.

Being free to move about from the clawbars, who were at the head, like the vanguard of an invading army, to the spikers in the rear, those cannoneers whose hammer blows resounded like an anvil chorus in the frozen plain, I had ample opportunity to observe the various operations involved in the process of laying steel. I could tarry as long as I wished with the tongmen, where my friend Nichola, too unwieldy for the clawbar or the spikemall and too strong to dilly-dally with an adze or a wrench, was lifting steel. His tall bony frame and his slow gait fitted him perfectly for this task. As the tongmen straightened their bodies after setting down a rail and strode forth to pick up another, Nichola's figure loomed above the rest like a pine tree.

Kozma and Toma, their diminutive bodies hidden in their warm coats, chipped at the ties with their adzes. They too were well suited to their jobs, since they could hew without even having to bend their bodies. Toma, with his hump rising above his shoulders, looked like a vulture digging into a carcass.

My father was a wrenchman, more a bundle than a man, a big wooly hunter's cap with ear flaps wrapping his head and face, his black mustaches white with hoarfrost, his breath coming out congealed like tufts of carded wool. My heart ached for him.

At one time the tongmen left the spikers some twenty rails behind. Then Pat, the foreman, called a stop in order to give the spikers a chance to catch up. Nichola walked over to where I stood planted in the middle of the track near my frozen pail and said cheerfully, "Well, well! And how's the *woda boy,* eh?"

"I don't want to be a water boy, Uncle Nichola!" I cried out. "I want to work!"

"You want to work? Just you listen to that! And what you call this what you're doing now? It's work, isn't it? Somebody's got to be a *woda boy.* Maybe there's not much to this *woda boy* job right now, but wait till it warms up. They'll be bleating for *woda* like ewes for their lambs."

"I don't care about that. I don't want to be a water boy now or ever. Somebody else can be a water boy. I can work. You know I can work."

"Now listen. You've been to school and you've got more reasonin' powers than anybody else got in this whole gang. I may be older, but you know things what I can't even dream and it ain't for me to be telling you things. I don't want to be a tongman either,

279

but I've got to. In this country you got to do what the Chewtobaccos says you got to do. Maybe you'd like better to wash dishes in the kitchen, eh? Maybe you'd like that better?"

"But I don't want them to say I get paid the same as the rest and I don't earn my pay."

"Who says? Who? Anybody been sayin' something like that?"

"Nobody yet. But they're bound to think it."

"Let them think what they like. It don't come from their pockets! Besides, nobody said a word. Let somebody say something, one word. Then I got something to say too. See?"

Nichola left me there standing in the track by my frozen pail and returned to his work. I resumed my march up and down the line, shouting *"Woda . . . Woda . . ."*

At noon I melted the ice and refilled the pail with fresh water from the tank, but I had made up my mind not to be the water boy. Ripping apart the old track and building it up better than it had ever been was more in line with my idea of America than carrying a water pail. I wished to work. In fact, I longed to put my finger to the steel, to inject my own youthful energy into the rebuilding of the line, to prepare the road for the mighty locomotives that roared across the continent.

As soon as the workers tore open the track and resumed operations, I put the water pail on the push car and walked over to Mitko.

"Where's your bucket?" he asked.

"I want to work!"

"What?"

"I want to work!"

"Then why don't you? Where's your bucket?"

"Carrying frozen water is no work. I want to lay steel like the others."

"Now listen, you're the *woda boy,* un'stand?"

"But nobody drinks water. And even if someone did ask for a drink there's no water. It's ice."

"Awright! What of it? They drink, they don't drink! We've got to have a *woda boy,* and you're the *woda boy,* un'stand?"

I resumed my beat, calling feebly, *"Woda . . . Woda . . ."* The men were too busy even to take notice of the incongruity of my calling out *woda* when there was only ice in the pail.

In a little while Mitko came over and said to me, "So you don't wanna be the *woda boy,* eh?"

"I want to work!"

"Come with me."

He swapped jobs for me with an old man who followed the tongmen and placed little pieces of steel between the rails as the tongmen laid them down in the track.

280

"Awright! You wanna lay steel! Here, take this bucket. These are shims, see! You hold one like this at the end of the rail and leave it there, un'stand?"

He gave my water pail to the old man and told him to be water boy. Then he turned to me again, "Now I hope you're *sa'sfied. Don't bodda* me any more because if you do I'm gonna send you in the kitchen to wash dishes, *un'stand?"*

The shims were as long as one's finger but wider, and they were bent exactly in the middle to form right angles. If you put two against each other, they formed a perfect square. As the tongmen set new rails on the track I placed a shim between each two rails and left it there.

At last I was laying steel! Little pieces of it, to be sure, but it was steel, and I was putting it in place.

And yet there was a hitch to it. I *was* laying steel and I was *not* laying steel. An old man with a chisel and a mallet dislodged the shims when the rails were spiked and bolted and brought back the shims to me to use over again.

I trailed moodily after the tongmen and as moodily squatted down and held a shim between each two rails. There, bitten by the new rails, was the steel I laid in the track. And that was gratifying, if only it stayed there to form part of the track, to perform a function, like the spikes, the bolts, the fish plates, the tie plates, to help support the trains.

But no, wherever I put steel there were little slits, little empty spaces, gaping. These empty spaces kept the rails apart, prevented them from touching. Each rail lay separate and apart. Held together by the fish plates and the bolts and the spikes, the rail formed a connected system, but every rail was alone, isolated from every other rail by the empty spaces I created.

There was nothing tame or gentle about this Montana country. It was one vast desolation. Only here and there a low mound bulged out like a blister on the monotonous flatness. The snow was not deep, for blades of last year's grass stuck above it. But the cold was all-pervading. There were no clouds in the leaden sky, and yet there was no sun. And this intensified the impression of a cloudless but sunless region. As air and sky were the same steely gray, it seemed there was no firmament on which the sun could rise. The hundred men, strung on the line, appeared to me like a tribe of pygmies lost in a glacial region and trying to bore their way out of it into a habitable world. With puny bodies, cumbrous in heavy wraps, and with steel implements, they defied the skin-cracking cold and the desolation itself. If I stepped on a rail or tie plate, the soles of my boots would stick to the steel, and I could hear the sizzle as though I had stepped on live coals. The cold was real; it was a living thing with teeth and claws. It needled my face, stung my eyes, penetrated to my feet, swaddled though they were in woolen socks, felt slippers, and booted in arctics. My feet thumped like clumsy, separate bodies, wobbling like hedgehogs. When the tongmen would stop to rest and give the spikers and the others time to catch up, I would walk back to see my father, watch him paw the bolts through his fur-lined mittens, fit them into the fish plates, thread the nuts and bend his body to the wrench till the nuts were tight, till they squealed like pups in the cold.

I looked ahead, or behind, or to the left, or to the right, and all I saw was a treeless, trackless white plain rolling away till it merged with the grayness, and I had a feeling that if we went out there to the edge of the plain we would see something. Only if I kept my eyes on what we were doing, on the bolts and the angle bars, I had a fair sense of my stature as a person. If I ranged my eyes over the immensity of country I instantly shrank to a dot.

The track ahead was but a thin stripe on the earth's white expanse. And on this band of steel the hundred men, like animated tumbleweeds, bent and twisted, bored and scratched. I reflected how on the white bosom of American earth we engraved a necklace of steel—set in tie plates, clasped with bolts and angle bars, brocaded with spikes. And there it lay secured to the earth, immovable.

Not a tree was on the plain, not a habitation in sight. Now and then a ground wind prowled over the surface, stirring the powdery snow, gathering drapes of it and twirling them about like the robes of spirits that seemed to weave and dance to the mysterious moaning of the telephone and telegraph wires and to the orchestra of bars and hammers.

The cold was there—ever present, glued to everything, pressing on the earth, stinging the steel itself.

I had always thought that the building of a railway was a complicated business, as mysterious as the building of a steamboat or a locomotive. And I had believed that we would be carrying the steel while others—Americans—would be doing the skillful work. Seeing now a hundred erstwhile plowmen and shepherds tear off the old track and build it anew as fast as they tore it down, the whole thing struck me as too simple to be true. There was the feeling in me that the hundred men, adults though they were, were just children pretending to be building a railway, over which maybe a toy train could pass but no real one.

There was not an engineer in sight, nor an American, to lend credence to this thing, to impute reality to what was being done. The Irishman boss bore the fantastic name of Pat—just Pat. Could a man named Pat build a railway? Besides, Pat did nothing anyway. Wrapped in his bearskin cloak that reached to his galoshes, in which his trouser legs were tucked, and on his head a beehive fur hat, he walked up and down the track, from the clawbars to the spikemalls, doing nothing, saying nothing.

Against the whiteness of the plain and the steeliness of the cold itself, Pat's ruddy, clean-shaven face was like a carrot—a lean, geometric face, with clenched jaws and a transverse scar on his nose, which was tipped in perpetual defiance. Tobacco juice dribbled from the corner of his mouth, making his chin look like a frost-cracked tomato streaking itself with its own rotted juice. Every now and then Pat splotched globs of the brown juice on the clean snow and looked at his watch, an open-faced watch the size of a small saucepan. Around eleven o'clock, when some sixty or seventy new rails had been strung on the line, Pat called a stop. A short time before he had talked with some distant place through a portable telephone, which he hooked on the telephone wire. Afterward he kept consulting his watch frequently and then ordered the clawbars to cease opening more track. The clawbar men stuck their bars in the snow on the embankment and sat on the tie stubs to rest their bodies. Some of them took out handkerchiefs to mop the cold dampness from their foreheads, for despite the cold their hair was moist from the labor and matted down to their skulls.

All others behind went on with their work, doing their tasks to bring the new steel to the point where the clawbars had stopped tearing up the old. When that was done, the men lay huddled like a flock of sheep while Pat and Mitko took over the business of the temporary closing of the track, which, like the whole process of laying steel, turned out to be a simple matter. The connection was accomplished with a switch point, the truncated end of which was joined to the nearest new rail and the bladelike point spliced against the old outcurving rail ahead.

I walked back to see Vasil, who was on a spiking team in the rear. The sight of him lent some credence to the reality of the railway we were building.

"Is this all there is to building a railway, Vasil?"

"It's simple enough here in a straight line but gets plenty complicated on curves, bridges, and switches."

"Why are we closing up?"

"I think for the Fast Mail. That's the train that carries the U. S. mail from St. Paul to Seattle. It's the fastest train on the line. If Pat stopped it for one minute we'd have a new boss tomorrow morning. Freight trains you can hold."

"So a train will pass over this track we just built?"

"And how."

"Why is it forbidden to hold the Fast Mail?"

"Because it costs the Great Northern one thousand dollars for every minute the Fast Mail is late getting into Seattle. It's in the contract. It's cheaper to the company for us to wait a whole day than for the Fast Mail to be one minute behind schedule."

"Do you have to have a contract with Uncle Sam to carry the mail?"

"Bet your life you do. The Great Northern and the Northern Pacific hold a race for the contract every five years. Both companies set off trains from St. Paul at the same instant and whoever gets to Seattle first gets the contract. The Fast Mail gets to Seattle from St. Paul faster than anything else moving on the earth, and nobody can hold the Fast Mail, not even old Jim Hill himself."

"Jim Hill? Who's he?"

"He owns the line. Used to anyway. He may be dead, but he's still the big boss."

Mitko and Pat walked up and down the track. The ground wind, which had winnowed the snow, had died down, and the plain, as if in hushed expectation of the Fast Mail, lay in frozen quietude. Only the telephone wires moaned continuously.

"We're getting paid for doing nothing," I remarked.

"It's the only rest we get except when we come to switches, and the Irishman will be scratching his head to figure out the position of the frog and the head block. But switches here are far apart. In summertime there'll be more trains—stock trains, fruit trains, specials. Stock trains you don't hold either. They're as important as the fastest passenger trains. The animals lose weight in travel, and the faster you get them to the Chicago stockyards the more money they bring."

The things this Vasil knew!

Pat's thin voice announced the approach of the train. "Here she comes, fellows. Everybody up now."

The men stirred, picking up their tools as they stood up. I looked up ahead to the east. And there, where the track vanished, a bundle of black smoke was visible. That and nothing else. But that was the Fast Mail. That patch of black smoke on the steel-gray horizon began to rouse the plain. We could detect a faint sound emitted by the rails.

By and by the bundle of smoke assumed the shape of an inverted cone, with its apex spinning on the edge of the plain. And soon I saw the engine, a black point on the rim of the horizon. There was now a distinct vibration on the rails, with the emission of an occasional sound as when you pick at an overstretched wire.

The men, holding clawbars, linebars, line wrenches, spikemalls, adzes, tongs, and standing on the embankment, looked like an armed savage tribe watching a vessel steaming up to the shore of their island. For me the approach of the train ameliorated the cold and the desolation itself, for it was bringing contact with the world, with St. Paul, with St. Louis. The approaching train seemed the only living thing on this broad expanse of lifelessness. I watched the locomotive grow bigger and bigger as it left more and more of the plain behind it. When the engine was a mile away I heard the explosion of the first torpedo placed on the rail by our flagman. A long warning whistle from the engine filled the immensity with its strident neigh. With reduced speed, the locomotive rolled on, the head of it rearing higher and higher as it came nearer and nearer to us.

Pat stood in the middle of the track highballing to the engineer to continue on with caution. Pat did that by describing low arcs with his arms. Two short blows of the whistle acknowledged Pat's signal, and he stepped out onto the embankment.

The engine appeared immense. Its cowcatcher was sculptured in ice, but its stack belched smoke, for there was a fire in the heart of the engine that no cold could stifle. And as long as the wheels stayed on the rails, the engine was a mighty power. It moved on, its wheels rolling with earth-shaking ponderosity.

There were only three mail cars attached to the engine, and these were loaded with letters and packages, with bonds, shares, gold certificates, with jewels and gold, and other precious stuffs. They would be delivered to the doors of houses, or into steam-heated offices in cities on the Coast, and some would be put on steamships to go to the Orient.

The pistons shuttled visibly like gigantic arms bending at the elbow to propel the wheels, under whose weight the rails bent into the frozen earth and sprang up in their resilience as soon as released.

The locomotive was still over old track, and the wheels turned slowly, cautiously, feeling their way, as if suspicious of the new track ahead. The engine itself sniffed, scented, its many valves spurting out jets of vapor shaped like the antenna of some giant scorpion.

The men withdrew farther down toward the ditch, and I too stepped back with them, but my eyes were on the front wheel, watching it come closer and closer to the point of connection. High up in the cab the engineer had slid open a section of the glass that enclosed him, and his goggled eyes held the rail below like a pair of binoculars.

285

My heart thumped in my breast as the front wheel turned onto the switch point. The next instant it was on the new rail made secure with the bolts and the fish plates, and on it rolled, over the new track I had thought was a toy.

I gave out an involuntary cry and then a chorus of a hundred voices waked the plain from its frozen lethargy. There was warmth and cheer in every voice, as if the locomotive were a rescue party from a peopled world come to us, forsaken on the nakedness of a cold and desolate America. The engineer gave out a prolonged, heartening whistle, and the train gathered speed on the new and firmer track.

I watched the Fast Mail disappear into the unknown west, and I felt less alone now, less cold. Some of the awe had gone out of the desolation, and the plain was not so unencompassable.

"All right, men, rip her up now," Pat yelled in his high-pitched voice.

A new energy seized the workers. The clawbars clamped the spikes with the iron fangs and jerked them out like frozen worms. The tongmen slung in the new thirty-three-foot rails with the lightness of sticks. I unclasped the metal hooks of my sheepskinlined coat so as to breathe more freely, and I took off my mittens that I might touch the steel with my bare hands. And then I felt as if a candle were suddenly lit inside me, glowing within me and warming my body. In crowded St. Louis I had never felt so close to America as I did now in this pathless plain. I knew that as I touched the steel, linking one rail to another, I was linking myself to the new country and building my own solid road to a new life.

5

Strung along the siding, the bunk cars looked like a row of uniform little red-painted cottages with smoke curling from the stovepipe chimneys above the roofs. Small windows let light into the interiors furnished with potbellied iron stoves, folding tables attached to the walls by hinges, coal boxes, washstands, benches, all made from lumber salvaged from the sawed-off upper bunks.

The space beneath each bunk served as storage for the occupant's suitcase and other belongings. The wall space above the bunk was fitted out to suit particular tastes. From this wall space one could read the character of the person who slept there. Some hung their best suits and hats, covered with newspaper to keep the dust out; others built shelves to keep knickknacks and toilet articles; still others hung up mandolins or banjos, while some papered the wall with pictures of Hollywood stars and bathing beauties.

The gang fell into a pattern of life and work no doubt evolved by previous groups. The cook, the baker, the flunkies, the three commissars who bought the provisions and kept the accounts had been chosen by vote. There was a tribal solidarity that made nominal Pat's power to discharge a worker. The company itself could not fire a worker without the gang's consent. It could fire only the whole gang.

Yet the gang was not organized in an industrial sense. The tribal, basic solidarity was understood by all and by the boss and the company. Nobody explained it to me. It was there and I simply grasped it. As I also grasped the fact that this cooperative, communal way of life had a leveling effect on all, sparing none. Young and old, learned and illiterate were equal; none was bigger than another. The only deference was toward those who performed the heavy tasks, such as the spikers, for the pay was equal.

Aware of this leveling, which put him on the same footing with men who drew crosses for signatures, the Philologian assumed a humorous attitude toward his position and presence in the gang and in this manner was able to salvage some of the air of erudition that had cloaked his person in St. Louis.

For some reason the man seemed to think that I, the youngest in the gang, had some special aptitude for understanding his learned phraseology. If I were not on hand, he would address the plain, challenging its mute enormity with his bombast. He sounded like an oracle as he made verbose comments about the spikes, the bolts, the angle bars, and the various tools, never calling them by their true and simple names. He would not even ask for a match in plain speech. A match to him was a "lighting stick."

Sometimes when talking to me he affected an archaic style. "Ah, my young colleague and co-toiler, didst thou ever, in that benighted land of our nativity, didst thou ever, as thou bestrode a quadruped with extraordinarily elongated auricular appendages— said quadruped being commonly denominated a jackass—didst thou then, while thus *acavalla,* ruminate upon the remote and incredible possibility of building iron roads in the American steppes?"

The man's big words made no more impression on me than the strokes of the hammers. My body was busy joining rails, my mind preoccupied with the multitude of details attendant to the new country, the new work, the new mode of life at camp. I was now reasoning things out for myself, as I could not go on forever asking questions. I was no longer a "greenhorn" but had been in America more than two years, had traveled across it from New York to Montana.

At work or in the bunks, my mind was never at rest but always taking the measure of things. It must know the why and wherefore of everything new. And many new things crowded on the mind, demanding to be understood in their true light and dimension. Names of tools, materials, operations—a whole railroad terminology—became absorbed rapidly into my fermenting vocabulary out of the very air itself, as if by some independent process, like osmosis. Each new word, at first striking the mind with the impact of its strangeness, in a short time became as familiar as bread and water. And it was there forever, to form a part of the new life. Every word and expression opened a door, illuminating areas, small or large, according to the connotative power of the word itself. Some words were like projectors splitting solid darknesses. And I could feel my being expanding, my scope widening, my intelligence reaching out into the vastness like a hand touching objects in the dark.

In the early part of May the pay car found us on the line and the paymaster handed us our April checks. On the very next day eleven men quit. By doing so they forfeited their free pass back east, but most of them were not interested in a pass east. They had, in fact, joined the gang for the sole reason of getting free passes west, and they stayed long enough to get a full month's pay. Some of them left for Portland, some for Seattle, and some for Butte to work in the smelters and the Anaconda copper mines. Only two returned east, and these two were loath to leave, but the wild oats which they had sown in St. Paul had germinated in their bodies. The whole venture was for them a total loss. It was best for them, and for the gang, that they should go where there were ready facilities for the relief of such distress.

Money in the pocket made other men arrogant. They now began to find fault with the food and make nasty remarks about it in the presence of the flunkies. "Tell it to the cook," said the flunkies.

"You tell it to the cook," barked a young man who had once worked in a lumber camp near Vancouver, British Columbia. He was now praising the steaks and chops and ham and eggs the Chinese camp cook had served the lumberjacks.

The flunkies did exactly what the young man asked, and presently the cook breezed into the dining car brandishing a large enameled dipper. He walked over to the erstwhile logger. "The frog saw them shoe the horse, and the frog turned up its foot," said the cook.

"Frogs make better fare than we get here," said the young man.

"And what did it cost for board at the lumber camp?"

"What's that got to do with it?"

"It's got plenty to do with it. What did it cost you?"

"A dollar a day."

"For a dollar a day I could feed you caviar, but oats is plenty good for you."

"I don't want caviar. I want steak."

"Oh? He wants steak. Now just you listen to that. The man wants steak. Of course. Tomorrow we shall have steak. Only for you, special. How do you want it done?"

"Aw, go jump in the Missouri."

The cook reached out with the dipper and tapped the young man's skull. "Sounds hollow," said the cook. "Absolutely empty."

Before real damage could be done at least a dozen men jumped to their feet. Some held back the enraged young man; others spirited the cook back into his kitchen. Once there he threw down the white hat and apron and vowed never to cook another stew.

"There's nothing wrong with me, is there—" he beat his chest

—"that I can't swing a mall or turn a wrench for my pay and work only ten hours instead of sixteen?"

Inasmuch as the cook coughed and gasped when he pounded his chest with his own fist, the others agreed with him that there was nothing wrong with him, nothing at all, that he couldn't, like the rest of us, earn his pay by working on the track.

"But," one said, "anybody can do that. The question is who else can perform such magic in the kitchen on eleven dollars a month per person?"

"I am well able," cried the cook, "to see through your crude flattery. You think the same of my cooking as that hollowhead there, only you show it differently. I'll have you know I've cooked stews and pilafs for beys in Ohrid."

It took much mollifying and a subtler form of flattery to induce the cook to restore the white hat and apron to their respective positions.

The incident was not without its effect. The commissars relaxed a bit on the economy, to the consternation of the pharisees. Twice during the next month there were ham and eggs for breakfast instead of just oatmeal and coffee and stewed prunes and bread. On three successive Sundays for dinner there was what passed for steak with those who had strong teeth. The others would rather have had a stew. Even so, the commissars managed to keep the cost of board down to twelve dollars for the month.

6

Not being occupied as much as the rest, I fell into acting as a kind of assistant to the temperamental Irishman. When we worked on stretches where the line was straight, I kept an eye on the joints. If the joints on one side of the track did not strike exactly the middle of the rail opposite, I noted the deviation and called Pat's attention to it.

On curves, where it was hard to maintain this relationship between the joints and rails of different lengths had to be used, I kept my head busy and offered suggestions that occasionally brought grudging praise from Pat.

Laying switches was a headache for Pat and me but a picnic for the men. They stood around talking, smoking, even playing leap-frog in the ditches, while Pat and I measured rail after rail, scratched our heads, and tried to figure out the position of the frog, the switch point, the guardrails. We tried to lay the switch in our minds before we started laying it on the blocks. The idea in laying switches was not to cut new rails. Anybody could lay a switch by cutting new rails to suit his purpose and by shifting around the head-block and the ties. But to lay the switch point over the head-block and to have the frog exactly where you wanted it without shifting all the double-length ties, and above all not to cut rails, that was another matter. And you must never, never, under any circumstances, cut a rail in the middle. If you had to cut, you *had* to, but then only a short piece, and you must bury the unused piece in the ground. You couldn't ship that piece back to St. Paul. Suppose Mr. James Hill, who owned the railroad, happened to be there in the yards while the scrap was being unloaded? Or suppose Mr. James Hill took a notion to take a walk over his line and came upon your broken piece of new rail?

We passed switch after switch. We cut practically no rails and did the least possible bit of block shifting. Nichola attributed this efficiency and expertness to my own "four eyes." He stood watching Pat and me scratch our heads, measure rails, make chalk marks on them. "Hey, hey, what did I say, what did I say?"

Our camp moved from place to place. You could hardly call these places towns. Often it was flung onto a lonely spur on the prairie with nothing around it but the vastness of the region and the flatness of it, broken occasionally by some solitary hill or rock looming up like a prehistoric monument.

A good many men left the gang when they had saved enough money to take them to the places they wished to go, but others came to take their places. Some of them became sick working for long periods underground in mines, and it was a kind of vacation for them to be on the railroad. Others came from homesteads where they had squatted through the winter and now wished to earn a few dollars to buy a horse or a cow.

From all of them I learned something of America, for every one brought with him his own America, which I added to mine, like little stones to a varicolored mosaic. And the pattern of America grew and expanded in my mind, so that I was greatly pleased with myself and with the work I was doing. Every time the Fast Mail swept like a whirlwind through the plain, carrying the United States mail and bags of gold from St. Paul to Tacoma, I felt elated that the wheels rolled on steel I had helped lay to the ground.

One of the newcomers moved into our bunk car to take the one unoccupied place. His name was Kobur, and he had traveled widely through the Northwest and knew people who had been to Alaska, but he himself had not ventured farther than Vancouver, where he had worked in lumber camps.

I was delighted that Kobur came to bunk with us and was much taken with him for the good reason that he had been to all those far places and was charged with that naïve and vital Americanness that was slowly seeping through my being. There was about the man something of the bigness and broadness of the Northwest. He was a square-jawed man with a compact, stumplike body, with broad shoulders and a huge head.

America had cast her magic spell over this sturdy fellow. No one I had met so far seemed so completely captured by America as he. His naïve trust in her, in her inherent righteousness, had something pathetic about it. In his wanderings through the democratic Northwest, in harvest fields and oil fields, in lumber camps, Kobur had heard of such proverbial shibboleths as justice for all, equal opportunities, pursuit of happiness. They were not just abstractions in which Kobur believed passively; they were the mighty pillars of a new and more just civilization. And Kobur preached them among the immigrants with as much effect as his limitations permitted. (Like Nichola, he was one of those unfortunate people for whom the art of reading and writing must forever remain an unfathomable mystery.)

Nor was Kobur timid or hesitant about mobilizing the formidable strength of his body whenever it became necessary to bring these sacred American principles to the attention of some native American who was ignorant of them or, knowing them, cared nothing about observing them. Being a strong man, Kobur took the hardest jobs on the track, glorying in lifting steel and never complaining of overwork. Hard work was to him one of the rudiments of good Americanism.

Judging from the way Kobur worked and the sheer physical strength he possessed, one would have thought him Spartanlike in his life. But it was not so, for he observed many refinements in the otherwise rough bunk life. While nearly all of us slept on blankets spread over the hard boards, or at most over burlap sacks stuffed with coarse grass plucked from the prairie, or with straw taken from some farm, Kobur had brought with him a mattress packed with cotton and a pillow stuffed with feathers. For covers he used soft, silky comfortables that looked incongruous in a track laborer's habitation. There was a cleanliness and tidiness about him, too, and an attachment to household duties that was anything but Balkan and must certainly have been acquired in America. To Kobur America meant clean clothing, clean bedding, abundance of food, good times, and, as he himself put it, "lotso vork."

All of these things about Kobur became accepted in the gang as time went on and the camp was moved from place to place. But on the day he moved into our bunk car something happened that all but started a fight.

After laying out the luxurious mattress and covering it with a white bed sheet, Kobur put on a pair of pajamas of the finest and softest silk, patterned with enormous flowers. These pajamas would have been fantastic for any man to wear anywhere, but in a bunk car in Montana, and to people who had never experienced the pleasurable sensation of silk touching the naked skin and who slept between blankets in their union suits, these pajamas seemed incredible and almost wicked. When Nichola saw them he was completely knocked out. He sat on the edge of his bunk with his jaw hanging down and stared and stared and would not say a word or utter a single exclamation. As a matter of fact, from the moment Kobur began preparing his bed and spreading his bed sheets, all eyes in the bunk were turned on him and there was very little conversation. When he put on the pajamas there was a long silence. After some moments the awful, oppressive silence was broken by an unhuman voice, by a kind of gargoylish giggle, a suppressed mocking laughter that refused to be suppressed. It came from Toma's corner. Toma lay there on his stomach, with his satyrlike face cupped in his palms and his eyes fastened on Kobur.

Kobur paddled across the floor in his pantofles and stopped before Toma's cot. "Look here, you, one more sneeze outa you and I'll flatten you to a pancake. I'll stifle the devil in that rotten hump of yours."

"He wasn't laughing at *you!*" Kozma came to his friend's defense. "We take you in our bunk and you start threatening people right off."

"You shut up. No one's talking to you."

Nichola gave me a knowing look. Neither of us made a sound for fear Kobur might misconstrue it.

After this incident there was no mockery of any kind about Kobur's way of life. The following Sunday, having laundered his pajamas, he hung them up to dry on a rope in front of the cars. Some of the men gathered there and stared at them curiously, but Nichola whispered something to them and they dispersed quickly before anyone had made a remark.

Kobur's one great sorrow was occasioned by his illiteracy. His inability to read and write filled his being with a boundless admiration for education. People with learning were cloaked with a dignity that evoked true worship from this simple man, who, no matter how hard he tried, always failed to learn to read or write. He had managed to read clocks and watches whether the dials bore Roman numerals or ciphers, but as for writing, he resigned himself to his fate and strove to make up for this irreparable deficiency in his life by surrounding himself with refinements and conveniences that he believed no educated person would do without. Kobur tried to live like an American, even under such adverse conditions as were imposed by a railroad camp—for who were better educated than the Americans? And in what other country were cleanliness and wholesome devotion to labor greater virtues?

If anyone cared to offend Kobur he had only to question the completeness of his Americanism. Kobur even considered it degrading to speak his native tongue and resorted to it only when he was angry, as when he spoke to Toma. He listened to his native speech when he was addressed in it but always replied in English, and a tortured, butchered English it was, since Kobur could pronounce no word without contorting his mouth, puckering his lips,

294

and growling the vowels from his diaphragm, whining and grunting the syllables through his throat and nose. That was the way the Americans spoke and there was no argument about it.

Kobur never wore patched clothes. The others mended their socks, their shirts, their overalls, going to extremities in the interest of economy, but Kobur considered patching and mending distinctly old-world and un-American. One could wear one's overalls torn but not patched, while to have a suspender fastened with a safety pin smacked of the American and Kobur contrived this even on a pair of new overalls.

Like Nichola, Kobur considered me a highly learned person and said repeatedly that I should earn my living with a pen in my hand instead of a bucket full of shims. He did not entertain the same exalted opinion of my shim job that Nichola did. My constant preoccupation with the English language and my study of it from books and not just by ear, like a parrot, were a constant source of wonder to him.

There was no literary task, in English or in Bulgarian, for which Kobur considered me inadequate. And soon enough he put me to the test. I regret to say that I not only disabused him of his illusions concerning me but also of his illusions concerning America, which was worse. We were being moved to Shelby, on the main line, from a place on the branch line connecting Great Falls with Havre. This was no flat country. A warm sun baked the land and the workers sat in the doorways or atop the tar-papered roofs of the bunk cars, enjoying the breeze.

I was one of those who were perched like crows on the rooftops, whence I could survey the expanse of rolling hills and plateaus on either side of the Missouri. Next to me sat Kobur. He kept reminding me that we were being paid for riding and enjoying the sights. Even without that comforting thought it was pleasant indeed sitting there on the spine of the roof and feeling the breeze, though the wheels banged on the rail joints and the cars rocked a little too much for comfort. The engine puffed and groaned, blowing showers of burning cinders over our heads. But one could not expect the best of everything.

The train twisted like a gigantic caterpillar, boring between high banks, skirting and hugging hills, retreating from the river in order to avoid some promontory that reared in front like a camel's hump. Again it returned to a precipitous bank, at the foot of which roared the river, muddy and foamy. At times it seemed dangerous the way that engine flung the camp about, like a snake flicking its tail. By now I had become impregnated with a cementlike trust in the stability of the railway system and the greater system of which it was a part. I questioned the worth or reliability of nothing that bore the company's insignia. The Chewtobaccos tested the structure and durability of everything before they permitted its use, and if the engineer thought it was safe to whizz with such terrific speed over these treacherous curves on the brow of this precipitous bank, beneath which the river groaned, then it must be safe. It was not for me or Kobur or any one of the others, acquainted as we were only with the mechanics of wooden carts drawn by oxen, to doubt the judgment of people who had built this dazzling mechanical civilization.

Such was my faith in America. And such was Kobur's too, for he sat there with me as unconcerned as though we were bumping along on a two-wheeled manure cart dragged by a team of oxen.

Our camp approached Great Falls, the most beautiful Montana town I had yet seen. The town lay in a hollow on the bank of the Missouri. Surrounded by barren, rolling hills, it presented a pleasant sight in the sunlit afternoon, an oasis in a dull, brown expanse of country.

Our bunks were switched into a siding in the yards, and the men got busy shaving, trimming themselves and airing their blue serge suits, for Pat had agreed to keep the camp in the yards for the afternoon and evening so that we might have a good time. Everybody acted much as sailors do when their ship pulls into port after a long and lonely voyage at sea. Some men had been in Great Falls before and knew the spots; there was a great deal of whispering going on, and money was taken from money belts and from the breast pockets of overalls where it lay secured by safety pins and was put in pocketbooks handy for use.

Even before the camp was sidetracked at the edge of the yards, the workers began to jump off and head for town.

I was lying on my cot with my nose buried in a grammar. "Are you coming, Little One?" asked Nichola.

"Not right away, Uncle Nichola."

Kobur had already gone, dressed to kill, his gold watch chain swaying from the lapel of his coat. Kozma and Toma were just leaving, both of them in clean overalls and freshly laundered blue shirts buttoned at the throats, without ties, their coats slung over their arms. Nichola started with them.

The cook and the baker and the helpers were also given the afternoon off, and there was to be no supper served at camp. So around four o'clock in the afternoon I locked the bunk car and went to town. Great Falls was clean and bright, with a neat little park in front of the railway station and a beautiful hotel facing the park. I spent some time sitting in the park and reading a copy of the Great

Falls Sunday *Tribune*. Then I walked through the main street, where I encountered some men from the gang. They gave me the "high ball," as it were, and went their way. I ate my supper at a lunch counter near the station and walked back to camp.

Toward nine o'clock Nichola arrived, alone.

"Did you have your supper?"

"Oh, yes. I was in town."

He hung up his coat and sprawled himself in his bunk. He was somewhat uncommunicative, considering that we were alone in the car, for usually he was quite voluble when we were by ourselves. I kept parsing sentences in the grammar by George Lyman Kittredge, which I had retrieved from a train wreck on the main line some weeks before. There was a sheepish look on Nichola's face. Every time I looked at him he averted his eyes.

Around ten o'clock the men began to pour into camp. They came in groups, and they were a lively and boisterous lot. Kozma and Toma stumbled into the bunk car with pint bottles in their hip pockets. They were carrying on brazenly about their experiences.

"And her skin was as smooth as a peeled egg," said Toma.

"Shut up, you nit," cried Nichola.

"What's the matter with him now? What's wrong? As though he didn't go himself."

"I suppose it's because of him," said Kozma, pointing at me. "He's no babe. Won't hurt him to know about such things. The fact is he's now old enough to go himself." But sobering up for an instant, he looked apologetically at Nichola.

In a little while Kobur came in. He smelled of cheap perfume.

By eleven o'clock everyone was back at camp and most of us were stretched in our bunks. We went to sleep as on any other night, though with full knowledge of the fact that during the night the camp would be picked up and transported to another spot in the boundless expanse of plateau and prairie. We had by now got used to the idea of going to sleep in familiar surroundings and waking up the next morning a hundred miles away, with the bunks switched in some yard behind rows of ugly boxcars, or in some spur shooting out into the plain with not a shack or a tree in sight for miles around. We felt as secure as though the quivering old boxcars, reared as they were on wheels and axles, had each been a solid structure planted immovable on rock foundations.

It was just past midnight when a terrific tremor passed through the camp. The experience at St. Paul was a mild jolt compared to the tremor the camp now suffered. Water pails leaped from their stands and spilled on the floor, lamp chimneys held to the walls by wire loops crashed to splinters, stovepipes dangled loose from the ceilings. But this time men's skulls were knocked against the walls or bodies tossed on the floors. Being asleep, we felt the intensity of the tremor far more severely than we would have if we had been awake, or been warned by the wave of noise that always preceded such shocks. On the other hand, had the boxcars been of more recent construction, they would have resisted the impact with some measure of resiliency. Mere wooden shacks that they were, super-imposed on wheels and axles, they all but flew into space.

It all must have lasted no more than a brief minute, but it seemed like the end of the world, at least to me, for I woke up with a feeling that the hills had descended on the camp in cataclysmic avalanches, or that the earth had split and we had sunk irretrievably into some abyss.

I walked to the door and looked out. Everything was peaceful and composed. The hills rose about in their undisturbed serenity beneath a passionless moon. The tracks were firmly bedded to the ground, and the bunks, except for a kind of sighing and moaning in their final effort to recompose themselves, remained upright, incredible as it seemed.

There was a volley of oaths against the engineer as soon as the men had recovered from the shock. But soon a sense of sobriety descended on them. Perhaps it was an accident, something that could not be avoided. One by one the men retreated to their bunks.

In our own car Kobur kept murmuring in English, "It's some driver wot tinks we ain't wort handlin' wit ker. He ain't gonna get away wit it eitter. I'll teach the swine a lesson he won't forget."

Kobur had reason to be angry. The spirit with which the engi-neer approached the habitations in which slept a hundred human beings was certainly not in keeping with Kobur's understanding of the American spirit of justice and fair play. And while the majority of the workers accepted the earth tremor with humility and resigna-tion, as helpless mortals accept the wrath of the powers above, Kobur was not going to let it go at that. Dressed in his gaudy pajamas, his feet in pantofles, he picked up an ax, jumped out on the tracks, and began to yell for all red-blooded men to join him in an assault on the engineer. He let out a profusion of oaths in the American language, and then in his excitement forgot his habit of not speaking his own tongue and reinforced his American profani-ties with a barrage from all the Balkan languages, which yield to none in this department of lexicography.

No one answered his call. "Cowards!" he shouted. "Dey tritted like sheep and dey stand for it!" Then brandishing the ax, he made for the engineer all by himself.

Whether from fright or to avoid trouble, or whether it was that he would have moved out at that moment anyway, the engineer pulled the throttle and the locomotive suddenly built up speed, the cars leaping over the frogs and switch points onto the line and rattling after the engine as it forged ahead, spitting fire in the night like an angry dragon.

From the doorway of our bunk I watched Kobur standing by the tracks. He did not even make an attempt to climb on. The cars were moving so fast he was afraid. As the train sped on I kept my eyes on the lone figure in the yards. In slippers and the garish pajamas, like a somnambulist, and with an ax in his hand, like a madman, he stood there in the moonlight, a quixotic figure defending his notion of Americanism and "equality." There was nothing I could do, or anybody else. The train roared ahead with great speed, and soon Great Falls was behind. I returned to my bunk.

"What happened to him?" asked Nichola.

"He was left in the yards."

Out of Toma's corner came devilish snickers, but the rest of the inmates were in a compassionate mood.

"What's so funny about it?" growled Nichola.

"Yeah, ain't funny at all," echoed Kozma.

Toma's snickers died out.

The first stop was some twenty miles from Great Falls. Everybody woke up as soon as the news spread that Kobur had been left in the yards. We came down and stormed the caboose. Some insisted that the train, or the engine alone, turn back and pick him up. But the conductor, who pretended to be surprised that a man had been left behind, refused.

"They did it on purpose," said a man in English.

"Sure ting! Lousy mustache-shavers, leaving a man in the yards in the middle of the night!"

"And with no clothes on!"

"That's right, no clothes, just pajamas."

"Dat's a lousy ting to do!"

"Listen, fellas," said the conductor, "they ain't no use cussing like that. If the man's got any sense he'd go to the station agent and tell him he belongs to Steel Gang Number Four and they'd put him on Number Forty-eight and he'd get to Shelby ahead of us."

"That's right boys," said Pat. "We'll talk to the dispatcher from the next station. He'll be put on Number Forty-eight sure thing."

"Better climb on the cars, fellas. I'll be giving the high ball in a minute," warned the conductor. We rushed for the bunks and began scrambling up the ladders.

In the morning the train stopped in a siding a couple of stations this side of Shelby to give us a chance to have our breakfast. The men limped toward the dining cars; a few had bandages on their heads. Some complained of pains in the ribs and shoulders and told Pat to tell the timekeeper about reports of their injuries and possible claims. But they soon forgot their own troubles, and Kobur became the sole topic of conversation. More men expressed ridicule than sympathy for the unfortunate fellow.

"They'd put him in jail."

"What else could you expect?"

"In pajamas and with an ax in his hand."

"And at midnight, too! They'd think he was nuts."

"Well, maybe he'd have wits enough to say he was stranded when he stepped out to answer the call of nature."

"That's right! Like Mohammed's Isha when she was left in the desert," said the Philologian.

"Why, the way he speaks English they'd give him a special train."

But we were in for a surprise when the camp pulled into Shelby and there, standing on the station platform, was Kobur in a pair of blue overalls and blue denim jacket. His pajamas and slippers were wrapped in a package.

The entire gang surrounded him and bombarded him with questions. What experiences he went through, where he got the clothes, how he reached Shelby ahead of the camp he would divulge to no one, not even to me. He seemed to have a grudge against everybody in the gang, but his only expressions were threats and curses directed against the engineer. There was no doubt that Kobur regarded himself as a grievously injured man. The America in which he believed would not stand for such injustice. There was some power somewhere that would readily rectify the wrong done him. But where? He was helpless, like a child. The foreman laughed at his threats of redress, and even some of his co-workers and compatriots, seeing that after all no harm had come to him, chuckled over his tragi-comic experience.

At last he took me aside and confided to me that he had gotten clothes from the section foreman at Great Falls, who happened to be a Greek. With him he went to the station agent and was put on the passenger train for Shelby.

"Now look," he said to me earnestly in our own tongue, "you must write a letter to Washington, to President Wilson. Something'll be done about this. This ain't right. Everybody's an equal in this country and everybody gets the same treatment." He said this in all seriousness, believing in his heart that such an outrage against his person and such a violation of his trust in American justice would not go unheeded by the powers that be.

I did not feel equal to such an exalted secretarial task and said

300

so, though I did not laugh at the suggestion and received Kobur's request with an appearance of gravity. Kobur was profoundly disillusioned. He did not say so, but it was obvious from his attitude that he had lost faith in education also, of which he considered me the immediate representative.

On the following day Kobur asked Pat for his time. He took the Skidoo back to Great Falls to work in the smelters. He did not take leave of anyone of us, even turning away from me when I proffered my hand.

When he had gone, Nichola said to me, "Maybe you should have wrote a fake letter, just to make him believe something was done. He'd have forgot soon and wouldn't have quit like this. It's too bad."

"I couldn't do that, Uncle Nichola."

7

The roadmaster dropped a message from the rear platform of the Skidoo and before Pat had had a chance to read it the men began to shout, "We're moving."

"All right, men," Pat announced, "we *are* moving. We close up right away."

It was to be the longest move yet. Moving was always exciting. It meant an interruption to the monotony of work; it meant riding across new country, to a new campsite, perhaps near a town where there might be a store, or close to the Missouri, in whose muddy waters one could take a bath on a Sunday. The moving was always done in the daytime and as a rule by a freight train, occasionally by a work train but never by a passenger train or by special engine. That meant slow going, and even if it was uncomfortable, we liked it because we got paid the same as if we had been at work on the track.

And yet it made no difference where the camp was parked. For it was the same everywhere, the same plain, the same earth rolling away in never-ending monotony. There were always the gophers peeping out from their holes in the brown earth to marvel at the strange people who had come to their community. Except occasionally when the track ran close to the Missouri, on whose banks grew some old willows and clusters of osiers, no trees relieved the ocean-like flatness. An occasional peculiar swelling of the earth, like a bump on a forehead, only tended to intensify the disklike flatness.

By four o'clock in the afternoon tools, handcars, push cars, switch points, and other equipment were loaded onto the flatcar and the camp was ready to be picked up at a moment's notice. With still two full hours before dinner, the men took advantage of the interval to indulge in hobbies and devote time to their personal appearances at the company's expense. Some took out their musical instruments; some organized card games on the grass before the cars; others set down backgammon tables and reclined on the ground. There were two barbers, and they both set up shop in the open, trimming hair at twenty cents a throw to earn an extra dollar. The cook was heard to argue with those who had lined up before the kitchen door with basins for hot water for shaving.

"We need the hot water for the dishes," the cook complained. But he kept filling the basins that were held out to him. "Why do you have to shave? Where do you think you're going, to Great Falls?"

I took soap and towel to the tank to save lugging water in pails to the washstand in the bunkhouse. Stripped to the waist, I enjoyed the warm sun on my back. It was ten days or so since my last shave, and now, rubbing my chin and the sides of my face, I decided it was time enough for another shave. One of the barbers said frequent shaving made the beard grow thicker, and on that score I thought I ought to shave more often whether I needed it or not.

I was drying my face when I heard the ring of the gong, an old fish plate hanging at the door of the kitchen. As it was too early yet for dinner, I wondered if because of the moving the meal might be served ahead of time. But then the ringing did not sound like the usual dinner call. The strokes were shorter and quicker, more beckoning and insistent, with a note of alarm in them. I hurried back, carrying my shirt on my arm and the towel around my neck.

"Is it for dinner?" I asked of a man standing in a doorway.

"It's for a meeting, for not to move at night."

All through camp the men were stirring. A score or so were already gathered before one of the dining cars, clustering about Vasil. I climbed into our bunk car, hung the towel on its nail above my bunk, put on a clean shirt, and was ready to go. Then I turned to my father, who was lying down.

"You coming to the meeting, Father?"

"No, I'll just rest. Let them thrash it out."

"You don't feel good."

"I don't feel bad."

When I got to the meeting nearly everybody was there. I heard a young man say, "Work animals get better treatment."

"Work animals have better sense than some of us." This was said by a dusky fellow with straight, coal-black hair. He was wearing a striped athletic shirt that left his strong, muscular arms exposed, browned by the sun to the color of roasted coffee. He was a spiker. A polka-dotted blue kerchief was tied to his throat.

"I never heard of any place where they paid you while you

slept," declared an elderly man, who as an adzeman did work that was play compared to spiking. The little pocket on the breast piece of his overalls had a bulge in it and was secured by two safety pins. This was his bank. Those who had no money belts kept their money in a wad in this little watch pocket of the overalls.

"That's just the point," said Vasil. "You won't sleep. These freight trains average about fifteen miles an hour and that means you'll be banged and bumped all night long. And you should be paid for it."

"That's too bad. Are we made of glass? It's unreasonable to demand pay for lying in your bunk. Whether you sleep or not."

"Here comes Mitko," someone said. The straw boss–interpreter was seen coming out of Pat's car.

"Are they going to move us at night?" asked Vasil.

"We'll be picked up around ten tonight." Mitko's straw-colored hair, freshly combed, was wet and stiff. He fingered the gold heads of several pens and pencils in his vest pockets. On hot days he would remove his jacket but never his vest, which he would wear unbuttoned.

"What about time?" demanded Vasil.

"Pat's got no authority to give time for night moving."

"Has he asked for authority?"

"There's no use telephoning. The answer will be no. It's the rule."

"The answer may be yes if Pat says the gang'll strike."

"Who elected you spokesman for the gang?" Mitko jerked out one of the fountain pens and waved it at Vasil.

"Nobody did," a thin voice chirped. "He rings the gong on his own. Now he says we'll strike. We've got something to say about that."

"Go stuff your mouth, you spouting idiot." The young spiker in the athletic shirt curled his lip disdainfully.

"Hey, hey," chided Mitko, "that kind of talk won't get us no-where."

"When a worker's not paid for his time his time's his own," argued Vasil. "And nobody has the right to budge him from his bed."

"Don't forget there's wheels and rails under your bed," Mitko answered. "Your bunk belongs to the company and the company can move its own property as it pleases."

"That's right," several voices echoed Mitko. "That's right."

"That's not right," said Vasil calmly. "We're in the bunks, see. And that makes a lot of difference. We're not property, we're human beings, not freight either. Look here, men, for myself I

304

don't care. A dollar one way or another don't make much difference to me."

"It don't to us either."

"All right then, it's not the dollar. It's whether it's right or wrong
for workers to be pushed around without compensation. The company owns the cars and the tracks, it's true, but the company don't
own us and shouldn't move us on our own time unless we are
willing . . ."

"We're willing," screeched a short, stumpy man with a solid,
cube-shaped body.

"We'll find out who's willing and who's not. We'll take a vote."

"It will do no good," counseled Mitko. "We're all for pay.
Nobody is against pay. But we can't get it. There's no authority.
St. Paul says no pay for night moving."

"We'll not vote for pay," declared Vasil. His words evoked some
laughter. And his own face twisted into an ironic smirk.

"What'll we vote for, cucumbers?"

"We'll vote on whether to strike."

"What'll we strike for?"

"For straight time, or time and a half, for night moving."

Many voices spoke up at once and it was impossible to make out
what was being said or who was for what. When in a little while
the clamor subsided some voices could be made out to say, "He's
crazy," "He's a gang-buster," "He don't give a damn if we all get
fired."

"We've been moved at night before, we never got paid. Why
now?"

Then a single voice was speaking. "We came here to work, not
to right wrongs. There's work elsewhere. Whoever don't want to
be moved at night he knows what to do."

Vasil remained calm. He stood there tall and lean, his face the
color of the brown earth. He was dressed as at work, in khaki
trousers girded tight to his narrow waist with an ordinary belt. His
faded blue shirt was open at the throat, revealing a large Adam's
apple and a tuft of hair beneath it. The sleeves of his shirt were
rolled to the elbows, and the hair on his forearms, bleached by the
sun, glistened like corn silk. He stood there speechless. What he
wished to say was going into his hands, causing them to close into
fists and open up, now one, now the other.

Then Vasil made a fresh start. "Look here, men, I know we came
here to work. I'm not against working. I am a worker. I'm speaking
to you as a worker. I'm not urging you to stop work. I am only
trying to tell you that when we are not at work our time is our own
and we shouldn't let ourselves be pushed around."

There was earnestness in Vasil's voice. If there was anger in him he did not let it go into his voice or into his words; he let it escape through his hands, which worked continually, clenching and unclenching.

I felt Vasil's strong belief in what he was saying. His words, while not tense or loud, rang with conviction. They were like the strokes of his spike mall, precise, compact, well aimed. I saw the hostility in some of the faces and the cold, steely eyes turned on him. And I could think of nothing to say that would carry any more weight than what Vasil was saying, yet I had a strong urge to add my own voice to his, and once or twice I did open my mouth to say something but said nothing.

"Who are we, a bunch of Balkanians, to be telling the Chewtobaccos what's right and what's wrong?" someone said. "They really ought to charge us fare for carrying us to a new place of work. Still, if they were to do that I'd say, yes, let's protest. But to ride on a train, just to ride on a train, and demand pay for riding on a train, I never heard of such a thing. And how about on pay day when they give us half a day with pay and take us to town on the work trains to cash our checks and do our buying?"

The young man of the polka-dotted kerchief pushed his way toward the man who spoke last and shook his fist at him. "You pharisee, why don't you go stick your head in a pint jar of vinegar and keep it there till it's good and pickled?"

Mitko put his arm out. "We don't want such talk here."

After much argument someone had sense enough to suggest, "It don't cost nothing to vote, so let's do it and stop this wrangling."

"Wait a minute. Why should a whole gang yield to Vasil?"

Of all people, this was said by the little "Avocat." As an intellectual it was least expected of him to raise such an objection.

"You're not yielding to me. We're to ballot and I'll abide by the majority opinion same as anybody else."

"The point is," pursued the Avocat, "according to Robert's Rules of Order you've got no right to rise and demand a vote. That's for a caucus to decide on."

There was a wave of laughter.

"Before it was a strike, now it's a kokos."

More people laughed.

When it was possible to be heard again, Vasil said, "We all know how clever *avocats* are with their points. But every stick has two ends. We're simple people and we wish to settle this matter by the simple method of voting."

"Then we're giving in to you," insisted the Avocat.

"You'd be giving in to me if we struck without first voting."

306

"But we *must* vote."

"Yes."

"Who asks for a vote?"

"I do."

"Then we are giving in to you. The whole gang must do what one man asks."

For perhaps a whole minute Vasil stood silent. Then he said, "Well, what do you propose?"

"I propose we first take a vote on whether to vote for a strike."

Many people scratched their heads, unable to grasp the fine point. Someone said, "Is that the *kokos?*"

"I never thought of it in that light," said Vasil. "Let's do it that way before somebody asks for a vote on the vote whether to vote for a strike."

"That would partake of the nature of filibustering." At long last the Philologian seized his chance.

"We've had enough of that," said Vasil resolutely. "All right, men. Now understand, we're not voting on the question of a strike but on whether we should vote for a strike. Those in favor of taking a vote whether to strike raise your right hand."

All right hands went up, including the Avocat's.

"That settles that. Now we shall vote again, but this time it's whether to strike or not to strike. This will decide it."

"Just a minute," a voice spoke up. "It's not against the law to strike, is it?"

"We have a legal right to strike," assured the Avocat.

"I just wanted to be sure we're not breaking any laws."

"All in favor of striking so as to get time for moving at night raise your right hand," said Vasil.

At least a score of men were counting hands, some inaudibly, some loudly. Thirty-one hands were counted.

"Those against striking raise your right hand."

Fifty-three hands went up.

"Okay, fellows, we move on our own time without pay."

It wasn't the first time. We had been through this many times. I was awakened as if by a powerful blow on my head—amidst shrieking of cars, jangling of water pails, the crash of lamp chimneys, the banging of tin basins as they swung off their nails. For a whole minute, it seemed, the cars groaned in a kind of mortal agony. And when after their protracted groaning the cars recomposed themselves into silence, I heard my father's groan across the aisle. The next instant Vasil, in his bunk next to mine, began to curse loudly.

307

The shock to the camp was even worse than the crew must have thought. The men asleep felt the tremor with greater severity. Some came to wakefulness with their heads banging at walls. When they realized it was not an earthquake and had divined the cause of the calamity, once again they stuck heads out of doorways and windows to give vent to their fury. What they said was unintelligible to the crew, who proceeded with their automatic signaling, ignoring even such profanities as were uttered in broken English.

The wrathful howling finally subsided with three lone voices, each sounding less vociferous than the other, and each in turn saying, after a brief pause, "Gaddem besterds . . ." "Sanamabeeches . . ." "Lassy Chewtobaccos." Men accept with equanimity the wrath of nature but become enraged when their own kind is the cause of their calamity.

The crew, still indifferent—as if these last voices were dogs wanting to give out a last angry bark before quieting—went on with their work of coupling the camp and getting it out onto the main line, which they now did without any undue roughness.

"There's going to be more of this and the safe way is to lie down," advised Vasil.

From the clanging of the wheels on the frog below I could tell the camp was getting onto the main line. For a while the train kept going, then it began to slow down, and finally came to a surprisingly easy stop. After a pause it began to move backward, so gently that the motion could be detected only from the squeaking of the wheels below.

"They're backing up to pick up the caboose," interpreted Vasil. "We'll be on our way now."

Shortly after there was a slight bump and the train came to a stop. Whereupon the engine gave out five whistles, each in quick succession.

"It's calling the flagman," Vasil interpreted the signal.

The train remained motionless for two or three minutes, following which two short whistles were heard.

"Get ready now," warned Vasil. At that instant there was a sudden stir, as if the engine were taking a deep breath. Our bunk was still, but from ahead, seemingly originating with the engine, I perceived the familiar wave of motion, like a tide, preceded by a vibration, as lightning precedes thunder, and rapidly communicating itself from car to car like the spinal movement of a reptile beginning to crawl. And this motion as it approached our bunk began to sound like a subterranean roar. The wave passed through the car and through my body as it went on backward to the end of the train. Reaching this, it reversed itself with such abruptness that

308

the movement forward seemed to derive its pulling power in the roots of my intestines. But being awake and having presensed the shock, we had steadied ourselves and remained in our bunks.

"By and by you learn how to take them," said Vasil. "You can feel them coming and get ready for them."

The train was rolling now, and the bunk hopped crazily on its ancient, squeaky springs. When the wheels below struck the rail joints the knocks had a way of causing repercussions in the brain. I doubled my pillow so as to cushion my head against the pounding of the wheels, but the train was gathering speed and the car tossed so impulsively that I couldn't keep head or body in place, and I sat up in bed.

About two o'clock in the morning we came into yards, where the crew must have done some switching, mercifully leaving the camp on a siding till all the switching was done.

When the journey was resumed, much to our surprise, even though the train went pretty fast, the cars did not rock and pitch so violently as before. I remarked to Vasil that perhaps a good many freight cars had been left behind in the yards, and the train, lighter now, went easier. But Vasil was of the opinion that the track here was newly surfaced and attributed the easier riding to that. Whatever the reason, it was now possible to lie in bed and even to fall asleep, though not for long.

The next time I wakened I could have sworn it was from another violent shock, for when I sat up for a moment or two I felt my body sway and the car vibrate. The window above my father's bunk was outlined by the light of dawn, and the interior was no longer pitch dark. I could make out objects and the men lying in their bunks. I walked to the door and opened it. There was no train or engine in sight; the camp was on a spur, and all about, quite visible in the blue-gray dawn, lay the plain, flat, treeless, exactly as at the place we had left. I did not know where I was, and it wouldn't have mattered if I did, for it was the same no matter where I was. I did not feel lonely or isolated or far away. It made no difference to me whether I was here or a hundred miles east or west. It was the same bunks, the same railroad, the same plain, the same state, the same country. I was where I was, and where I was was America.

8
———

At night I had dreamed of the shims. In one of my dreams the shims grew bigger and bigger until they became as long as the rails and they became the rails and it was on them the Fast Mail and the Orient Limited sped on their way to Spokane, Seattle, and Tacoma. Another time I kept piling up shims, one above the other, like cubes, until I built a high tower that collapsed with a tremendous roar and I woke up shouting.

I kept at my task with a troubled head and a cheerless heart. I said nothing to Mitko about my discontent. At least it was better than carrying the water pail. Besides, my shim job kept me with the tongmen, close to my friend Nichola. What I disliked about the job even more than the conviction that I was not helping rebuild the line was that I was called a shim boy. And I had to leave St. Louis to become a shim boy!

When the tongmen would sit down to give the spikers a chance to catch up, I would sit down on the tie stubs with Nichola.

"Hey, hey, just think, Little One [I never resented Nichola's calling me Little One], who'da thought in the old country we'd be building roads for the train, eh?"

"I build nothing, Uncle Nichola, nothing! The steel I lay, little that it is, doesn't stay there. You know they take out my *shimsi* as soon as the rails are spiked and coupled. There is nothing where I put the steel. It's empty. I make the only empty spaces on the line."

"Well, now, just you listen to that! And how do you know the *shimsi* aren't needed there as much as anything else? The Chew-tobaccos won't be putting them there unless it was necessary. There's got to be a good reason for them *shimsi*, for them empty spaces they make."

The first intimation I had got of the importance of the shim in

310

the scheme of laying steel was when the cold had let up. The leaden grayness had gone from the sky and on the blueness there the sun had appeared. The plain had lain in breathless quietude, disturbed only by the chiming of hammers and the jangling of bars and wrenches.

Each succeeding day the sun had grown warmer. As more and more of the wintriness had gone from the air, dark patches had begun to appear on the land—as welcome a sign as the emergence of the sun had been. One could perceive the earth stirring under its white coating, its warm breath thawing out the snow, reaching up to give man reassurance.

With the noise of the work now mingled the voices of the workers, talking as they performed their tasks. Especially the Philologian seemed to thaw out with the snow. In his long, worn-out black overcoat, with the collar turned up, he had looked comical. Unlike the others, he had not fortified himself with woolens and furs in St. Paul. He was the only one to wear a felt hat, and since this had left his ears exposed to the stinging cold, he wore earmuffs, little black velvet things that looked like leeches applied to his ears. The Avocat, too, had presented a pathetic sight, his round, cherubic face a splenetic blue, his short legs twirling on the snow as he dragged after him a burlap bag of tie plugs.

Nichola's usually clouded visage opened up, like the sunlit plain, and his body seemed taller. Men and tools were seized with passion to bind the prairie with new and stronger steel. The sun also dispelled the store of profanities with which Pat contaminated the air. The Irishman's hunger for track laying was at last gratified, for the men, freed of wraps and mittens, rent the old steel belt away and swung in new girders like men possessed.

Pat came over to me with a new supply of shims of a different size, thinner than the ones I had been using. "Here, you use these. It's getting warmer." Saying that, he pulled a thermometer from his pocket and looked at it for some time. Then he put the thermometer back in his pocket and walked away.

It was quite plain now that the thermometer had something to do with the shims. Immediately I began to believe that the shim must be an important factor in what we were doing. The moment the tongmen sat down to rest, I rushed to Nichola.

"Listen, Uncle Nichola, you were right! There *is* something to the shim. I am using a different size now because it's warmer. It's all according to a thermometer. You know, a *gradus!*"

Nichola smiled broadly. "Now, what did I say? There's a lot more to this shim business than people think. Lots more. So you go by a *gradus,* eh?"

"Yes, Pat has the *gradus.*"

"Tse . . . tse . . . I knew it. Didn't I say the Chewtobaccos don't do nothing for nothing, didn't I say? Now listen! The Chewtobacco'll give you that *gradus* before another week goes by. Then you'll know more about it than the Chewtobacco himself. That I know! Hey, hey! Who'da thought it in the old country!" He went back to his work.

Was I really doing something more important than lifting steel? Regardless of the temperature, the men lugged the same kinds of rails, drove the same types of spikes, wrenched the same bolts, but what I did was conditioned by the weather. A vein of quicksilver in a glass tube had to be watched, and according to the way it stretched or shrank, the sizes of shims I inserted between the rails changed.

Emboldened, I kept at my task, changing shims at the direction of Pat, who kept sole consultation with the *gradus.*

And Nichola must have been a prophet, for at the end of a week I was promoted. Pat explained the whole thing to me, and I had no difficulty in understanding it. I could now read the *gradus* and figure out for myself the size of shim I should use. And with this knowledge I was initiated into the mysterious relationship between shim and thermometer, between steel and weather. This made me feel proud to be carrying the old lard bucket with the small pieces of steel in it. I felt exalted so high above the mortal spikers and the clawbars and the wrenchmen that I began to think of myself as a kind of junior engineer.

Nichola, too, was proud and overjoyed. "Didn't I say? I knew it!" He magnified the importance of the shim and the *gradus* until he began to believe that I held the key to the whole scheme of building the line. He strutted about like a peacock. "The Little One, he knows everything. To hell with the Chewtobacco!"

I was anxious that he should share with me the knowledge of the connection between the shim and the thermometer. "No use telling me," he said. "How can I understand such things?"

"But it's simple, Uncle Nichola. In hot weather the steel expands, in cold weather it contracts. The rails today are longer than they were when it was cold. When it gets hotter in the summer they will become even longer. Then all the empty spaces where I put the *shimsi* will fill up. If there are no empty spaces there would be no room for the rails to stretch into. In such a case the steel would kick here and there, buckle out, and the whole line might go in the ditch."

"So it's the empty spaces that hold the line together?"

"Not entirely. You need the fish plates, the bolts, the spikes. They have to hold."

"Hmmm. But they'd be helpless without the empty spaces?"

"Yes. It's the shim that does it!"

"You know, it just goes to show you that there's a lot to magic. It seems that what's not there, what you don't see, counts for more than what you do see."

I sat there pensively and, like Nichola, began to magnify the importance of the shim. Put there between the rails and taken out after a few minutes, the shim left a space wide enough to insert a dollar and thus kept every rail separate and alone. But it was that empty space that held the whole structure together. It was like a spirit, a spirit that binds things more firmly and more strongly than the strongest matter, the soundest steel.

9

On a nail above the bunk in which my father lay hung the old Turkish watch with the winding key on the heavy silver chain. The watch looked out of place here in the bunk car in Montana but no more so than its owner, now lying on his back and staring at the low ceiling.

"You'll soon get well, Father. You need rest and some good food. I'll go ask the cook if he's got something special." Regularly I brought his meals from the kitchen car and set them on the little folding table between our bunks, but it was no fare for a sick man. There was a farm visible from camp perhaps a couple of miles away, and the cook said if I could get a chicken he would make broth for my father, who had been sick now for a week and worried me because both of us were losing wages. He had not been well for months but kept on working. He was a wrenchman, and it wasn't hard work tightening bolts to the fish plates; still, I asked Pat if I could switch jobs with my father, but he insisted he needed me where I was, close to the tongmen so I might keep an eye on the joints and assist him with the measurements on curves, bridges, and switches. So Pat switched jobs for him with an elderly fellow who with a small chisel and mallet was taking out the shims I was putting between the rails. I was worried that the move might cause wise-cracking about my putting in the shims and my father taking them out. But Pat wanted it that way.

My father hadn't been well in St. Louis. I first realized it one evening on returning to the flat, where I found him sitting in the kitchen.

"You'll have to sleep on the floor tonight," he said.

"I don't mind that. You don't feel well?"

"I don't feel bad, just that I am tired. I'll go back to work tomorrow evening."

"Maybe you should go to a doctor. You've been feeling poorly lately."

"Doctors are butchers here, my son. Your finger hurts, off it goes. You leg hurts, they chop it off."

The next evening my father went back to work and so long as his legs would carry him he would go to work despite his weakened condition.

Now in the bunk car I said to him, "As soon as you're strong enough to travel we'll go back to St. Louis. You shouldn't have come here in the first place."

In a bowl I brought him a mixture of raw eggs and evaporated milk that the cook had whipped into a creamy consistency. But he took a couple of sips and shook his head.

"The cook says chicken broth is what you need. There's a farm by the river a mile or two away and if you'll go to sleep I'll go get a chicken."

"It's no use, my son."

"Then maybe we should send for a doctor. Pat says he'll send the section foreman with the motorcar to fetch a doctor. It's only twenty miles."

"To send for a doctor that distance! He'll charge a month's wages."

"What does that matter?"

"It's cheaper to buy a chicken, and it may do more good."

I struck out across the plain. There was no road, only wheel tracks leading to the farm. I spoke to some gophers as I went through the plain. While I was perhaps a hundred yards from the farm a dog began to yelp, and presently a woman appeared in the doorway, watching me. A child of about five was beside her. The woman called the dog to her but kept her eyes on me.

A few paces away from the door I stopped and took off my cap. And I was about to state the reason for my call when the woman, in a sharp, fretful voice, asked, "What do you want?"

I answered in my best grammatical English, "Please, I desire to buy a chicken."

I spoke to the woman but I looked at the boy, amazed at his extraordinarily fair complexion. His round, cabbage-shaped head looked as if it were thatched with white straw. The woman, who wore a plain dress of some dark, coarse material, was as unlike the boy in appearance as I was myself. Her dark hair was severely drawn over her scalp, and her face was like her voice, thin and sharp.

"We haven't any to sell."

The dog didn't bark or growl but kept his small eyes on me. The child stuck his right hand under the breast piece of his overalls and shifted his weight from one leg to the other.

"Is for a sick man. My father."

The woman made no reply. She stood there with one hand on the dog's neck, the other on the boy's woolly hair.

"What ails your father?"

"Don't know. Is very sick."

A calf tied to a stake gave a low, plaintive moo. The woman turned her eyes toward the pleading calf. Then she looked back at me. "Well, wait a minute." She went into the house.

She reappeared with a bowl of grain. Walking toward the barn, she called to the hens by making a clucking sound with her tongue. A score of hens and a few roosters rushed toward her from several directions. She dropped grain close to her and soon the whole flock was at her feet, pecking at the grain and at one another. The next instant there was an alarming squawking and hens and roosters scurried frantically in all directions. But one of the flock, a rooster, was in her hands. This she took to a shed, followed by the dog and the child. In a little while she came out carrying the headless rooster. By this time I had extracted a dollar bill from my pocket-book and held it out to the woman when she handed me the bird.

"You keep your money. The bird is not for sale."

"Please. I desire to pay."

"It's for a sick man, isn't it!"

It occurred to me to pay for the rooster by making a gift of the dollar to the boy, but the mother objected. No, she said, give him a nickel or a dime.

The boy refused to touch the money.

"Please, let him take the dollar. It's not pay for the rooster, just a present." And I pressed the dollar bill into the boy's palm. He kept looking at his mother, his eyes pleading for her consent.

"All right, take it, and say thank you to the young man."

Pat sent the section foreman for the doctor. A hot sun was beating down on the roofs of the bunks, overheating the interiors. Still the sick man was chilled. I put his overcoat over the blanket.

"The doctor will be here soon."

"Doctors don't know much," he whispered. "They look at your tongue, listen to your heart, stick a *gradus* in your mouth and ask for money or send you to the hospital. Pull the covers from my chest, my son."

"Is it too hot for you?" He had to stop between words for breath. I uncovered his chest.

"In the vest, in the lining," he whispered.

316

On the left side of his vest against the lining there was a patch pocket with a flap secured by a small safety pin. I unfastened the pin and took out a well-padded envelope.

"Is this what you want?"

"Yes."

"You want me to keep this for you?"

"Will you send one hundred dollars to my sister Kyra and tell her I didn't forget her?"

"You can send it to her yourself when you get well."

"Will you do what I ask? Will you?" The voice was weak and hoarse, like the voice of a cracked bell. He rested a moment, and then again in a faint voice: "I've been angry with you . . . and said things . . . in my anger. . . . You are a good son. . . . I am not worrying about you. . . . I've been a burden to you. . . ."

The section foreman's motorcar was coughing on the sidetrack, and I climbed down the bunk's ladder to meet the doctor, who turned out to be surprisingly young. He had no beard and no mustaches and wore a loose-fitting gray suit. The only thing to inspire confidence was the little black leather bag with the shiny metal clasp.

"I am Dr. Wainer. Is it your father who's sick?"

"Yes, very sick."

The doctor shook the *gradus* and put one end of it in my father's mouth and with the thumb and forefinger of one hand held my father's wrist.

"Help me undress him."

We undressed him to the waist. The doctor wound a band around one arm and pumped air into it and listened through some metal clamps he had in his ears while his eyes were fastened on a clocklike instrument. When all this was done he took out another instrument also with "listeners" and a "feeler," which he kept moving over the patient's chest while tapping it.

I kept my eyes on the doctor's face, anxious to read his thoughts, but his face was blank as an unprinted page. He put his listening devices back into his bag and then carefully pulled the blankets over the patient's chest and motioned me to follow him outside.

"How long has he been sick?" It was as if a mechanism spoke and not a human voice.

"A week or ten days, like this, but he hasn't been well for a long time."

"Has he seen a doctor before?"

"No."

"He should be in a hospital, but the nearest hospital is in Great Falls and I cannot take the responsibility of moving him under these

317

conditions. It may not help anyway." The doctor spoke without feeling. If he was angry he did not show it.

"Doctor, will my father die?"

The doctor seemed abstracted; he did not appear to be considering my question. His phlegmatism extended even to the matter of his fee. Failing to think of the word *fee* and unable to phrase my question more delicately, I said, "Doctor, how much you charge?"

"Oh, it doesn't matter. Ten dollars will do."

He took the ten-dollar bill and put it in his pocket without even bothering to glance at it. Then he walked up to the waiting car and the section foreman drove him off.

I would wake several times through the night to listen to my father's breathing. His breathing, or rather his gasping for breath, was the only sign that he was alive. He never stirred. His breathing was so labored that every time he wheezingly breathed out I feared he would have no strength to breathe in enough breath to keep him alive.

When the others in the bunk would go to bed around nine o'clock I would put the kerosene lamp on the floor and turn down the wick so the glare wouldn't interfere with their sleep. I myself lay awake in my bunk, my whole being tuned to my father's difficult breathing, picking it out from among the somnolent exhalations and inhalations of the others. Around midnight I would fall asleep only to wake fitfully to make sure my father was alive.

On the third night after the doctor's visit I wakened around two o'clock in the morning and as usual listened for my father's breathing. I tried to separate it from other respirations as I was wont to do on waking, but now I couldn't. I lay there quietly, fully awake, and listened intently, so intently that after perhaps two or three minutes my ear picked up the clean, metallic tick of the old Turkish watch hanging on the wall above my father's bunk. That gave me a momentary reassurance. I could not conceive of that old watch ticking without my father's breathing. My childhood memories of my father were connected with that old Turkish watch. My earliest memory of sounds was not of the village bell or my mother's voice but the bell-like ticking of that watch as my father held it to my ear. I still had visions of my father twirling the watch on its silver chain before my tearful eyes. The golden rays that it emitted as it turned would stop my tears and bring a smile to my face. Then I would laugh and stretch my arms to try to catch the dangling watch, but my father would put it to my ear so I might hear the sound it made. Every night when I was put to bed my father had to hold the watch close to my ear and wind it with the little silver key. Then the watch sounded as if there were a cricket inside it that chirruped excitedly at every turn of the little key. No, it was impossible to think of that watch ticking and my father not breathing.

I rose and picked up the lamp from the floor and turned up the wick. I put the lamp up on the narrow folding table between my own and my father's bunks. The flame cast a weak yellow light on his face, which looked as if he had fallen into a deep, dreamless sleep. I leaned over and listened for his breathing. Instead, again I heard the ticking of the watch on the wall above. And again it seemed unbelievable that the watch should tick and my father not breathe.

My father was not breathing.

I went over and touched Vasil. "Vasil," I whispered. "Vasil."

Vasil sat up and stared in the semi-darkness.

"I think my father is dead, Vasil."

"He died?"

"He's not breathing."

"God's been good to him. *Bôg da prosti* [God have mercy]. Guess we should wake the others."

"Yes."

Slowly and silently the band of men moved across the open plain behind the coffin of rough pine boards borne on a farmer's cart. The farmer on the driver's seat, with his team of horses, alone seemed of this place. There was something incongruous between the strange procession and the peopleless plain. I paced directly behind the "hearse," Vasil at my side. I was dressed in my brown suit and wore my felt hat. I did not weep. In all the sadness that hovered over me there was inside me a numbness of feeling and a profound unsuspected sense of relief.

The cart creaked along; as they turned the tall wheels made a track on the untrod earth. The silence of the procession was occasionally broken by some man coughing, a horse nickering, or a prairie dog barking from the mouth of its burrow. The trodding feet hardly made any sound. I was thinking of my mother, of how different her funeral had been. The procession here through the treeless plain was unreal and unbelievable; there was something incomplete, unfinal, about this burial, as though we were burying a man not quite dead. This was no way to return a man to his eternal resting place. No bell tolled; no priests in braided vestments swung fuming censers or intoned chants; there was no avenue of tall Lombardy poplars flanking a roadway leading to a cemetery encircled by pointy, dark-green cypresses and shaded by Homeric oaks and walnut trees.

319

For a whole hour the outlandish procession trod in a straight line across the plain to the small burial ground fenced off by barbed wire to keep the cattle from tramping on the dozen graves. It was a lonely and remote spot for anybody to be buried in, and yet a more fitting burial place could hardly be found, for the little graveyard was at the foot of one of those monumental mesas that rise sheer from the plains, like temples, to heights of two and three hundred feet. No one could be in the shadow of this majestic tableland without being aware of something mysterious and supernatural abiding on it. One had the feeling that the mystery of the mesa more than compensated for the lack of religious rites. That and the Philologian, who now took on the role of priest, church, and ritual. Tall and gaunt, in his well-worn dark suit, he stood silent for a few minutes at the head of the coffin. He appeared to be communing with the spirits that dwelled on the inaccessible tableland where it seemed that no human had set foot. When he began to speak he surprised everyone, perhaps even the dead, with the unwonted simplicity of his funeral speech.

"Now I know you all feel that we are burying one of our own in a strange land. But that is not so. The departed felt a stranger here only in life. He is no stranger here now. He is not being buried in an alien land. Nothing brings to the mind of man so powerfully the sense of the earth's being common ground as when he lays his dead in the earth. The earth is one. The earth asks no credentials of the dead—only that they be returned to her. Only the living divide the earth and themselves upon the earth. We are not committing our departed to a strange and hostile earth. His spirit shall not be troubled because others lying here, early settlers, pioneers, perhaps Indians, spoke different tongues. They did that in life; in death there is a universal tongue. In death all men are brothers, as they should be in life.

"To this land that was strange to him in life our deceased has pledged his son. And his spirit shall hover over this broad plain. Only a fortnight ago he was bending over and removing from the rail joints the little pieces of steel that his son had been placing there only minutes before. Wherever there was a shim on the line there is now an empty space. Like one of those shims he too has now been removed from the track of life by a hand from above and there is an empty space where he was. We are all like the shim, put on earth for a while to serve a purpose in the scheme of the Master Builder and then to be taken up to leave behind empty spaces, some smaller, some larger, depending on the climate of our lives and the purpose which they served."

10

We strung thousands of rails across Montana, strung them across bridges, and fitted them around bends. The vastness and bleakness of the region, the utter desolation, was intensified by the cluster of track hands laboring away in the all-embracing loneliness. The gang hovered on the curving bosom of the earth like an antheap. Puny men, with steel implements, bent and twisted their bodies, bored and scratched, and crawled on inch by inch, embroidering the ribbon of steel on the broad surface of the plain. The hammers struck the new spikes with a dull compact sound. When a hammer missed the head of the spike and banged on the rail a bell-like sound chimed in the desolation.

There was nothing tame or gentle about the Montana country. There were no trees, except some old willows along the banks of the Missouri. On either side of the river the earth rolled out in never-ending monotony, rolled out until it merged with the purple horizon. Here and there a hill lifted out of the brown expanse like a camel's hump, or a precipitous flat-topped rock rose sheerly to a great height and brooded sphinxlike, an Indian monument looming up as a reminder of the days before this great land had reached across the seas to bestir peoples in far corners of the world.

Thus we stitched the earth, hobnailed it with iron pins, brocaded it with tie plates and spikes and bolts. The ties were embedded in the earth, tamped with gravel; and there upon them the steel lay fastened, immovable, but made resilient by my shims. Day after day the steel belt stretched ahead, zoning the plain, binding the earth, bringing the earth closer to itself, bringing me closer to the earth, closer to America. For the trains from east and west—freight trains, stock trains, passenger trains, special trains—came flying over the rails I had touched with my fingers. I had touched every rail with my finger. To every rail laid in its permanent place in the roadbed I had held a shim.

Daily the Skiddoos shuttled between the division points. Numbers One and Two, the fastest passenger trains bound, respectively, west and east, had deluxe observation cars at the end with round luminous signs like huge medals. In them rode well-dressed men, clean-looking, important-looking fat men with round necks and bulging stomachs. Black men in spotless white uniforms waited on beautiful women in the parlors and dining cars. To the workers down in the ditch between the track and the fence these women looked like remote creatures of legend. Soft and white and delicate they were, as though they had not been touched by sun or wind or by the hand of man. They looked out of the windows with curiosity at the workers who stood with bars and hammers and wrenches in their hands like an armed savage tribe.

The Fast Mail carried only a couple of baggage cars and no passengers. Its crew was armed with blackjacks and rifles. This train did not clatter and jog along like the freight trains, nor did it roar and rumble like the passenger trains. It came blasting through the plain like a gale. You could not see the wheels roll nor the pistons or the rods of the engine move. The engine and the two or three cars whizzed before your eyes like a rocket and disappeared into space on the rails that I helped pin to the earth.

And there was I, a speck in the vastness of the country, but a speck that dreamed of the luxuries that were on those trains and in the cities whence they came and the cities to which they were bound. My mind traveled with the trains, faster than the trains. It went from coast to coast, if ramified in the many directions in which the railways branched out. For I was young, and America was big and incomprehensible, and you could ride on any train in any direction and have all the luxuries you wished.

I was forever preoccupied with the English language. Word by word, idiom by idiom, the language revealed itself to me, each word unveiling its meaning like a woman lifting up her veil to expose her features. And each word with its specific meaning illumined some dark corner of the new civilization into which I was stitching myself inextricably. With my growing knowledge of the language America itself grew before my vision, etched itself out more clearly, and captivated my soul more enduringly. There began to seep through my being, like a strong potion, a vitalizing American serum. My young body became possessed of a passionate yearning to be absorbed by America. I longed, like a youth in love, to lay my head on the breast of America.

322

It was on a hot day. I placed the thinnest shims between the rails. Even so, as soon as the man behind scraped them off, the narrow slits between the rails filled in. The spikers were reeking with sweat, and the clawbars complained of dizzy heads. The spikes would not come off as easily as when the weather was cold. The prolonged yanking with the bars and the resultant jerking of the heads, with the hot sun beating down, had caused dizziness.

Toward the end of the working day a cool shadow fell on the broad plain. The foreman shouted at the clawbars to stop tearing the track, and they rushed to the push car for their jackets to throw over their drenched shoulders.

The spikemalls still pattered over the remaining unspiked stretch of new track when the tongmen started to cut an old rail with which to close the track for the day.

I sat on a tie stub nearby and watched the operation. The Irishman held a chisel at a point on the rail at which it was to be broken, while a young worker struck at the chisel with a fifteen-pound sledgehammer. As the sharp edge of the chisel sank into the steel, the foreman moved the chisel a little farther on for the next blow. The sinewy arms of the young worker brought the sledge down over the cutting implement. Bit by bit, when a groove was engraved on the rail, like a bracelet, the water boy spilled a bucket of cold water over it and the tongmen lined up for the lifting.

"Up high . . . up high . . . up high . . ." called out the Irishman. At each call, the tongmen, who had taken hold of the short end of the rail with their bare hands, raised the rail higher, until they lifted it above their breasts, above their shoulders, and finally held it above their heads. Then at the word *down* from the foreman, they let go the rail and scurried away to avoid being hurt in case the piece they were trying to break off should leap out from the track.

The rail fell on the two fish plates placed one above the other athwart the track to serve as a kind of fulcrum. The lifting operation was repeated once again with no result.

"Guess we'll have to do some more cutting. The steel's too hot today, won't break so easy," said Pat. And again he retraced the indenture with the chisel. The tongmen stood about ready for the lifting. The sledgeman's body vibrated from head to foot as his arms raised the sledge above his head and swung it down with all his strength. The harsh metallic sound produced by steel striking steel rang with a strident cry.

Then suddenly a heart-rending human cry drowned the cry of the steel. And at that instant Nichola's right hand snapped against his right eye, and he dropped to the ground like a felled oak.

Men rushed to the spot where Nichola lay groaning. Quickly

they tied a kerchief to his eyes and stretched his long body on the push car. He lay there silent and rigid like a tree trunk.

I picked up the chisel the foreman had left in the track near the unbroken rail. A nick on the sharp edge of the implement revealed that a small piece of steel, as big as a grain of corn, had chipped off the edge during the hammering. I realized what had happened, and in that instant the whole plain became covered with a thick, impenetrable darkness. I sat down in the middle of the track with tears streaming down my face.

"It's nothing, nothing. He'll be all right." Some men tried to comfort me. But the vision of the piece of steel darting like an angry wasp for Nichola's eye and lodging there filled me with grief, and I kept crying disconsolately.

My friend lay prostrate on the push car, bearing his pain with fortitude. After the first wail and moan he did not utter a sound.

In a little while the work train came. Several men lifted Nichola like a corpse and carried him into the caboose. The train started, and through eyes blurred with tears I watched it disappear into the twilit plain.

"They'll take him to the hospital in the city. He'll be all right. There is nothing serious."

My grief slowly was turning into anguish. Why did it have to be Nichola? Why? There were a hundred people in the gang and some of them devils, like Toma.

The days that followed were utterly cheerless. A murkiness had descended on the vast country, and the solitary mesas rising in the midst of it brooded sadly and ominously. When I looked at the sixteen tongmen lifting rail after rail and did not see the familiar tall figure of Nichola rising above the rest, I felt an immense emptiness within myself. Even the vastness of the land and the immensity of America, which always filled me with awe and heart, failed to dispel the gloom that had settled over my head.

It was a month before Nichola returned to camp. On the grass in front of the bunks he waited for the gang to come from work. I saw him from the switch, standing there like a charred oak, his lean, bony frame slightly stooped, but there was no bandage around his head. When I came near him I was afraid to look at his eyes. Suppose there were a hole where the eye had been; suppose the eyelids had drooped into the socket to hide the hole. Then I shot a quick glance at the eyes and my heart sang with joy when I saw both of them intact.

Oblivious of all others who rushed to greet him, Nichola bent down to embrace me. "Ai, Little One," he whimpered like a child, "are you all right? You look fine! Nobody's been mean to you, eh?"

324

"Of course not, Uncle Nichola."

"Who'd be mean to him? Everybody's been so good to him he's spoiled," someone said, laughing.

The workers shook hands with Nichola. No one spoke of the accident. They all said they were glad to see him back, as though he had been away on vacation.

As the men shook hands with him and Nichola looked at them I noticed a certain lifelessness and immobility, a kind of glassy stare, in the right eye. The other, the left one, was full of warmth and living light.

After supper Nichola and I sat on a pile of ties near the track. He knew what was on my mind and spared me the pain of asking.

"It's really not very bad." He tried to be casual about it. "I can see just as well as I could with both eyes. God was kind to me. I can see you, and I'll be able to see my children and our village."

"You mean you can't see at all with the other eye?"

"No. How could I? It's not my eye. It's an American eye, a made eye."

"But it looks exactly like the other."

"I know it. Didn't I tell you in St. Louis they can make anything here? Didn't I say they made eggs in factories? They can make anything. Sure it's a *made* eye. But you can't see with it; they can't put light in it. That they can't." And here my friend grew emotional. "Yes," he said, "they take your eye with the light in it that God put there and they give you a new one made in a factory."

My eyes became blurred with unwept tears. Nichola suddenly checked himself. "Oh, it's well enough. Now don't you go feeling sorry for me. I don't like that. Besides, the company'll give me two thousand dollars. They said they would. They wanted me to sign a paper. Two thousand dollars is a lot of money for just one eye, 'specially when you can see with the other just as well."

"Did you sign the papers?"

" 'Course not! I got nothing to do with any writing or reading, and I'd put no cross on no paper till you read it. I'll put my cross on those papers if you say it's all right."

We were silent for a moment. Then Nichola began again. "It's a lot of money. I figured it out. There's enough for both of us. We'll take the money and go right back to the village. I think we're lucky to lose only one eye. Something worse may happen, God forbid! People lose legs, arms."

"You shouldn't have come to America in the first place, Uncle Nichola. But what's done is done. Now you must go back. This is no country for you."

"Nor for you neither. You'll come back with me."

"No, Uncle Nichola. I'll have to stay here."

Nichola looked at me and a tear from his good eye wet his cheek.

"You mean you aren't coming back to our village, ever?"

"I guess not."

"No, you mustn't say that. There's nothing but steel and iron here. We don't belong here. We belong to our land, in our own country. Here? Here we are . . . we are like the *shimsi.* They just use us awhile, then where are we? We aren't part of things. There's just empty spaces where we were, like where they take out your shims from."

My mind was full of thoughts, but I could neither express them nor had I been able could Nichola have understood them. I sat there, silent. Nichola, too, became speechless for a while. His eye, the good one, was tearless now, and it glistened with a warm, living light. He wiped the wet spot on his cheek with the rough skin of his wrist. My refusal to go back with him was too much for him. The whole thing was bigger than he could understand. He had confidence in me, however, and something deep inside him must have told him that perhaps I was right.

"Well, you know better. I just thought, what's there in our country for you to go back to? Our land has been sucked dry, like a ewe that lets many lambs suckle her. Maybe the best thing for you is to stay here. And maybe some day I'll send my Peter here, and then you'll look after him, eh?"

"Of course, Uncle Nichola."

A few days later the claim agent came to camp. After some haggling he increased the compensation to twenty-five hundred dollars. With my consent Nichola put crosses on the papers. On the following day he took the Skiddoo for Havre, there to catch the express for St. Paul. I went with him as far as Havre, where we parted on the station platform.

"Remember," he said, "I am here always, looking at you. Always. My right eye is here in America, always to watch over you, eh? What did I say?"

"Yes, Uncle Nichola, I'll be all right. I am not a Little One any more. I am grown up now. Don't fear for me. And don't worry about yourself. An agent of the line will meet you at the station in St. Paul and will put you on the train for St. Louis. You give him the paper with your brother-in-law's address and he will send him a telegram to meet your train in St. Louis."

He boarded the coach and stuck his head out the window. The train pulled out and as long as it was in sight I stood on the platform and watched the head at the window get smaller and smaller. I could feel Nichola's good eye fastened on me until I too became invisible to him.

11

___

In mid-November the gang disbanded. Most workers returned east
on passes for the winter. Some paid fares to cities on the West
Coast, and a few remained on the division as section hands for the
winter. The men had had enough of laying track. Their money belts
bulged at their waists, and they were anxious for the life in the
colonies in the cities back east. I hated to see the gang break up;
I did not fancy the idea of returning to St. Louis to work in a factory
after the months of the open, pleasant life on the prairie. The
railroad was not like the factory. You had a sense of being part of
it. Vasil went to Spokane, to rejoin Pat's gang the following year
and to lose his life in the treacherous Missouri.

Pat urged me to stay in Montana, either with him on his section
in Chinook, to which he returned for the winter, or anywhere on
the division. In the spring he again would be put in charge of a steel
gang. I wanted to have the winter free to study, so Pat fixed things
with the roadmaster so that I could have his bunk for the winter and
have it moved wherever I wished on the division. I chose Great
Falls because it was the largest and most beautiful town and there
was a Carnegie Library there. I rearranged the bunk car to suit my
convenience, built a work table and a bookshelf, as well as a stand
for the first dictionary I ever owned, an unabridged Webster I
picked up secondhand. I felt proud of that great book, reposing
with its burden of infinite knowledge on the pedestal in all its
lexicographic dignity. I hibernated in the bunk car alone, enjoying
my hermitage and devoting myself to the study of the language.
Long into the night I burned the company's coal and coal oil.
Sometimes I was marooned by blizzards on my spur at the edge of
the yards for days and nights and ventured forth only when my food
or fuel or water gave out. I did not forget Paskal's advice regarding

327

the study of the language. I applied myself to it with the diligence of a scientist. When I got tired from poring over the dictionary and the grammar, I read books and newspapers and magazines. I read whatever I could get hold of. I never threw away a package or a can or a box without reading whatever labels were pasted on them. The words that were unfamiliar to me I wrote on small square pieces of paper in red pencil. These I tacked to the walls of the bunk until every available inch of space was covered. In whatever direction I looked I saw words. Every week or so I went along the walls and culled out the words that had become familiar and friendly to make room for new and strange ones.

It was not as dull a process as it may seem. The language was full of mysteries and adventure. Every new word I learned brought to me something fresh and exciting. From that book, reposing on the pedestal like an old sage, emanated the spirit of a people.

For it was not alone as a mere instrument of communication that I studied the English language. It was to me the source and symbol of a people's culture, the spokesman of its habits and of its creative spirit, the expression of its collective personality, which more and more invaded and colored mine. Since my contact with America and its people was limited, through the language I sought to link myself with them. If I mastered the speech, though I were ignorant of all else—and that was impossible—I felt certain I would come nearer to attaining my ideal. I knew then, as I know now, that the language was the passkey to my America, my chart and guide to it.

When America casts her spell over those who have transplanted themselves in her soil, she makes them eager and willing to transform themselves into whatever they believe represents the American. To Kobur the American was one thing, to me another, to Pat the Irishman still another. The track hands who came to Montana for the summers and returned east to the colonies for the winters had little in common with America, with mine or with Kobur's or with Pat's. They were in America corporeally. Spiritually, mentally, they were in the old country. Many had been in America for years, and still they were strangers in this country. They lived in hermetic colonies, special worlds fashioned after their old country. They thought old-country thoughts, spoke only their native tongues, were interested in the political and nationalist movements of their own peoples. They sat in their coffeehouses sipping Turkish coffee and playing cards and backgammon, talking old-country politics.

All of them were interested in making money, and that was their contact with America. If ever an American ventured into their coffeehouses, he caused a stir. It was as much a novelty for him to enter their coffeehouses as for him to appear in a village of the old country. There they were, like actors on a set. The American world was inchoate. Of its complicated pattern they could discern not a single stitch, let alone begin to trace the design itself. A few perceived a faint thread in the tapestry. In time the pattern might emerge and the warp and woof of its design seize the soul, but for the time being, the colony was the limit of their vision.

12

I remained in Montana for two years. One day I stood for the last time before my father's grave. And Vasil's. There was nothing strange or remote now about the little fenced-off burial ground, or the looming mesa, or the vastness. From the border of North Dakota, where the Yellowstone flowed into the Missouri, to the western edge of the great plain, where the mountains met its rolling flatness, I had lived in a hundred spurs and sidings. After months of the monotonous, never-ending prairie, it was inspiriting to come within the shadows of the mountains. But I had learned to love the plain and felt at home on it; I knew scores of small and larger towns along the five-hundred-mile stretch of main line. Often in the loneliness the telephone wires sang a whining, moaning song to me. I rode Indian ponies on the reservations and I was never far from the Missouri, along the banks of which the previous summer I had paced for two days looking for the body of my friend Vasil, whom the unruly river had swallowed before my eyes.

On a hot Sunday afternoon a dozen of us had gone to bathe in the river. We had chosen a spot where, after swirling past gnarled twisted trunks of old willows, the river widened and shallowed. Its opaque waters were not swift, and we could wade some distance before coming into deeper water. What we didn't suspect was that there were deep holes in the channel where the water eddied without any surface sign. It was into such a hole that Vasil's body was sucked. We did not catch sight of the body until two days later, when miles downstream we discerned something that looked like bleached driftwood caught in a clump of osier on the opposite bank. We were fifty miles from my father's grave, but I insisted that my friend be carried there to be buried. We laid him in the earth girded by the belt with the embossed silver buckle and the ten-gallon hat with the band of tooled leather within reach of his hand.

On this final visit, before turning from the graveside, I happened to take out my father's watch, which I had made my own. As I looked at it, I felt humbled and ashamed, for though I wore the old watch, I had all along been embarrassed to wear this vestigial ornament of my foreignness. I had gone to a jeweler in Havre to have it renovated into a modern, open-faced American watch. The jeweler persuaded me that I possessed a valuable heirloom, and in an unsatisfactory personal compromise I discarded only the stout silver chain, replacing it with a fine threadlike gold one. But hanging to it was the little silver winding key with which my father had beguiled my tears and had put me to sleep when I was a child. That memory filled me with shame.

The same day I took a passenger train for Chicago, and as my body rode ahead, my mind prowled back over the region I was leaving, over the winters I had spent in bunk cars listening to the roar of the wind, over the summers I had stood by the tracks in my blue overalls, holding a line wrench or a clawbar, and recalling the women on the luxury trains as unearthly creatures with delicate, flowerlike complexions. Often the trackmen standing on the bank as the cars glided slowly over the temporary junction whistled and shouted like a company of soldiers at the fairylike creatures sitting on the observation platforms. And then I would be angered because I saw myself in the future riding on the trains with my lady by my side, and I didn't want a bunch of Bohunks to behave that way. Often I would wonder what those people up there thought of us trackhands standing by like some savage tribe. Or did they think of us at all! Might we be to them something like the snow fences, the telephone poles, or the rails and the ties, just so much necessary equipment to make the trains go? But I was not a fencepost or a guardrail; I had eyes to see and a mind to think and dreams of achieving the kind of life that was on the luxury trains. I rode on sitting in the plush chairs, sipping cool drinks, and a fair lady was by my side.

More than the people who rode in them, the trains spoke to me of America. I would copy the names on the Pullman cars on a piece of paper, later to look them up in my unabridged Webster's. The names of Pullman cars came from mythology, American history, geography, Indian tribes. It was from the sides of these cars that I first learned of rivers with such singing names as the Susquehanna and the Monongahela and of such historic landmarks as Ticonderoga and Saratoga. The freight trains were equally instructive, for while the engines that hauled them were always Great Northern engines, the boxcars would belong to a score of different railroads. Reading the writing on the cars, I learned the names of nearly every railway company in America. And since most railways bore the

331

names of the regions they traversed, the boxcars passing before my eyes were like placards advertising America. In time I came to recognize the different carriers by their initials alone, such as C.B. and Q. (Chicago, Burlington and Quincy) or by the color of the paint on the cars, or by some slogan or trademark, such as the goat within the circle and the SEE AMERICA FIRST on a Great Northern boxcar.

American symbols, places, landmarks, American dates and events, American historical and legendary figures were evoking emotions. From the niches in the hallway of memory, *haiduks* and *komitadjis* stubbornly gave way to Paul Bunyan, Buffalo Bill, Jesse James, General Custer, Sitting Bull. The new was so much bigger than the old. America elbowed about, pushed out the mind's barriers to make room for her great contours. The plains were no longer vast enough to contain my dreams and my desires. There came then the hunger and thirst for an America that I could not nail down with a spike or bind with a band of steel. And it was in quest of this America that I was now journeying. Every now and then my body quivered as my mind would envision the massiveness of the yet unseen Chicago's "Loop," for that was where I was headed. I was young, and I was healthy, and I knew what I wanted. Others might dream of wealth, of power, of splendid careers, but at this time, as I rode the train east, I wanted nothing more than to be a fully realized American. Whatever life held in store for me, whatever at all I might achieve, must have its basis in me as an American.